DARK OF THE MOON

Books by John Dickson Carr

DARK OF THE MOON
PANIC IN BOX C
THE HOUSE AT SATAN'S ELBOW
MOST SECRET
THE MEN WHO EXPLAINED MIRACLES
THE DEMONIACS
THE WITCH OF THE LOW-TIDE
IN SPITE OF THUNDER
THREE DETECTIVE STORIES
The Arabian Nights Murder
The Burning Court
The Problem of the Wire Cage
THE DEAD MAN'S KNOCK
A JOHN DICKSON CARR TRIO
The Three Coffins
The Crooked Hinge
The Case of the Constant Suicides
FIRE, BURN!
PATRICK BUTLER FOR THE DEFENCE
CAPTAIN CUT-THROAT
THE THIRD BULLET AND OTHER STORIES
THE NINE WRONG ANSWERS
THE DEVIL IN VELVET
THE BRIDGE OF NEWGATE
BELOW SUSPICION
THE LIFE OF SIR ARTHUR CONAN DOYLE
THE SLEEPING SPHINX
HE WHO WHISPERS
TILL DEATH DO US PART
THE EMPEROR'S SNUFFBOX
DEATH TURNS THE TABLES
THE CASE OF THE CONSTANT SUICIDES
THE MAN WHO COULD NOT SHUDDER
THE PROBLEM OF THE WIRE CAGE
THE PROBLEM OF THE GREEN CAPSULE
THE FOUR FALSE WEAPONS
TO WAKE THE DEAD
THE BURNING COURT
THE MURDER OF SIR EDMUND GODFREY
THE ARABIAN NIGHTS MYSTERY
THE THREE COFFINS
THE MAD HATTER MYSTERY
HAG'S NOOK
DEATH WATCH
THE EIGHT OF SWORDS
THE BLIND BARBER
CASTLE SKULL
POISON IN JEST
THE LOST GALLOWS
IT WALKS BY NIGHT
THE CORPSE IN THE WAXWORKS
THE CROOKED HINGE

John Dickson Carr

*

DARK OF THE MOON

HARPER & ROW, PUBLISHERS

NEW YORK, EVANSTON AND LONDON

FIRST EDITION

LIBRARY OF CONGRESS CATALOG CARD NUMBER: 67-28824

K-R

FOR

DAVID HIGHAM

Dear David:

You are in England, three thousand miles away. But I believe you have visited Charleston, and may need little warning about the book I offer you in token of thirty years' friendship. This is a work of fiction; as another friend of ours would say, it's all a damn lie. The house in the story may have been suggested by Boone Hall, Mount Pleasant, but only in certain features of its appearance. There is no Davy's Restaurant and no Joel Poinsett High School, though other places mentioned by name are real enough. The photograph which provides a clue may be seen in the museum at Fort Moultrie. All the characters are imaginary; friends and neighbors must not appear in such reprehensible goings-on. But it is hoped that some hint of the atmosphere has been invoked, and some tribute paid to the most fascinating of American cities.

Yours as ever,
John Dickson Carr

Greenville, South Carolina
October 1966

DARK OF THE MOON

1

Dark clouds scudded across a moon which had not quite reached its full. The warmth of the Carolina night lay on James Island at the entrance to Charleston harbor. Jessamine and magnolia added their scents of early May. And emotion stirred here too.

Maynard Hall, on the northern shore of the island, faced due east. Its side was towards beach and water. If you had been standing in the broad sanded drive which led to the front door, you would have seen the four tall columns of the portico white and ghostly against the Hall's central face, with north and south wings in time-mellowed red brick raising two floors of moon-silvered windows at either side. Just above these, a mansard roof for a smaller top floor showed lights at its two middle windows.

On your left, as you stood in the sanded drive, would have been gardens extending to a boundary wall parallel with the drive, and to Fort Johnson Road beyond the boundary. On your right, northwards past smooth lawn, an earthen terrace carpeted with white, finely crushed oyster-shell stretched between the side of the Hall's north wing and a short row of poplar trees, overlooking the slope of beach and the surf of the incoming tide.

Rather more than a mile away, diagonally across moonlit water, the lights of Charleston glimmered above the long dark line of the

Battery. But emotion in these grounds stirred elsewhere.

At one particular place, for instance . . .

Just inside the entrance-gates of the Hall, some fifty yards from the front door, six magnolia trees towered up, three on either side of the drive at its beginning. In shadow under the magnolias, momentarily all but lost to the world, a man and a girl stood locked together in frantic embrace.

Unless you had been very close you would not have heard their voices, which whispered. The man's voice, a youthful baritone, contrasted with the light, breathless speech of the girl. The thick air was alive with passion, with a kind of desperate frustration; and also, less romantically, with mosquitoes.

Nobody troubled about mosquitoes. The girl whispered: "Darling, this oughtn't to be! But don't stop!"

The man whispered: "I know it oughtn't to be, but I can't stop; I never can." Suddenly his voice rose. "Oh, God, Madge! If your father should come down here now . . . !"

"Sh-h!"

"All right." The voice became a whisper again. "But if your father—!"

"Daddy? He won't come down here!"

"Why not?"

"He won't, silly, unless you shout as you did a second ago."

"I asked you—!"

"Because he never does, that's why!" The girl called Madge gestured towards the two faintly lighted windows at the top of Maynard Hall. "He's always up there at his eternal calculations. Or sitting on the terrace," she gestured to the right, "with more books and papers. But—!"

"But what?"

"Well! If you care for me as much as you say you do . . ."

"*If* I care? *If* I care!"

"Darling, why must we go on being so awfully furtive? Why can't it be as we want it to be? Why don't you just speak to Daddy?"

"Because I can't speak to him! And you know why I can't, don't you?"

"Well . . ."

"You know why, don't you?"

"Maybe, but I don't care."

"I care." Once more her companion was galvanized, though he did not raise his voice. "Madge, listen! Didn't you hear a car in the lane just now?"

"There wasn't anything to hear, you foolish boy. Come back to me!"

"I'd better go, I think. I can slip out through the side gate towards Fort Johnson Road."

"Now?"

"Madge, what chance have we got tonight? It's not late, you know. In addition to your father, people can turn up all over the place."

"And we know who'll turn up tomorrow, darling." The soft, cajoling voice seemed to wind round him, making his nerves jump like a hooked fish. "But you won't be jealous of *him,* will you?"

"I'll try not to be. There's only one person *I'm* jealous of."

"Oh? Who's that?"

"It doesn't matter. And I must go now, Madge. Good night."

"Oh, don't leave me this way! *Don't!"*

"I've got no choice, my sweet. It's a hell of a thing, but I've got no choice. Good night, Madge."

Head down, nerves twitching, he strode away through shadow towards the gardens on the left. Madge Maynard, twenty-seven years old, made the baffled gesture of one who would cry, "Everybody puts me off!" A few moments more Madge herself remained in shadow. Then, her own twitching nerves now composed, she stepped out into the moonlight.

Under middle height, sturdy but shapely, she wore a sleeveless white dress which clung to her figure. Moonlight drained color from the glossy fair hair, from a complexion which in daytime would be white and gold, and made her luminous brown eyes appear black. The face she turned up to the moon, so healthily pretty that it was almost beautiful, seemed intense, trustful, and very guileless. But she was not happy.

"Oh!" blurted Madge, spinning round.

Whether or not she had heard a car in the lane which curved down from the main road to the gates, she could now hear someone approaching on foot. There was a sharp slap as the newcomer whacked at a mosquito on his left forearm. Between iron-grilled gates wide open, through the shadow of the magnolias and out into moonlight, sauntered a tallish, lean, loose-limbed young man perhaps two or three years older than Madge. He wore gray slacks and a white sports-shirt with a silk handkerchief knotted round his neck inside the collar. So far as could be judged in this light, he looked extremely intelligent, if also lazy and easy-going: his features clear-cut and aristocratic, his hair dark and thick.

Madge and the newcomer stared at each other. A thin whine of insects droned round them. From the direction of the beach they could hear the soft, shaky ripple of the tide washing in. Then Madge spoke.

"Why, Yancey! Yancey Beale! What on earth are *you* doing here?"

Yancey Beale swept her a great bow.

"Evening, honey. At your service, as usual."

"You sneaked up, did you?"

"Who sneaked up, little 'un? Drove to the gate like a proper-minded suitor, that's all. Who was here with you a minute ago?"

The girl lifted shining eyes. "There was nobody here, Yancey."

"There wasn't? Could have sworn I heard somebody galumph away. Still! If you say there was nobody, honey, that's my pleasure and my belief."

"You're nice, Yancey!" Struggling against laughter, Madge made a mouth at him. "But you're a sweet-talking Southerner just the same!"

"You reckon *you're* no Southern girl, Madge Maynard?"

"I've never considered myself one."

"Now don't you start talkin' foolishness, honey! You were born in France, maybe, and brought up in New York and Connecticut. But your daddy's a Maynard of South Carolina . . ."

"The last of the doomed Maynards, were you going to say?"

"Honey, that's still foolish talk. No, nothing so fancy as doomed-anybody! Your daddy's a Maynard, I said; your mother was a Wilkinson from Georgia. If that makes you any kind of a damnyankee, then my name's Tecumseh Sherman."

"Still as eloquent as ever, Yancey. How's the law-practice?"

"Few clients, little profit, no prestige at all. Like to be twenty years 'fore I get a partnership, if then. Who'd pay any mind to the likes of me, anyway?"

"*I* might, if you spoke to me nicely. But you still haven't told me what you're doing here."

Mr. Beale smote at another mosquito.

"Well!" he said. "Tomorrow, bright and early, I'm to be here for the first week of my vacation. Old Playford wants to get away in June, which is the time I usually take, so that gives Br'er Rabbit two weeks in May. Meanwhile, thought I'd just run over from Charleston and ask how're things on this side. Mark Sheldon's been wondering too; so has Valerie Huret. How are things, by the way?"

"Just as usual."

"Oh?"

Madge tried to hold herself in and failed.

"Uncle Dick died in March," she said explosively. "We've been installed here for less than a month. But it's just the same, just exactly the same, as it always was in Goliath, Connecticut. Lonely and dreary, Yancey; you'll never guess *how* lonely and dreary! I'm not old enough to be a hermit like Daddy."

"Easy about hermits, sweetness; your daddy's a very wise man. Leastways, he is to the people who appreciate mathematics and science; though damn me if I could ever understand the stuff, even! You just pick yourself a devoted husband—me, for dealer's choice—and don't fret your head 'bout anything else. Old Yance'll be here from tomorrow, as I say. And your Yankee friend'll be here too, they tell me."

"You mean Rip Hillboro?"

"I guess so. Another ornery lawyer: wouldn't you know?"

"You don't like Rip, do you?"

"Easy, sweetness! Only met the fellow once, when he came down with y'all in April. He is goin' to be here tomorrow, isn't he?"

"Yes, we expect Rip," Madge answered casually. "And Camilla Bruce, who's a *real* friend, and later in the week an old crony of Daddy's from Goliath. Both Camilla Bruce and Mr. Crandall are what you would call Yankees too. You met them both when *they* visited us in April, and you seemed to like *them* well enough. But poor Rip—!"

"Now don't get me wrong, honey!" begged the other. "Your much-admired Rip Hillboro's all right, I guess. He's the only Yankee I ever really thought of as a damnyankee. But who am I to pass judgments? All I said was: don't you fret your head about anything, anything at all!"

But Madge was fretting none the less. For some reason the jessamine-scented air seemed to press down with thicker heat, even with a breath of the sinister. Then something rumbled in the sky, distant sound-waves rising and falling. Madge suddenly threw her arm across her eyes and shrank back into shadow. The young man strode after her.

"Did you hear that, Yancey? Like ghost-guns at Fort Sumter out there! What was it?"

"Only a little thunder, honey. We often get it in these parts, even when the sky's clear. Pay no mind to that, honeychile! All the same—"

It was as though the disquiet had been communicated to Yancey too.

"Now listen, sugar!" he continued with a kind of heavy gentleness. "I said don't fret and I meant it, you hear? All the same, something mighty damn funny's goin' on hereabouts. *I* know that, even if I can't tell you what it is. Just remember I'm always on tap if you need me. And you may need help, Madge. You see . . ."

Again thunder rumbled; Yancey broke off. Fifty yards away, inside the four white columns of the portico at Maynard Hall, there was a small stir to draw their eyes. Though the great front door stood open, its screen door had been closed. An indistinct figure in a gray suit opened the screen door, closed it behind him, crossed the porch, and descended steps to the broad sanded drive between the lawns.

Madge did not speak; she only breathed.

The indistinct figure, approaching along the walk, took shape as a spare, wiry, vigorous man in his late fifties, carefully dressed without ostentation or dandyism. He had been smoking a cigarette, which he flipped away across the lawn. His hair shone clear silver-white. Under that silver hair he had the same thin face and high-bridged nose which could be seen in the family portraits. You sensed other qualities too. Whether affable or moody (he could be both, as Madge well knew), Henry Maynard was clearly a man of intellect and of strong feelings held in check by discipline or a sense of fitness.

Though he could not have seen the other two, who remained in shadow, he seemed to know they were there.

"Madge!" he called a little uncertainly. And then in a louder voice, "Madge!"

"Yes, Daddy?"

"Forgive me, my dear. I don't want to interfere, but—"

Madge stepped out into the moonlight. Her young companion followed. Henry Maynard stopped as though he had run into a wall.

"Evening, sir," said Yancey Beale.

"Is that you, Yancey? It really *is* you?"

"It's me, sir, your obedient servant aforesaid. Is that so very surprising?"

"Not surprising, no." Henry Maynard stared at him. "Don't you know you're always welcome here, Yancey? Don't you know that, my boy?"

"Glad I'm not in the way, sir. I'm right sorry to have disturbed you, though."

"You didn't disturb me. You puzzled me badly."

"Sir?"

"I was up in my study. The air-conditioner was off, and the window was open with a screen in it, or I couldn't have heard you at all. You said something to Madge; you spoke very loudly. I don't recall the exact words . . ."

"Yes, sir?"

"They were to the effect that it might be disastrous if I discovered you here." Henry Maynard drew in his breath. "Yancey, I've known your father for forty years. Don't you know you're always welcome in my house? Good God, boy! That I of all people should be angry if . . ."

"But I didn't—!"

"Didn't what?"

Madge seemed about to speak; Yancey shushed her.

"Must have been wool-gathering," he replied. "Just can't remember sayin' it, that's all." Yancey slid his arm across Madge's shoulders. "Little lady's a bit upset tonight, sir; must've upset me too."

"Madge has fancies. I'm well aware of it."

"Please!" Madge burst out. Henry Maynard paid no attention.

"The past is too much with us, as it always is in Charleston or anywhere nearby. A touch and then the deluge; old superstitions sweep us away. Yes, Madge has fancies . . ."

"Like her ghost-guns at Fort Sumter?"

"Not that; she knows it's only thunder; much more. What happened to the first Maynard in 1698, when something or somebody followed him through the swamp at the other side of the island? What happened to his descendant of 1867, when Commodore Luke Maynard, formerly Confederate States Navy, had his skull crushed down there on the beach, with no weapon to be found, and wet sand for ten yards in every direction unmarked by any footprint except his own? What evidence was faked or omitted from that account, to invoke the seeming supernatural and stun minds too credulous? Nonsense; worse than nonsense! So if Madge has been thinking about the thing that follows and leaves no trace . . ."

"Please!" the girl cried again. She shook Yancey's hand off her shoulder. "You're always shutting me up, Daddy. You tell me to run away and play like a good girl; that's what they all tell me. But I will say this if I never say anything else! *I'm* not thinking about the thing that follows and leaves no trace. *You* are."

"I am, Madge?"

"Don't deny it; I know you too well! You've been thinking and thinking and thinking."

Henry Maynard drew himself up.

"In a sense, my dear, you are quite right. Must I repeat it? These old superstitions have no force or value for a logical brain. I would give anything, anything in my poor power, if I could write Q.E.D. and destroy them forever."

For several seconds nobody spoke, while a light breeze from the harbor ruffled treetops in the park. Then their host addressed Yancey Beale.

"I had hoped," he said almost plaintively, "things would be so different at the Hall. And they will be; I promise they will be! Life has been very dull for Madge; I know that, and I propose to remedy it. As we grow older, my boy, we find seclusion holds fewer and fewer charms. Once upon a time I was acquainted with many persons in Charleston. If I have lost touch with most of them, younger people like Mrs. Huret and Dr. Sheldon should provide welcome company. We must invite them to dinner more often. And already I have taken steps towards ending seclusion with a small house-party."

From his inside breast pocket he took out a small leather-bound diary, and from his side pocket a pencil flashlight, directing the beam on the diary as he opened it. There was nothing written there; the master of Maynard Hall sought a date.

"*Sunday, May 2nd,*" he read aloud. "That's today, 1965, and it's almost gone now. The first guests arrive by air tomorrow. Apart from yourself, Yancey, they are people we knew at a town called Goliath, not far from Hartford in Connecticut."

"I know, sir; Madge was telling me!"

"Permit *me* to tell you." Henry Maynard lifted one shoulder. "Young Ripton Hillboro, whom I believe you met, has got leave of absence from his law-firm in Hartford. The other guest arriving tomorrow is a charming girl named Bruce, Camilla Bruce, whom you also met. I might add that at Goliath there are two institutions of learning, Colt University and Lydia Stone College for women."

"Apropos what, Mr. Maynard?" demanded Yancey. "It's no problem rememberin' Camilla, no problem at all. She seemed quite a gal, in her quiet way; anybody could see she had possibilities. But why bring up Colt and Lydia Stone? Is she connected with the women's college?"

"Not officially, no. Camilla is a tutor; she coaches slower-witted girls in mathematics. I'm not sure what you mean by 'possibilities,' but I hardly like to conjecture."

"Forget it, sir! Only me and my big mouth!"

"Madge will be glad to see Camilla, I feel sure. The blight of my own presence here—"

"Daddy," Madge exclaimed, "what on earth *is* all this?"

"The blight of my own presence, I say, can be removed for a day or two. On Wednesday I must go to Richmond on business; my late brother's affairs were not left in quite the good shape he thought they were. Meanwhile . . ."

"Look, sir! Isn't there a Mr. Randall or Crandall, a newspaper reporter or something?"

"Mr. Robert Crandall, Yancey, was formerly owner and editor of the Goliath *Sentinel,* one of the few small-town (or city) papers solvent enough not to have been swallowed up by any of the big combines which own everybody and everything in newsprint.

Though he's rather younger than myself, he retired this spring after finally selling out to the Shaw-Marketer chain. It's been on his conscience, I think. We don't agree about many matters, and he's a bad chess-player because he won't concentrate; but I find his company entertaining. Cheer up, Madge; don't look so sulky! With such a trio of guests to while away the dull hours . . ."

"Camilla Bruce, Bob Crandall, and good old Ripton Hillboro! All of 'em Yankees, eh?" chortled Yancey Beale, now beginning to burlesque himself. "Man! We goin' have a ball, ain't we?"

Madge rounded on him.

"Yancey, for heaven's sake! A Yankee is someone from New England; you want to make it anybody living north of Virginia or Maryland. Camilla's a Philadelphian, Rip was born in New Jersey, and I think Mr. Crandall originally came from the Middle West."

"I stand rebuked, honey, and offer my apologies to any damn-yankee *not* born in New England. Is that everybody, sir?"

"It's everybody who will be staying at the Hall. I neglected to tell you, Madge, that nearly a fortnight from now, Friday the 14th,"—having found that date in the little diary, a stately Mr. Maynard put away both diary and flashlight,—"we shall entertain two more. From one of them I need advice badly. Madge, do you by any chance remember Alan Grantham? Two years ago, if memory serves, he called on us several times in Goliath when he was the guest of Chancellor Livingston at Colt. Do you remember Alan Grantham?"

"Yes, I remember him. So does—" Madge stopped.

"For the past year he has been at King's College, Pearis, at some not-very-onerous academic job. Pearis, South Carolina, is in the Piedmont some two hundred miles from here."

"I know!"

"He has fallen completely under the spell of Charleston, as some people do. Towards the middle of next week a friend of his will fly from New York to Pearis. On Friday the 14th Mr. Grantham is driving this friend down from Pearis so that he can show his visitor the sights of what was once Charles Town. I invited them to stay with us, of course; but they made polite excuses; I think they prefer the freedom of a hotel. You won't mind seeing Alan Grantham again, will you?"

"No, I won't mind a bit. Alan's nice, and *he* can be entertaining when he tries. But there's somebody else who'll want to see him a good deal more than I ever would or could."

Yancey touched her cheek. "No foolin', pet? Who'll want to see the fellow as much as all that?"

"Camilla will. Oo-er!" breathed Madge, cradling her arms and then extending them. "Camilla's supposed to be the brainy one and she really is, but—oo-er! She's got it so badly for Alan you'd be embarrassed if I told you. And of course, Daddy, Valerie Huret's been making eyes at you; Valerie doesn't like being a widow . . ."

"Now really, Madge!"

". . . but she'd have to do a strip-tease in your study before you noticed. I was talking about Camilla, though. Oo-er! If I ever lost my head over a man, do you think *I'd* be willing to shout it from the housetop and let everybody know?" She stamped her foot. "I'd be too proud to demean myself, so there!"

"Your naïveté, Madge, is refreshing in a jaded age. However! Since you are scarcely an authority on anybody's affairs of the heart . . ."

"Daddy, why do you *want* advice from Alan Grantham? He's concerned with literature and history; he's on the arts side, which you've always distrusted. Why do you want advice from *Alan?"*

"I don't want advice from him; I include him as a matter of courtesy. The man whose counsel I must have is the friend who will accompany him to Charleston."

"Oh? And who's that?"

"A distinguished travelling Englishman, Dr. Gideon Fell. You must remember, my dear. He lectured at Goliath in February; you met him at tea afterwards."

"Madge, there are your ghost-guns again," Yancey Beale interposed, as the sky seemed to tremble with distant noise. "Hear 'em, honey?"

"Ghost-guns?" Madge's voice poured with scorn. "Currents and cross-currents, you mean! All of us bumping together in the water, not for a moment knowing where we're being carried!"

"Madge . . ."

"Yes, I remember Dr. Fell. He lectured on *Murderers I Have Met.* And there's just been the most awful murder in Westchester County, outside New York, some actress shot with a crossbow-bolt or whatnot, and Dr. Fell was the one who . . . Daddy, what *is* all this? Do you think there's going to be a murder here? Or do you just want him to explain how Commodore Maynard died on the beach a hundred years ago? Sometimes I feel it's not worth . . ."

A kind of convulsion crossed the older man's face. "Madge, stop! For God's sake, stop!"

The cry boomed and rang under the magnolias. Then, instantly, Henry Maynard had himself under control.

"Who said anything about murder, my dear? The advice I need concerns you."

"*Me?* How can it concern me?"

A tortured figure looked down at her.

"Everything I do," he said, "is for you and your happiness. You may not appreciate that, you may not even understand it, but by this time you must have some cause to believe it." His voice sharpened. "Let's have no more of the other talk: do I make myself clear?"

"Yes," Madge whispered after a pause.

"Yancey!"

"Sir?"

"I had almost forgotten the weather hereabouts. Tonight has seemed too warm for the beginning of May. But a change is coming; it will be chilly before long; Madge and I had better go in. Have *you* any questions, my boy?"

"Plenty of questions, sir. What follows people and crushes their skulls without any trace to show how?"

"Good night, Yancey! We shall see you tomorrow."

"Something funny goin' on here, I said!" muttered Yancey Beale.

Ghost-guns rolled and tingled along the sky.

2

Friday, May 14th.

At nine o'clock in the morning the Imperial convertible, open, bowled out of Pearis by way of Pinckney Road to Highway 276, which presently would become Interstate 26 past Columbia, the state capital, south-east to the coastal plain and Charleston.

Alan Grantham—who, had he known it, was spiritual kin to Yancey Beale—drove at a steady legal 65. Mountainously piled into the back, too large to be accommodated by the bucket seat beside the driver, was his friend Dr. Gideon Fell.

The fate of Alan Grantham in his mid-thirties might have been envied by many. If Alan himself would not have agreed, it was because he fretted over much in his mind. In addition to the problem presented by the Maynards at James Island, there was the recurrent emotional crisis with Camilla Bruce. Camilla, night or day, was never out of his thoughts. But the enviability of his position had been stressed by Dr. Fell not long after the latter's arrival on Thursday afternoon.

Alan had been on the platform when the big Eastern Airlines Whisperjet, non-stop Newark to Pearis, trundled in at Pearis-Athenstown Airport. Dr. Fell, wearing a shovel hat and a black cloak as big as a tent, came lumbering down the aircraft steps and rolled across on his crutch-headed stick. Pink face already steaming, bandit's moustache downturned and eyeglasses skew-wiff on the black ribbon, he shook hands heartily with a middle-sized, active young man in slacks and a sports-coat.

"Heh!" chuckled Dr. Fell. "Heh-heh-heh! Forgive me, my dear fellow; a blaze of sun has few elements of humor. Do you mind if I remove this incarnadined cloak?"

"Mind? The temperature is 74. I'm wearing a coat only in deference to my alleged academic standing. It's early in the year, of course; the thermometer hasn't really started to rise."

"It has risen far enough," Dr. Fell retorted sternly. "Archons of Athens! In England, as you are well aware, any temperature above 70 constitutes a paralyzing heat-wave. Mightn't we . . . er . . . ?"

"Drink? Of course. You don't want whisky, do you?"

"The man who would drink whisky in this weather," boomed Dr. Fell, "would don flannel underwear in the tropics and call for hamburgers at a Lucullan feast. No, God forbid! Why do you ask?"

"In this state, Magister, hard liquor mayn't be sold by the glass. We may—and do—buy all we want at liquor stores to guzzle at home. If you crave bourbon (in the South always bourbon, though Scotch is not unpopular either), we must wait till we get to my apartment. If beer or wine will do . . ."

"Beer, by all means! Forever beer! There is a place?"

"Here at the airport. This way."

Air-conditioning stroked marble beyond glass doors. In the dusky, pleasant cavern of the bar, with tall glasses of Alt Heidelberg on the table between them, Alan lit a cigarette and his guest an obese meerschaum pipe.

"Nunc bibendum est!" rumbled Dr. Fell, lifting his glass and blowing out sparks like the Spirit of the Volcano. "I knew you in England, Alan, when you were at Simon Magus, Cambridge. One thing I don't know: it never occurred to me the matter was important enough for enquiry. But in this country, I have discovered,

the first question every American asks another is where he comes from. Let joy be unconfined; I bow to custom: where *do* you come from?"

"Wilmington, Delaware, the shrine of the Du Ponts."

"Now, then! This academic standing you mentioned: to what do you attribute it?"

"I said 'alleged' academic standing, remember. None of my friends, believe me, can find it half as funny as I do."

"A commendable attitude, but try to answer. To what do you attribute it?"

"My M.A. Cantab," replied Alan. "A master's degree from Simon Magus seems to have powerfully stimulating effects."

"What, precisely, are your duties here?"

"At King's College, which celebrates its two hundredth anniversary in 1967 and whose name remained unchanged even when Richard Pearis, its first Tory backer, was chased out of town at the time of the Revolution, I have been delivering the Hughes Burwell Memorial Lectures in English Literature. Only twenty lectures need be given throughout the year; my stint is finished until just before commencement in June."

"Oh, ah! Are you a good lecturer?"

"I have enthusiasm, that's all. As a lecturer, I suppose, I can't be more than indifferent. Camilla would say . . ."

"Camilla being Miss Bruce? The young lady you talk of so frequently? What *would* she say?"

"A good deal. Because I can't admire our present-day sacred cows, the much-touted Prousts and Joyces with reputations overblown out of all proportion to their merit, I'm supposed to be an old mossback interested only in sensational melodrama or slapstick farce."

"Is it true?"

"To a certain extent; only a certain extent. They don't seem to mind at King's, though. They've asked me to stay on next year as a regular member of the faculty, which I have every intention of doing."

"I gather from your letters," said Dr. Fell, "you're rather fond of the South?"

"*Rather* fond of it? This, very definitely, is the place for your obedient. I like the people; I like their easy-going ways, and the freedom from pressures so incessant in New York or thereabouts. In short, I feel at home."

Wheezing, rumbling, brushing ash from the vast slopes of himself, Dr. Fell sat back and blinked at the other through lopsided eyeglasses.

"Has it never occurred to you, Alan, that you are a very fortunate chap?"

"Well . . ."

"Consider! Yours is an independent income. You need no academic post if you don't want one. You have youth, health; yes, and beyond doubt enthusiasm: it bubbles or roars through every word. Has your extreme good fortune never occurred to you?"

" 'Wheresoever a man liveth, there will be a thorn-bush by his door.' "

"Your particular thorn-bush being—?"

"Camilla. Or mainly Camilla. If only the damn woman could be persuaded to take some interest in me!"

"And she won't?"

"I don't know, Magister; shall we drop the subject? And an anti-mathematician like me mustn't monopolize the talk. How goes it with *you,* Dr. Fell? Has the case at Richbell been wound up?"

"Wound up satisfactorily, or reasonably so, when a police-lieutenant named Spinelli shot the guilty party at an amusement park. I only hope—"

"You hope you're not walking into another one? Is that it?"

"Frankly, my dear fellow, I have no notion where I may be walking. The good Mr. Henry Maynard, for instance: what does he want of me? He won't say; he continues to hint. Can you supply any illumination?"

"I don't know either; I'm merely horse to your Lady Godiva. But the Maynards . . ."

"*Sat prata biberunt!*" intoned Dr. Fell, finishing his beer and whacking down the glass. "This Maynard business, it seems to me, has more than one curious feature. With your permission, however, we will drop THAT subject until it obtrudes itself on our notice."

And so, at nine on Friday morning, in Alan's Imperial they left town by Highway 276. It was a fine day with a breeze. Dr. Fell in the back had his crutch-headed stick propped in front of him, hands folded on top. He had laid aside his hat, which wouldn't stay on against the wind; his great mop of gray hair blew wildly, as did the ribbon on his eyeglasses. But the pink face beamed all over; chuckles animated his several chins. At intervals he would bend sideways and catch Alan's eye in the rear-view mirror, a living image of Old King Cole.

They had left Pearis far behind when he spoke.

"By the way," he said, "where are we staying in Charleston? We have both declined Maynard's invitation, I gather?"

"Yes. There are two luxury hotels: the Francis Marion at King and Calhoun Streets, and the Fort Sumter on Murray Boulevard overlooking the harbor. Both are first-class; if I prefer the Francis Marion, it's because I have stayed there often and I'm familiar with it. Anyway, I've reserved rooms there."

"Good! Clever-good! The Francis Marion let it be."

"There was something else you started to say, Magister?"

"Oh, ah!" agreed Dr. Fell, in his absent-mindedness looking rather half-witted. "I myself (harrumph!) am not altogether ignorant of the South, though the lecturer's path lies mainly through large cities: Richmond, Atlanta, New Orleans."

"Then you've never visited Charleston?"

"On the contrary, I was there once some years ago, but for so brief a time that I scarcely saw it."

"What can you tell me about the place?"

Dr. Fell squinted at the sun, which always seems to be in your eyes no matter which direction you drive.

"Without wishing to sound like a handy guide," he replied, "I can inform you that the city of Charleston—called Charles Town for King Charles the Second in the later seventeenth century; it did not become Charleston until it was incorporated after the American Revolution—is built on a peninsula between the Ashley and Cooper Rivers, whose waters unite in a harbor ringed with sandy islands and ancient forts. Hazily I recall a quiet city of pastel colors and graceful church-spires, of houses with double piazzas and gardens in tropical bloom. I recall a very long if rather narrow thoroughfare . . ."

"King Street."

". . . knifing straight down through from the northern suburbs to the Battery. But always," wheezed Dr. Fell, looking still more half-witted, "this dull old brain returns to buzz like a fly round those islands in the harbor. Permit *me* to ask a question or two."

"Yes?"

"Sullivan's Island with Fort Moultrie, of course, is famous in song and story. So is Fort Sumter. Where precisely is Fort Sumter?"

"A little way inside the mouth of the harbor, on an artificial island of its own."

"It is notorious (harrumph!)—it is notorious that before daybreak on April 12th, 1861, the Confederates fired on Fort Sumter and inaugurated the unpleasantness between North and South. But how did they fire on it? From a ship?"

"No, Magister. From another fort."

"Another *fort?*"

"Yes. From Fort Johnson, at the eastern tip of James Island less than two miles away. You visit Fort Sumter by water; a little steamer makes the excursion every day."

"And the other islands?"

"There are bridges to them all. You can't visit what remains of Fort Johnson; they've built a marine research station at that tip of James Island. But Maynard Hall is very close to there, off Fort Johnson Road. You see where this leads us, Dr. Fell? It leads straight round in a circle to the Maynards, their friends, and our own present embarrassment. Shall we discuss the subject at long last?"

"Oh, ah! We had better."

"I won't go into the history of the Maynards; Mr. Maynard himself can tell us much more than I've been able to find by digging in libraries. Anyway, it's the present situation that seems to be causing a lot of grief."

"And what is the present situation, my dear fellow?" boomed Dr. Fell. "Maynard wrote that he meant to assemble what he called a small house-party. But that was to begin almost a fortnight ago, on May 3rd. Surely the party must have broken up long since?"

"Not a bit of it. They're all still there."

"Archons of Athens! *Who* is still there?"

"Henry Maynard, his daughter (her mother died soon after Madge was born), my Camilla, a former newspaper-editor called Crandall, and a pair of fledgling lawyers, Northern and Southern: respectively Ripton Hillboro and Yancey Beale. Two others not house-guests but paying frequent calls are a young medical man, Mark Sheldon, and a youngish woman, Valerie Huret, who married the scion of an old Huguenot family and was widowed three or four years ago. The party's still in progress."

"How do you know this?"

"From Camilla. She writes regularly, if coolly."

"And you spoke of 'grief.' What grief?"

"Say alarm and confusion, then; exactly what remains obscure. Camilla's been cryptic, as cryptic as Henry Maynard, so cryptic I can't be certain of one damn fact. Camilla's upset, though. Something rather sensational occurred last Friday night, the 7th, when Mr. Maynard was away on a business-trip to Richmond. Up to then, it seems, he himself had been despondent and down in the mouth. When he returned Saturday morning he was a changed man, hearty and full of beans. The guests were supposed to leave at the weekend; he wouldn't hear of it, and persuaded 'em to stay. Except that Camilla is upset, which bothers me a good deal, that's all I can tell you."

Then Alan burst out. Though normally a driver who kept his

eye strictly on the road, he flashed round a look before turning back.

"What do *you* make of Henry Maynard, for God's sake? Outwardly he seems stuffy, but I'm willing to bet he's not stuffy at all. There's an explosive personality behind that façade."

"Agreed without a struggle," grunted Dr. Fell.

"How well do you know him, Magister?"

"I have met the man just once. And you?"

"I've seen him only three times, and two years ago at that, when I called on 'em at Goliath in Connecticut. There's a daughter named Madge."

"Oh, ah; I know. Well?"

"Madge radiates sex-appeal," Alan said. "Like the late Gaby Delys, she has an eye that can open an oyster at sixty paces. Madge isn't conscious of this; it's as natural to her as breathing, and she never quite guesses the effect on every male within yards. I might have fallen for her myself, which is why I went there three times, if I hadn't met Camilla and . . . and . . ."

"And what?" demanded Dr. Fell, now looking pinkly distressed. "Forgive the curiosity of an old duffer, but why such reluctance to speak of the lady? Is it merely that you have fallen? You're in love with her?"

"Yes, except when I want to murder her. Or, which is more accurate, when she wants to murder me."

"Wants to murder you, does she? Surely a hopeful sign, by thunder!"

"No, it's past hope. Camilla's different from other women."

"In what way is she different?"

"Not anatomically; I can swear to that. For sheer sex-appeal, in my view, she outdoes Madge Maynard and any other woman alive."

"Then what, pray, is the nature of the difficulty? Hang it all! Can I persuade you to be a little more explicit?"

Alan pondered.

"There is no subject calling for an opinion," he said, "where we don't collide head-on. Camilla's a mathematician, mathematics being my pet abomination. Politically she's a liberal concerned about social welfare; I'm a reactionary conservative who couldn't care less. She's got some fairly far-out views on letters and art; I see no virtue in butchering the English language or spoiling canvas with a nightmare. The best we achieve is an armed truce; wait and see."

"Are you sure (harrupmh!)—are you sure you understand the lady? For instance, have you mentioned your more than tepid feelings for her?"

"No; Camilla wouldn't be interested." Then Alan burst out again. "But I wish I knew what's happening at Maynard Hall. If the ghost of a dead pirate is still alert to stalk somebody and smash his head with the blunt side of a tomahawk . . . !"

It was as though he had flung a bucket of water into his companion's face.

"One moment!" spluttered Dr. Fell, gasping and choking for breath. "Will you repeat that, please? If the ghost of a dead pirate is still alert to WHAT?"

"It's only a legend, Magister. Founded on fact, but the rest whisper and rumor: all cloud."

"Cloud or moonshine, my lad, let's have it!"

Alan studied the road ahead.

"The first Maynard to be granted land by the Lords Proprietors of the Province of Carolina (in 1685, I believe) was called Richard. The names Richard, Henry, and Luke keep recurring to the present day.

"No longer a young man, our first Richard seems to have been something of a swashbuckler. But he had bought five hundred acres on the north shore of James Island; he married, started a family, and settled in to grow rice and sea-island cotton. Then came his bitter feud with Big Nat Skeene.

"Nathaniel Skeene, though decently bred and educated, was a tangle-bearded ruffian of the most vicious sort. He had sailed with pirates and lived with Indians; but nobody could prove the former, and of the latter he boasted. He lived then in a stone hut beside a swamp on the south shore of the island, not far from what is now Folly Beach. We don't know why he hated Richard Maynard and threatened to (quote) 'have his guts out'; Richard returned the hatred in full force.

"Joseph Morton, Governor of Charles Town Colony, had been looking for an excuse to get rid of Skeene. The years rolled; he found his excuse. Big Nat had two Indian wives who actually were slaves; the law forbade slavery for Indians if not for Negroes. One day in 1692 Governor Morton dispatched his military aide, Captain Waring, to give Skeene walking-papers and turn the man out. Captain Waring crossed from the mainland in a small boat, but wasn't sure where to find Skeene. Richard Maynard offered to guide him.

"They rode over on the embryonic trail which was the only path that then existed. No sooner had they dismounted than Big Nat came rushing out of the house, his arms loaded with primitive weapons. Paying no attention to the governor's officer, he directed all venom at his old enemy. He flung weapons at Richard's feet, bellowed the sort of challenge no Maynard could refuse, and charged in hell-roaring.

"Quite a battle must have danced on those lonely sands beside the swamp. They fought Indian-style with knives and tomahawks, knife in the right hand and tomahawk in the left.

"Richard Maynard, a good swordsman but unused to butcher's work like this, had great speed or great luck. He was far from squeamish; he didn't mind fighting with the knife. But to split any man's skull with a tomahawk, whether thrown from a distance or used hand-to-hand, seemed to him bloody barbarism. He dodged Skeene's first rushes, then lost *his* head and waded in.

"The tomahawk, you know, was only a smaller hatchet with a flat surface, no hammer-head, on the side opposite its cutting edge. Even the blunt side was deadly enough. Skeene charged again, striking upwards with the knife for his opponent's belly. With the tomahawk turned in his hand, blunt side inwards, Richard whacked hard at the right side of Skeene's head. Skeene failed to parry with knife-arm; the blow struck him senseless or worse; even as he was falling Richard stabbed him to the heart.

"They buried Big Nat at the edge of the swamp where he fell. Since Captain Waring had witnessed everything, Richard Maynard's 'trial' was no trial at all. The jury discharged him almost with a vote of thanks, certainly with recorded thanks that Skeene had been given Christian burial. So far the story's true; it's a matter of record; you can find it under sign and seal. But afterwards, Dr. Fell . . . afterwards . . . !"

Dr. Fell, who had been listening in cross-eyed absorption, here reared up.

"With exemplary patience," he said, "I have heard very tolerable sensationalism. Cheerfully will I continue listening. So far, however, there has been no puzzle to keep us awake o' nights."

"Richard Maynard, they say, was kept awake o' nights."

"Well?"

"Again the years rolled on," Alan continued. "No trace, apparently, remained of Big Nat Skeene. His hut fell to ruin; his wives returned to their Tuscarora tribe. Except for an influx of settlers, then as later, James Island remained the same. It was Richard Maynard who gradually changed.

"Never very genial, he grew so morose and edgy that his children were afraid to go near him. To anyone who would listen he complained that something or somebody was following him everywhere. He would go through the roof at a suddenly opened door; he dreaded the hour of dusk, and couldn't bear the night.

"One day in 1698 he rode again to the other side of the island. Nobody knows why he went there. His horse returned that night; he didn't. At dawn they found his body in the swamp a few hundred yards north of Big Nat's grave. The right side of his head had been battered in: not with a cutting edge, but as though by repeated blows from the blunt side of a tomahawk. His own footprints, only his, were in the soft mud roundabout. No weapon of any kind could be found.

"There's the story, Dr. Fell. Make of it what you like; I apologize for such foolishness. But Nathaniel Skeene living was no fit associate for anybody. Nathaniel Skeene dead would have been still less desirable company."

Dr. Fell had shut his eyes tightly and was groping in the air.

"Stop!" he boomed. "I think I have heard . . . Isn't there a subsequent story rather like that one, about two hundred years later?"

"If you mean Commodore Luke Maynard in 1867, we have almost as little evidence about him."

"Almost as little evidence? Archons of Athens! Surely there were newspapers?"

"Oh, yes. But—"

"But what?"

"Commodore Luke Maynard, a grim sort of swashbuckler and as fire-eating a Confederate as ever lived, commanded one of the Southern raiders which wreaked such havoc on Union commerce. Everybody has heard of C.S.S. *Florida* and C.S.S. *Alabama.* Luke Maynard commanded C.S.S. *Palmetto,* like the others built in England and fitted with guns at a port far from Britain. She was finally accounted for by U.S.S. *Pontiac,* of much heavier tonnage and gun-power; the two warships sank each other in a running fight off Jamaica in 1864. Luke Maynard stayed with his ship when it went down, but was picked up by a boat-load of Confederate sympathizers from Port Royal.

"If he didn't die under the guns of the enemy, he might well have died in a duel after the war. Down came the stars and bars from the flagstaff outside Maynard Hall. The grip of reconstruction squeezed Charleston hard; Union troops occupied the then-Citadel on Marion Square; there were damnyankees at every corner, and Commodore Maynard had no even temper. Yet he didn't die by a bullet either.

"One night in April of '67 he was walking west along the beach below and at one side of the Hall. They found his body at low tide next morning. Though he lay above the highest reach of the tide, the sand was damp for thirty feet around him in every direction. Right side of the head battered in, no footprints except his own, no weapon there either.

"I said the newspapers weren't very helpful. They're still preserved in the basement at Charleston City College Library. But you can understand why they're not very helpful. The Confederacy had endured four years of horrors, including Sherman's gentle march from Atlanta to the sea, and afterwards into the Carolinas too; the Confederacy had supped full. Newspaper accounts of Commodore Maynard's death are so discreet it's hard to tell what happened. The one point they do mention is hardly informative. On the sand at a short distance from the body, twelve or fifteen inches from his head and ten inches above it, lay a little tangle of seaweed."

"Seaweed!" Dr. Fell suddenly boomed. "O Lord! O Bacchus! O my ancient hat! Did you say *seaweed?*"

"Yes. It's often found on beaches, you know."

"Oh, ah; of course. I was wool-gathering again." Dr. Fell blinked at the countryside flowing by. "Incidentally, where are we now?"

"Past Columbia and the hundred-mile mark. In another hour and a bit . . ."

They said little more for the rest of the journey. With cross-eyed concentration Dr. Fell studied, hands folded on his stick. Alan smoked cigarette after cigarette, an image of Camilla in his mind. He saw the chestnut-colored hair, the glow of her complexion, the dark-blue eyes that would never quite meet his own.

At a quarter past noon they were negotiating the gritty industrial area north of Charleston's center. Alan made a right-hand turn through thickening traffic.

"This is King Street," he said, "the very long thoroughfare you mentioned. Now ten minutes or so of fast-changing traffic lights. When the light turns green, you must be almost the next car in line or it's red again before you get there."

"Must we search all over town for the hotel?"

"No. You'll see it presently on the right, at the corner of Calhoun Street opposite Marion Square. Watch for a large red-brick building with the entrance to the parking space beside it in this direction.

"As I tried to indicate long ago," he said ten minutes later, "Henry Maynard should be able to tell us more family history than there is in the record." Disquiet smote again. "But nothing very bad can be going on now, or we should have heard of it! There can't be anything wrong, can there? This is where we turn in."

"Well," said Dr. Fell, "somebody seems to be hailing you. The young lady . . ."

Alan's heart jumped. He drew up at a white-painted barrier across the entrance to the open auto lobby. With his left hand he pressed a silvered knob on the box-mechanism that controlled the barrier. The mechanism rang, yielding up a punched slip of paper; the barrier rose, and he drove through.

Then he saw her.

Slightly taller than Madge Maynard, perhaps a little more slender though with much the same figure, she wore a blue-and-white summer dress of somewhat formal aspect, and raised a pair of sun-glasses at him.

"Camilla!"

"Alan!"

"It's all right, isn't it? They haven't been using a tomahawk, I hope?"

"No, not lately," said Camilla. She seemed a trifle flustered, no doubt from the warmth of the day. "If you're referring to those horrible old stories, there's a tomahawk in the weapons-room. But it's gone out of fashion nowadays, even as something for you to use on me."

"On *you?"*

For the first time Alan noticed somebody else, and caught himself at once. Behind Camilla towered a burly man in dark suit and dark tie, beginning to put on weight as his years neared fifty. He had a hard jaw but a good-natured eye; his manner was deliberate and ruminating. Camilla's attention remained with Alan.

"*I* haven't done anything wrong, have I?" she asked. "You said you'd be at this hotel, and get here about twelve-thirty. Oh! Forgive me! This is Mr. . . . Lieutenant . . . Captain . . ."

"Captain Ashcroft," interposed the burly man, "Charleston County Police." His eye woke up. "Mr. Grantham? Dr. Gideon Fell?"

In the back of the car Dr. Fell arose and bowed, an impressive spectacle. Captain Ashcroft addressed him with great formality.

"When you've checked in, sir, you and Mr. Grantham, I'd be right glad of a word off the record. Fair enough, sir?"

"The word, sir," Dr. Fell returned with even more powerful formality, "shall be obtained at lunch. Meanwhile, allow me to frame the question with which my young friend has been struggling. Has there been any disturbance at Maynard Hall?"

Captain Ashcroft deliberated.

"Well . . . now!" He extended a hand as though to make mesmeric passes. "Nothing to get excited about, maybe. But you *could* call it a disturbance if you wanted to. Anyway, somebody stole a scarecrow."

3

"Would you mind repeating that, Camilla? About last Friday night?"

"The whole story?"

They had finished lunch in the air-conditioned coffee-shop at the hotel. Camilla Bruce, Alan Grantham, and Captain Ashcroft sat at a table for four. Across the road, beyond a wall of plate-glass window giving on King Street, amid Marion Square's greenery and flowers, John C. Calhoun on his tall column looked south over a city of what Dr. Fell had called pastel colors and graceful church-spires.

Alan, across the table from Camilla, was very conscious of her nearness. Complexion cream and rose, rich brown hair worn almost to her shoulders, dark-blue eyes straying towards the window whenever he tried to catch them, Camilla fidgeted badly. He had been wrong about the formal appearance of her dress; at close range Camilla's figure made it anything but formal.

"The whole story?" she repeated. "Really—!"

Captain Ashcroft put his elbows on the table.

"Now, ma'am," he was insidiously persuasive, "you just do what Mr. Grantham tells you to do. Yes, the whole story; I'd like to hear it again myself. Not about the scarecrow, maybe. To my way of thinking that's not important. The no-counts of this world would steal anything! They got your scarecrow, ma'am; nobody else did."

"The scarecrow," Alan interjected, "wasn't in a cornfield, then?"

Camilla's gentle voice held a note of pain. "Oh, Alan, you're thinking of *The Wizard of Oz!*"

"Am I?"

"How often have you seen a scarecrow in a cornfield? People put up scarecrows wherever they think the birds may do some damage. This one, as I've tried to explain, was in the garden at the back of the Hall. Madge put it up when they first came there in April; I helped her. She found a bag of salt that was just the right size for the head. She took one of her father's good suits and hats. Mr. Maynard didn't like that; he didn't say much, but you could feel him breathing annoyance as soon as he saw it."

"I don't blame him, Camilla. Dandyism in a scarecrow seems out of place."

"Realism isn't out of place, surely? The colored gardener gave us a kind of bib-thing to hold it together. Madge and I stuffed the scarecrow with straw; maybe *we* were thinking of *The Wizard of Oz.* We pinned the bib-thing inside the coat, and tied the arms and legs together with twine. It was a *beautiful* scarecrow."

"I'll bet it was."

"Alan Grantham, will you please stop sitting there and sneering every time I open my mouth?"

"I wasn't sneering, Camilla."

"You were; you know you were; you always do! I can't say one word without being picked up on it!"

Captain Ashcroft made a massive and pacifying gesture.

"Now, ma'am," he said at his most fatherly, "you forget the scarecrow. What bothers me is all that hoo-ha in the middle of the night. Yes, yes, I know the others have given me their versions! Suppose you tell us yours again, as you told Dr. Fell a while ago?"

"Where *is* Dr. Fell?"

"You've not forgotten, ma'am, he was called to the phone hardly three minutes ago? And that reminds me. Mr. Grantham, do you know a man named Spinelli, Lieutenant Carlo Spinelli, in Westchester County outside New York?"

"I don't know him. I've heard Dr. Fell mention him."

Captain Ashcroft shook a graying head.

"Twenty years ago and more I was in the Army with Carlo Spinelli. You ought to hear *him* about Dr. Fell! Thinks the world of that blundering man-mountain, Spinny does; and now I've met the man I'll go along with it. Come on, Miss Bruce! You don't mind telling me, do you?"

"I don't mind telling *you,* Captain Ashcroft. You're very easy to talk to, not like some people I could mention."

"Now, now, ma'am!"

"But I didn't think you were going to be like this at all." Camilla pushed back a lock of hair. "Rip Hillboro persuaded Mr. Maynard to get in touch with the police, which he didn't want to do. When Madge said there was a detective coming from Charleston . . ."

"Scared you, did it?"

"I was frightened to death; I wanted to run and hide. In the stories . . ."

"I know, ma'am, I know! If we carried on like what they do in those detective stories we'd be in a heap of trouble every time we turned around. Lots of people seem to have it in for us: *po*lice always wrong, any old crook always right. It's a hard job and a thankless job and it don't pay hardly anything, but we're not such a bad bunch in the long run; you hear?"

"Captain Ashcroft," Camilla said gently, "may I ask *you* a question? You know Mr. Maynard fairly well, don't you?"

Captain Ashcroft may have been a strong man; he was not a silent one.

"I've known the Maynards," he answered, "almost since I can

remember anything at all. They've been gentry for near on to three hundred years; I'm not that, exactly, though my great-granddaddy *was* chief gunnery-officer of the *Palmetto* when Henry's great-granddaddy commanded her."

Here, with a motion of apology to Camilla, he bit off the end of a King Edward cigar and lighted it.

"In the last generation there were only two of 'em, Richard and Henry. Richard, the older one, died unmarried a couple of months ago; he had inherited the property, and there was still plenty of property to inherit.

"But Henry, who's eight or ten years older than I am, never had to worry. He was his mother's favorite; you know what that means. They sent him to a swell preparatory school up north, then to Williams or Amherst or one of those places; I wouldn't know. His mother left him so well fixed he could suit himself and live abroad, which he did almost until Hitler walked into France.

"That's my part of the story, and I'm right happy to tell it. Early last Saturday afternoon, the 8th, we get a call at the office; there'd been a rumpus on James Island the night before. 'Joe,' the chief says to me—I don't let this get out usually; my first name's Josephus for Josephus Daniels of North Carolina—'Joe,' he says, 'we can't tell what this is, probably nothing at all. Still, you know the folks. You're no Lord Chesterfield or Beau Brummell, but you won't throw soup in their faces or jump up in the air just to land on somebody's toes. You hike out and see.'

"Now, little lady, it's *your* turn. You've got no call to be scared, anybody as sweet and pretty as you are. It happened 'most a week ago, didn't it, and you've already told it once this morning? I don't want to crowd you, believe me! But I agree with young Mr. Beale: something mighty damn funny goin' on over there, and I'd be grateful for any extra help you can give."

"All right," Camilla agreed.

She still fidgeted badly, the strain showing in her eyes. Alan had lit a cigarette for her when he lit his own, but she put it out at once. Camilla clasped her hands together. She looked out the window, as though intent on the rap of heels along the sidewalk; then she turned back.

"Mr. Maynard," Camilla began, "was away in Richmond that night. Valerie Huret and Dr. Sheldon came to dinner, and Bob Crandall had arrived from Goliath. After dinner we had coffee in the back garden. When we went indoors about ten o'clock, we can all testify the scarecrow hadn't been touched."

Now it was Josephus Ashcroft who displayed anguish.

"Pardon my language, ma'am, but did you hear what I said about that God-damn scarecrow?"

"It's the theft of the scarecrow you're investigating, isn't it?"

"I don't know what I *am* investigating, ma'am. That's just the trouble. Go on."

"Well, we went indoors about ten o'clock. Valerie Huret and Dr. Sheldon left together at that time. The rest of us, Madge and Yancey and Rip and Bob Crandall and I . . ."

"Whoa, ma'am; whoa there! Take it easy, and not so fast." Captain Ashcroft spoke with a certain excitement. "You're not saying . . . you can't be saying . . . ?"

"Saying what?"

"Mark Sheldon's got a wife of his own; they've been married for less than a year, and a very fine person she is. Blow me down! You're not suggesting there's something between Mrs. Huret and that young doctor?"

Camilla was appalled. "Saying it? Suggesting it?"

"Ma'am?"

"I'm not even *dreaming* it. Neither is anybody else. They're casual acquaintances, that's all. They 'left together' because they live near each other, somewhere down around East Bay in Charleston. She'd be too old for him anyway, even though she doesn't look it. If Valerie's interested in anybody, Madge thinks, she's interested in Madge's father."

"Or in Mr. Crandall, maybe? That'd be my own guess; I could

be far wrong. Also, speaking of who's got a fancy for whom, Miss Maynard says that you . . ."

His eye flickered briefly round the table. Camilla's color came up; she held herself rigidly.

"Madge says—what?"

"Nothing, ma'am, ab-so-lutely nothing! However! Since you're in the young lady's confidence and can probably guess . . ."

"I'm not in Madge's confidence. Madge doesn't confide in anybody, really. She's a sweet girl, as you would put it. But she has moods. You mustn't take her moods too seriously or regard her as an authority on anything relating to me."

"I won't, ma'am. Still! Even if you did have a fancy, where would be the harm in it?"

"Now listen, Mr. Jehoshaphat Ashcroft . . . !"

"Josephus Ashcroft! Just 'Joe' will do."

"Please!" Camilla begged, more than half docile again. "I don't know anything about policemen, especially policemen like you. But what are we doing, really? Are we discussing some rather frightening experiences last Friday night or are we just fishing for idle gossip?"

"You'd be surprised, ma'am, how much real evidence can be buried in idle gossip. I don't say the funny business at Maynard Hall comes from somebody fooling with the wrong woman, or with any woman at all. But it's much more likely to be caused by that, now, isn't it, than by anything that happened many years ago?"

"Well . . ."

"We can discuss the frightening experiences, ma'am, if you'll just get on and tell 'em while I think."

"I'm sorry, Captain Ashcroft! Where was I? Oh, yes!"

Camilla put her hands flat on the tablecloth and drew a deep breath.

"Madge and Yancey and Rip and Bob Crandall and I came indoors, then. It was warm during the day, but it had turned cool with twilight. A mist rose off the water, as they say it often does. The five of us went to the library, which is the big room to the left of the front door and down four steps, with the books behind wire gratings and early Victorian furniture padded in yellow satin. Then they started telling ghost stories."

"Who told the ghost stories?"

"Yancey and Rip. Yancey began on a dreadful one out of M. R. James; Rip countered with the severed hand that has a life of its own and crawls across things to strangle people. Ever since Monday, you see, Rip and Yancey had been trying to top each other's remarks and impress Madge; they're still doing it."

"Not much love lost between those two, is there?"

"No, none at all. But they both began by being heavily polite to each other, much too polite when you remember Rip's aggressiveness; and they've continued that too."

"Both of 'em gone on the young lady, aren't they?"

"Oh, yes. I'm betraying no secret when I say that. Given the least opportunity, either will buttonhole you and explain at length."

"Which one does she favor?"

"I don't know. I'm Madge's closest friend; she's been kept so much in cotton-wool that maybe I'm her only friend. But, as I told you a while ago, Madge doesn't confide things like that; she keeps her own counsel far better than—" Camilla stopped.

"Anyway, on and on went the ghost stories! Bob Crandall tried to lighten the atmosphere by giving an account of life on a small-town newspaper in the old days before they had teletypes; a reporter at the typewriter would put on head-phones and take dictation from what was known as a 'pony-call.' And he quoted some typographical errors that were real beauties, though I've no intention of repeating them.

"It didn't matter. Whichever way we turned, whatever we started to talk about, back it came to something wickedly supernatural. Really, I ask you! Ghost stories in the space age! It was absolutely ridiculous, don't you think?"

"Well . . . now!" Captain Ashcroft said in his ruminating way. "I wouldn't just like to go as far as that, no. There's more things in the world than we know about, maybe. What do you think, Mr. Grantham? Agree with the lady?"

"It's not the least bit of use asking Alan," Camilla said sweetly, "because he'll only disagree on principle. All he ever does is ignore me or sneer at me."

Alan jumped to his feet.

"For God's sake, Camilla, when have I ever done that?"

"When haven't you done it? What are you doing right now?"

Alan studied her, mouth and eyes and figure.

"If I told you what I'm thinking at this minute"—he sat down again—"you might feel still less cooperative than you already are. I won't do it, Camilla! Just go on with the story."

Camilla fixed her attention on Captain Ashcroft.

"Yes, it was ridiculous," she insisted. "But the atmosphere had been established too well. Start thinking of horrors, especially at a place like Maynard Hall when the time's close on midnight, and you'll have the horrors in spite of yourself.

"It was affecting Madge badly. Yancey saw that and stopped talking; nothing could stop Rip. Towards twelve-thirty, when we were getting ready to go up to bed, Rip said, 'Madge, do you know about the thing that follows and leaves no trace? At the Library Association they say the story's found in only one book, called *Sea-Island Ghosts.*' Madge said, 'Rip, there's no such ghost.' 'I know there isn't,' said Rip, 'but what if it tapped at one of our doors in the middle of the night?'

"Yancey shouted, 'You shut your mouth,' and for a second I thought there would be trouble. But there wasn't. Madge ran out of the room and up to bed; she told me later she took two sleeping-pills. Yancey said, 'God help me, I started this.' Then *he* turned around and *almost* ran out of the room; anyway, he went.

"The rest of us followed more slowly. I was in as bad a state as Madge; I can't defend myself. In the upstairs hall on my way to my room I looked out of a window facing north over the beach. The mist had cleared; the moon was shining. But all I could think of was poor Commodore Maynard with his head battered in.

"We'd had rather a lot of wine at dinner, and whisky in the library afterwards. I hoped it would put me to sleep, but of course it didn't. I was wide awake—and worse.

"My room is on the south-western angle at the back of the house, above a weapons-and-trophy-room behind the library on the ground floor. When Mr. Maynard's elder brother partly rebuilt and modernized the Hall in the late nineteen-forties, he added a private bathroom to every bedroom, and put an air-conditioner in one window of every bedroom. That air-conditioner is necessary, or at night the mosquitoes would drive you crazy.

"Yes, I was in a state. I had some sleeping-tablets of my own; not the heavy kind Madge uses but some lighter stuff, called Dormez-Vous, you can buy without a prescription at any drugstore.

"I had locked the door. I took two pills; I got undressed; I paced the floor, smoking cigarettes. It would take about half an hour for the pills to work, if they worked at all. Meanwhile, every creak and crack of the woodwork brought fancies I oughtn't to have had. I picked up the bedside book; it was called *Sea-Island Ghosts*.

"I threw that book across the room, and scared myself with the noise it made when it hit the wall. At about one o'clock I thought I might be feeling drowsy. My watch has a luminous dial." Camilla held up her left wrist to show the gold band. "I put it on the bedside table. I turned out the overhead light, crawled into bed, turned out the bedside lamp, and hoped for the best.

"Well, the pills worked—after a fashion. I lost consciousness, at least. There were dreams of some kind. Then my eyes were open again.

"This, it developed later, was at half-past three in the morning. I didn't turn on the light or look at my watch. My eyes were open, yes. But I was confused and only half conscious, with the fears pretty well dulled.

"The moon had set. What drew me to the window it's impossible to say. That room has two windows above the back garden, with the air-conditioner blocking the lower part of the left-hand one. In bare feet and pajamas I blundered over to the right-hand window. I looked out and then down.

"The weapons-room below has a big French window, two leaves to the window, opening on the garden. What I could just barely see in such a light made me push up the bedroom window; it slid smoothly and without noise. The leaves of the big French window, below me and to my left, had been pushed or drawn partway outward. There was somebody standing in the aperture between them."

Captain Ashcroft shifted in his chair and struck two fingers on the edge of the table.

"I've asked you before, ma'am . . . !"

"I know you have; they all have. But what can I say?"

"Description, ma'am?"

"It was a man, or at least I suppose it was: who else can it have been? He stood sideways, facing to the left away from me. I have an idea, rightly or wrongly, there was some kind of stocking-mask over his head and face. He didn't move; I couldn't tell whether he was going out or coming in. That's all the description I can give."

"Did you think it was a ghost or a burglar?"

"I didn't stop to think; I wasn't that coherent. All the fears rushed back, and I panicked. I grabbed up robe and slippers, turning on every light I could reach. Then I ran down the hall and hammered at Madge's door.

"Possibly I should have gone to one of the men first. It wasn't a reasoned thing; it was instinctive. Madge's heavier sleeping-pills hadn't served any better than mine; if you're used to them, she says, they won't keep you under for more than a few hours. Out she came in *her* pajamas. We must have talked loudly, almost shouted; in a short time we'd waked up the other three.

"We didn't rouse the servants, who sleep on the top floor at the back. The men were all for burglars: Yancey and Rip stalked downstairs with their fists clenched, and Madge clinging to

Yancey's arm. I followed with Mr. Crandall, who'd turned grumpy at that hour of the morning. You know what we found.

"There was no burglar in the house, and nothing had been stolen from it. The French window in the weapons-room was now closed, but not locked; no window there is ever locked. To me it was beginning to seem weird."

"Weird, ma'am?"

"That was the word. Whoever had been at the French window, it couldn't have been somebody from inside the house going out; we were all there. And it couldn't have been somebody from outside the house coming in; where was he? But to the others, after we'd searched until daylight without any result, it wasn't weird in the least. Yancey just patted me on the back and said, 'Honey, you were dreaming.' "

Camilla clenched her hands.

"That's what they all thought and still think, though they won't always come out flat with it. Good old Camilla! Too much impressed by the ghost stories, she took sleeping-pills on top of alcohol and had only been hysterical!

"It's true that Rip Hillboro, hunting through the garden when it got light enough to see, found the scarecrow was gone. But that didn't help much.

"And it didn't help at all when Mr. Maynard arrived back Saturday morning, on an early flight from Richmond that got him home in time for lunch. He'd gone away moody and depressed (I think I wrote this to Alan), but he came back as cheerful as all getout. It's even changed his habits a little. He still sits on the terrace in the afternoon and in his study during the evening, but he doesn't always seem to be calculating something. We'd been supposed to leave at the weekend, all of us; he begged us to stay on; and he's got a way with him. He hadn't any trouble persuading the others, and I stayed because . . . well, I stayed. May I have another cigarette, please?"

Alan lit one for her. Acknowledging the favor with a slight nod, Camilla expelled smoke hard.

"*Mr. Maynard* thought I was dreaming. The only one even

partway inclined to be serious was the hard-headed Rip. When Mr. Maynard pooh-poohed the idea of phoning the police about anything, Rip said: 'Probably the poor girl *was* hysterical, sir. The scarecrow *was* taken by a sneak-thief, as you think, and has nothing to do with this. Still! Suppose she wasn't dreaming; just suppose it! In case something or somebody should pay us a visit we don't want, why not be on the safe side and let the cops know?' Am I making myself clear this time, Captain Ashcroft?"

"Can't complain about the clearness, ma'am; not a bit! It's just that . . ."

"You don't believe me?"

"I didn't say that either."

"You yourself, Captain, won't hear a word about the scarecrow. But Rip Hillboro's no fool. With your permission, please, I should like to use an argument Rip used to Mr. Maynard. Supposing me to be an undeceived witness, which *I* know I am, can you really think the scarecrow and the prowler aren't in any way related? Isn't it far too much of a coincidence that the night the scarecrow was stolen was the night I saw somebody going in or out of the house?"

"Now, now, ma'am!"

"Yes?"

"The argument works both ways, don't it?" asked Captain Ashcroft, grinding out his cigar in an ashtray. "Anyway, why so much hoo-ha? If your prowler wanted something in the house, why swipe the scarecrow? If he just wanted to swipe the scarecrow, why bother to go anywhere near the house?"

"Well!" Camilla said.

Except for themselves, the dusky restaurant was deserted. With a lithe motion Camilla rose to her feet. She took half a dozen steps towards another table, then swung round and stood looking at them with eyes strained and lips half parted.

"We may be out of the woods; I hope so. Nothing unpleasant has happened since last Friday. Unless it happens tonight or tomorrow night, on Sunday we shall be off home with no more to worry about. But I do wish I could have made my story more convincing! I'm not silly and I'm not hysterical—not, at least, about things like that. Doesn't *anybody* believe me?"

"I believe you, Camilla," said Alan.

"Oh, dear God! If *you* start again, Alan Grantham—!"

Alan got up and went over to look down at her.

"Women, Camilla," he said, "don't seem to be half as perceptive as they have a reputation for being. Should it occur to you that I am sneering or being facetious or speaking anything except the literal, painful truth, you can't see what's there to see and has been there for some time. I believe you because you're you; it couldn't be any other way. Whatever you say, I am solidly on your side."

Briefly she looked him full in the eyes.

"And if *I* could believe *that—!*"

"Camilla . . ."

"I also," boomed another voice, "may be enlisted solidly on Miss Bruce's side."

All of them jumped; Alan retreated.

Dr. Gideon Fell, who had almost walked straight into the doorpost on entering the coffee-shop, altered his direction in time. Hat in one hand and stick in the other, he loomed majestically with eyeglasses again lopsided and big mop of hair over one ear.

"The word 'solid,' " pursued Dr. Fell, surveying the slopes of himself, "is perhaps superfluous. And I stray from the point. Teenage girls in America, we are told, will freeze to the telephone for hours at a time. They can go on at no greater length, I fear, than Henry Maynard of Maynard Hall, even when he ends by communicating very little. Might I trouble you, Alan, to drive this old carcass to James Island? He would like to see us as soon as may be convenient. And if he failed to credit Miss Bruce's story of a week ago, he may now be persuaded to change his mind."

"Change his mind? Why?"

"It would seem," said Dr. Fell, "that something else has happened."

4 *•

"This way, please," requested Henry Maynard.

The time, Alan afterwards remembered, was almost half-past three. And the weather seemed to be changing a little.

Captain Ashcroft had not accompanied them; he had other business, he explained, which wouldn't wait. With Camilla beside him, with Dr. Fell again in the back, Alan drove by way of Calhoun Street and the Ashley River Bridge. James Island, though largely residential, bustled with traffic at the beginning of Folly Road. Once you had made a left-hand turn off the main thoroughfare, and driven for five minutes through the countryside, its whole aspect changed.

How long had it been since anybody grew cotton here? At either side of them, great trees bearded with Spanish moss reared a canopy through which stipplings of sunlight danced on the road. They might have been miles from any human habitation, shut away as though by walls.

"I say, my dear fellow!" wheezed Dr. Fell. "Have you visited Maynard Hall before?"

"I've driven past the grounds, that's all. I've never been inside them."

"How much farther now?"

It was Camilla who answered.

"Fifteen minutes or so," she said, craning round. "There's another left turn at a little crossroads store; then straight on along Fort Johnson Road. We pass real-estate developments with some good-looking new houses, most of them not finished yet. We pass a high school. Just before the road ends in the fence around the research station, Maynard Hall is down on the left and sideways to the beach. Dr. Fell!"

"Oh, ah?"

"Since questions seem in order again, what did Mr. Maynard tell you? What's happened there since this morning?"

"My dear young lady, you are acquainted with your host."

"Am I? Sometimes I wonder!"

"Let me repeat," said Dr. Fell, "that he communicated very little. The man has positive genius at evasion; for politics he would be what you call a natural. But he must speak out soon, by thunder! When the Sphinx propounds a riddle, we have a right to demand just what the devil the riddle is. If he had not been so urgent, I should have preferred to spend the afternoon exploring Charleston or visiting Fort Sumter. However!"

"Did he seem—upset?"

"Such was my impression, at least."

They all fell silent. Glimpses of greenery flashed past and fell away. So did several real-estate developments, elaborate but skeletal amid gravel. To the right of the road, set well back, a two-storey building of orange-yellow brick had carved across its façade the letters *Joel Poinsett High School* and the date *1920.*

Alan wondered about this, but had no time to indulge the speculations in his mind. Less than a quarter mile beyond the school loomed a wire fence with signboards forbidding you to enter. To the left of the road . . .

Down a dirt lane that curved between live-oaks, trailing creepers of the gray moss that would strangle them, Alan drove through iron-grilled gates set open in a brick wall. Beyond this, beyond magnolia-tree sentinels inside the wall, a very broad sanded path ran fifty yards straight ahead to Maynard Hall.

The car had been idling; Alan stopped it when they were still some distance away, and indicated the four tall columns of the portico.

White shutters were folded back from windows on the ground floor, against dark-red brick and thick wisteria; black shutters were folded back from smaller windows of the floor above; the little mansard-roof top floor displayed no shutters at all. The whole front rose up darkish against a westering sun, and at that moment the sun slid behind cloud.

"Feels a little clammy, doesn't it?" Camilla asked of nobody in particular. "Did I—did I mention atmospheres?"

"Oh, atmospheres!" growled Dr. Fell, who had been muttering to himself. "The atmosphere, which does very much exist, seems mainly a pressure of piled-up emotions; I keep wondering what emotions. Harrumph! Over on our right, now . . ."

On their right, beyond a lawn clipped to putting-green smoothness, the terrace overlooking the beach stretched for some thirty-six feet between a row of half a dozen poplar trees and the side of Maynard Hall's north wing. Below it the beach sloped steeply out to the froth of the receding tide. Separated from the slope of the beach only by a miniature chain fence with dwarf posts less than six inches high, the terrace was half as broad as it was long. In the middle stood an iron chair and a little iron table, both painted green. It was this terrace which had caught Dr. Fell's fancy.

"Archons of Athens!" He pointed with his stick. "It's not paved; at least, not with flagstones or the like. The surface of that terrace has every appearance of sand. It is white, pure white, unlike the gray beach we see out there. And yet it must be sand, surely?"

"Not sand," Alan corrected. "It's bleached and crushed oyster-shell."

Dr. Fell gaped at him. "Bleached and . . . *what's that?*"

"In the earliest records of Charles Town," said Alan, "you'll find the tip of the peninsula referred to as 'White Point' or 'Oyster Point' from quantities of bleached oyster-shells that had accumulated there. The name has been preserved in White Point Garden to this day. According to the guide-books, some Maynard at the end of the eighteenth century had a notion to use an oyster-shell surface for his terrace. He put down a thick layer of the stuff, manufactured for him; it's been added to occasionally since then . . ."

"And the gardener smooths it down every day," interjected Camilla. "If these old things have any interest for you, Dr. Fell . . . ?"

"Madam, they interest me."

"Then *I* can add one or two. Look at the north wing of the Hall. Almost at the end of the wing!" Rather excitedly Camilla pointed ahead. "You see the flagstaff? Planted in the ground a little way out from the house, on the side towards us?"

"Yes?"

"From that flagstaff—no, not from *that* flagstaff; from one like it; don't confuse me, Alan!—they had to haul down the Confederate banner when Union forces entered Charleston in February of 1865. Past the flagstaff and the end of the wing, there," she swept out her arm, "a flight of wooden steps led down to the beach. And from the beach, a century ago, there was a jetty built well out into the water. That's where they carried the cotton for shipment across to the big docks at Charleston."

"I see no jetty now."

"No, Dr. Fell; it's been gone for many years, Madge says. There are still steps down to the beach, though of course I can't say whether they're the original ones. And there's somebody on the beach now!" She looked at Alan. "If any persons are down there, you can't see them from this position unless they walk out toward the surf. But a moment ago I was sure I heard voices: Madge's and Yancey's and Rip's."

Alan touched her shoulder. "Do they use the beach for swimming, Camilla?"

"On this side of the island? No! The water's filthy, Madge says. It's going to rain shortly, you know. But I'd better go down and join the others; Madge will need support, or at least a referee between those two. May I get out here?"

"Sit still for a moment," said Alan, putting the car into gear. "I'll drop you off at the porch, and you can go down the famous steps. Steady, now!"

The car rolled forward to the house, where the sanded drive divided in two before the front steps. Camilla slipped away and almost ran. Dr. Fell and Alan descended on the other side, Dr. Fell with considerable effort. He then reared up majestically, waving his crutch-headed stick.

"For the life of me," he said, "I can't see the place as an ogre's den. But its impressiveness I grant you. Whatever awaits us, have at it!"

A dignified elderly Negro in a house-coat admitted them to a lofty and spacious hall, all polished white-painted wood, with a graceful black-and-white staircase curving up at the rear. Large doors opened off the hall left and right. The door on the right led to the dining-room; Alan glimpsed a vista of mahogany and silver against pale-green walls. Over a fireplace in the same wall as the right-hand door hung a three-quarter-length painting of a man in the full-bottomed periwig of the later seventeenth century.

Then Henry Maynard himself emerged from the door on the left.

Alan had not forgotten that spare figure, the thin face and high-bridged nose dominated by chilly-looking blue eyes under silver hair. If Henry Maynard had strained nerves, he did not betray it.

"Thank you, George; that will be all," he said to the major-domo, and rather stiffly shook hands with his visitors. "Good afternoon, gentlemen. It was very kind of you to come."

Dr. Fell and Alan made appropriate noises.

"Considering the circumstances," their host continued, "I won't bore you with a guided tour of the house. However! Here behind me . . ."

He set the door partway open. Briefly Alan saw, down four steps, one room Camilla had described. Confederate-gray walls set off ceiling-height bookcases with wire doors and rosewood furniture upholstered in yellow. Henry Maynard closed the door again.

". . . behind me is the library, which has been much photographed, and it would be churlish if I *avoided* the subject of the Hall."

Here his eye caught Dr. Fell gaping like an idiot between the portrait over the fireplace and a chandelier like a glass castle.

"Dismiss from your minds, gentlemen, any notion that the original settlers in this part of the country had greatly to rough it even at the beginning. (Yes, that is the first Richard in the portrait; we believe Kneller painted it.) They brought luxuries from England; here on the spot they could buy and train slaves. Barring Indians, pirates, and Spanish enemies to the south, barring plague or fire or crop-failure, they led a comparatively easy life. By the time this house was completed by the first Richard's great-grandsons in 1787, Maynard Hall bore much the same outward aspect it bears today.

"That is enough, I think. If you see anything that interests you or stirs your curiosity, don't hesitate to ask questions. Otherwise, since we have at least one matter to discuss, I will ask you to accompany me to my lair on the top floor. This way, please."

In single file, Alan following their host and Dr. Fell bringing up the rear, they mounted the staircase to a floor with ceilings almost as high as those below. At the top of a second stairway—narrow, enclosed within walls—Dr. Fell was puffing heavily. Outside the windows the sky had grown dark, and tingled with distant noise.

"Thunder," remarked Henry Maynard. "What my daughter calls ghost-guns. But it will be a brief shower, if it comes at all. Here we are."

"I think, sir," panted Dr. Fell, "you said your lair?"

"I did. The house-servants sleep on this floor at the back. I myself have a self-contained suite of rooms (why, in South Carolina, *will* they say suit of rooms or suit of furniture?) running all the way along the front. You see this door towards the front, in the middle of a long blank wall?"

"Oh, ah?"

"It is the door to my study. Beyond the wall, as you shall see, two rooms open off the central one on either side. To the right of the study, bedroom and dressing-room with bathroom attached. To the left of the study, billiard-room and lumber-room. And now, with appropriate conjuring, for the study itself. Behold!"

He threw open the door, an unexpectedly and unnecessarily dramatic gesture. Perhaps he thought the study was empty. It was not empty.

The study, a good-sized room of very fair ceiling-height, was panelled in dark oak. Open shelves of meticulously arranged books occupied much wall-space, where Alan saw pictures of a nautical sort. From its wall-bracket hung a ship's bell, brass surface inscribed with the faded name "C.S.S. *Palmetto.*" There were easy chairs of padded brown leather, straight chairs, a cluttered writing-table, and an antique desk inlaid with ivory. In one of two windows, both closed, an air-conditioner buzzed softly.

At a chess-table under the other window, where pieces had been arrayed on the board, a meditative man sat peering at the woman opposite. His dark-blue suit, white shirt, and gray tie looked formal enough for a visitor but informal enough for the visit. Though he could not have been much younger than Henry Maynard, there was no gray in his dark hair. He had a sharp profile softened by the tolerance of the eye or the good-humor of the mouth. He also had considerable intensity.

At the other side of the chess-table, risen from her chair, stood a tall, slender woman with red hair and a coaxing manner. The flower-design dress clung to her body. Before windows dark with threatening rain she had just raised her hand to the chain of a floor-lamp. A switch clicked as the door opened; light flooded the study; both the man and the woman swung round.

"Why, Henry!" said the woman.

"Hello, Hank," said the man.

Their host drew himself up.

"Dr. Gideon Fell; Mr. Alan Grantham," he intoned, "Mrs. Valerie Huret; a very old acquantance of mine, Bob Crandall. And be good enough, Bob, not to call me Hank!"

"Wounds your dignity, does it?"

"Bear witness," said Henry Maynard, "that I have never been called a stuffed shirt. Your vulgarisms, those limericks and the collection of typographical errors, have their proper place; at the right time I welcome them. But I object to a personal vulgarism when it's totally unnecessary. You have literary pretensions of a sort, Bob. Would Henry Fielding have been called Hank? Or Henry James either?"

Mr. Crandall sighted along an extended forefinger.

"Henry Fielding," he retorted, "signed himself Hen. And don't call me a liar; I can show you a copy of the signature! If that's not worse than Hank in anybody's calligraphy, I'll eat *Tom Jones* page by page. Why, I remember, when I was a boy on the old *Times-Dispatch* in La Force, Indiana . . . !"

"Spare us!" said Henry Maynard. "Spare us another anecdote of wit or wisdom, and the perfection that may be attained with life on a small-town newspaper."

"Taking the good with the bad, Henricus, it's just about true. All right: I'll be serious. No limericks! No typographical errors! Will you hear wit and wisdom too?

"Among our literary scenes,
Saddest this sight to me,
The graves of little magazines
That died to make verse free."

"Hear, hear, *hear!*" applauded Alan.

"You agree, Mr. Grantham?"

"Heartily, Mr. Crandall. You must recite that to Camilla Bruce. Afterwards, if she hasn't poisoned *my* coffee . . ."

"I was quoting a forgotten bard, who learned epigrammatic style on a small-town paper. Believe it or not, Henry, our very best light verse has come from those who began as members of the fourth estate. I'm out of the game now; I've retired, in my sere and yellow, with a bigger chunk of dough than I ever expected or deserved. But one four-line stanza, only part of a long and fine piece, sticks in my head when everything else has gone."

Bob Crandall rose to his feet. His voice rolled out:

> "Under the broad bright windows
> Of men I serve no more,
> The grinding of the old great wheels
> Thickened to a throttled roar . . .

"To anybody who's ever heard the presses begin to roll, especially just before daylight, those are words of description that strike home. And do you know 'The Chop-House in the Alley, When the Paper's Gone to Press'?"

Valerie Huret stirred, the lamplight kindling her sleek skin and hazel eyes.

"I don't think he *wants* to know it, Bob. What are we doing here, anyway?" She appealed to their host. "He asked me for chess; I told him I can't *play* chess . . ."

"Neither can Bob," said Henry Maynard.

"There are lots of things *much* more interesting than chess. I'll tell him about them, if he asks me nicely. But hadn't we better go downstairs, Bob? In the first place, we're trespassing. We *are* trespassing, aren't we, Henry?"

"Frankly, Valerie, I'm afraid you are. Remember, Bob: as usual, one game before dinner, and I'll trim you again. Be here promptly at seven, just as it's beginning to get dark . . ."

"Forgive me!" boomed Dr. Fell, looking particularly half-witted. "But your climate can still hold surprises for the stranger.

At this latitude, in the middle of May, does it begin to get dark at seven o'clock?"

"In these parts, Dr. Fell," their host informed him, "we are not on daylight-saving time. Forget the clock in New York and everywhere else. I am not accustomed to making inaccurate statements."

"In the second place," cried Valerie Huret, who had struck a pose like the Goddess of Reason, "at any moment it's going to *pour* with rain. I've just remembered; I left my car around the side of the house. It's a convertible, and open. If anybody else has an open car . . ."

Alan made a move towards the door. Henry Maynard stopped him.

"Gently, both of you! There is no need to go; George will see to it. When you have visited us more often, Valerie, you will learn that no car suffers rain-damage with George in attendance. However! Any storm will be brief, but it may be violent." Alarm rang through his voice. "Where's Madge? Where are the two boys? Where's Miss Bruce? She accompanied Dr. Fell and Mr. Grantham; I saw her from the library. But . . ."

"The last time *I* looked," Valerie pointed to the window, "they were down on the beach. Yancey Beale and that tough-looking light-haired boy were throwing stones out over the water to see who could throw farther. The girls were with them."

Henry Maynard's lips tightened.

"For almost two weeks, ladies and gentlemen, I have been wondering when they would start on baseball. My brother, himself once captain of the Little Potatoes Hard to Peel, was patron and Maecenas of a teen-age team called the Bearcats. There is baseball equipment all over the cellar. And, since Rip Hillboro fancies himself as a pitcher . . ."

"You're a dried-up old bastard, Hank!" Bob Crandall said without rancor and almost with affection. "What's the matter with baseball?"

"There's nothing the matter with baseball, if you happen to like it. I don't. I was merely wondering—"

"And in the third place," cried Valerie, sticking insistently to her main theme, "let's us go downstairs, Bob! *You're* not a dried-up old . . . what I mean is, let's us forget chess and baseball too." Her tones grew coy and honeyed. "There *are* other things, aren't there? While I sort of hint at it, in a nice way, you can just tell me some more limericks and typographical errors. You *have* got some more of those, haven't you?"

"Woman, I've got a bushel of 'em. Come along."

Henry Maynard drew a breath of relief as they left the study. But he had not in any sense heard the last of them. Due to the carelessness either of Mrs. Huret or of Mr. Crandall, the door did not quite close. A confused murmur, no words distinct, could be heard from the enclosed staircase to the floor below. Then, suddenly, something else jabbed through serenity. Valerie Huret's voice went shrilling up.

"You're a nice man; you're too nice, really!"

"Now look, Semiramis!"

"You don't know what's happening here! I can't bear it!"

"Sh-h!"

"I can't bear it, I tell you!"

But they heard no more. They would have heard no more in any case. A deluge burst; the windows blurred and grew darker with driving rain.

More emotional pressures, but from what source? It was no use speculating, Alan decided. He turned back, and was looking round the walls when Henry Maynard caught his eye.

"It will have occurred to you, Mr. Grantham, that this room has a nautical flavor foreign to my essential tastes. Yes, that is the ship's bell from the *Palmetto,* rescued like her logbook when she sank in the Caribbean. There over the Sheraton desk—head and shoulders, full beard, gray naval uniform—is Luke Maynard himself. It is not a water-color, though it appears to be. Actually it is a photograph, enormously enlarged and tinted by hand. You, Dr. Fell, are goggling at the picture as though it stunned you. May I ask your thoughts?"

"Why, sir . . . (harrumph!) . . . to begin with, I was thinking of colors."

"Colors, sir?"

"Various Confederate uniforms (harrumph!) which in past days I have seen at museums here in the South. Their colors varied considerably."

"Yes?"

Rain roared against the windows. Dr. Fell poked at the carpet with the ferrule of his stick.

"Some were of the customary and conventional gray. Others looked so close to what nowadays we should call air force blue that without C.S.A. on the belt-buckle I might have ascribed the uniform to the wrong side." A sniff rumbled in Dr. Fell's nose. "Then, again, as any human being must, I was thinking—O my hat!—of Commodore Maynard and his violent death on the beach."

"That happened so long ago, Dr. Fell, that surely it need not detain us?"

"To a degree, I fear, it must always detain us. And in the third place, as Mrs. Huret would say," he whacked his stick on the floor, "my thoughts (or feelings) are purely personal. I have come from some considerable distance in response to your letters of weeks ago. I arrive from the hotel, not a little dishevelled, in response to the urgency of your telephone call. *Confound it, sir, what do you want of me?*"

"Ah, yes. What I want of you!"

Here their host took on a bustling air.

"Sit down, gentlemen; make yourselves comfortable. You will find cigarettes on the writing-table. Or a cigar, if Dr. Fell would prefer one? . . . There, that is better. At least you have sat down.

"Speaking of Commodore Maynard, there on the wall towards the billiard-room *is* a water-color: some contemporary artist's conception of the *Palmetto* leaving Charleston harbor on her last voyage. Observe the flag she flies at her mizzen-peak.

"Though most people are acquainted with only one Southern

flag, the famous battle-flag of stars and bars, at various times the Confederacy adopted four different ones. That flown by the *Palmetto*—you will also see it in pictures of the *Alabama*—was the second to be adopted: a white ensign with the smaller square of the battle-flag in the upper left-hand corner. Firebrands objected to this as looking far too much like a flag of surrender. They said—"

"During a recent affair outside New York," boomed Dr. Fell, "some argument and confusion arose relating to the number of stars in the Confederate flag. But why, by thunder, are we entangled with flags *now?* What does this mean?"

"It means," replied Henry Maynard, standing beside the writing-table and brushing the finger-tips of his right hand gently over its surface, "that I am straying from the subject. And you deserve better than that. I will stray from the subject no longer.

"I was disturbed, Dr. Fell. I was badly disturbed, and I confess it. This arose at lunch-time, after Joe Ashcroft had driven Miss Bruce to the Francis Marion Hotel to intercept Mr. Grantham; at her own request, a whim of Camilla's.

"George—you remember George, the butler, who admitted you? —thought he had seen someone skulking in this room. I feared for certain papers in the Sheraton desk over there. Precipitately I rushed to the telephone and rang the hotel. I asked you, I all but entreated you, to come here at once. And now I ask you . . ."

"Yes?"

"I ask you," answered Henry Maynard, "to forget that phone-call entirely."

5 *•

Yellow lamplight fell strongly on the man's intent face. He took a cigarette from a silver box on the table, but thought better of this and put it back. The rain had slackened; it was still sluicing and splashing down the house, but the buzz of the air-conditioner could be heard again. Dr. Fell reared up in his leather chair.

"Forget it, you say?"

"If you will be so good. I was very foolish; I confess that too. I should have realized nobody could have gotten at those papers without smashing the desk to pieces; they are in a secret drawer. And they are still there, safe and untouched."

"May I ask, sir, the nature of these papers? For instance, are they some 'calculations' of yours?"

"Certainly not!" The other looked genuinely astonished. "Why do you ask?"

"Miss Bruce mentioned—even insisted upon—the fact that, though you still sit up here in the evening and on the terrace in the afternoon, you seem no longer preoccupied with 'calculating something.' "

"The papers, Dr. Fell, relate only to my late brother's estate. Since there has never been any mystery about the disposition of the estate, they are of no real importance at all. Believe me, they could be lost or burnt without the slightest ill-effect to Madge or to me or to anyone else on earth."

"Then why should a threat to them upset you?"

"Because, if the truth must be told, like my daughter I suffer from moods. Have you never said to yourself, 'I *must* find such and such a document; it is vital to have that document; what if it were missing?'—though it is not vital and you know it. I seldom admit this foible; the cold reasoner must not seem a sham or a fraud. But I go to an extreme—and then change my mind."

"It is not the first time, I believe, you have changed your mind in the past fortnight. May I revert to that presently?"

"If you insist. Meanwhile, you are thinking . . . ?"

"It would be difficult," grunted Dr. Fell, puffing out his cheeks, "properly to formulate such thoughts as exist. 'Blow hot, blow cold,' or perhaps blow the whole business. This won't do; it won't do at all! Is my quest of a thousand miles to end in moonshine and wild geese? And you were so very urgent! If you had not been so urgent, I told my friends on the way here, I should have preferred to spend the afternoon exploring Charleston or visiting Fort Sumter."

"Oh, Fort Sumter!" Henry Maynard said abruptly. "Come with me, please."

All his tight-lipped reserve had gone. Beckoning them to their feet, he conducted them to a door in the left-hand wall. This opened into a good-sized billiard-room, also oak-panelled, with a covered table, a rack of cues, and a padded seat under the two windows facing front. With a conspiratorial air their guide led the way through it into the farthermost room on the top floor at the front of the north wing.

A lumber-room of dingy white-plaster walls and bare board floor, it was as littered with old trunks, with discarded household effects, as the other rooms had been swept and neat. Unlike study or billiard-room, there was an air-conditioner in neither of two windows. Both were open, with fine-mesh screens hooked into place.

"The rain has stopped," said Henry Maynard. "It lasted hardly more than ten minutes, as I predicted; the sun is coming out. Look here!"

He bustled to the far window, and put the tip of an extended forefinger against the wire screen.

"There *is* Fort Sumter, Dr. Fell."

"Where?"

"Where I am pointing. Over the top of that flagstaff below the window, take a line bearing slightly left out across the harbor. You see the smallish dark-gray mass against the water? One moment!"

Opening the top of a cabin trunk near the window, he fished out a pair of heavy field-glasses in their leather case. He took the glasses from the case and handed them to Dr. Fell.

"Put these to your eyes; adjust the focus . . ."

"The focus, sir, is already adjusted."

"Then take the line I have indicated. Move the glasses to your left . . . so! Have you got it now?"

"Oh, ah!" Dr. Fell was puffing with concentration. "I have got the fort; I see it clearly. Some kind of small steamer appears to be drawing away from it."

"That's the excursion-steamer returning. You would have been too late for it today in any case; it leaves the Municipal Yacht Basin at two o'clock. You can always go tomorrow, of course. Meanwhile, if a distant view will suffice . . . ?"

"The distant view," said Dr. Fell, "will do admirably. Harrumph! A Union officer named Major Anderson, I understand, surrendered Fort Sumter to the Confederates in April of '61? When did Federal forces retake it?"

"They never did 'retake' it in the sense you mean."

"Oh?"

"At the beginning of '65 the fort was a wreck. It had been under heavy bombardment for almost two years, notably from a monster Parrott gun on Cummings Point. But it was still defensible, with a garrison of six hundred. In February Sherman marched north from Georgia. Sumter's garrison, fearing they might be cut off if Sherman struck at Charleston—which he never did—slipped out and joined what remained of the Confederate Army. And Brigadier General Anderson, formerly Major Anderson, returned to raise the flag he had lowered four years before."

Henry Maynard swept out his hand.

"I set little store by history, gentlemen. The past is dead; let it remain buried; don't rattle the bones! And yet certain comments are called for."

"What comments, sir?"

"To the Union, from the very start of the war, Charleston and Fort Sumter had been symbols of Southern defiance they would have given anything to recapture. And they were always trying.

"But by water they hadn't a hope. Any attacking ship could be caught in a murderous crossfire between Sumter and Moultrie. In April of '63 Admiral Du Pont tried to force a passage with nine Federal ironclads. The ironclads took a beating without even getting close; five were disabled and one destroyed. This led to the combined land-and-sea attack by General Gillmore and Admiral Dahlgren. In August they tried again with ironclads; again they failed, as they failed in every direction until the defenders had abandoned all works. Your own comments, Dr. Fell?"

Dr. Fell lowered the glasses and straightened up.

"For one so scornful of the past, sir," he said, "you seem remarkably well informed about it."

"I am conscientious; no more than that. I consider it my duty to be informed."

"And have you no other duty?"

"To whom?"

"Come!" Dr. Fell inclined his head towards the window. "Look down there, I beg, much closer at hand than Fort Sumter."

"Yes?"

"There is the beach spread out below us, dark gray from rain. On that stretch of beach, only two years after the time about which you have been so glib, an ancestor of yours was brutally done to death in unmarked sand. But you won't discuss this; you won't touch it, you won't go near it!"

"Did I say I would not discuss it?" Henry Maynard drew himself up. "I said only, if memory serves, that the subject need not detain us. We lack full evidence for a solution. Lacking such evidence, which has been distorted or suppressed, we can do little more than travel in a circle. However! If you insist on rattling *those* dead bones for our present pleasure, I shall be happy to supply you with what few details I have beyond the sketch in the newspaper account. Is there anything else?"

"Is there anything else?" thundered Dr. Fell. "Archons of Athens, is there anything *else?* Well, yes. There is the situation in this house.

"Last Friday night a scarecrow was stolen from the garden. Call that ludicrous, if you like. Miss Bruce saw, or claims to have seen, some prowler entering or leaving a downstairs room. Call that ludicrous too; say she was drugged or dreaming. Today you yourself are thrown almost into a fit by the report of someone 'skulking' in your study.

"These ludicrous instances are piling up. Do you ask me to whom you owe a duty? To your daughter! To your guests! Even to yourself! Your daughter is reported as jumpy; Camilla Bruce is jumpy; Mrs. Huret is distinctly jumpy; you, sir, are as jumpy as any of them. Surely there is something here worth investigating? And yet all you can do is tell me to forget it entirely!"

"Now, there," retorted Henry Maynard, touching the careful knot of his tie, "there again I must correct you. I said to forget the *phone-call;* I said no more than that. I distinctly recall observing, just before we came upstairs, that we had at least one matter to discuss. And so we have: the source of all my worry to begin with. Back to the study, please."

Taking the field-glasses from Dr. Fell, he replaced them in their case and returned the case to the trunk. With some dignity he led the way through lumber-room and billiard-room, carefully closing each door when Dr. Fell had maneuvred through sideways. In the study, after switching off the floor-lamp by the chess-table, he went to the antique desk below the colored photograph of Commodore Maynard, and ran his finger-tips over its sloping lid.

"In here," he went on, "I have an old exercise-book containing a diary for the year 1867 kept by Miss India Keate of Charleston, then eighteen years old.

"Luke Maynard was not my great-grandfather, as some suppose. He was my great-grandfather's younger brother, and a bachelor. In '67 the head of the family, my great-grandfather Henry, seems to have been a character even more stern than Luke. But he was hospitable, as stern characters of the day so often could be.

"India Keate, a close friend of great-grandfather Henry's youngest daughter, spent part of the month of April in this house. Her diary contains the only supplementary details we have about Commodore Maynard's death. I will give you the diary, Dr. Fell, for your consideration at leisure."

Then his voice sharpened.

"But that must wait! My own constant worry, which goes on and on interminably, may be expressed in one word. Madge."

"And my question," returned Dr. Fell, "may also be expressed in one word. Why?"

"It's not easy to explain."

"Will you try to explain?"

Henry Maynard turned from the desk and faced them, his eyes growing unsteady.

"Madge is so innocent!" he said. "Or, if not altogether innocent in thought, let's agree she is warm-hearted, well-meaning, and rather naïve.

"She was born in Paris in 1938, registered at the American consulate, and baptized at the American Church in the Avenue George V. Her mother, whose portrait hangs above the mantelpiece in the library downstairs, died about a year later. Early in 1940 I brought the child to America in charge of an English nurse who remained with us only for a year or two. Madge was brought up in New York; we moved to Connecticut just under a decade ago.

"But I never know what the girl is thinking, or quite how to deal with her. I feel constrained; today they would say inhibited. Am I over-protective too?

"Young men have been flocking around Madge since she reached her teens. Recently the field, if I may so express this, has narrowed itself down to two: Rip Hillboro and Yancey Beale. I want her to marry, of course. But I want her to make the right choice. It is bound to be Rip or Yancey; who else is there? Unless—" he stopped.

"Sir," demanded Dr. Fell, "may I ask just what is *worrying* you so much? The situation confronting you has confronted every father since time began. If it is only a question of finding a suitable husband . . ."

"Oh, suitable!" the other said with some bitterness. "Both young men are suitable enough. For my own reasons I should prefer Yancey. He has certain natural advantages denied the other. But I should give my blessing to Rip too; I am no snob. Rip worked his way through my own college and through law school. He is with the best legal firm in Hartford and has a brilliant future. If sometimes he seems a little too aggressive for quiet tastes, shall I hold this against a young man making his way in the world?

"What happens next, I ask myself? Where are we going? Where will it end? It is enough to . . . it is enough to . . ."

"No!" roared Dr. Fell. "It is NOT enough to haunt and hag-ride you as so obviously it does. What else is there? Out with it, man! Have you brought me a thousand miles merely to act as marriage counsellor? And is it the young lady or the father who can't decide?"

Henry Maynard, who had been pacing beside the writing-table, stopped short.

"With your permission, Dr. Fell, I will now address myself to Mr. Grantham. *You* don't mind, young man?"

"No, of course I don't mind. What is it?"

"Forgive me," said their host, "if I seem abominably ill-mannered. Forgive me also if I sound like prosecuting counsel at a trial. Mr. Grantham, where were you on the night of Sunday, May 2nd?"

Alan stared at him.

"Sunday, May 2nd," repeated the other, "just twelve days ago. About ten o'clock at night, say. Where were you then?"

"I'm trying to remember, that's all!"

"Were you by any chance in the grounds of this house?" Henry Maynard pointed. "Under some magnolia trees by the front gate? Embracing my daughter there?"

"Good God, no!" said the flabbergasted Alan. "And I've just remembered where I was."

"Yes?"

"In Pearis, two hundred miles away. At ten o'clock I had just finished having dinner with Dr. Leffingwell, the President of King's College, his wife, and three members of the faculty."

"You're sure of that?"

"If I had to prove it in court, Mr. District Attorney, I could bring at least five witnesses. I wasn't embracing Madge or anybody else. What makes you think I was?"

"I don't think you were. It was an unworthy suggestion, and again I apologize. But it did strike me that once upon a time you seemed *rather* interested in Madge. For want of another candidate, I wondered."

Candidate? Candidate? Now just how, Alan was thinking, is anybody supposed to answer a remark like that?

('I could say,' he continued to himself, 'just possibly Madge might have had another conquest if I hadn't seen Camilla and gone head over ears down the drain. But I can't very well tell the old boy that; and, anyway, what the hell is this all about?')

He was spared the necessity for answering anything.

"There is another difficulty," said Henry Maynard, taking out a key-ring and twirling it round his finger. "I had thought no harm would be done if I told both of you everything. There would still be no harm in this. The trouble is that I can't do it; literally, physically I can't do it! Will you think me over-squeamish, Mr.

Grantham, if I ask you to leave us while I tell the rest of the story to Dr. Fell? Would you mind very much?"

"I'd not mind at all, Mr. Maynard. Excuse me."

"One moment!" The key-ring stopped twirling. "Whatever I may think of your judgment, Mr. Grantham, I have the highest respect for your discretion. You won't pass on to Madge any words that have been spoken here?"

"I won't tell Madge or anyone else," said Alan. "Now excuse me."

And he marched out simmering.

Alan didn't particularly mind being exiled from the conference; he had half expected it. But nothing was more unlikely than that he should go to Madge and say, "Look here, little one: your father thought I might have been making passes at you (or more than passes) under the good old Southern magnolias. Who did make passes, Madge?"

No, nothing was more unlikely. Had Papa Maynard really imagined he would tell Madge?

And so Alan simmered, his thoughts back with Camilla again. He was descending the enclosed stairs, where light struggled through a little staircase window, when he almost bumped into somebody on the way up.

The newcomer, a shortish, thick-set, handsome young man of about thirty, wore a conservative charcoal-gray suit and carried a black medical bag in his left hand.

"Afternoon!" he said in a pleasant voice. "You're Alan Grantham, aren't you? I'm Mark Sheldon."

They shook hands. Rather ruefully Dr. Sheldon held up the black bag.

"Dunno why I took this out of the car; I'm not here professionally. Force of habit, I guess; it *is* my afternoon round. Do you think I might intrude on the paterfamilias and tell him something?"

"Unless you've got something very important to tell him, I

don't advise it now. He's talking to Dr. Fell, and he's not in the mood."

"Well!" Mark Sheldon hesitated. "In one way it's important; in another way it's not. Reckon it'll have to wait. Yes," he continued, as they tramped together down the stairs, "I heard Dr. Fell was here in all his glory. Have you met the others?"

"I already knew Camilla and Madge. We met a Mrs. Huret and a Mr. Crandall."

"Valerie's not here now. As soon as the rain stopped, they tell me, she grabbed her car and buzzed off in a hurry. Old Rhadamanthus . . . do I mean Rhadamanthus . . . ?"

"Rhadamanthus, the judge or critic? Otherwise Bob Crandall? Yes, that will do."

"He's in the library, orating to beat the band. Madge and Camilla are with him. Speaking of Camilla, what have you been doing to her?"

Alan exploded. "So it's *Camilla* now, is it?"

Passing the bedroom floor, they were descending the main stairway to the big main hall. The handsome young doctor had great ease of manner, and wiry hair of so dark a red that it looked almost black.

"Sometimes," he said, "I think everybody in this house needs a tranquillizer. No offense was intended, take my word for it! Camilla's in a state, that's all, and Madge thinks you're responsible. Yancey and Rip are in the cellar, probably looking murder at each other. Make my excuses to the others; I've got to run. You can tell where *they* are, can't you?"

Alan could. In the lower hall a grandfather clock, its ticking unimpaired after more than two hundred years, indicated the time as twenty minutes past four. The door to the library stood wide open. Dr. Sheldon took his hat from a table and left the house, letting the screen door bang after him. And Alan made for the library, towards the sound of an upraised voice.

In the library, with its four big windows facing front, Madge

Maynard in a brown-and-beige dress sat on a yellow-upholstered Victorian sofa with her yellow head bent forward, intently listening. Behind the grand piano in one corner sat Camilla, listening less intently. Bob Crandall stood at the other side of the piano, declaiming. He was in mid-doggerel and mid-flight; the syllables rolled and soared.

"Delve in problems philosophic,
  How did Adam lose his rib?
What's the chance of war in Europe?
  Has the *Herald* scooped the *Trib?*
Oh, our present world is better;
  Still, a longing I confess
For the chop-house in the alley,
  When the paper's gone to press."

Here he interrupted himself, hooking his thumbs in his belt and looking lofty.

"Yes," he informed Camilla, "it's pretty poor stuff, as you were saying. And yet I've always liked it. I'd have liked it still better if the would-be poet hadn't said 'scoop.' No newspaperman has ever said scoop, just as he never says 'front' page; he says 'first' page. We called it a beat when we called it anything at all. But it's been forty years or more since I can remember one. With some God-damn big syndicate grabbing up every God-damn paper in town, what chance have you got?"

Madge raised her head. "Mr. Crandall, must you be so very *serious?*"

"Yes, young woman, when I feel strongly about anything. Mine is a simple, primitive nature. I can't help howling when I get kicked or cussing my head off when I get mad. And there's a lot to make us mad in these days."

Alan went down the four steps into the library. Above the fireplace, in that impressive room, a full-length portrait in oils showed a graceful, fair-haired, blue-eyed woman in an evening gown of the mid-1930's. Alan scarcely glanced at this. He was looking at Camilla, who had risen partway from the piano bench before sitting down again. Her resemblance to a Botticelli angel, pink and white, could not be marred even by an expression more lofty than Bob Crandall's.

"Did I mention the word 'big'?" Mr. Crandall demanded. "That's all we hear today. Big syndicates! Big government! Big taxes! Big brother!" Then he yelled. "With the God-damn government on its God-damn socialistic course, a man—"

"You mean a God-damn man, don't you?" Camilla asked gently.

"Something tells me," said Mr. Crandall, "we have here a sugar-candy flibbertigibbet with a taste for smart cracks. All right! Say a God-damn man; he'll deserve the adjective when our left-wingers have finished with him. Sooner or later, so help me Jinny, he'll need permission from some bureaucrat to change his job or sleep with his own wife."

"Are you married, Mr. Crandall?"

"No, thank God! I was saying—"

"We know what you were saying," Camilla assured him. "And *of course* Alan agrees with you. He'd like to be back in the eighteenth century too. When Alan finds a situation he doesn't like, he never tries to use his reason or even approach it. He just loses his temper and swears."

Alan was in the wrong mood for this.

"Then how ought I to approach the situation, Camilla? Would you be better pleased if I worked it out mathematically?"

Camilla dropped her lofty manner.

"Don't you say anything against mathematics!" she breathed. "In the higher mathematics, for those who can understand, it's the most romantic and imaginative conception ever dreamed of! Mathematics gave us the space age . . ."

"Hoo-ray."

". . . and other things reactionaries sneer at because they hate progress! In the higher mathematics . . . not that I ever got that far myself . . . !"

"Well, *I* never even got within shouting distance. To me mathematics means the activities of those mischievous lunatics A, B, and C. In my time they were always starting two trains at high speed from distant points to see where the trains would collide somewhere between. Which, as the man said in the story, is a hell of a way to run a railroad."

"Does it *say* that?" flashed Camilla.

"Say what?"

"Does the problem anywhere say the two trains are on the same track? It doesn't; you know it doesn't; you won't stop to think! All the book wants to know is where those two trains will pass!"

"And why does the book want to know that? So one engineer can wave to the other or give him a raspberry in passing? Why?"

"Why, why, why? You're like a little boy in kindergarten! All you can do is ask why!"

"*Somebody's* got to ask. You know, Camilla, it suggests a legal ruling once said to have been made in Arkansas about a disputed right-of-way. 'When two trains approach this intersection, both shall stop; and neither shall proceed until the other has passed.'

"That's just about as sensible as most decisions now handed down by the United States Supreme Court. But we haven't finished with your tireless friends A, B, and C. When the silly dopes weren't wrecking trains or computing the ages of their children without seeming to know how old the brats were, two of 'em had a passion for pumping water out of a tank while the third poor mug pumped water into it. Camilla, how many afternoons do *you* spend doing that?"

Camilla leaped to her feet.

"I won't hear any more of this! I'm s-sick of your damn trains and water-tanks! I could kill you, Alan Grantham! And I'd do it, too, if I didn't—!"

"Didn't what? Look down and despise me from your Olympian height?"

"You've guessed *that,* have you?"

"All right!" exclaimed Madge, getting up from the sofa. "If that's how you really feel, Camilla, you despise him as much as you please. But hadn't we better get on to something less controversial?"

"An inner voice," Bob Crandall declared oracularly, "an inner voice tells me almost anything between those two is likely to be controversial. *You* pick a subject."

Madge deliberated. Always she seemed a little apart, lost in some world of her own. Her golden-white skin stood out vividly against gray walls and towering wire-meshed bookcases.

The fireplace was in the back wall of the library, westwards. To the right of it a big door gave on the room which must be the one Camilla had described as the weapons-room. Though the door stood open, Alan could see little beyond the threshold; shutters or curtains had been closed there.

Madge made half a gesture towards the weapons-room before turning back.

"Alan, what has Dr. Fell been saying?"

"Very little so far. He's persuaded your father to do the talking. By the way, Dr. Sheldon dropped in . . ."

"Yes; we saw him!"

". . . and asked me to make his excuses. There was something he wanted to tell your old man, but he thought better of it."

"*I* know what he wanted!" said Madge. "Poor Mark! He's so anxious to do the correct thing! Never mind Mark." She made another half-gesture towards the weapons-room. Then her brown eyes travelled round the group before fastening on Bob Crandall. "You remember that awful fuss last Friday night?"

"We're not likely to forget it, young lady."

"It wasn't only that they took my lovely scarecrow, the one I called Mr. Christopher. But in there—outside the French window, anyway—Camilla said she saw somebody at half-past three in the morning. Camilla dear, I'm most awfully sorry! I didn't believe you then; I thought you were dreaming too; and I wasn't very nice."

"You didn't believe her then. But you believe her now; is that it? Why do you believe her now?"

"Well, because," answered Madge, "because last night I saw something too."

6

"If you want *me* to handle this," declared the ex-editor, "fair enough. But don't say I didn't warn you! A good reporter has got to ask the same questions as a cop. Who? What? How? When? Where? Why? Do you understand that, young woman?"

"Oh, I understand!"

"*You* saw somebody at that window?"

"Good heavens, no! How could I have? My room's at the front, practically over the front door. Anyway, if I'd seen something *at* the house or anywhere near it, I think I'd have had a fit. This may not have had anything at all to do with us. But I couldn't help wondering . . ."

"Suppose you start at the beginning. What did you see? When and where did you see it?"

"We were rather late getting to bed last night, you remember. With—with Daddy keeping us in our places, there was no talk of ghosts or anything to get nervous about. But you told that story about the young girl from Jersey City . . ."

"Is this another limerick?" demanded Camilla.

"No, dear, no; *you* remember. The girl from Jersey City! Before they put her in jail she had thirty-four husbands in three years, or practically one a month. Mr. Crandall was just beginning to speculate about what methods she used . . ."

"Anybody knows what methods she used," said Mr. Crandall. "Remind me to tell *that* one to Valerie Huret!"

"Valerie'll be awfully pleased, I'm sure. Anyway! You were just wondering how she could keep one husband from meeting another—Camilla wanted to hear and I know I did—when Daddy shut you up. But it took a long time, didn't it? It must have been half-past twelve or later when we all went upstairs."

"All right. Take it from there."

Madge stood with her hand on the back of the early Victorian sofa. Her gaze roved round the library, as though seeking somebody who wasn't there.

"It must have been half-past one," she went on. "I'd taken my sleeping-pill some time before, but it hadn't worked yet. I was standing at the window and looking out: first at the front gates, and then down at the beach on the left.—Alan," she broke off suddenly to ask, "what's a gibbous moon?"

"A what?"

"In stories," said Madge, "the moon is always gibbous. To me it conveys something scary, like 'ghostly' or 'gibber.' But I've never looked it up. And is it ghibbous or jibbous?"

"Jibbous, Madge. Soft g, usually, before e and i. There's no suggestion of the supernatural. The word means convex: bigger than the semicircle, but not the full-moon circle complete."

"Well, this moon was smaller than that. Much past the full and waning, and yet with light enough to see by.

"I'm not sure when I first saw him. And don't ask me what he looked like; I was too far away to tell. It was just a man walking along the beach below the terrace, walking from west to east. He was looking out towards the harbor, with his head turned, and carrying something like a sack over his right shoulder.

"For a second or two it gave me quite a jump. But he was too far away to *hurt* me, I thought. Then I thought it was probably some stranger who had no connection with us—just there by accident."

"What did you do?"

"What *could* I do? I wasn't going to yell and alarm the house; it didn't scare me enough for that. And I hate being turfed out when *I've* gone to bed, which is why I was cross with poor Camilla last Friday. I closed the curtains on both windows, with the air-conditioner going full blast. I jumped into bed, and I must have been asleep in two minutes. When I opened my eyes again it was nine o'clock in the morning, with bright sunlight to make everything normal.

"I wasn't going to tell anybody about this; I haven't mentioned it until now. Then I began thinking. We said Camilla was seeing things, when she'd taken much lighter sleeping-stuff and hadn't drunk much either. Was what I saw only a coincidence too? Couldn't the man on the beach have been a part of something much scarier?"

"Frankly, the court rules against." Bob Crandall lifted an orator's forefinger. "Just for the hell of it, my wench, I'd almost welcome sinister doings and bodies falling out of walls, like the plays I enjoyed so much as a boy in the nineteen-twenties. But I didn't believe 'em then; I don't believe this now. It's all bunk, Madge! Let's talk about the young lady from Jersey City, shall we?"

"I'm willing," said Madge.

"I'm not," said Camilla, "though at any other time I'd be glad to. Whether you believe it or not, Mr. Crandall, there's a perfectly *horrible* situation working up. What if something else happens?"

"Forget it, Camilla! And I'm afraid, Madge, you've missed the whole point about Jersey City's pride and joy. I was just going on to explain this point when Hank shut me up.

"In evaluating her case," proclaimed Bob Crandall, as though writing an editorial, "we must remember three facts: that it happened ten years ago, in 1955; that she was only twenty-two when she landed in the sneezer; and that in most states the maximum sentence for bigamy is seven years.

"She probably got time off for good behavior; she'd have had few opportunities for her favorite sport in a women's prison. But even if the judge threw the book at her, even if she didn't get one day off her sentence, she'd have been released no later than 1962—still under thirty, ready for more and raring to go.

"What's happened to her since then, Madge? Where is she now, and how many husbands has she accumulated? That's the whole point, my girl; I could have dwelt on it with wit and eloquence. But Hank's suspicious of every word I utter; and, as you say, the son-of-a-bitch shut me up."

"Who's a son-of-a-bitch, Bob?" demanded a loud voice.

They all turned.

Into the library—into it, at least, as far as the little wooden platform with the steps leading down—had marched two young men of about the same age, height, and weight. Both wore slacks and open-neck sports shirts. There all similarity ended.

The first newcomer, though not ill-looking, had a jaw so large that the rest of his features seemed small and squeezed-up. He was not a bad sort, Alan thought, though he might do his best to seem the opposite. His right hand juggled a regulation baseball, throwing it up and catching it. From his left wrist by their straps hung a fielder's glove, a catcher's mitt, and a catcher's mask. The dark-haired young man behind him carried a bat.

With clacking footfalls the first newcomer descended and strode towards them, shoulders at a challenging angle.

"Old Bob Crandall, the People's Oracle!" he said. "Old Bob Crandall, the Watchman of Goliath! Who's a son-of-a-bitch, Bob?"

"You are, Rip; didn't you know it? Rip Hillboro, meet Alan Grantham."

"Grantham? Grantham? Hi, Grantham! You must be the right-wing diehard Camilla's been telling us about, aren't you?"

"Yes."

"Then you'll get along just dandy with Bob. You'll get along still better with Stonewall Jackson here." Rip jerked a thumb towards his loose-limbed companion, who had followed. "He's been wanting to call *me* a son-of-a-bitch for almost two weeks. Come on, Stonewall; let's be natural for once. Why not call me a son-of-a-bitch and get it off your chest?"

"I haven't called you anything yet, son, though I may be workin' around to it."

"And do you take my bet, Stonewall? (Alan Grantham, Yancey Beale.) Five gets you ten I can strike you out with—no, not three pitches, but before the umpire can call a fourth ball. I'm not Sandy Koufax, maybe. But I'm good; I know I'm good, so why deny it?"

"You'll never deny it, son," said Yancey Beale, "as long as there's a horn to be tooted. Forget the five-ten; I'll take it for twenty at even money. Mr. Grantham, I'm at your service. Madge honey, how are you?"

"Look!" exclaimed Rip, working himself up. "Somebody's been acting suspiciously, and somebody's a son-of-a-bitch. That's what Bob said, and I want to know—"

"Oh, Rip!" Madge burst out. "Must you use such *language?* It's all right for Mr. Crandall; he's a privileged character. But it doesn't come so well from a young lawyer with his whole career ahead of him." She broke off. "And *you,* Yancey!"

"What's that, honeychile?"

"I'm not made of stained glass, you know! But it seems every man in the South just looks down at me and tells me not to trouble my pretty little haid."

"Have you met every man in the South, honey?"

Again Rip yelled for silence.

"Look!" he repeated. "We've got ourselves a bet here, with Stonewall Jackson taking me on for twenty bucks. The trouble is, there's no catcher. What about it, Bob? You're in pretty fair physical shape, we've got to admit . . ."

"That's been demonstrated, hasn't it?" Mr. Crandall was definite. "On Tuesday afternoon, when you and Beale were both trying to impress your little blonde by arguing which of you could climb the side of the house by holding to projections in the brickwork . . ."

"I know!" snapped Rip. "You showed us; you just walked out and *climbed* the damn house without saying another word. All right; you can catch for us, can't you? Why not get behind the plate and stop 'em?"

"No, thanks, Bull of Bashan. Having demonstrated my fitness by one fool stunt already, I'll leave baseball to those of fewer years and less dignity. But don't count me out either. If you can find a catcher anywhere, I'll be glad to get behind the plate as umpire."

"And I," said Alan, "will do the catching with pleasure."

"You!" cried Camilla. "I never knew you concerned yourself with baseball, Alan. At Oxford I thought you played cricket."

"It was Cambridge, Camilla, and I did have a try at cricket. But my first and only sports-love has always been baseball. I was no great shakes as a catcher, admittedly. And yet how I enjoyed it!"

"Is that so, now?" Bob Crandall asked with interest. "As one who's tried both, where do you stand in the vexed argument of baseball versus cricket?"

"There's no real argument at all. I maintain, rightly or wrongly, that each side would fail at the other's game because each side would have to unlearn its own basic principles. The first rule in baseball is to let the bad ones go by; in cricket it's to let nothing go by. The baseball player on a cricket-pitch would be bowled in about two minutes. The cricketer who says hitting a baseball's as simple as hitting a full-toss would be fanned by any pitcher with a fast one and a good curve."

"Look!" Rip shouted. "Can't you people stick to one subject, any subject at all, for two consecutive minutes? About this question of somebody acting suspiciously, *I* was going to say a word. But I won't; it can wait; we've got other business. If you'll do the catching, Grantham, that's swell and thanks a lot. I've got a glove and a mask here, as you see, and there's another mask in the cellar for the umpire. But there's no chest-protector or leg-guards."

"I don't want any of that apparatus, thanks. Just a mask to keep off foul tips. If the umpire wants a mask . . ."

"Not *this* umpire, old socks," said Mr. Crandall. "Any foul tip will flatten the catcher before it bothers me. All right! If everybody's ready, what are we waiting for?"

With powerful gallantry Yancey addressed Madge and Camilla.

"You ladies like to go along, maybe? Or would you rather—?"

"Sit here and tend to our knitting?" flashed Madge. "There you go again, Yancey, treating us like figures in a stained-glass window! We'll go with you, of course. Where do you mean to try all this?"

"The drive in front of the house," Rip answered before Yancey could speak, "will do well enough. I get it, Madge! You want to see me fan Stonewall and win his twenty bucks. *I've* got a fast one he won't like. But the Oracle of Goliath is absolutely right: what are we waiting for?"

And he strode out, with the other five trooping after him. From a table in the hall Yancey caught up a silver tray to serve as home plate. They emerged under the portico with the four tall pillars, and down the front steps into cool light.

The sanded walk or drive was still soaked from the rain, but it offered firm enough footing. Alan's car stood well to the left where he had parked it, its top now closed. The front garden on the right glowed red and purple with azaleas. Bob Crandall took a refreshed survey of their surroundings.

"You're all crazy, and I'm as bad as anybody," he said, "though you might be a good deal crazier still. At least you had sense enough not to try roping Hank into this. He's a fisherman, I know. But asking Hank Maynard to play baseball would be like asking Robert Browning to compose limericks for an Elks social. Just thank your stars he's otherwise occupied!"

"Will he stay occupied, I wonder?" asked Camilla. Her voice rose. "Yancey, where are you putting home plate?"

With the others trailing, Yancey had shambled away almost fifty yards towards the front gates. He stopped at a point just before magnolias rose at either side of the path. He put down the silver tray on the sand and stood to the right of it, slowly swinging his bat.

"There! How's that?"

"Facing the house?"

"Sure, facing the house! Who wants to chase a lost ball in those woods the other side of the lane? That's Charleston College's research station, fence and all. Land a ball in there, Camilla, it'd take a police posse to get it back again."

"But—*facing* the house? What if you break a window?"

Yancey replied by addressing Madge.

"If I bust a window, honey, I'll replace it with stained glass of the kind you were talkin' about. And an image of you in the window, like the angel you never were. How's that?"

Madge said nothing. Rip, putting down catcher's mitt and mask beside Alan, drew the fielder's glove on his left hand and paced off the distance to an imaginary pitcher's box.

"There'll be no windows broken, Madge! He won't get a sniff of the ball, he won't even *see* it, with Old Smoke Hillboro on the mound for the Yankees. What's the good word, Stonewall? Like to cover a little side-bet?"

"I'll cover any damn bet you want to make! But I'm gettin' *God-damn* sick and tired of—"

"Easy, you two!" yelled the umpire. "If you've got to fight the Civil War all over again, for Pete's sake do it on your own time!"

Out from the house, opening the white-painted screen door and letting it slam, came Dr. Gideon Fell. Hatless, in his black alpaca suit and leaning on the crutch-headed stick, he lumbered down the steps and blinked his way towards them. It was unnecessary to introduce Dr. Fell; everybody knew who he was, and accepted him from the start. Yet his presence, if anything, added to a tension that already existed.

"Alan," said Camilla, "what are *you* doing?"

"Only taking off my coat. Forgive the suspenders."

"That's a Savile Row suit, isn't it? Don't they make English suits for belts?"

"Yes, of course, but this particular tailor won't make 'em."

"What are you doing with the coat?"

"Putting it down over here, that's all. I can't—"

"On that wet grass? Don't be silly! Here, give it to me and I'll hold it for you."

"Thanks."

Leaving the mask where it was, Alan pulled the big glove on his left hand and moved behind the improvised plate.

"I can't give you signals," he called to Rip, "because I don't know what you throw. Like to warm up?"

"Look, Grantham, I'm always warmed up! However! Just to show 'em this damnyankee knows his stuff, I'll give you one strike and warm the plate. Stand back for a second, Stonewall! Ready, Grantham?"

"Fire away."

There was no elaborate wind-up, as Alan had expected. Rip's motions were very easy. Weight on the left foot, ball cradled close, he flung forward and uncorked his fast one.

It *was* a fast one. The ball blistered across the plate and whacked into the glove six inches above waist height. Alan, who had not touched a baseball in years, almost fumbled it. But you don't forget, he was thinking, any more than you forget how to ride a bicycle. He threw back to the pitcher. Picking up the mask, he adjusted its elastic over his head and crouched behind the plate.

"All right!" proclaimed the umpire. "Now will you guys quit stalling and get with it? Play ball!"

What sun remained was well behind Maynard Hall; they had no trouble with the light. Dr. Fell withdrew to the right of the path, the two girls to the left. Yancey advanced negligently, bat waggling.

"If he *does* break a window—!" Madge burst out.

"He won't, Madge; didn't I tell you?"

"I hope my father doesn't see it happen! I hope—"

"Play ball!"

Down came the pitch, a whistling duplicate of the first. Yancey's bat did not move. The umpire's arm did.

"Str-rike one!"

"Like it, Stonewall?" carolled Rip. "Just because you were a hot-shot hitter at some *parvenu* school like William and Mary . . . !"

"*Parvenu* school, for God's sake?" echoed a hollow voice. "*Parvenu* school, burn my britches to a cinder! Son, they were learnin' their letters at William and Mary a hundred years before *your* damn place was hacked out of the wilderness it ought to have stayed in. I'm tellin' you—"

"I'm not telling you, Stonewall; I'm just showing you. See?"

Down it came: very fast, but high and inside. Alan did fumble this one; the mask seemed to provide a more restricted view than he remembered, and his own throw back was so high Rip had to jump for it. The next pitch, a slow curve with a wide break outwards, was also called a ball.

"What's the matter, Stonewall? Won't try for anything, eh? Bat stuck to your shoulder, or what?"

"Put it *here*, son! Just put it *here!*"

This time indulging in an embryonic wind-up, Rip fired with every ounce of weight—a pitch so debatable, a little high and inside but perhaps below the shoulder, that Alan himself would hardly have known what to call it.

"Ball—three!"

Rip straightened up on receiving the throw, his face not pleasant.

"How's your eyesight, umpire? Wouldn't it be better to get some pencils and a tin cup?"

"Want me to slap a fine on you?" howled the irate umpire, doing a little dance behind Alan. "Now shut your God-damn mouth and play ball!"

"I'll do that, Bob. We'll get you a seeing-eye dog when this is over. Meanwhile, though . . ."

By the look on the pitcher's face Alan guessed what it would be: Rip's fast one again, dead in the groove. The ball thudded into the glove exactly where he was holding his hands.

"Strike—two!"

Rip's spirits bubbled up.

"See that, Madge? I thought I could get him with my fast one again, and I was right. He won't swing at anything; he's too afraid of missing! Now what shall we feed him for the third strike? Something different, maybe?" Rip settled the weight on his left foot. "Always keep 'em guessing, that's the thing. Always . . ."

"Camilla," Madge burst out, "I don't like this!"

"It's all right, dear. There's nothing wrong."

"There *is* something wrong! I know! I can—"

Crack!

Yancey had stepped into the fast one and swung.

"Jesus H. Christ!" whispered the umpire.

In actual play it would have been a line drive over second base, too high to be speared or knocked down. The ball, a white streak like unwinding yarn, whistled straight between the two inner columns of the portico just as Henry Maynard, a book in his left hand, pushed open the screen door and emerged in its path.

It could not have hit him—it was far too high—but he would scarcely have known that. He dropped flat on his face, not at all a ludicrous spectacle to those who watched. The ball whacked against brick a foot or two above the front door, and rebounded out into the drive, where Rip Hillboro danced to field it. Henry Maynard picked himself up, briefly brushed at his knees, gave them all one look from a distance, and with much dignity went back into the house.

Rip hastened to join the others, pushing the ball into his hip pocket.

"That's the end of the exercise, I think. If we don't want thunders from Sinai, we'd better knock it off here and now. You know, Stonewall, maybe it's a good thing you and I are both leaving tomorrow."

"Yes, son, I guess it is too."

"Look, Stonewall, here's your dough: a ten and two fives. You made a fool of me, all right; I don't like it one bit. But you smacked that last one fair and square; you made a fool of me with all my talk, and I admit it! Here's the dough."

"Well . . . now!" said Yancey Beale. "I didn't much want your money, son. Up to this minute I meant to tell you just where you could shove it. Still! If you're bein' a good sport, that's different. Reckon I said things *I* oughtn't to have said, and maybe that clout was mostly a fluke. Shake hands?"

"Sure; why not? We can be civilized again, can't we?"

Rip and Yancey, together with Dr. Fell, Bob Crandall, and Madge too, moved towards the house. Alan removed mask and glove and approached Camilla, who stood motionless with his coat over her arm.

"Alan—!"

"Yes?"

Camilla's face had grown rather flushed, and there was an odd look about her eyes. For an instant she seemed quite literally to sway towards him. Then the impression was gone, a burst bubble or an illusion.

"What a lot of *children!*" she said. "You know, Alan, it's really too bad about the hit that . . . that . . ."

"That almost beaned Madge's old man?"

"Yes. When Yancey hit that ball, I was looking at Dr. Fell's face and at Bob Crandall's too."

"What about it?"

"They were both hoping he *would* break a window." Camilla made a gesture of despair. "Oh, God save us! *Men!*"

In silence Camilla and Alan followed the little procession up the steps, across the porch, and into the main hall. Putting down mask and glove on the table, where Rip had put his own glove and Yancey the bat, Alan took his coat from Camilla. There was no sign of Henry Maynard, for which he felt profoundly grateful.

"Honeychile," Yancey exclaimed to Madge, "where's your daddy?"

"If you ask me, he's up in his study doing a little sulking. Yancey, wait! Where are you going?"

"That salver thing we were using for home plate: I left it out in the sand! And he's as mad as a hornet already! I'll just—"

"No, let it be! George will bring it in!"

"Yes, Stonewall," advised Rip Hillboro, "you let it be. *I've* got something to say."

A subdued Rip, who had made handsome apology, clearly could not remain subdued. He had reared up again. His fair hair in a crew-cut seemed only a knife-edge of hair.

"Just before we went out there," he said, "I started to ask a question. And I'll ask it now come hell or high water. Follow me."

This time the procession poured after him down into the library, Dr. Fell bringing up the rear. Rip assumed a commanding position in the middle of the room.

"A remark was made—in what context I don't know and can't say; the Oracle of Goliath wouldn't tell me—that somebody has been acting suspiciously. Here's my question, ladies and gentlemen, and I think we'll all be interested in the answer." Dramatically he stabbed a finger towards the door on the right of the fireplace. "Which of you stole the tomahawk out of that room?"

7.

A lightning-bolt just outside the windows could have produced no greater effect.

"Tomahawk?" blurted Madge.

"No!" Camilla whispered. "No, no, no!

"Somebody acting suspiciously?" she continued to Rip. "You heard something when you came in here with Yancey. But it wasn't what you think you heard."

"Wasn't it?"

"Mr. Crandall was telling us about a girl from Jersey City. Madge's father is suspicious of the stories he tells and the language he uses, always afraid he'll come out with something dreadful—"

"—which he often does, let's face it," concurred Mr. Crandall, addressing Dr. Fell. "Maybe I'm out of place in good society. My father was a cabinet-maker; he apprenticed me to a cabinet-maker when I was fifteen years old. But I didn't stay apprenticed; there was too much printer's ink in my veins. I'm a crude kind of fellow, *au fond,* though I've picked up a good deal over the years. I can be very refined when I want to be. When it's absolutely necessary, I can be as refined as all getout! You see—"

"Not," Camilla interrupted, "that there hasn't been suspicious behavior, everywhere and all the time. Considering what happened at half-past one this morning, when Madge saw a man on the beach . . ." Rapidly she recounted Madge's story, to the cross-eyed absorption of Dr. Fell. "And now, to top everything else . . . !"

Madge herself, lost in some unhappy dream, did not seem to be listening. She ran across to the open door of the other room, which remained dark, and groped just inside for a switch. Light glowed from a crystal chandelier. The others followed Madge inside.

It was as lofty as the library, though a good deal narrower between this door and a big double-leaf French window, flanked by a sash window on either side, in the opposite wall at the back. Both French window and sash windows were masked in rich red curtains patterned with gold.

Against walls of polished white wood more Maynard ancestors looked down from portraits. But first of all, on those walls, you saw the weapons.

The firearms, set out in tiers, ranged from an early flintlock musket down through heavy eighteenth- and nineteenth-century rifles to a Winchester repeater *circa* 1898, with pistols of corresponding dates. All were well-cared-for but dark with age. Along the right-hand wall stretched a rack of swords. Beside the French window, incongruously, a blackboard stood on its easel.

"Yes, the curtains are drawn," observed Dr. Fell, as though someone had commented on this. "May I ask who drew them?"

"There's nothing funny in that!" replied Madge. "*I* drew them. Or, rather, I told Sylvia to do it. There are three maids: Sylvia, Judith, and Winnie Mae. The afternoon sun fades the carpet and the drapes, that's all. But if you asked *me* who's been behaving very oddly, I'd have to say my own father. Why did he want to know how tall you are, Yancey? And how tall you are, Rip?"

Rip Hillboro pointed.

"There," he said, "is the famous Kentucky rifle, called a Kentucky rifle because it was made by German gunsmiths in Pennsylvania. All right, Stonewall, all right! I know it was *used* in

Kentucky and Tennessee, and played hell at the Battle of New Orleans!

"And over there, on the wall above the swords, we have bayonets arranged in an incomplete circle. The circle's incomplete at the top because that's where the tomahawk hung. And somebody's lifted that tomahawk as clean as a whistle. Who stole it?"

"Don't look at *me,"* said Yancey Beale. "Maybe you did."

"Or could it have been Pa Maynard himself? He wasn't at all happy, Stonewall, before he left for Richmond. Three days in the Confederate capital restored him as miraculously as though he'd drunk the Water of What's-its-name or seen Jeff Davis restored to the presidency. But we haven't done him any good today. I feed you a baseball, and you slap it back straight in his face. Hadn't we both better look a leedle oudt?"

"Oh, don't be *absolutely* silly!" cried Madge. "What could he have against you two, of all people? Even if he had something against anybody, which he hasn't . . ."

"I wasn't being quite serious, Madge. You're a literal-minded little devil, you know."

"Even if he had," Madge pursued, "can you imagine him using a *tomahawk?* He might work out something very subtle and mathematical, but he'd rather be dead than crude. Forget Daddy! And yet the tomahawk is gone; somebody took it. It *is* horribly worrying, isn't it? What do you think, Dr. Fell?"

"Yes, that's an idea." Rip fingered his large jaw. "What did Bob call you? Gargantua, wasn't it? Speak up, Gargantua; give us the long view! We know you're the old maestro."

"Sir," replied Dr. Fell, "I am the old duffer. Forgive an apparent inanity which all too often is real inanity. However, since you both ask my opinion, I can do no better than quote a series of incidents already quoted to Mr. Maynard himself, adding two more of which I was unaware half an hour ago.

"Last Friday night the scarecrow is stolen; early in the morning somebody is seen at that window there. Nothing to excite remark happens for almost a week; then it all happens at once. Last night, or rather at half-past one this morning, Miss Maynard from her bedroom window sees an unidentified man trudging from west to east along the beach. Today, at some time before lunch, an invaluable major-domo named George thinks he sees somebody 'skulking' in Mr. Maynard's study. (You didn't know that? I have been so informed, and I believe it.) Presumably also today, as though to point an old story of men slaughtered without a trace in soft mud or sand, the tomahawk disappears. Confound it! When to all this we add emotional pressures building up like steam in a boiler with the safety-valve closed . . ."

"You think there's menace around?" demanded Rip.

"I fear so."

"O.K., Gargantua! Who's being menaced?"

"Now that," argued Dr. Fell, "is precisely the point on which I can't make up my mind. It might be one person, it might be another. However! You, Mr. Hillboro, discovered that the tomahawk was gone. When did you discover it?"

"This morning after breakfast, when I went through here on my way out to get some air."

"Did you mention it to anybody else, up to the time you told us?"

"No, I did not. Hell's bells, Gargantua! When did Madge mention the man on the beach, carrying a sack over his shoulder? I never even heard that one until Camilla repeated it to you not five minutes ago! Now, I'm a lawyer; I think I can weigh and assess evidence. But what *is* evidence? What's important and what's not important? A lot's been happening, as you say."

"And yet when it began happening last Friday night, I understand, you were inclined to dismiss the matter and treat Miss Bruce's story lightly?"

"Wrong, Gargantua! Dead wrong! If you ask Camilla herself, she'll tell you *I* was the one who persuaded Pa Maynard to phone the cops. He didn't want to, but I got around him. *Maybe* she'd had too much bourbon or too many sleeping-pills; then, again, maybe she hadn't. Always play it safe and be on the safe side: that's my motto! I was the one who did take it seriously. How's about that, Camilla?"

"Yes, it's quite true," agreed Camilla. "I told the story twice at lunch, Dr. Fell!"

"Actually," Rip reported in a loud voice, "the one who made light of it and laughed ha-ha was old Stonewall Jackson there, after he'd started the whole business by telling ghost stories. And yet up to that time he'd been muttering under his breath that there was something damn funny going on in this place. True or false, everybody?"

"Couldn't we go back to the library?" interposed Madge, who was looking rather white. "This room's only a kind of museum, with no place to sit down. *Couldn't* we go back to the library?"

Yancey Beale came to life. "Yes, honey, you do just that. Here!"

To Alan's astonishment Yancey took Madge by the shoulders. Gently, but insistently and powerfully, he impelled her through the doorway while himself remaining there with the others. He closed the door and stood with his back to it.

"She's our hostess!" he said in a fierce whisper. "You can't just tell the hostess to get lost, or go and make us a pitcher of iced tea, when there's something you want to confide in the visiting crime-specialist."

Yancey himself was under a great strain. His eye wandered round the white room of black weapons and black portraits, and came to rest at a point between Alan and Dr. Fell.

"If Hillboro's looking for a son-of-a-bitch," he said seriously and earnestly, "I expect it's me. Sometimes I think I'm a worse son-of-a-bitch than that ol' bastard Sherman himself. Yes, I started it! I started it all!"

"By telling the ghost stories, sir?"

"Before that! Long before that!"

"Oh, ah?"

"It all started, you might say, on the Sunday night just before the house-party. It was May 2nd; Mr. Maynard read the date out of a pocket diary. He and Madge and I were out in front near the gates. It was a funny kind of night, with Madge gettin' the jim-jams from no cause I could be sure of. I asked Mr. Maynard what was the thing that follows and leaves no trace. He wouldn't answer; he never does answer, though I looked it up later. But it hadn't shed any sweetness and light.

"And if that weren't enough, as Hillboro will tell you, on Friday night I must open my big mouth and tell 'em 'The Treasure of Abbot Thomas.' Yes, I led off with the ghost stories! And *of course* I laughed ha-ha, though not very loudly, when things started to happen later on. It's Madge: you think I want that little gal any more upset than she has to be? She's no walloping Amazon; she's delicate; she can't take it. I hoped I could jolly her out of being scared, even if it wasn't much of a success. Didn't you see her face just a minute ago, when we were all goin' on about tomahawks?"

"Then in justice to Miss Maynard," rumbled Dr. Fell, "may I suggest you open the door so that we may join her?"

Yancey opened the door. Rather self-consciously Dr. Fell lumbered into the library, followed first by Camilla, then by Alan, then by Yancey himself, with Rip and Bob Crandall.

Madge in the brown-and-beige dress had seated herself again on the yellow upholstered sofa. Yancey and Rip marched to the sofa, where they stood like grenadiers. Dr. Fell took up a position with his back to the fireplace, and addressed Alan.

"Any ideas, my dear fellow?"

"No ideas as yet. Whatever you've got yourself into this time, it must have a very odd solution."

"Sir," returned Dr. Fell, wheezing and puffing past the ribbon on his eyeglasses, "it is not merely the solution. This is a very odd problem, even considered as a problem."

"You mean," cried Camilla, "the thing that follows and leaves no trace?"

"Not necessarily. I refer to an aspect which does not seem to have occurred to you. Archons of Athens! May I crave your corporate indulgence while this old scatterbrain attempts to concentrate for a moment or two?"

And he leaned on his crutch-headed stick, blinking at the carpet. Bob Crandall moved uncertainly. Camilla drifted to the grand piano and sat down behind it. Alan followed her by instinct, very conscious of her nearness.

The silence stretched out. There was no music on the rack of the piano, but Camilla needed none. While still nobody spoke, softly she began to play. The keys rippled and rang in the big room. And suddenly Dr. Fell raised his head.

"Mendelssohn!" he roared.

Everybody jumped. Camilla's hands fell from the keyboard.

"It's not Mendelssohn, Dr. Fell! It was a bad try at a Chopin prelude; I don't play very well, I'm afraid. And I didn't know you were musical?"

"Musical, hey?" repeated Dr. Fell, regarding her in half-witted fashion. "O Lord! O Bacchus! I have but one recollection of what even remotely might be described as music. Once upon a time I had a passion for standing with boon companions at the piano and bellowing out 'The Road to Mandalay' or similar catches beyond the patience of the most indulgent neighbors. No, really, it won't do!"

"What won't do?" demanded Rip Hillboro. "Look, Gargantua, what *is* all this?"

With his stick Dr. Fell pointed to the front windows.

"There is a car coming up the drive," he announced. "I rather think, though I am not sure, it is Mrs. Huret returning."

"Yes!" agreed Madge, rising partway from the sofa to look. "It's Valerie, all right! She ran out of here as though she couldn't bear it any longer, but nothing really discourages her. Here she is, Mr. Crandall! Here's your girl-friend back again!"

"My girl-friend, is it? *My* girl-friend, for Jesus Christ's sake?"

"At least, sir, you conceal your transports," observed Dr. Fell. "Come, this won't do either! Let us gird ourselves to receive the lady with what suavity we may."

But they did not receive her; for the moment, at least, they did not even see her. Since the door to the hall stood wide open, they heard the outer screen door open and close. They heard Valerie Huret's voice say a word or two to somebody, presumably George. Her heels rapped along the hall and up the stairs at the rear.

"Now I wonder," Camilla said, "I wonder just why she came back?"

"Oh, Camilla," exclaimed Madge, "does it matter why she came back? She's always welcome, of course, no matter what man she's currently making passes at. *I* was hoping Dr. Fell had some enlightenment for us. Have you, Dr. Fell?"

"Miss Maynard, that depends. I was wondering . . ."

Madge had become extraordinarily animated, perhaps feverishly animated.

"You were wondering about the blackboard, weren't you? Why there's a blackboard in that museum? And about the tomahawk?"

"Madge honey," said Yancey Beale, "can't you forget that damn tomahawk?"

"It's a real eighteenth-century one. I never associated them with anybody except Indians. But did you know, Camilla, that during the French and Indian War British troops in this country wore tomahawks just as they wore bayonets? It's a little hatchet, really; it was used to chop a way through underbrush. But I never knew that," Madge said rapidly, "until the week just before the house-party.

"They—they asked Daddy to give a speech on antique weapons to a small group of high-school seniors. Six of them, with their history teacher, came here on a Friday afternoon: that would have been April 30th. Daddy put up a blackboard in that room there . . ."

"Forgive me, Miss Maynard," interrupted Dr. Fell. "On our way here, hardly a very long stone's throw from this house, we passed rather an elaborate high school building of orange-yellow brick, with the date 1920. Did your group of seniors come from that particular school?"

"From the Joel Poinsett? No, of course not!"

" 'Of course' not?"

"Nobody goes there now; it's closed, though a man in a nearby cottage keeps an eye on the place. It's past use, they say, and they've got funds for a modern building on the same site. Next month they'll begin tearing it down, and replace it . . ."

"I know; don't tell me!" Camilla cut in. "They'll replace it with one of those ghastly one-storey structures we see everywhere, as cheap-looking and flimsy-looking as somebody's henhouse, but very popular because they're mostly glass and cost a fortune to build."

"Camilla," said Alan, "is it possible there's something modern you don't like?"

"Alan," cried Camilla, "is it possible there's anything modern you *do* like?"

"Yes. That's a personal subject I'd like to discuss with you in private."

"I see. You want to sneer at me in private as well as in public, do you? Well, you won't get the chance! *You* were saying, Madge?"

Madge remained intent, as though buoyed up by some inner spirit.

"I was telling you," she answered, "about the lecture on old weapons to the high-school seniors. Six rather nice children, three girls and three boys with their history teacher, were here in the afternoon. Daddy loves lecturing, although he'll never admit he does; he loved standing at that blackboard and explaining things with figures and diagrams. When he'd finished he told George the blackboard could stay where it was, for the time being; and it's been there ever since. I heard that lecture too; that's how I know tomahawks were once a part of colonial troops' equipment." She broke off. "For heaven's sake, Rip, what's the matter with you?"

"There's nothing the *matter,* Madge. But don't you see this just leads us around in the same old circle?"

"Leads us where?"

"Straight back to Pa Maynard. Look, Madge: don't get me

wrong. I'm not saying a word against your old man—!"

"You'd better not!"

"But are you sure you understand him?"

"Do *you* understand him, son?" asked Yancey Beale.

"I flatter myself I know human nature." Again there was an aggressive set to Rip's shoulders. "Madge says he'd rather be dead than crude, and she's right. But suppose (just suppose, Stonewall!) he's got it in for you, or for me, or for anybody else you can think of? And suppose he's figured out some way a man can walk over mud or wet sand without leaving a trace? *That'd* be subtle enough, wouldn't it?"

"Mr. Hillboro," interposed Dr. Fell, "are you making a serious accusation against the gentleman whose hospitality you have accepted?"

"Good God, no! Since Madge is so very literal-minded, I'd better repeat that this isn't to be taken seriously at all."

"Yes?"

"In a question of reading individual character, I'm just suggesting what he *might* do if he were driven far enough. When I say he's tricky or slippery, I don't mean tricky in the way we usually mean it. There's a whole lot of things he wouldn't and couldn't do. Pa Maynard wouldn't cheat you: he wouldn't sell you a worthless stock or a used car you couldn't depend on. But if he thought he had cause he might just possibly slip poison into your bourbon when he was sure you weren't looking. I'll go further than that; I'll say—"

"Yes, young man?" demanded a harsh voice.

It was as though the room had been struck with physical chill.

On the little platform inside the library door stood Valerie Huret, with her red hair and her white skin. But they hardly noticed Mrs. Huret now. They all looked at Henry Maynard, who stood just in front of her.

His wide-open eyes had acquired such fixity that a ring of white showed entirely around the iris. He hardly seemed to breathe. Shoulders back, elbows as his sides, he stood rigid, drawn up, the picture of a perfect gentleman holding in check the flaming temper of a fiend.

"Yes, young man?" he repeated. "Let's both go further, shall we? Since you insist on theorizing about my many shortcomings and my basically murderous impulses, hadn't you better share the theory with me?"

8 *

Early evening light, with a broad red glow in the west, was settling over James Island as Alan drove back the way he had come. Again Dr. Fell occupied the rear of the car; there was nobody else. The trees of Fort Johnson Road sped past overhead; the clock on the dashboard pointed to ten minutes past six.

And a certain feverishness was still on Alan.

"Do you see the time, Dr. Fell? Actually, it hasn't been a full ten minutes since the old boy turned up at that door like an avenging ghost. I thought there was going to be the great-grandmother of all rows!"

"The same thought occurred to me," confessed Dr. Fell. "But young Hillboro, it would seem, is not quite the indomitable figure he tries to be. Faced with a direct challenge, you remember, he covered confusion by laughing and apologizing, and a reminder of his careful preface that he had been joking all the time."

"Which Mr. Maynard accepted, to everybody's surprise, without protest and with only one comment." Here Alan mimicked Henry Maynard. " 'It will decrease friction, Rip, if you and Yancey see less of each other from now on; and if I see still less of you too.' They both said, 'Yes, sir,' like obedient schoolboys. Back upstairs he went, with some remark about a book he'd forgotten.

"And that was all. But *was* it all? Valerie Huret stalked over like Juno to capture the attention of Bob Crandall; you instantly made excuses to get us out of there . . ."

"Promising," supplied Dr. Fell, "that the old duffer would be on tap if they needed him. In candor, I was concerned to avoid more rows. What did you write on that card you gave Miss Bruce?"

"The name of the restaurant where we're going now, one I particularly want you to visit. I asked Camilla to go with us; she wouldn't. It's not quite six-fifteen at the moment, but it will be nearer seven when we get there. Do you mind an early dinner?"

"Sir, I enjoy dining at any time; even, malcontents have hinted, at breakfast-time. What is the restaurant?"

"A place called Davy's, adjoining the Dock Street Theatre in Church Street."

"No Englishman," said Dr. Fell, "can be stunned to find the Dock Street Theatre in Church Street. At the same time . . . !"

"It's not as confused as it sounds. Queen Street, formerly Dock Street, is just around the corner. By the way, speaking of Camilla—"

"Do you still think she can't bear the sight of you? Archons of Athens! 'Somebody asked the Sergeant's wife.' "

"Asked the Sergeant's wife what? How did the Sergeant get into this anyway? Are you beginning on cryptic remarks again?"

"No remark of mine, properly considered, is ever cryptic," Dr. Fell informed him with a certain stateliness. "It may be misinterpreted; it is not cryptic. Is there anything you especially want to know?"

"I want to know everything. But I'll be content with such hints as you feel you can drop. Can't we talk about this business at Maynard Hall? Is there any reason why we shouldn't discuss it freely?"

"On the contrary, there is every reason why we must and should discuss it as freely as circumstances permit. What others may think is anybody's guess; but by thunder, sir, it frightens *me!*"

"What frightens you?"

"Emotional pressures," said Dr. Fell. "Certain remarks and attitudes of several persons, notably of Henry Maynard himself."

"Do you think Rip Hillboro's right? That the old man might just possibly have some kind of murderous design?"

"Come!" the big voice boomed. "Tut, tut, and out upon it! Are there no emotional pressures but those that lead to murdering somebody? More often, surely, they may be directed to the happier course of not murdering somebody? For the most part, I concede, our information has come from atmospheres, suggestions, innuendoes. But the atmospheres, suggestions, and innuendoes have been extraordinarily revealing!

"As for Henry Maynard, something haunts and hag-rides the man. I told him this in your presence. The twenty-five minutes or so I spent alone with him, after you had gone downstairs and before I myself descended to watch the baseball challenge, I devoted mostly to hammering him with questions about what could be doing the haunting or hag-riding."

"And—?"

"It has something to do with the conduct of his daughter," replied Dr. Fell. "But that, on the surface at least, would seem the most puzzling point of all. She is a well-behaved girl, is she not?"

"Madge is all of that. Even in Goliath (and there's no whispering gallery like a college town) the worst of the damned prying minds had nothing against her. She hasn't liked being kept so much in cotton-wool, like a fair-haired princess in a fairy tale. But that's not strange; it's only human!"

"Then what can she have been up to that worries or frightens him so much? Does nothing suggest itself?"

"No; nothing."

"Perhaps it will help," wheezed Dr. Fell, "if I recount what he told me in reply to my questions. Later this afternoon, I seem to remember, Yancey Beale mentioned an occurrence that took place on the night of Sunday, May 2nd. This is what Henry Maynard had already told me:

"On the night of May 2nd, he says, he was in his study with the air-conditioner turned off and one of the windows raised. Madge and some young man—whom her father supposed to be Yancey Beale because Yancey lives close by in Charleston, and Rip Hillboro had not yet arrived—were under the magnolias out in front.

"He could hear only a distant murmur of talk, and not always that. The situation appeared to be growing a little impassioned, though not at all dangerous, when suddenly the visitor lost his head and cried out something to the effect that it would be disastrous if Madge's father discovered them there.

"It took Henry Maynard off balance, or so he says. If his daughter becomes anybody's wife, he would prefer her to be Yancey Beale's. The notion that the boy should suppose himself unwelcome really shocked our listener on the top floor. Down he went in a hurry. Yancey *was* there. When asked why he had made so strange a remark, Yancey—perhaps carrying chivalry too far, as he is inclined to do—did not deny using the words. He merely said he could not remember saying them.

"But . . .

"Henry Maynard is no fool. He wondered at the time, and afterwards felt certain. Yancey Beale, a highly cultivated young man, affects broad Southern speech; it is the only affectation I myself have discerned in him. There had been, as our friend Maynard put it, 'something different about the voice.' It was not Yancey who had been with his daughter at the time. Who was it?"

"He accused *me,* damn him!" Alan burst out. "He thought *I* was the one, even though—"

"Tut!" protested Dr. Fell. "He did not really think so. It occurred to him, or so he says, merely because you, once admittedly an admirer of Madge, were a mere two hundred miles away instead of a thousand miles or more.

"And yet this disturbance, surely, is all cry and no wool? The girl was being 'embraced,' his own word; nobody suggests it went further. Truth must be told, as I indicated to Maynard. Queen Victoria is dead; President McKinley has long since departed the White House. Is he afraid she will make an unsuitable marriage?

Even so, why the disturbance? What is there about the bearing of this girl, Madge Maynard, to hint at devils howling down the wind or direful voices in the wilderness? So far as we know, nothing whatever. And yet, unless the man has been a complete liar in *everything,* which I refuse to believe, there is an explanation somewhere. That is our problem, or the greater part of it."

"What else did he tell you, Dr. Fell?"

"Nothing germane to the purpose. Stop! It seems almost an irrelevance," bumbled Dr. Fell, fishing out of his capacious side pocket a battered old exercise-book bound in cardboard, "if briefly I execute a flip-flop back over nearly a hundred years, and to Commodore Maynard battered to death on the beach."

He held up the exercise-book. The wind caught and riffled yellowed pages of spidery script in ink that had turned brown.

"I have here—as Maynard promised, remember?—the diary kept for the year 1867 by one India Keate, then eighteen years old, who for a part of April was a guest at Maynard Hall. She was very much there on the night of April 16th, when somebody so mysteriously struck down the victim.

"I glanced through these pages on my way downstairs from the study. India Keate noted several significant points, though she did not realize she was noting them and never thought of the matter; well-brought-up young ladies were not encouraged to interest themselves in brutal murder. Most significant, it seems to me, are the names and activities of those staying at the Hall on April 16th–17th.

"The head of the family was our own Maynard's great-grandfather Henry. Great-grandfather Henry, our host told me this afternoon, was born in 1810. He had three sons and three daughters. Two of the sons had been killed in the late conflict; the third —our Maynard's grandfather, incidentally—was a mere boy of fourteen. The two elder daughters had married and left home. The youngest daughter, Ariadne, was that friend of India Keate who entertained India at the time.

"Present at the Hall on the night of April 16th, in addition to

Miss Keate herself, were Great-grandfather Henry, his wife, his son, his daughter, and his younger brother Luke, the stern and moody ex-commander of C.S.S. *Palmetto*. Finally there was Jack Maynard, a cousin from Mobile, Alabama. Jack Maynard seems to have been something of a ne'er-do-well. He followed the sea in less formal fashion than the commodore, and had been a blockade-runner during the war. But similar pursuits had not endeared him to his cousin Luke; there was bad blood between the two, as India Keate's gentlest references seem to indicate. Jack Maynard twitted the commodore about a real or supposed weakness in the latter's right eye, saying he wondered that a gallant Confederate captain had been able to see the enemy, still less engage the enemy; and once, after Luke had refused to lend Jack money, there was a quarrel that came very near a fight."

Dr. Fell, puffing out his cheeks, made a hollow noise like wind along a tunnel.

"Now mark what follows; use your wits on it!

"On the afternoon of the 16th they had an early meal, all of them, at half-past five. At about high-tide—say between six-thirty and seven o'clock—Luke Maynard went for his customary walk along the beach. Nobody worried when he did not return; his solitary habits were known and accepted.

"Nobody worried, that is, until a laborer found his body next morning. The line of his footprints showed that he had gone as far as Fort Johnson and returned, walking rather high up the beach. At some point below the terrace of crushed oyster-shell he had veered towards the water, as men on an idle walk will do, apparently without reaching what at that hour would have been the edge of the surf. Commodore Maynard lay on the beach with the right side of his head crushed: not as though by repeated blows, but as though by one massive blow from a blunt weapon."

"Yes!" Alan agreed, when Dr. Fell hesitated like a man whistling for attention. "All that was in the newspaper account!"

"Then hear what India Keate says. Before Commodore Luke left for the walk the previous evening, Jack Maynard, on the plea of exercise, had taken a small rowboat and left the then-existing jetty with the intention (he said) of rowing around James Island. At the crucial times, we observe, Luke Maynard was near the water and Jack Maynard was on the water in a boat. Note that well: *in a boat.*"

Alan, in a rush of whirling thoughts, almost drove the car off the road before he recovered.

"Dr. Fell, it won't do!"

"What won't do?"

"Your theory won't do. Luke Maynard was walking west, it's true. He had his right side towards the harbor: agreed. But if you're suggesting that ne'er-do-well Jack, with a small boat in very shallow water, approached on Luke's blind side and struck before his victim apprehended danger, it's out of the question. I told you this morning that the body lay above the highest reach of the tide; no boat could have come so close. It's more than out of the question; it's fantastic!"

"Did I say how the murderer approached?" demanded Dr. Fell. "I asked only that you use your wits and remember the facts."

"But it leaves us worse off than before; there's *no* way!"

"When water is near, keep your eye on water. But perhaps," grunted Dr. Fell, closing the exercise-book and slipping it back into his pocket, "perhaps I should not have brought the matter up. What have we to do with these old shades? Out upon them! Our problems lie at Maynard Hall in 1965. Think of the people you have just seen there, of the Hall or associated with it!"

"I'm trying to think."

"There are several—this I do suggest—who might be called enigmatic. But by far the most enigmatic is Henry Maynard himself. Henry Maynard, to whom all roads lead! Have you any notion about *him?*"

"I was wondering . . ."

"Yes?"

"Dr. Fell, two of my lectures at King's College dealt with the Victorian novel. I maintain, in spite of Camilla's derision, that the

Victorians wrote novels better than anybody before or since. One of their stock figures was the heir to an estate who isn't really the heir; if some curious personality turns up in the story after long absence from home, you can bet your shirt he's an impostor. Our own Henry Maynard seems almost too good to be true. What if Henry Maynard isn't the real Henry Maynard at all? Or is that, as Camilla would say, too wild even for me?"

"As a matter of fact," Dr. Fell sounded guilty, "it was the first thought which occurred to me. And the notion is not wild; it is merely mistaken. I had a word aside with Captain Ashcroft at the hotel. Henry Maynard really is Henry Maynard and nobody else; kindly accept that or we shall be nowhere! But it does lead directly to another thought, if you follow me. And, speaking of the hotel," pursued Dr. Fell, waving a hand ahead as they emerged into fast traffic on Folly Road, "surely that is the bridge and the approach to Charleston? Do we return by way of Calhoun Street and our hotel?"

"No. In getting to the restaurant, we'll swing all the way downtown and come up again. The tricky thing is to remember the one-way streets; where you may turn and where you mayn't. In about twenty minutes, now . . ."

Twilight was thickening above old roofs and pastel-colored house fronts as Alan, having parked his car a little distance away, led Dr. Fell into Church Street.

There is always a hush at this hour. On the west side of Church Street, which stretches seven blocks from St. Philip's to the Battery, thin pillars of brownish sandstone supported a wrought-iron balcony across the face of the Dock Street Theatre. No lights showed there tonight; apart from fragile street-lamps, the whole thoroughfare seemed dark.

Alan pointed.

"The first Dock Street Theatre, Dr. Fell, was opened in 1736. It burned down; so did a succeeding one. On that site, in 1809, they built the once-celebrated Planter's Hotel, a place of luxury where so many bets, love-affairs, and duels originated in the old

South. Thirty years ago its shell was restored into still another playhouse, with a Georgian auditorium and as many relics as possible, including those pillars and the balcony above them, from the Planter's Hotel. That pink-fronted building to the left of it is Davy's."

"Davy who?"

"That's the surname: Parsifal Davy, a restaurant-keeper of the early nineteenth century. If the head-waiter I'm acquainted with is on duty tonight . . . "

The head-waiter was. With some ceremony they were ushered from the foyer into a spacious restaurant, gratefully air-conditioned, with walls panelled in native black cypress and ante-bellum décor not overdone. Electric table-lamps, fashioned to resemble oil-lamps in gray silk shades with gilt fringes, shed soft light on napery and silver. At a table against the right-hand wall, where a window looked into the courtyard of the Dock Street Theatre, Alan ordered food and drink any host could depend on.

She-crab soup, a Charleston specialty, was followed by succulent lobster à la Davy and strawberry shortcake for dessert. The wine, a medium Anjou, padded mind and heart. Over the coffee, with a mist of tobacco smoke arising, Dr. Fell jerked his thumb towards the window beside them.

"Those premises adjoining," he said. "They've had a romantic history, then?"

"Romantic and sensational too. In 1838, when the place was a hotel, Junius Brutus Booth, the actor, got roaring drunk as usual and tried to murder his manager by beating the man's head in with an iron firedog. He—" Alan stopped abruptly.

"I see. You don't suggest," asked Dr. Fell, "that beating somebody's head in is a common practice hereabouts? At the same time, when we remember Maynard Hall . . ."

"When we remember Maynard Hall," Alan insisted, "we mainly remember that accursed jumpy atmosphere. Dr. Mark Sheldon, whom I met on his way to deliver a message he decided against delivering after all, said everybody there needed a tranquillizer. I wish Camilla had come with us; I wish *she* were out of the atmosphere. You and I are out of it, at least."

But they were not out of it. At that moment none other than Mark Sheldon himself, minus black bag but with a distressed forehead, hurried into the restaurant and wormed among tables towards them.

"Evening, Mr. Grantham. You, sir, can't be anybody but Dr. Fell." He introduced himself. "When you've finished dinner, Dr. Fell, could you get back out to the Hall as soon as possible?"

Dread struck Alan like a dart in a board. "Don't tell us some other damn thing has happened!"

"No, no, they're all right! Only . . ."

"Will you have something to eat? Or join us for coffee?"

"Thanks, but I can't. I'm due home, and I've got to hurry. At the moment I'm just a sort of errand-boy. The message is from Madge—Miss Maynard, you know."

"Yes?"

"I don't know them at all well, either Madge or her father. So I don't know what's happening, and there's no reason why they should tell me. But—'Get Dr. Fell!' Madge said. 'Get Dr. Fell!' said Camilla Bruce. 'He and Alan Grantham are at Davy's Restaurant; the name's written on this card.'

" 'Telephone him!' I said. 'Davy's may look like an Old South Museum, but they're up to date; they've got plug-in phones so you don't even have to leave the table.' But you know these women! Once they get an idea in their heads, nothing will do but that you must drop everything and do it in person."

"Sir," Dr. Fell intoned majestically, "I am at their service, of course. Still—what troubles the ladies *now?*"

"It seems they're being badgered by the police."

"By the police?"

Despite his evident haste Dr. Sheldon drew out a chair and sat down. From his pocket he took out one of those small, flat, tilt-the-box puzzles; tiny quicksilver pellets must be rolled into holes, a feat which the steadiest hands find difficult. Mark Sheldon inclined the box this way, inclined it that way, then put the box on the table and ran a hand through his wiry dark-red hair.

"By a fellow named Captain Ashcroft," he continued, "who's not a bad sort but a persistent dog when he digs his heels in. He got there not long after you left. It seems somebody stole a tomahawk, though how he learned it was stolen I can't say; nobody at the Hall told him. But he takes it seriously; he—"

"Sir," thundered Dr. Fell, "what do they want of ME?"

" 'Get Dr. Fell!' said Camilla. 'He's the only one who has influence over Jehoshaphat Ashcroft.' His name's not really Jehoshaphat; it's Jesus or Jerusalem or something biblical, and they're putting all kinds of variations on it."

"Influence over Captain Ashcroft, sir? This is entirely ridiculous!"

"Well, they think you have. Camilla Bruce does, anyway. 'Dr. Fell,' she said, 'can restrain him if he claims we've got a murderer in our midst. Which is absurd, or is it? And get Alan too,' she said. She particularly requested your presence, Mr. Grantham."

"Camilla," demanded Alan, "requested *my* presence? Are you quite serious and quite sober?"

"I'm sober, worse luck." Mark Sheldon picked up the puzzle, tilted it helplessly, and put it down again.

"The situation out there," he went on, "would have had *me* rattled if I hadn't been so concerned with other things. They're all avoiding each other as if each thought everybody else had some contagious disease, except that Valerie *will* follow Bob Crandall wherever he goes and whatever he does. The paterfamilias is a man apart, as he always is. He's sitting alone on that terrace, or he was when I left just before dark, and even old Ashcroft didn't have the crust to go near him. 'He sat there lonely as a cloud, that floats—' I've got the quotation wrong, haven't I?"

"Archons of Athens!" said Dr. Fell.

The whole restaurant had become a blatter of talk from tables pretty well filled, which may be accounted fortunate. Dr. Fell surged to his feet, taking little trouble to lower his voice.

"Archons of Athens!" he said. "Was I unutterably stupid to leave that house, suspecting what I did suspect?"

"Well," inquired Dr. Sheldon, "what did you suspect?"

The other did not seem to hear.

"How far can we pre-judge? How far *dare* we pre-judge, by thunder? Am I my brother's mind-reader, with so little except impressions to go on? And yet it may be so. Suppose he had decided not to do it? And then (suppose this) somebody else discovered the evidence, discovered what had been so carefully hidden, and turned all guns the other way? He didn't mean to do it, and had made up his mind. *He* did mean to do it, and had made up *his* mind too!"

"Look here!" protested Alan.

"I've got to go!" said Mark Sheldon. "My wife's waiting; I'm late already. Excuse me."

He picked up the puzzle, slipped it into his pocket, and was off across the crowded room.

"Look here!" Alan repeated. "Your use of pronouns alone, Dr. Fell, is confusing enough by itself. Just what the hell are you talking about? Whoever *he* is, what had he made up his mind to do?"

"Whatever was to have been done." Dr. Fell came to life with a kind of groan. "But don't ask me what that is, I beg, because I haven't the least idea. Do I hear a great devil howling, the worst I have heard these forty years? Or am I only wool-gathering, as usual? After all, we can't say it's happened; nothing whatever has happened so far! Absolutely nothing has—"

"Dr. Gideon Fell?" asked the head-waiter, appearing suddenly at their table. "You're wanted on the phone, sir."

"Oh, ah? Where is your phone?"

"Here, sir." And the head-waiter, like a conjurer, produced one from behind his back. "I'll just put it on the table and plug it in, shall I? I'm afraid it's . . . never mind."

He faded away. Dr. Fell, still standing, took up the telephone, spoke into it, and instantly held it three or four inches from his ear. Out of it, every syllable audible to Alan, issued a heavy voice speaking a little more loudly than was necessary.

"Joe Ashcroft here," it said. "The girl's all right; leastways," it added argumentatively, "she'll be all right in a day or two. It was a bad shock and a bad sight, though there was no blood and no mess. Maybe Mark Sheldon oughtn't to have left here. But he's not their own doctor; their own doctor came over from town as soon as he could. She's under heavy sedation, and she'll stay that way. As for him, poor bastard, he's still on the terrace where he got it."

Now it was Dr. Fell who quarreled about pronouns.

"Yes?" Dr. Fell demanded, with a face of collapse. "*Who* is under sedation? *Who* is on the terrace?"

"His daughter's under sedation; didn't I tell you? And Henry Maynard who got it. Somebody came up behind him, and— The right side of his head's practically crushed; though, as I say, there's no mess and no blood except in his nose. Might have been done with a baseball bat; might not.

"He's on the terrace," Captain Ashcroft continued, "but he won't be there when you get here. The wagon will take him away; they'll have finished with the photographs and the plaster casts. But that's just the hell of it! I hope . . ."

"What did you say?"

"That's just the hell of it; I hope history's not repeatin' itself. That oyster-shell stuff is still damp from the rain this afternoon. There's his own footprints, all fine and clear and dandy. But there's nobody else's footprints. Not on the terrace, not on the beach down below, not in any damn place at all! How soon *can* you get here, anyway?"

9 *

A waning moon rode high above Maynard Hall, so that four white columns stood out ghostly against the darker background of the house. But it was not the only light here in the grounds.

In the broad sanded drive, a little distance out from the front steps, a police car had been parked completely sideways, facing north. Its headlamps, full on, shone out across cropped grass, across the crushed-shell surface of the terrace, and across the slope of the beach beyond.

"There!" called Captain Ashcroft's voice, from the gloom on the other side of the police car. "That'll do; that's far enough; stop there!"

Alan would have had to stop there in any case, with the other car blocking the way. He switched off the engine and his own headlamps. Still a little nauseated from the news—how would Camilla take it?—he crawled out of the right-hand side. Dr. Fell descended massively on the same side.

Captain Ashcroft, a large flashlight in his right hand, strode round the front of the police car to join them. Momentarily his shadow ran out towards the scene of disorder on the terrace.

"We (harrumph!) we made good time from the restaurant, I

think," grunted Dr. Fell. "No comment on this distressing business need be made. Who found the body?"

"*I* found the body," said Captain Ashcroft. "I'll tell you about that in a minute. They've carted him off, as you can see. This way!"

The way led across cropped grass to the inner edge of the terrace overlooking the beach. Captain Ashcroft—face heavy, brows lowering—switched on the big flashlight and used its beam like a pointer.

"In actual distances by tape-measure," he said grimly, "it's just thirty-six feet from the nearest of those six poplar trees on the right to a point just inside the edge of the house on the left, where a path runs past the side of the house and down some wooden steps to the beach. It's just half that distance from where we stand to that tiny little miniature barrier, chains strung between iron pegs not six inches high, for what we'll call the beach-side boundary.

"Thirty-six feet long by eighteen feet wide; get it? You see the tracks *he* made? You see the tracks my men and I made and then messed up? There's the table he sat at and the chair he fell from. Get that too?"

Particles of shell glittered like glass in the strong glow of the headlamps. That afternoon Alan had observed the heavy iron chair and the round iron table, both painted green. Though midway in the length of the terrace, they were a good deal more towards the little chain-barrier than towards the terrace's inner edge, so that anyone sitting there would have a good view out over beach and harbor.

Across that white surface footprints made by narrow and fastidious shoes went out in a diagonal line from the grass-verge to the chair. The indentation of the surface between table and chair showed where somebody had toppled or slid down. There were other marks: messed up, as Captain Ashcroft had said. But those made by the victim stood out with brutal clarity against the night.

"Never knew what hit him!" Captain Ashcroft said now,

"He'd been reading until the light started to fail. Then he put the book in his pocket; leastways, we found it in his pocket; and was just sitting there. Somebody sneaked up behind him and swung for the side of the head. Why the *side* of the head?"

"Sir," Dr. Fell blinked round, "I don't think I understand."

"Any cop knows about head-wounds. Yes, and dreads 'em. At one time or another in your life you've got to hit somebody on the head because you've got no choice. When you do that, never for God's sake hit the *top* of the head: that's how you can kill or hurt badly when you don't mean to. The man who did this job meant murder—it was one hell of a swat—and yet he hit the side of the head from choice. Maybe that's not important; maybe it's something only a cop would think of. What *is* important, what's given me pink nightmares already, is just how in the name of Jesus he managed to do it?"

"Is it still true," asked Dr. Fell, "that before you and your men took over there were no marks or footprints on the terrace except Mr. Maynard's own?"

"None on the terrace, none on all that beach down there," the beam of the flashlight swung out, "none on any damn place a mark could be made. Have we got space-walkers that can hang maybe a foot up in the air while they float out and hit like Babe Ruth? Not in this county we haven't!"

Mosquitoes sang thinly. Alan slapped at one and missed. Captain Ashcroft began to pace back and forth on the grass in front of the car's headlamps, his shadow appearing and disappearing across the terrace.

"And don't tell me about tomahawks either! Wasn't any tomahawk did what was done to Henry, sharp edge or blunt edge whichever; plenty o' mess and blood if you used that. Might have been a baseball bat, as I said on the phone. Might have been a rounded piece of iron, like what you can pick up off the ground in any junk-yard. Might 'a' been anything.

"In the Army, twenty-odd years ago, ol' Carlo Spinelli—he was the top-kick; I was only a corporal—he'd tell me not to get excited and lose my head. Me," yelled Josephus Ashcroft, "*me* get excited and lose my head? I'm older now; I'm always calm and detached. I'M SO GOD-DAMN CALM AND DETACHED . . ."

"Sir," said Dr. Fell, "you have convinced me of your detachment and calm. May we have more facts? For instance! Dr. Sheldon, who dropped in briefly at Davy's, told us you arrived at the Hall soon after we left. May I ask why you paid the visit, and how you learned of the missing tomahawk?"

"Dr. Fell, we've got more'n a murderer in this business! Somebody else actin' mighty mean too."

"Yes?"

"Anonymous phone-tip," replied Captain Ashcroft. "I was in my office, a little past five o'clock, when the switchboard says somebody wants me and asked for me by name. I said, 'Yes?' Somebody breathed hard a couple of times, and then a voice whispered. I'm not kidding! A hard kind of whisper; you couldn't tell whether it was a man or a woman; but you couldn't miss a word either. 'Find out,' it said, 'find out who took the tomahawk from the weapons-room at Maynard Hall. You find that out.' I said, 'Who's this? Who are you?' Somebody said, 'I might be Nat Skeene, mightn't I? You'll hear from me again,' and hung up before I could get a trace on the call." Captain Ashcroft broke off. "Nat Skeene? Who's Nat Skeene? I don't know any Nat Skeene, and I thought I'd met everybody connected with this. Yes, Mr. Grantham?"

"The only Nat Skeene in the business," Alan told him, "has been dead since 1692. He was the murderous ex-pirate who fought the first Richard Maynard with knives and tomahawks on the sand at Folly Beach. His ghost—"

Alan stopped. Mosquitoes sang around him.

"You know," declared Captain Ashcroft, lifting the flashlight, "I sort of guessed it was a funny joke like that. All right! But that's all; that's enough; I don't want any more of it, you hear?"

"It wasn't meant to be taken seriously, Captain. It was only . . ."

"I know. But don't you see, Mr. Grantham—don't *you* see, Dr.

Fell—it's just the kind of craziness we've got to avoid? 'Joe,' I've said to myself, 'don't let this business throw you. If *you* start thinking about murderous ghosts and whatnot, things that follow and kill without leaving a trace, you'll wind up in the nut-house before you write your first report.'

"Now I'll tell you what I did discover about that phone-call. Somebody (not the murderer, but a mighty mean somebody, as I say) has been makin' trouble and may go on at the same game. We'll take things as they come. But, whoever made that call at a little past five this afternoon, it wasn't made from Maynard Hall."

"Captain Ashcroft," demanded Dr. Fell, "are you sure of that?"

"Dead sure, and I'll tell you why. There's only one telephone at that house: in the lower hall downstairs; no extensions at all. As soon as I got there I had a talk with George: George Dyson, his name is. They can say what they want to about conditions nowadays," Captain Ashcroft shook the flashlight in the air, "but George—who's over seventy, and was brought up there—is absolutely devoted to the Hall and the people in it; he'd do *anything* for 'em.

"And George keeps an eye on things, as you may have noticed. Not a soul used that phone, Dr. Fell, between the time Henry himself spoke to you just after lunch and the time I got there at maybe a quarter after six. If George had been lying I'd 'a' got it out of him, but he wasn't lying. If we want to know who's been up to funny jokes, if it can interest us at all after every other damn thing that's blown up in our faces, we've got to look outside the people who were in that house all afternoon."

"It has been somewhere remarked," and Dr. Fell reared up, "that every little bit helps. Did you discover anything else, my dear sir? Was your visit in general a fruitful one?"

"Not so's you could notice it, it wasn't," said Captain Ashcroft, resuming his usual weighty manner. "I didn't come out here, mind, as soon as I got the phone-call. I sat and thought, and sat and thought. Tomahawks, eh? The more I thought the less I liked it. A tomahawk wasn't used, as it happens; but how was I to know that or know anything else?

"Out I came sky-hootin'. There was Henry himself, sitting at that table with his back to me and a book in his hand. I didn't stop to talk to him. He's dead now; St. Peter's doing the talking if anybody is; but nobody ever got any change out of Henry 'less he decided to talk his own self.

"So I went in and tackled George, who told me what I've just told you. *He* knew about the tomahawk; thought it must 'a' been taken the night before, but that's all he could say.

"The two young ladies were in the library; I could hear their voices. Also, when I went in, Yancey Beale was in a big chair in the corner.

"Well, I pitched in about the tomahawk. Maybe I spoke sharper than I needed to, and I was sorry afterwards; both those girls were on edge and ready to scream. They told me what I reckon you already know: they hadn't heard anything about a tomahawk until late in the afternoon, after the baseball-do when Henry himself nearly got clobbered. Yancey Beale said it was Rip Hillboro who'd drawn their attention to the tomahawk. I said, 'Where is he?' And Yancey said, 'I don't know; Mr. Maynard made us promise to stay away from each other; I think Rip went upstairs.'

"Just as I was on my way to have a word with that smart young Yankee, Mark Sheldon drove his car up to the front door. *He* can't have any connection with this, so I didn't stop to question him. On the second floor, where there's a big corridor through the breadth of the house past the front bedrooms, Mrs. Huret—Mrs. Gilbert Huret—was standing outside a closed door down at the north end. That lady always embarrasses me, sort of, though I couldn't tell you why. So I didn't stop there either. I asked her if she'd seen Mr. Hillboro, and she said he was on the top floor.

"Then . . ."

For a moment Captain Ashcroft brooded on something. Mosquitoes now sang round all three who stood on the grass beside the terrace; all three slapped briskly. Captain Ashcroft raised his head.

"On the top floor," he continued, still brooding, "the door of Henry's study was wide open. There was nobody in it, but I could hear pool-balls click from the next room on the left.

"Young Hillboro was there, practising shots on the pool-table. Funny thing, you know. It had just started to get dark a little. As I stuck my head inside the door, he reached up and turned on the lights over the table. Then he looked at me in that way of his. 'Well, well,' he says, 'if it's not the Procurator of Judea! Been winning any chariot races today, Ben-Hur?'

"Is it mind-reading, like what they try to do in North Carolina? He wasn't at the Francis Marion Hotel today; he wasn't within miles of us when Miss Bruce made that slip o' the tongue. If it goes on this way they'll be callin' me a Jewish so-and-so, me that's been a good Episcopalian since the day I was born! Still, have I made the story clear so far?"

"Your recital," Dr. Fell proclaimed, "is both lucid and admirable. Be not troubled, I beg, by tasteless remarks about your supposed ancestry."

"Oh, I took him down a peg or two; he's not as tough as he looks. It'll be different, that's all, if anybody gets funny after a murder's been committed. He said, pretty reasonably, he hadn't mentioned the tomahawk until late afternoon because he couldn't be sure it was important. And there's other things I hadn't heard about, like the man on the beach with a sack over his shoulder.

"That's almost all, though I don't much like the part that comes next. Down I went to the ground floor. Nobody in the library, and Dr. Sheldon's car gone: the whole house might 'a' been deserted. It wasn't dark, but it was getting dark. I went out the front door. There was Henry in his gray suit, on the ground between the table and the chair. I hurried to him, and took care not to step in his tracks. He was as dead as a mackerel, but only just dead if I'm any judge.

"I was bending over him when something made me look up

and around. There on the porch stood Madge Maynard, with her mouth open and her eyes big enough to drown in.

"She ran a-flyin' towards Henry, but stopped on the grass here as if her legs wouldn't support her much farther. I said, 'It's bad news, girl; I'm afraid he's a goner.' For a second she just stood there. Then she let out a screech they could have heard across at the Battery, and keeled over in a dead faint."

Captain Ashcroft switched off the flashlight.

"Afterwards, what with all the fuss and uproar and running around—carry her in the house, get her up to her room, phone the doctor to see how bad it is—what with all that . . . Dr. Fell!"

"Eh?"

"Dr. Fell," roared the harassed detective, "have you heard one word I've said?"

"Frankly . . ."

"You've been in a kind of a trance, with your eyes out across the water as if you could see something we couldn't see. It's only the lights of Charleston over there; they won't help us!"

"You are quite right, sir; they won't. I was wool-gathering again, I fear. You see—"

But Captain Ashcroft had embarked on a grievance.

"What with all that," he said, "I haven't had a chance at one single witness. Where were they? What were they up to? I've got to get at 'em soon, unless I want worse trouble than we're already in. —Mr. Grantham!"

"Yes?"

"Will you hop in the house and round up the witnesses? Ask 'em to wait in the library. This murderer took one hell of a risk, unless he's invisible as well as lighter than air. *Somebody* must have seen *something*. I'll be there in a minute or two, as soon as I've had a little private confab with Dr. Fell. Will you do that, young fellow?"

"Yes, of course."

Alan strode off under the high, incurious moon, not without a feeling that something besides mosquitoes might be on his track.

The front door still stood wide open. Through the screen door soft light glowed out from the crystal chandelier of the main hall. In that white and glistening cavern, where the grandfather clock ticked and the portrait of the first Richard looked down, all baseball equipment had been removed from the table, and the silver tray put back.

Camilla Bruce, her hand on the banister-rail, was just descending the black-and-white staircase at the rear.

"Hello, Camilla."

"Hello, Alan."

She completed the descent and moved towards him. Even at that inappropriate time he noted the clear complexion, the dark-blue eyes and pink mouth, the supple figure set off by a clinging dress. But she was also pale and distraught; his heart smote him.

"Camilla, Dr. Sheldon gave us your message, or at least *a* message. He said you wanted to see Dr. Fell, and see me too."

"Did I say I wanted to see you? Yes, I believe I did."

She extended both hands, and he grasped them. For a moment they stood and looked at each other.

"Alan, this is a *ghastly* business! Poor Madge!"

"How is she?"

"Sleeping. She won't know anything until tomorrow morning; then she'll remember all over again. And we haven't a hope of getting away at the week-end, any of us! Not that *I* should go in any case, with Madge feeling as she does. But we'll stay and face the music whether we like it or not. Captain Ashcroft's made it very clear, even if he hasn't said much; he seemed quite exercised about it."

"That's not the only thing he's exercised about. Apart from a murder under completely impossible circumstances, which has brought him to the verge of raving lunacy, he doesn't much like these Old Testament names."

"It's my fault, I know!"

"How could you help it? Your tongue slipped and you called him Jehoshaphat. But—"

"The restaurant wasn't the only time. You and Dr. Fell left here at not much past six o'clock, just before poor Mr. Maynard went out to the terrace. Madge and Yancey and Rip and I were in the library. You hadn't been gone ten minutes when another car drove up. I looked out of the window and said, 'Be on your best behavior, everybody; here comes Jehoshaphat Ashcroft!' Rip said, 'I'm getting out of here, good people; I ought to have gone long ago.' And he went.

"Captain Ashcroft talked to George out in the hall. Then he marched in here and carried on about the tomahawk without telling us how he knew the tomahawk was gone. After about twenty minutes he left to tackle Rip upstairs. Yancey said, 'I'm gettin' out too; old Melchizedek's on the warpath for fair.' Yancey went out through the weapons-room into the back garden just as Dr. Sheldon arrived and hung over Madge as solicitously as though he were trying to qualify for her fan club. He said he was going back to Charleston, and had some errands on the way. I asked him, I practically begged him, to get you and Dr. Fell. And I think—I'm not sure, but I think—I must have called Captain Ashcroft 'Jehoshaphat' *again*."

"Camilla, stop worrying about it! Which reminds me. Our biblical friend told me to 'round up' the witnesses and put 'em in the library. Where is everybody, by the way?"

"They know! They know there's to be an inquisition, that is. They're coming (all except Madge, of course), and they'll be here at any minute! Meanwhile, about the other thing . . ."

Reluctantly he had released her hands.

"As I say, Camilla, forget the other thing. It doesn't matter a hoot what you called Captain Ashcroft two or three hours ago, so long as we can restrain people's sense of humor now that there's been real trouble. The next one who addresses him as Herod Antipas or Moon of Israel is going to get it in the neck.

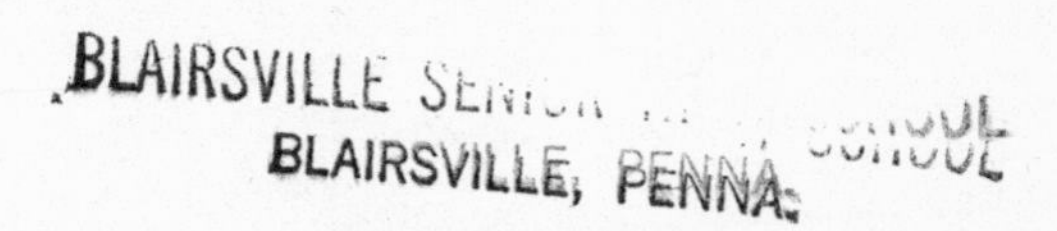

Barring that, what difference does it make? It was only a slip of the tongue to begin with . . ."

"But it wasn't a slip of the tongue," cried Camilla, "even to begin with! His name is Josephus Daniels Ashcroft. I knew that perfectly well, just as I know you were at Cambridge and not at Oxford. He annoyed me, that's all. I—I get cross with people; I say things I had no intention of saying, or at least that I'd give years off my life to take back! You must think I'm a pretty dreadful person, don't you?"

"No, Camilla, that's not my view at all. But suppose you and I open the ball by adjourning to the library now. Then, when the Tetrarch of Galilee arrives for his investigation . . ."

"Alan, don't *you* start!"

"All right; sorry."

He led her to the library door, down four steps into that gray room of books with fine bindings, where the light of many lamps shone on furniture upholstered in yellow satin. As though by instinct Camilla went to the grand piano and sat down on its bench.

"Do you know," she said, "that nobody's had a bite to eat all evening? *I* don't want anything, and neither does anybody else. The cook prepared a dinner, but—"

"If I drove you as far as the main road, you could at least get sandwiches and coffee. There was a lunch-wagon of sorts beside the gas-station."

"I meant it, Alan!" she assured him earnestly, putting her hand on his arm. "I simply *couldn't* eat a thing; after what's happened, it would choke me. Was there anything else on your mind?"

"Well, yes. If you feel up to it, you might tell me what happened just before the murder was discovered. It's the first thing the Tet—it's the first thing Captain Ashcroft will ask."

"I'll try. What did you want to know, exactly?"

"Captain Ashcroft went up to the top floor to see Rip Hillboro, and did see him. Dr. Sheldon arrived, stayed for a short while, and left. Did you and Madge remain here?"

"Yes, for a time."

"What about the others, Bob Crandall and Mrs. Huret?"

"Mr. Crandall had gone upstairs before Captain Ashcroft got here; Valerie followed him. I rather gather they weren't *exactly* together afterwards; but there's been too much rumpus to learn what anybody was doing. Madge was horribly restless. Finally she said she was going up to her room; she went out, and I heard her go upstairs. I stayed here."

"All the time, Camilla?"

"Yes, all the time! Madge seemed to want to be alone; I didn't know *what* to do. I prowled and prowled. I sat down here at the piano, but that didn't seem to be right, somehow. I opened one of those wire bookcase-doors, and took down a book at random. It was *The Prophet Isaiah and His Message;* I put it back again. Just to occupy myself—I can't tell you why, really!—I went over there."

Rather shakily Camilla gestured towards the closed door of the weapons-room.

"When Yancey went out to the back garden through that room, he must have opened and closed the French window without disturbing the curtains; they were still closed and in place, and the room was dark. I was just inside, reaching for the light-switch to the left of the door, when I heard heavy footsteps coming down the stairs out in the hall.

"It was a distinctive tread; it couldn't have been anybody but Captain Ashcroft. I thought, 'Dear God, more questions!' So I didn't turn on the light; I just stood there. And it *was* Captain Ashcroft. He looked into the library, but didn't see anybody and must have decided we'd all gone. He stayed in the hall for a few moments, muttering to himself; then he went outdoors and let the screen door bang.

"I thought, 'We're rid of him.' But we weren't.

"Well, I got out of the weapons-room in a hurry, and closed the door as you see it now. Then I heard Madge coming down the stairs. At least, I supposed it was Madge, and I know now it was. *She* went out on the porch. It couldn't have been thirty seconds later that Madge screamed. She screamed so horribly that I almost felt I knew, though I couldn't have known anything at all.

"I ran out of the library and out on the porch. Over by the terrace Madge was lying on the grass in a faint. Everybody else seemed to be pouring downstairs into the hall, including servants, though for the life of me I can't remember who was there. Madge wasn't coherent at any time afterwards, even when she came out of her faint. All she'd say was, 'Why did God take *him?* Why did God take *him,* of all people?' And that's all I can . . ." Camilla broke off. "Alan, don't leave me! Where are you going?"

"Only to the weapons-room."

"Why?"

"Camilla," he said, "forgive me for intruding brutal details; I'm afraid there'll be enough of 'em before we've finished."

"Yes? What is it?"

"The side of Mr. Maynard's head was crushed with one heavy blow. It wasn't done with a tomahawk; we know that now. If something else has gone from that room, say a musket or one of those rifles . . ."

Thick, airless night had closed in with almost physical pressure. As Alan moved towards the weapons-room, Camilla clinging to his arm, the door opened.

In the aperture stood Yancey Beale, his right hand on the light-switch and his left shading his eyes. The lights were full on behind him, silhouetting the lanky figure.

"Come in, old son," Yancey said in an odd voice. "Come as far as the door, anyway! Got something to show you."

With Camilla clinging and pressing, Alan went no farther than the door. He put his arm around her and held her.

Beyond the threshold he saw not only white room and black weapons. Yancey, with a look still more odd on his clean-cut features, was pointing to the blackboard on its easel by the French window. As though in response to Alan's thoughts, letters had been printed with chalk on the blackboard for a message that leaped out at him.

NO, THERE IS NO OTHER WEAPON MISSING. YOU MAY LOOK FAR BEFORE YOU FIND IT. BUT BE ASSURED OF MY ASSISTANCE AT ALL TIMES.

And it was signed *Respectfully present, N.S.*

"More fun and games, eh?" demanded Yancey Beale. "You want to bet the 'N.S.' don't stand for Nathaniel Skeene? He's respectfully present, is he? And it's another one for the late Dr. M. R. James; you want to bet that too?"

Heard clearly, through two open doors and around the corner, fluid chimes rang from the grandfather clock out in the hall, which struck a single deep note. Alan glanced at his watch. It was half-past nine.

10.

Once more fluid chimes rippled from the grandfather clock in the hall; it struck eleven-thirty.

At the end of the inquisition, which after all had been a fairly easy inquisition, four persons remained in the library. Dr. Fell's bulk was piled on the sofa. Captain Ashcroft, notebook on knee, occupied an armchair in the north-west corner of the room, under towering walls of books. Camilla and Alan sat side by side on the piano bench. It was the same group who had lunched at the hotel.

As the clock struck, Captain Ashcroft rose to his feet. Beefy, red-faced, grizzled at the temples, he corked down his temper and addressed Dr. Fell.

"Then what it amounts to," he announced, "is just this? Nobody saw anything—anywhere, any place, any time!"

"Is it so very surprising?" asked Dr. Fell. "They were used to our friend Maynard being on that terrace. Once his presence was established, they forgot him. Nobody ever went near him; nobody so much as thought of him . . ."

"Except the one who killed him."

"Oh, ah. We must always except the murderer."

"They've gone to bed now. Leastways," said Captain Ashcroft, "they've gone upstairs, whether or not they do much sleeping. What did you make of *that* bunch, Dr. Fell?"

"We-ell . . ."

"What beats me, what sticks in my craw like something you might think of in a graveyard, is that we've probably been talking to the murderer all the time!"

"Probably," said Dr. Fell, "although not necessarily."

"And at least," the other argued, "at least the women are disposed of. Henry's daughter full of drugs and sound asleep! Mrs. Huret on her way home! We've disposed of 'em, that is, except . . ."

His eye strayed towards Camilla, who sat up straight.

"I'll go, of course, if you tell me to," she said. "I don't *want* to go; I don't want to be alone. Still, if you order me out—!"

"Well, now, ma'am, I can't see you're doing any great harm where you are. You're *comfortable,* sort of, though maybe Mr. Grantham wouldn't agree." He turned back to Dr. Fell. "The women are disposed of, I said. Whatever we think, whichever way we turn, one thing is certain-sure: no woman is concerned in this business! Don't you think so too?"

"It depends on what you mean by 'concerned.' "

"How's that?"

Dr. Fell drew in his breath and exhaled it in a vast puff.

"If you mean," he returned, "that no woman committed this crime or is concealing guilty knowledge of it, then despite the fog on these wits I most heartily agree. Yes, by thunder! But there are other ways of being concerned. We must seek roots; we must go after first causes."

"Yes, and that's another thing! Always go for motive, Dr. Fell; it's my motto, and it's a pretty safe rule. But you can name anybody you want to, anybody in the whole case so far, and yet there's not one damn sign of a motive!"

"Sir," said Dr. Fell, "are you sure?"

"Well, look at what we've got!"

Here Captain Ashcroft held up his notebook.

"Take Yancey Beale, to begin with. Now, I know the boy; I know his daddy. I'd hate to think *he* did what he oughtn't to do, and deep down inside I know he didn't. He swings a mean baseball bat; that's about the worst you can say.

"After I'd talked to him and to Madge Maynard and Miss Bruce here in the library, I hiked upstairs to see Big-League Pitcher Hillboro. You all heard what Yancey told us. He went out to the back garden by way of the weapons-room there—not turning on the lights—and prowled around without doing much of anything. In fact, he walked as far as the old slave-cabins."

"That, if I may mention it here," intoned Dr. Fell, "is the part about which I am not clear. What slave-cabins?"

"About a hundred yards west of that garden," Captain Ashcroft answered, "there are ten brick cabins set in two rows of five each. A hundred years ago the house-slaves—as opposed to the field-hands, who were on another part of the estate—lived in those cabins. They're still in a pretty fair state of repair for places nobody uses or has used since the old days.

"All right! Yancey went as far as the cabins, just messing around all by himself. He was on the way back when he heard the young lady scream. He didn't know what it was, but he knew it was bad. And he didn't return the same way he went out; he ran around the north side of the house to the front. He was with the rest of 'em (*I* remember that) when I carried Miss Maynard upstairs. He stayed nearby—you might say he hovered over her—until Dr. Wickfield got here from town and said she was in no danger.

"Out he went again, by the front door and around to the back where he'd been. 'Kept thinkin' about it,' he says; and smoked about half a pack of cigarettes. But he remembered how I'd said nobody must leave here, and I wanted all of 'em in the house for questioning as soon as the hoo-ha had died down a little. So—"

"If only to demonstrate that my memory at least is unimpaired," Dr. Fell suggested rather ghoulishly, "may I supply the ending?"

"Well?"

"Mr. Beale's final move," said Dr. Fell, "was to return by way of the French window into the weapons-room. It had been pitch dark for some time. He groped across the room, switched on the light, and was confronted by that jeering message on the blackboard."

"Oh, the message. Sure! Sure! Sure! You were sayin'?"

"Sir, what do we know of the message?"

"I know it makes me mad. It makes me *so* mad—"

"Gently!" begged Dr. Fell. "And let not your wrathful passions rise. There are times, Captain, when you sound amazingly like an old friend of mine, former Superintendent Hadley. You don't mind a throat being cut, but you can't stand a leg being pulled."

"Who says I don't mind a throat bein' cut? Or a head bein' smashed in either? That makes me madder still. IT MAKES ME SO GOD-DAMN MAD—"

"No doubt. At the same time, if you will indulge me, I asked what we know of the message and not how it affects you emotionally. May I explain?"

"Course you can explain! I'm from South Carolina, and I'm an even-tempered fellow. You just go ahead and explain!"

Dr. Fell took out a meerschaum pipe and began to fill it from a fat pouch.

"We have postulated two persons: (a) the murderer and (b) some joker affecting to be the ghost of Nathaniel Skeene. About five o'clock this afternoon an anonymous phone-call in a voice unidentified and unidentifiable informed you that the tomahawk had been taken. This call did *not* come from Maynard Hall. There seems little doubt that the phone-call and the message on the blackboard originated in the same brain. And yet, unless a sinister Chinaman from the camp of Ho Chi Minh crept in and printed those words at some time this evening, they must have been printed by somebody very much here at the Hall. How do we explain this apparent contradiction?"

For a moment Captain Ashcroft looked at him. Then, wheeling round, he stalked to the door of the weapons-room and threw it wide open. Alan on the piano bench could see him cross to the easel with the blackboard. On the ledge of the easel lay a stick of chalk and a length of grimy rag. Captain Ashcroft picked up the rag. Carefully he erased the printed words, so that the surface of the blackboard shone damply under overhead lights. Afterwards, with a sort of bursting dignity, he stalked back to confront Dr. Fell.

"Yancey Beale," he said, "can't remember whether there were any words on it when he went out through there the first time. The curtains were closed and he can't be sure, but he thinks not. The likeliest time for somebody to 'a' printed that stuff was in the uproar after Miss Maynard fainted.

"For the only evidence we've got, you heard what George Dyson said. The blackboard was set up in there when Henry gave a talk to some high-school kids on April 30th. The chalk and the old washrag have been there ever since; the washrag's been as dry as a bone for two weeks. But it's not dry now. Somebody damped it for this very funny caper tonight; maybe for more capers too. Explain it, you say? Explain it, for God's sake? I'd kind of hoped *you* could help out there. Can you?"

"I was pursuing the Socratic method. If you don't want me to pursue it—"

"Not now I don't, and I'll tell you why. We've got ourselves sidetracked! The one with the sense of humor," declared Captain Ashcroft, hunching his shoulders ominously, "can wait till I get my hands on him later on. Our subject was Yancey Beale.

"That's the story Yancey tells; I believe it; I think you believe it too. There's no confirmation, but does it need any? How he behaved was how I'd 'a' behaved my own self, in the days when I was young enough to go courtin'. He's really gone on that little blonde daughter of Henry's, and I'm just sentimental enough to hope he gets her when this is all over."

"Continue!" Dr. Fell had lighted his pipe, and was blowing smoke and sparks like the Spirit of the Volcano. "At the moment, sir, no comment from me is either needful or desirable. Continue!"

"Next," said Captain Ashcroft, "there's Big-League Pitcher Hillboro."

"What do you make of *him?*"

"I'm not keen on him: he's too smart for his own good. With him it's the big 'I'; what *he* thinks, what *he* knows. Practical experience, eh? He don't know B from bull's foot! And there's nobody as bad as a smart Yankee who won't shut up. But—"

In one corner of the library was a big globe-map on its wooden stand. Captain Ashcroft strode to the globe-map, struck it and set it spinning, after which he turned back once more to Dr. Fell.

"Hillboro *says* he was at the pool-table the whole time, until he heard the young lady scream and ran downstairs. He didn't look out the window before then, but wouldn't have seen anything if he had. He'd put the lights on, as I can testify myself. With lights on in a room, you can't see out the window when it's started to get dark. There's no confirmation of his story either, but is there any good reason for us to doubt it?"

"You answer."

"No, there's no reason to doubt it! Hillboro had his eye on the girl, all right. If you ask me, he had his eye on Henry's money too. Still! Both he and Yancey Beale had what my old grandmother would 'a' called honorable intentions. Even if you could figure out how he committed the murder, he wouldn't endear himself to Madge by knockin' off her old man. I can't pin a murder on somebody just because the guy gripes me. Finally . . ."

"Yes?" prompted Dr. Fell.

"Finally," said Captain Ashcroft, "there's Bob Crandall and Mrs. Huret."

"Both of them interesting personalities, don't you think?"

"Yes, you can say that again—specially 'bout the ex-newspaperman with the fund of anecdote! Make every allowance for the fact that he'll talk your ears off; still and all, he's a pretty good sort when you come right down to it. What's more, for somebody who professes to be such a cynical so-and-so he's not very suspicious-minded."

"The man is a romantic," said Dr. Fell, "like other newspaper folk on both sides of the Atlantic."

Captain Ashcroft opened his notebook and leafed through it.

"There's no need to remind you what Mr. Crandall says. He claims Henry told him to come up to the top floor for one game of chess before dinner, and you and young Grantham confirm that. At about six-ten or six-fifteen, just before *I* arrived, he went up to his own room and didn't leave it until the young lady screamed an hour later.

"His room's on the second floor front, the end room on the left-hand side as you face front. He says he went up there to wash his hands and (quote) 'prepare.' That's all he did say until Mrs. Huret chipped in.

"He didn't know she was on his track and following him. She went up and hung around outside the door, which is where I saw her. She never left that corridor; she was never very far from the door the whole time. All he did, she says, was pace back and forth looking at a very thin book with a bright cover, called *How to Win at Chess*. She knows this, Mrs. Huret says, because she looked through the keyhole and watched him. He'd pace past the keyhole to the other side of the room, and then pace back again. Remember?"

"Perfectly."

"The only thing that flustered him, it seems, was the notion he'd take any special pains for a chess-game with Henry, who always beat him. Afterwards he said to Mrs. Huret, 'The door wasn't locked,' he said; 'why the hell didn't you open it and come in?' She said that wouldn't have been 'nice,' or 'right,' or some word I didn't catch."

The burly detective wheeled towards Camilla.

"Now, Miss Bruce, I let you stay for the questioning. Maybe I had a reason; maybe I'm a craftier devil than anybody takes me for. Sometimes a woman's what-is-it—intuition—will jump through to the truth where a man can't see at all. What's *your* opinion of Mrs. Huret?"

"I like her!" Camilla said instantly. "You'll get all sorts of views from other people, I know. They tell you she's 'obvious' or 'blatant' or other terms that only mean they won't say what they mean. *I* say she's natural, which is how a lot of us would like to behave if we just had the nerve. And I believe her; don't you?"

"Yes, ma'am, that's just what I do. 'Pears like I'm arguin'," declared Captain Ashcroft, lifting the notebook with an oratorical flourish, "wasn't anybody at all did this murder. But that's how I see it, right or wrong. We can say, of course, those two were in cahoots together. But I don't see a woman concerned in this, and Dr. Fell agrees. I don't see Crandall killing Henry because Henry beat him at chess, or for any other reason either. He's not the type; I just don't believe he did it."

"As a matter of fact, I didn't," said a new voice.

They faced round at Bob Crandall himself, in hard-leather slippers and with a lightweight dressing-gown over pajamas. Tousle-haired, drawn of expression but quenchlessly vital and alive, he clacked down the four steps into the library, shying a little as he saw Camilla.

"Excuse these duds, my dear. The captain's right; I *couldn't* sleep. On the other hand, it's nearly midnight; I can't take late hours as I used to. In about two minutes, if they don't kick me out before then, I'm going to get a big drink of liquor from the dining-room; and that'll do the trick of sending me off. You know, Captain Ashcroft, being on the receiving-end of a police investigation is very different from just reporting it. Do you want me to tell my story again?"

"I don't think we'll need that, Mr. Crandall."

" 'For this relief much thanks.' And I didn't kill Hank, so help me Jinny I didn't! Hank and I never quarreled because we always argued, if you'll accept the paradox. I can't even get used to the idea that he's dead. At any minute I expect to see him walk in here and freeze to an icicle when I recite the limerick about the young girl from Detroit, who, when asked how she liked it, said, 'Quoite.' "

"Sir," suggested Dr. Fell, "may we hear the whole limerick?"

"Just once, believe it or not, I've got no taste for limericks; Hank's ghost would haunt me. Also, believe *this* or not, I liked the old bastard and I'm sorry he's gone.

"Then there's another thing," pursued Mr. Crandall, lifting an admonitory forefinger. "I heard you people talking about Valerie Huret and me; I couldn't help hearing you. That's some woman, that is, even if she does look through keyholes. Now so far there's been a good deal of discussion about backgrounds, and where this or that person came from. Captain Ashcroft, what's *her* background?"

"Before she married the late Gilbert Huret, she was a schoolteacher in North Charleston. Any special reason for asking?"

"Well! No special reason, maybe. But that's quite a woman, I repeat. She grows on you; you don't think she will, but she grows on you. 'What's she thinking?' you say to yourself. 'Is she thinking what I think she's thinking? Because, if so—' Be very funny, wouldn't it, if at my age and at my state of congealed cynicism and distrust . . . oh, never mind! Forget what I'm saying; the hell with it!"

"Mr. Crandall," interposed Dr. Fell, "your customary loquacity seems considerably diminished. Now I, for my sins, used to know something of newspaper work in England. If we may not hear a limerick, may we at least hear another anecdote?"

"At this hour of the night? Nary an anecdote, I'm afraid. But I'll tell you something about your English papers, Dr. Fell," Bob Crandall said in his surprisingly youthful voice, "that you must know only too well already. Bar the *Times,* bar the *Telegraph* and one other—it's morning papers, mostly—they'll dish out more sensationalism and muck-raking than any paper in this country has ever printed or would dare to print. If the story's good for a scarehead and it's not too libellous, they'll shoot the works on anything.

"This afternoon, here in the library, I quoted one short verse from a screed written in England more than fifty years ago. It likens Fleet Street, home of your own Fourth Estate, to the old

Fleet Prison for debtors in Dickens's day. And it's true of the present Fleet Street; every word is gospel truth! You didn't hear that one verse, Dr. Fell; if you think I've blown my stack I won't deny it; but in sheer journalistic honesty I think I'll give you the rest.

"They did not break the padlocks,
  Or clear the wall away.
The men in debt that drank of old
  Still drink in debt today;
Chained to the rich by ruin,
  Cheerful in chains, as then
When old, unbroken Pickwick walked
  Among the broken men.

"Still he that dreams and rambles
  Through his own elfin air,
Knows that the street's a prison,
  Knows that the gates are there;
Still he that scorns or struggles
  Sees, frightful and afar,
All that they leave of rebels
  Rot high on Temple Bar.

"All that I loved and hated,
  All that I shunned and knew,
Clears in broad battle lightning
  Where they, and I, and you,
Run high the barricade that breaks
  The barriers of the street,
And shout to them that shrink within,
  The Prisoners of the Fleet.

"And that, ladies and gentlemen, concludes our entertainment this evening. Now a big slug of whisky for your obedient servant; then bed and dreamland before I say something I'll regret. Good night."

With a curious kind of dignity he ducked them a little bow,

turned, clacked up the four steps and across the hall to the dining-room opposite.

"Ahem!" said Dr. Fell, whose pipe had gone out. "The man's right, you know," he added rather inconsequentially. "Whether or not it is an unprovoked attack on the press of Great Britain, I fear he's right. But journalistic reflections are hardly to our purpose now. The time has come . . ."

"Well?" prompted Captain Ashcroft.

Imbued suddenly with volcanic energy, Dr. Fell dropped the pipe into his pocket and towered to his feet on the leverage of the crutch-headed stick.

"Captain, I need your help. You have an authority denied to me, and resources beyond my command or ken. The time has come, I say, to clear away certain mists and obfuscations which cloud the glimmering landscape to our sight. If the others will excuse us, I suggest a conference *à deux* in the weapons-room. Do you dig?"

"Oh, I dig!" Captain Ashcroft made a kind of pounce. "This is what I've been waitin' for: the moment in any case, as Carlo Spinelli would say, when Old King Cole unlimbers the heavy artillery and lets fly. Give me one hint, just one hint, of how the murderer did this . . . !"

"Now, there," said Dr. Fell, "there, I fear, I can be of no assistance whatever. With regard to the mechanics, by all the archons of Athens, I am so far in my usual dull state: bewildered, benighted, bamboozled! But there are other aspects equally fetching and fascinating; I would point them out. You say you see no sign of a motive anywhere. If you had been here earlier this afternoon, if you had seen and heard certain things it was given us to see and hear, then indications of a motive, believe me, would have shone like the village drunkard's nose on a brisk Saturday night at the pub. I wish we could question Miss Maynard. I wish we could learn who was with her under the magnolias on the night of May 2nd. Since we can't question her and we don't know, we must remember Mendelssohn and do the best we can with him."

"All right, all right! At least," proclaimed Captain Ashcroft, throwing open the door of the weapons-room, "I can get SOME sense out of a business that don't seem to make any sense at all. Now we're goin' in here," he continued to Alan and Camilla, "and, whatever happens, don't anybody disturb us till we come out again. Don't anybody disturb us (you hear?) or I'll show myself a lot less easy and indulgent than I've been so far. This way, Dr. Fell."

Dr. Fell ruminated.

"Thank'ee." He looked at Camilla. "Indulge your instincts, madam!" He looked at Alan. "And you, my dear fellow, always remember that somebody asked the Sergeant's wife. Now pray excuse us; I shall not long detain the captain from his labors."

The door closed.

In the night stillness, side by side on the piano bench, Alan and Camilla looked at each other. The latter, as though reminded of something, got up suddenly but rather uncertainly and wandered to the middle of the room, where she started to turn back. There was not far to turn; Alan had risen and followed her.

"Mendelssohn again!" Camilla said. "And I'm to indulge my instincts, am I? What was *that* all about, do you think?"

"Except for the cryptic point about the Sergeant's wife—it's not the first time he's mentioned her—I may have more than a glimmer of an idea. Also, from something Captain Ashcroft said when he kept hammering at ways of committing murder without leaving a trace, it's just possible even a no-detective and anti-mathematician like myself can see how the thing might have been done. But you wouldn't believe that, I suppose?"

"I've called you many things, Alan; I've never called you stupid. How *might* it have been done?"

"That's the trouble: this whole case is too infernally personal. The idea I had, if it can be dignified with the name of idea, is in the abstract; it's not meant to apply to any particular person. But it won't seem abstract. As soon as I mention it, somebody will jump up and say, 'You mean So-and-so, don't you? You're accusing So-and-so of the murder?' So I'd better keep quiet, for the moment at least. And, anyway, that's not the main consideration."

"Well, what is the main consideration?"

"It's you, Camilla. You seem in a different mood tonight. What shall I call it? Pliant? Approachable? Almost . . ."

"You think so too, do you?"

"Think what?"

"What Madge thinks. Oh, now you *are* being stupid!"

"Maybe I am; maybe not. I don't know what Madge thinks; does it matter? Allow it's the wrong time; allow you're worried about her and everything that's happened. But, while Dr. Fell communes with the law, couldn't we go for a stroll outside? There's a moon of sorts, and the grounds have a certain charm of their own. Camilla, will you walk?"

She had turned away, with the light of many lamps on glossy brown hair worn almost at shoulder-length. Then the blue eyes swam up at him as she looked over her shoulder.

"Well!" Camilla whispered. "We'll be eaten alive by mosquitoes; you must know that. Still! If you feel you can bear my presence, and bear to be alone with me . . ."

"Bear your presence? Bear to be ALONE with you? Camilla . . ."

"Yes?"

They were not destined to say more. Both had been too preoccupied to hear a car approach the house. Both were taken off guard when footsteps rapped through the hall and on to the little platform of the steps into the library. Valerie Huret, who had changed her flowered dress for a dark one, stood there like a tragedy queen. Carefully she closed the door behind her and descended the steps.

There were dark circles under Valerie's eyes; she breathed as though she had been running. But it did not seem to be shortness of breath, or any kind of excitement except one. So far as Alan could see, it was stark fear.

"How many times," she began, "can any woman make an idiot of herself in one day? Rushing back and forth? Running in and out? I'm sure I don't know why I came back here at this hour of the night. And now I wish I hadn't, because I've just seen something up there." Her gesture indicated the ceiling. "Somebody with a tiny little flashlight, somebody so furtive I hate to think who it may be, is creeping through the rooms on the top floor."

11.

"Maybe that's an exaggeration," Valerie continued, beginning to address Camilla but speaking past her at Alan. "I didn't actually see the light in any room except the one poor Henry used as a study. It was the awful *furtiveness!* Is—is that captain of detectives still with us?"

"Yes. He's in there talking to Dr. Fell."

"Then I'd better get him at once, hadn't I?"

Alan caught her left arm as she started towards the door of the weapons-room.

"Frankly," he said, "I don't advise it."

"Are you stopping me from going into that room?"

"I won't stop you if you insist. It's just that I don't advise it. Captain Ashcroft's blood-pressure is dangerously high now. If you barge in when Dr. Fell is telling him who had the best motive for killing Madge's father, he may blow up."

" 'Who had the best motive for . . .' Oh, God, this is worse than ever! Do you understand what's happened and is still happening? With a murderer loose now?"

"It's not yet midnight, Mrs. Huret."

"Do you need to be so formal, Alan? Can't you call me Valerie?"

"It's not yet midnight, Valerie. So far, when there has been dirty work during the dark hours, it's never been before one-thirty A.M., or at least at a time when everybody could be expected to be asleep. Just because somebody goes into a room with a flashlight, it's not necessarily the murderer a-prowl. Anyway, I'll go up myself and have a look. Care to come along?"

"I wouldn't *dream* of it!"

"May *I* go with you, Alan?" asked Camilla. "I don't like this any better than she does; I loathe it; but I don't mind so much if I'm with you. May I go too?"

"Yes, of course."

"Please!" cried Valerie. "What am *I* to do?"

"Stay close to the door of the weapons-room. If any maniac comes in brandishing a baseball bat, you've only got to yell and they'll be out in half a second. This way, Camilla."

The lower hall, bathed in soft light from its crystal chandelier, had a hollow, unreal look at the turn of the night. The hands of the grandfather clock stood at three minutes to twelve; the painted eyes of ancestor Richard Maynard seemed to turn in that direction. Through the doorway of the dining-room they could see Bob Crandall at the sideboard, putting down a tall glass with the appearance of one who has just finished a second large drink and has decided to call it quits. They were halfway up the first flight of stairs, treading softly by instinct, when Camilla spoke.

"You know, Alan, you're a callous devil."

"I'm not in the least callous. Whether this is wise may still be a debatable matter. Maybe you'd better not go after all."

"Don't send me away now! *Don't* send me away now!"

"Take my arm, then."

Camilla did so. The second floor was dark; they passed it through thick shadow and struggling moonlight. In the enclosed stairway to the top floor, where the eye of the moon penetrated through a solitary window, Alan could not deny that his pulses were jumping or that his legs felt light. But he did not speak; neither did Camilla.

There were two corridors on the top floor: one parallel with the front, past a wall pierced by the door to Henry Maynard's study, the other corridor stretching back west through the servants' quarters. Here, too, only the moon entered. But inside the open door of the study showed the reflection of a motionless firefly glow.

Now on tiptoe over a floor carpeted in straw matting, his right hand gripping Camilla's left arm, Alan edged sideways along the front corridor. After one glance into the study, he stopped with a shock of what might have been anticlimax or relief.

The "prowler," so-called, was Madge Maynard. But this provided a shock and a puzzle of its own. She had put down the little flashlight on the writing-table in the middle of the study, so that its beam shone across at the antique Sheraton-desk against the right-hand wall. The lid of the desk had been lowered. In bare feet and a thin nightgown, her golden hair dishevelled and her head turned away, Madge was running her fingers over the little doors and pigeon-holes revealed inside. Her voice, soft and stupefied, went wailing up against stillness.

"Where is it?" she said to nobody at all. "Where's the drawer and how does it open? He never told me!"

As that frantic note reached him, Alan became aware that Camilla had seized his right arm and was urging him insistently back towards the enclosed stairs. He yielded and followed her. Once inside the shelter of the staircase, Camilla put both arms around his neck, dragging his head down for a fierce whisper.

"How did she get there? What is it?"

Woodwork creaked and cracked; Alan's own whisper was barely audible.

"They gave her too much sedation, that's all. She woke up in a drug-fog, not knowing what she was doing, and wandered up here on some wild idea of her own. We can't leave her there; we've got to get her back to her room."

"Won't it be dangerous to wake her up?"

"She's not sleep-walking, you know; she's semi-conscious now."

"Alan, what's she *after?*"

"I don't know. Looking for the secret drawer in the desk, probably; her father said there was one. But why bother about that? Anyway, we can't leave her there; she may fall and hurt herself!"

Still moving quietly, though with less secrecy now that small need for it remained, they returned to the door of the study. How, Alan was wondering, did you handle a situation like this? Did you treat Madge as though she were in her right senses, with the no-nonsense attitude of a policeman telling the crowd to move along? Or did you pick her up without ceremony and carry her downstairs?

Both moon-silvered windows were closed; he heard the buzz of the air-conditioner. And then, suddenly, Madge faced round from the desk and saw them.

"I can't find it!" she said, extending her arm towards Camilla. "Maybe it's not important; maybe it's only a silly idea of mine; but I do so wish I could find it!"

Whether she recognized them in semi-darkness nobody could have told. It was a creepy business, and became more so.

Little comprehension shone in Madge's eyes: only the edge of a thought that eluded her. Forgetting the desk, she floated across in her white nightgown and picked up the flashlight from the edge of the writing-table. Camilla and Alan had come into the room; by this time Alan was willing to swear Madge recognized them both.

"Silly old Commodore Maynard!" she continued, directing the beam of light at the colored photograph above the desk. "Silly old Commodore Maynard, and the silly old bell from his silly old ship! Why must everything be so complicated for *me?*—There you are, my dear!" she broke off to add.

The thin beam was pointed through the doorway into the corridor, at a point past Alan's left shoulder. He whipped round; there was nobody behind him.

"You're not really there, I know!" Madge almost sang. The light was switched off; then it reappeared, dancing wildly across the ceiling. "And *you* wouldn't have hurt him, would you? But you wouldn't speak to him either! I begged you to be frank and tell him everything. What harm could there have been in that, even if things *were* as they are?"

"Madge . . ." Camilla began.

"Yes, Camilla, I know you! You and Alan have come to help me, haven't you? But you can't help me. Nobody can help me, though I've only done what I had to do, and not so very much at that. You might think good intentions would count for something in this world, mightn't you?"

"It's all right, Madge," Camilla assured her; "you're among friends, and it's all right!"

"It's not all right," cried Madge, sending the beam of light wabbling into Camilla's face. "And they don't count; they don't count one bit!"

It was at this point that Alan heard a trampling of feet somewhere below, the voice of Captain Ashcroft and the voice of Dr. Fell; but above both, crying out in an enclosed space, the voice of Valerie Huret.

"I'll say it again," Valerie was declaring. "I'm most awfully sorry if I came in and interrupted you. But Alan Grantham's up there, probably getting himself killed; and poor Camilla *would* go too. *Please* hurry!"

Madge heard none of this. She had reached a kind of exaltation, but she was faltering.

"Isn't it ridiculous," she cried, "that the road to hell should be paved with them? They told me so when I was a little girl; I never believed it, any more than I believed most things. And yet it seems to be true! That's where I am; that's where I'll stay; that's where . . . that's where . . ."

Her voice faltered too. The electric torch slipped through nerveless fingers and dropped to the floor without breaking. Madge swayed, her knees giving way; the whites of her eyes rolled up; Alan took a long stride forward and caught her just before she collapsed.

Small, sleek of body, she lay inert in his arms as Captain Ashcroft and Dr. Fell appeared in the doorway across the path of light from the torch, with Valerie Huret lurking behind them.

"What's happening?" Valerie blurted. "Is the murderer . . . ?"

Alan held out the inert figure.

"There's no murderer here. Only a girl too full of sedatives and wandering in both senses."

Rapidly, with Camilla's assistance, he explained what had happened. Captain Ashcroft, finding no switch inside the door, first picked up the fallen flashlight and then turned on a green-shaded lamp on the writing-table.

"Nice goings-on, I must say! Henry at the morgue, this girl here, and ten generations of 'em probably turnin' over in their graves! We'll take her down to her room; better get the doctor again, just in case; then we can use this room while old King Cole finishes what he's got to say. Want *me* to take her, young fellow?"

"No; she's easy enough to carry." Momentarily Alan blinked against the light. "If you and Dr. Fell will stand away from the door . . . ?"

"I'll do better than that. I'll go ahead with the flash; there's no light on those damn stairs; and I ought to know where her room is by this time. Fine business, eh, when a cop's got to act as nursemaid? Never mind; a cop's got to be a little of everything."

Dr. Fell alone remained behind when the others descended. The bedroom floor was now softly illuminated by wall-lamps behind buff-colored shades. Camilla and Captain Ashcroft led the way to a door in the middle of the transverse corridor across the front.

In a large, many-frilled room of the sort which would be called dainty, one dim lamp burned beyond a big four-poster bed with tumbled sheets. Madge, unconscious but breathing easily, was lowered to the bed; Camilla bent over the sleeping girl and arranged the sheet around her.

"Great God in the bushes!" said Captain Ashcroft. "Let's hope that's the end of it for *one* night.—Mrs. Huret!"

"Yes, Captain?"

"Probably no need for it. Better be on the safe side, though. Ma'am, will you please go down to the telephone and get Dr. Wickfield? Dr. J. S. Wickfield, the one who was here before? His number's written on the pad beside the phone."

Valerie, standing sideways, had been eyeing her statuesque image in the mirror over the dressing-table. Now she seemed to emerge from obscure thoughts.

"*I* know Dr. Wickfield, thanks. And I'll do it at once, of course. But—what was Dr. Fell saying about a piece of string?"

"How's that, ma'am?"

"I was outside the door, you know. I didn't hear very clearly, but I couldn't help overhearing *just a little*. Dr. Fell said something about a piece of string, or the great importance of a piece of string. He did; I heard him!"

"Now, ma'am, you shouldn't listen at doors. Just take my word," Captain Ashcroft seemed in a kind of restrained agony, "you heard it all wrong and all mixed up. Wasn't anything 'bout string in the way you mean. Anyway . . ."

"If it's police business, of course, I know you can't tell me. And I'll go now." Valerie crossed to the door. "But we're all concerned in this; we've all got something to fear; we can't help it if our nerves jump and we want to scream." Hand on doorknob, she gestured towards the bed. "*Madge* is in no danger, or is she?"

"Danger from shock, you mean?"

"Danger from the murderer," said Valerie—and made her exit.

There was a little space of silence. Alan fidgeted; Camilla drew up a chair beside the bed. Captain Ashcroft began to pace between the door to the hall and another door on the north side of the room.

"Now burn my britches to a cinder!" he said, using a favorite exclamation of Yancey Beale's. "I'm no greenhorn at this game; I oughtn't to let a damnfool woman rattle me or put me off. If Dr. Fell's right, Madge Maynard is the last person on God's green earth who could possibly be in danger. And yet I've said it before: some mighty mean people sneakin' around here, whether they bat a man's head in or just write smart messages on the blackboard. Also, if Dr. Fell's right, that little girl may know a heap too much for her own good. Leastways, we'll make sure there's no danger. Miss Bruce!"

"*I* haven't gone anywhere, Captain Ashcroft."

"You know, Miss Bruce, I meant to ask whether you'd sit here and stay with her until the doctor comes. But I don't ask it now. She's out cold; there's nothing you can do; and, anyway, I'd rather you didn't. One of my men is here now; he came back, as I told him to. So we'll just . . ."

He opened the door to the hall. Outside, patiently waiting, stood a wiry, hard-jawed young man in plain clothes.

"Sergeant Duckworth!"

"Captain, sir?"

The big police-officer turned back to Camilla, surveying the room.

"Both windows shut and locked; curtains closed; air-conditioner on. That door over there is only the door to the bathroom, ain't it? Any other way in here, ma'am, except the door to the hall?"

"No; only the door."

"You hear, Duckworth? That's Miss Maynard on the bed; the other young lady is Miss Bruce, who's just leaving. You pull up a chair outside this door; keep your eyes open. Dr. Wickfield ought to be here before long, if they get him at all. Don't let anybody else in without you have my say-so. Now, ma'am . . . and you, Mr. Grantham . . ."

Camilla and Alan were formally ushered out. Sergeant Duckworth closed the door and fetched a carved Jacobean chair.

"Be good, you two!" enjoined Captain Ashcroft, assuming a

hearty manner. "I'm off upstairs to see Dr. Fell; excuse me."

And away he went, turning off several wall-lamps so that a certain gloom descended.

Clearly there was something on Camilla's mind. Taking Alan's arm, she impelled him away from the stolidly seated sergeant, away from the transverse corridor and into a side passage that led to the enclosed stairs. Again she drew down his head and spoke in a whisper.

"He's gone, hasn't he? Listen, Alan! Let's creep upstairs, just as quietly as we did before, and listen to what those two are saying! Will you?"

"I'm not keen on it, Camilla."

"What's the matter? Have you a priggish opposition to eavesdropping?"

"I haven't got a priggish opposition to anything. It's the idea of being discovered at that game. Dr. Fell may not mind, but old Mordecai Ashcroft would cut up rough if he caught us."

"Then he mustn't catch us. Please! This isn't just curiosity; I have a reason. It has to do with somebody being jealous. I couldn't believe my ears when I heard the words; or, rather, the tone they were spoken in. Please, Alan! Can't I persuade you to do it?"

"You could persuade me to do anything in the book or out of it. All right; let's go."

They went up on tiptoe; the stairs were solid and did not creak underfoot. The upstairs corridor was dark except for light streaming out of the door to the study. Camilla shrank against him; his arm was around her and her head against his shoulder as they risked a look inside.

Dr. Fell and Captain Ashcroft stood facing each other in profile at opposite sides of the lamp on the writing-table. Dr. Fell, an empty pipe in his mouth, removed the pipe and spoke past his companion as though addressing the colored photograph of Commodore Maynard on the wall above the Sheraton desk.

"So much that's cloudy!" he wheezed. "So much obscure! So much I ought to see and don't! Blast these wits of mine, where did I miss the turning?"

"If you ask me," Captain Ashcroft said with a certain awe, "you haven't missed much so far."

"I have missed the method! I have missed the mechanics! I have looked out to sea; I am lost."

"Well, keep lookin'. The theory you outlined to me," Captain Ashcroft was beginning to rave, "is the damnedest thing I ever heard in my life. I don't like it; I don't like it a bit; there'll be big trouble soon. But it hangs together; it makes sense when nothing else does. Allow we can prove it, which we ought to be able to do: where do we go from there? What's next?"

"Next?"

"You've given the motive, or at least *a* very strong motive. But which one of 'em does it apply to? There's not one single indication of who the murderer is!"

"You think not?"

"Well, I don't see one. All it tells us is something else about Henry himself. And he's dead; he can't help now."

"Sir," returned Dr. Fell, pointing his stick at the antique desk, "are you sure he can't help now? This afternoon, to Alan Grantham and myself, he spoke of certain papers—perhaps only a paper; he was not clear—in a secret drawer of that desk. He *said,* of course, the document related only to family matters."

"And you didn't believe him?"

"Candidly, I did not believe him for one moment. In that respect, as in other respects, he lied in his teeth. Always provided I am right, a certain important paper—*not* relating to family matters, to himself or to Madge either—was in the secret drawer this afternoon. Again provided I am right, it may still be there. But it won't stay there, believe me."

"The murderer'll steal it, you mean?"

"I do. Madge Maynard, who distinctly is not the murderer, tried and failed to find the secret drawer and its contents. Who else might succeed where she failed?"

"Just a minute! Hold on, there! If the murderer already knows where the secret drawer is, wouldn't he have swiped that damn paper long ago?"

"Perhaps, but I doubt it."

"Why?"

"So long as Henry Maynard was still alive," declared Dr. Fell, with the air of one making himself radiantly clear, "the prospective murderer had no reason to steal the document and every reason not to steal it. With Maynard dead, the whole picture changes. If the murderer has anticipated our thoughts and got here before us to take the document, we are royally snookered; there is no more to be said. If he hasn't (and I suspect he hasn't) then our course is clear. Can't you make some excuse to impound that desk and remove it from the house while we ourselves investigate?"

"Yes," yelled Captain Ashcroft, "and I can do better that that. There's a man in the C.C.P.D. whose hobby is antique furniture. He's bats on antique furniture; there's nothing he don't know about it, like a minister knowing the Bible. *If* there's a secret drawer with a paper inside—which is a mighty big 'if,' but I'll go along with you—Jerry Wexford will find it. How far that'll help us is anybody's guess. We're still in one hell of a mess . . ."

"As you rightly point out," Dr. Fell agreed, "we are still in one hell of a mess. But the mists commence to thin a little, do they not? And Henry Maynard can still be of assistance. The late lamented gave us clues in spite of himself; at no time did I like the way he was behaving."

"I don't like the way *anybody's* behavin'! Take Mrs. Huret, for instance."

"What about her?"

"Do you know she was listening a part of the time when you and I talked in the weapons-room? I COULD MURDER PEOPLE WHO LISTEN TO PRIVATE CONVERSATIONS. Never mind: nobody listenin' to *us*. In the weapons-room you said—remember?—you wondered how many boy-friends Madge Maynard kept on a string."

"I said suitors, not boy-friends. But we will not argue the point."

"Well, Mrs. Huret picked up the word 'string' and latched on to it. She thinks, or says she thinks, Madge herself may be the next one in danger. That's not likely; considering what we know, it's the unlikeliest thing of all; but she had me rattled for a minute. She also claims you said the solution of the case depends on a piece of string."

"Sir," Dr. Fell announced majestically, "it is not the first time today I have been misunderstood. However, since you mention the lady, I confess to a certain curiosity. She was here in the house when Grantham and I first arrived this afternoon. Subsequently, we are told, she departed in something of a hurry, only to return shortly before six. Paying no attention to your obedient servant or anyone else in the library, she headed straight upstairs and descended with our host.

"What did she want on that occasion? During a questioning-session between about a quarter to ten and eleven-thirty, you yourself asked her the same question. She replied that she had something to tell Henry Maynard. But she failed to elaborate, and you did not press her."

Captain Ashcroft shook his fist.

"I didn't press her," he said, "because what would have been the good if I had? Her attitude is, 'It's-only-poor-me-I'm-not-responsible-am-I?' There's a lot of women like that. They make you mad and you can't get through to 'em. But they're harmless, mostly. And we agreed, didn't we, Mrs. Huret's not mixed up in the funny business?

"I've got something about her that's not entirely negative. The only servant we questioned in the library was old George. But once, you remember, I excused myself for ten or fifteen minutes? I hiked down to the kitchen and cornered the other four house-servants: the three maids and Ben Jones, the cook."

"Isn't there a gardener called Sam? The one who keeps the surface of the terrace smooth, and in fact smoothed it down this morning so that it took perfect footprints after the rain?"

"Yes. But Sam—Samuel Butler, his full name is—don't live in the house. The servants were as bad as the guests; nobody saw or heard anything. Oh, except just a little bit! One of the maids, Winnie Mae, was on the top floor for a minute or two when Mrs. Huret went up to see Henry. Winnie Mae says they both seemed angry, and Mrs. Huret called Henry a fraud. Winnie Mae didn't stay any longer; she was afraid to, and ran down the back stairs.

"Well, now," Captain Ashcroft went on argumentatively, "in one way Henry *was* a fraud, though Mrs. Huret couldn't have known that in the way we now know it. He was the real Henry Maynard, but in one sense he was a fraud; he may have been a fraud in others too. Anyway, I can't see it means much. These people are a mighty casual bunch; they run in and out, they run back and forth, not always with a good reason for doin' it. Was there anything else on your mind?"

"Yes, to a degree," said Dr. Fell. "There is one rather enigmatic character who seems to have attracted no attention at all. I refer, of course, to Dr. Mark Sheldon."

Captain Ashcroft stared at him.

"Great God in the bushes! Mark Sheldon's got nothing to do with this, you know. You're not suspectin' *him,* are you?"

"I did not say I suspected him. I say merely that he also is conspicuous among those who run back and forth. He called with a message for Mr. Maynard which he failed to deliver. Unlike Mrs. Huret, he has not returned twice. He did return once, and seems to have departed again before the murder. On neither occasion was his errand explained. But no doubt we can forget him, if you would rather."

"Yes, frankly I think I'd rather. He's a fine young fellow with a mighty nice wife; he'd no more be mixed up with murder than he'd be mixed up with drugs or abortion! The thing we've got to get after," Captain Ashcroft turned to point, "is that desk and whatever's inside it. Thank God there'll be no more funny business for one night! No more o' *that,* anyhow. No more—"

Then the screams began.

From somewhere below, probably the ground floor, they went shrilling up in a wordless, almost mindless terror; they jabbed the nerves like a needle under a tooth. Alan's left arm was around Camilla; he raised it under her shoulder, swinging her round and almost swinging her off her feet. They were flying back down the stairs on tiptoe before Dr. Fell or Captain Ashcroft could move.

Constantly, as they stood so close together and listened, he had been tempted to press her still closer, lift her head, and kiss her at some length. Now, with screams piercing up at that dead hour of the morning, he knew it would have been the wrong moment.

That they did not stumble may be accounted something of a miracle. The bedroom floor swam in half-light. Sergeant Duckworth had risen from his chair beside Madge's door; otherwise he had not moved. Rip Hillboro, in candy-striped pajamas, seemed to materialize from nowhere. Alan and Camilla had reached the head of the main staircase when they heard Captain Ashcroft plunge down the enclosed stairs like a charging bull. Dragging Camilla after him, Alan descended the remaining steps.

In the lower hall Valerie Huret, the back of one hand pressed to her open mouth, stood rigid with incipient hysteria. In reply to Alan's look she stabbed her finger towards the door of the library; then, as he made for it, she ran past him and pointed frantically at the door of the weapons-room, which stood wide open. Alan reached the weapons-room with Camilla only a step behind him.

The crystal chandelier still glowed. On the blackboard from which Captain Ashcroft had erased one message, there was now another. In that room of white walls, with block letters carefully punctuated, the white letters stood out against blackboard, black portraits, and black weapons.

> THE MAN TO BE SOUGHT IS MADGE'S LOVER. FIND HIM; DON'T SO EASILY BE PUT OFF QUESTIONING HER. AND, IF YOU WOULD LEARN ABOUT THE MURDER, MORE TOMORROW. I HAVE NOT FINISHED.
>
> *Ever yours to command,* N.S.

12 *•

That had been Friday, May 14th. Despite all omens of good weather, the sky over Charleston looked dark and threatening on Saturday morning.

At half-past nine Alan, in his room on the seventh floor of the Francis Marion Hotel, awoke to the ringing of the telephone. It was Dr. Fell, who himself had been roused by a summons shortly before.

They breakfasted in the coffee-shop at ten o'clock, after which Alan's car took the now-familiar road to James Island. There was very little talk on the way. Damp, smoky-looking clouds curled low above Maynard Hall as they drove into the grounds at just past eleven.

Yancey Beale, a silk scarf knotted round his throat and thrust into the open neck of his shirt, emerged from the screen door and descended the front steps with an air of repressed excitement.

"He phoned you, didn't he?" Yancey demanded. "Old—no, wait! Got to stop callin' him Hezekiah and Judas Maccabaeus and the Prophet Ezekiel. Wasn't very funny even at the start. Now, with Pa Maynard dead and Madge still so prostrated the doctor won't let her get up, you've got to have a peculiar sense of humor if you can split your sides over biblical names. But he did phone, didn't he?"

"Yes, he phoned," replied Dr. Fell, "though with nothing to explain the urgency. "Did something else happen after we left here?"

"There was quite some rumpus before you left, wasn't there?"

"Indubitably; but—"

Yancey lifted a quizzical eyebrow.

"Let's see if I've got it straight," he continued. "Last night, after some of us had gone to bed, Madge went wandering in the attic and collapsed again. Captain Ashcroft posted a guard at her door and sent Valerie Huret downstairs to phone Dr. Wickfield. Right?"

"Right," agreed Alan.

"After Valerie phoned, she went back upstairs. The sergeant of the Sanhedrin wouldn't let her into Madge's room. Even Valerie didn't have the nerve to rout somebody out of bed, and she didn't dare go to the attic when the sergeant told her Dr. Fell and old Caiaphas were in close conference.

"But she had to have company of some kind. She grabbed the telephone again; she called practically everybody she knew, one person after another, and kept it up for some time. The last person she called didn't like being waked up at one in the morning just to be asked how things were, and told her to get lost.

"Valerie stalked away from that phone, not knowing quite what to do. In she went, first to the library and then the weapons-room. There she walked into a *second* blackboard message (I don't understand that message!) writ large in ghostly hand. She hadn't seen the first one, but that did it. Valerie lost her head and screamed the house down.

"By that time I was awake; we were all awake. You people left not long afterwards. I'm the only one who saw Captain Ashcroft and the sergeant carry that Sheraton desk down the back stairs and smuggle it out of the house like their own guilty secret. I haven't mentioned it so far; police business is their own business; and nobody else noticed because Valerie was still having a fit in the library."

"Sir—" Dr. Fell began portentously.

"Takes a lot to discourage that gal, though. She was the last to leave last night; she's here again today. Her car's around the north side of the house, near the garage with Pa Maynard's three cars. The others are having breakfast now; Valerie's with 'em. Captain Ashcroft is here too. He—"

"Mr. Beale," thundered Dr. Fell, "may I cut short a twice-told tale to repeat my question? *Has* there been some other development?"

"Compared with what's happened already," said Yancey, "you can't call it much. Still, there was at least one other incident you'll want to hear about. Come with me."

In his loose-limbed stride he led the way round the south side of the Hall, past the wing with library and weapons-room. From the middle of the house's back a smaller red-brick wing had been built out westwards. Through glass doors giving on a flagstone terrace they could see the modern furniture of two modern rooms like lounges. This newer wing divided the back garden into two parts. The south side, the only one now visible, stretched away in a riot of bloom. At its fringes rose cypresses and weeping willows, romantic or funereal according to your mood.

Down a sanded path, with benches on either side and a sun-dial in the middle, Yancey went on talking over his shoulder.

"Forgot to tell you," he said. "The cops are releasin' me today. *I* can go home, that is, because I live in Charleston and I'm still available if anybody wants me. The others can't go; they mustn't leave town, it seems. But Ashcroft and Co. can't keep 'em here forever. The inquest's on Monday; after that, maybe, the bloodhounds will relent. Meanwhile, about last night . . ."

The western boundary of the garden was marked by an eight-foot evergreen hedge with an arch cut in it. Beyond, at the end of a beaten-earth path which straggled for perhaps a hundred yards through coarse grass, loomed up ten little one-storey houses, five on either side of the path. Formerly slave-cabins in the bad old days, their red brick had faded to a dull pink blotched with white like the white of the cement between the bricks. Over peaked roofs, irregular red tiles also sun-bleached, great trees drooped their foliage behind the cabins.

Yancey ducked through the opening in the hedge, took two strides farther on, then stopped and turned to face his companions as they followed him.

"You were saying?" prompted Dr. Fell. "About last night?"

Yancey cast up his eyes.

"Last night?" he repeated. "Gettin' on for two o'clock in the morning, more like. You people had gone long ago; Valerie was gone too. Rip Hillboro had turned in to get the rest of his interrupted sleep; so had Bob Crandall, who's not very good-tempered if you keep wakin' *him* up.

"The only ones left were Camilla Bruce and myself. Oh, and Sergeant Duckworth! After he helped the high priest carry that desk down to the car, old Ashcroft posted him to stand guard for the rest of the night outside Madge's door. Camilla said to me, 'About time you and I turned in too, don't you think?' I agreed it was. She went to her room, which is at the back of the house and faces in this direction; but in one second flat she ran out again yelling fire."

"Yelling what?" demanded Dr. Fell.

"May I answer that?" interposed Camilla's voice.

And Camilla, her allure no whit diminished that overcast morning, hurried through the arch in the hedge. She wore a fleecy tan sweater and a brown skirt, with tan stockings and brown shoes. To Alan there seemed something different about her manner; for a moment he could not place it.

"I was not yelling, if you please," she said. "It seemed to me I was quite reasonably calm. But I looked out of my window. Out here, just beyond the farthest slave-cabin on the right, I could see something burning. It was not a large blaze, though it seemed a fairly fierce one. So I told Yancey, as I tell you now . . ."

"Yes, Miss Bruce," encouraged Captain Ashcroft, ducking through the hedge to join them and straightening up massively, "you've told the others; you've told me; now tell Dr. Fell." He looked at Yancey. "And you, young fellow—!"

"Well!" said Yancey. "What could I do but charge out here, as it seems I've been chargin' at something every night for about two weeks? Come and see what I found."

He strode ahead, with the others following. Alan ranged beside Camilla, who this morning would not look at him.

A little way beyond the farthest slave-cabin on the right, whose door hung drunkenly open, there was a large bare patch in the grass. Litter indicated that trash had been burned there at some distant time, as well as charred and blackened fragments of a burning much more recent.

The earth still breathed a dull, dead scent of cloth not quite consumed. There was another odor too.

"Kerosene!" said Captain Ashcroft, squaring himself. "Cans of it in the cellar, they tell me. All right; I was wrong!" He bent over the debris, and picked up a crumpled piece of straw burnt only at one end. "Wasn't any sneak-thief took that scarecrow after all. Look here! Look at these cabins!"

He pulled the door of the nearest cabin wide open, poked his head inside, and turned back again.

"Littered with junk, every one of 'em. Old boxes, busted furniture, every kind of odds and ends. There's even a discarded horse-trough in this one. You know, Dr. Fell, I ought to turn in my badge!"

"The step, sir, seems both drastic and unnecessary. Why should you turn in your badge?"

"Because by this time I must be old and useless; I've got softening of the brain. I was so dead-set hypnotized with the notion some no-'count sneak-thief took the scarecrow for the value of a suit of clothes . . . I was so hypnotized, damn my britches, I never did search these cabins as I ought to 'a' done! We see now, don't we?"

"I think so," agreed Dr. Fell.

"See what, please?" cried Camilla.

Captain Ashcroft just stopped himself from raving.

"The murderer," he answered, "had a use for that scarecrow. God knows what use, but he had one. He stole it on the first Friday night you were all here. He hid it, maybe in one of these cabins. If he upended the horse-trough over it, he could have hid it in this cabin; and I could have looked in without seein' anything at all.

"By late last night he'd finished with it. He hoped he could destroy it so thoroughly that anybody who looked at this scrap-heap would think any remains were old trash burned long ago. So he poured kerosene over the scarecrow and touched a match to it. *But—*" Captain Ashcroft wheeled on Yancey Beale. "When you ran out here, son, was it still burning?"

Yancey nodded in some excitement.

"It was still burning, though not with anything like a roar. I beat out the flames with a dead tree-branch, and hadn't any trouble killing 'em. I think I see the drift of this. Cloth like the cloth of Mr. Maynard's suit won't burn as easily as somebody expected; maybe he used too little kerosene. But what was his game, whoever he was? What in hell's name did he *want* with the scarecrow?"

"Maybe this; maybe that." Captain Ashcroft's eye ran round the group. "Still! It's just possible we've all started to wake up a little and can use our heads instead of behaving like a bunch of sleep-walkers. Yes, Mr. Grantham? What's on *your* mind?"

Alan stood transfixed. What hitherto had been only a cloudy idea was beginning to take definite form and shape.

"Captain Ashcroft," he asked, "you didn't question Madge this morning, did you?"

"I couldn't; the doctor wouldn't allow it. It'll be all right this afternoon, Dr. Wickfield thinks. Anyway," the other said heavily, his eye turning towards Dr. Fell, "I can't ask the *real* questions until we get some information we may be lucky enough to get this afternoon too. Any questions *you* wanted to ask her, Mr. Grantham?"

"Just one. Before she went to bed the night before last, Thursday night, Madge looked out of her window and saw our mysterious man walking east along the beach, carrying 'something like a sack' over his right shoulder. Could that something like a sack have been the missing scarecrow?"

Captain Ashcroft uttered an exclamation.

"It could have been! Damn me, I'm beginning to think it was! But I feel like Yancey Beale there. What was the murderer's game? What did he *want* with the damn scarecrow?"

"He wanted it for a rehearsal."

"A what?"

"We've just been reminded," said Alan, "that the scarecrow wore a suit of Henry Maynard's clothes. It was therefore the same height and build, though far from the same weight, as the prospective victim. Madge was frightened when she saw the prowler on the beach; she closed the curtains immediately, she told us. If she had looked a little longer, she might have seen the whole rehearsal with a doll or dummy representing Henry Maynard."

Alan broke off for a moment.

"I may be wildly wrong, of course," he continued. "It struck me last night, as I told Camilla, that there was one strong indication of how the crime may have been committed. I didn't carry it further at the time; it would have looked as though I meant to accuse somebody, which wasn't the case at all. And so, until you see it for yourself—which you'll soon do; it's easy enough—I'd better not carry it further now."

"You think so, do you?" Captain Ashcroft enquired with a kind of ferocious affability. "You'd better not 'carry it further,' eh? Is that what you're givin' me?"

"Well . . ."

"This is no Emily Post Book of Etiquette," raved Captain Ashcroft, doing a little dance beside the remains of the bonfire. "This is MURDER, son, in case it hadn't occurred to you. Never mind how an idea 'looks,' for God's sake! We can't be as finicky as that; we can't afford to be gentlemen. If you know or suspect anything, no matter how wild it seems, it's your duty as a responsible citizen to spit it out and leave the interpretation to me. All right! Will you tell me what's on your mind, or do I have to get tough after all? Since there's no way to explain what the murderer did—!"

"There *is* a way," retorted Alan, now convinced he must be on the right track. "Let's go to the front terrace again, and I'll try to show you."

Back he went, through the arch in the hedge and through the luxuriant garden beyond. Camilla, in her fleecy tan sweater and brown skirt, fell into step beside him. The cool, poised, haughty Camilla this morning was a different person from the pliant one of late last night.

"Really, Alan!" she said in a low voice, and glanced back over her shoulder at the other three following. "This is hardly like you."

"What is hardly like me?"

"Trying to play the great detective! It's quite unwarranted and a little silly, don't you think?"

"I'm not trying to play the great detective. Anyway, last night you didn't think it was silly."

Camilla shivered, like one putting away a distasteful memory.

"I didn't think at all," she told him. "I made a dreadful fool of myself last night! Or I—I almost did!"

"Why? Because you behaved like a human being for once?"

"Here it is again, Alan; you see?"

"See what?"

"You can't come near me, you can't say ten words, without beginning to sneer and trying to provoke a quarrel. But I won't quarrel with you; I'm above quarreling. Since you seem determined to stage some demonstration or other, please go ahead and do it. When you make a fool of yourself, as you undoubtedly will, don't say I didn't warn you."

So the infernal woman was in another mood, was she?

Never mind! He couldn't let her disturb him; he couldn't let her put him off. All five of them had come round the south wing to the front of the house. Dr. Fell, with the baffled gesture of one in despair, leaned on his stick and blinked at the ground. Captain Ashcroft, followed by Alan and Yancey, strode across the sanded drive and across the northern sweep of lawn to the edge of the white-surfaced terrace, with its single line of footprints leading to green-painted table and chair.

"Now, then!" declared Captain Ashcroft, hitching his shoulders like a prize-fighter getting out of a bathrobe on entering the ring. "Now, then, young fellow! Here we are, but where are we?"

"The problem, I take it," said Alan, "is how the murderer could have approached his victim without leaving any trace?"

"Well, yes." The other spoke with powerful restraint. "You might say that's a kind of a problem and not be too far out. *Holy, jumpin' Judas Iscariot!* Look there!"

"I'm looking."

"Nobody on earth could have come at poor Henry from in front, up over hundreds of yards of unmarked sand down on that beach. There's a grass verge to the left, towards the house. There's a grass verge to the right, towards those six poplar trees in a line. There's a grass verge to the south, where we're standing now. Do you see the distances?

"An Olympic-games athlete in good condition," continued Captain Ashcroft, "*might* have taken off in a running broad-jump from one of those three sides. He *might* have landed somewhere near where Henry was sitting. But, even if he could have swung a weapon while he flew through the air, he had to land somewhere; and he didn't land at all. Bar ghosts, bar space-walkers and the likes of all that, just where the hell does it leave us?"

"Nowhere at all," Alan admitted, "if we assume the murderer had to be standing beside his victim. But suppose there are no marks because he never went near Mr. Maynard and didn't need to go near him."

"How's that again?"

"Shall I show you?"

"I'd be right grateful if you would. I'm ravin' and I know it.

But, before they send the wagon and cart one cop to the bug-house for the rest of his natural life, you just tell me *anything* that makes a single grain o' sense!"

Remaining on the grass, Alan moved off to the right, eastwards, and then forwards to the first of the six close-set poplar trees standing sentinel along the beach-front. Next, turning his face west towards the house, he began to edge back and still farther back, putting more distance between himself and the chair where Henry Maynard had sat.

"They're not very high, as poplars go," he pointed out. "Say twenty feet or a bit more. About the same height as that flagstaff there, which rises two or three feet above the sills of the windows on the bedroom floor. And the row of poplars is in line with the flagstaff. I can't get quite the position I want. The trees prevent me from going a little farther north, and therefore . . ."

"Yes?" bawled Captain Ashcroft. "Therefore what?"

"The trees prevent me," Alan said, "from being in a direct sideways line from somebody we'll imagine to be sitting in that chair with his right profile towards me. But I can almost manage the place I want. I draw still farther back from the imaginary victim . . . this position will do . . ."

"It'll do for what? You've drawn back one hell of a distance, haven't you? How far is it?"

"Call it sixty feet six inches," replied Alan, "or the distance between pitcher's box and home plate. One other point. I seem to remember Dr. Fell saying that Commodore Luke Maynard, a hundred years ago, had trouble with the sight of his right eye. Did Henry Maynard have any trouble with *his* eyesight, Captain?"

"No, not with the sight of either eye! Never wore glasses in his life; never needed to. Henry was proud of that. He was always bringing it up; he'd talk you to death about it if you gave him a chance."

"Well, the point doesn't really matter. Imagine it's yesterday evening, and getting dark. The victim's sitting there looking out across the harbor; he doesn't see me, and there's no reason why he should. You've said, Captain, Mr. Maynard never knew what hit him. You've wondered how the murderer could seem to get close without alarming him. This may be the answer."

Alan could feel Camilla's eye; he could feel all their eyes. But he was committed; he had to go through with it.

"Finally, imagine I'm the murderer. In my right hand I've got a regulation baseball, and I cut loose with a blazing fast one. A baseball weighs only five ounces, but it can be a lethal weapon. It can kill, it *has* killed, with no outward damage to the victim's head except a degree of bleeding from the nose. In actual fact I've been a catcher, not a pitcher, though I think that with practice even I could throw to kill. All the same! Whether this makes sense or whether it doesn't, do you see why I haven't been anxious to tell you?"

"Yes, *I* see!" exclaimed Yancey Beale, who was hopping from one foot to the other. "You thought we'd all jump up and accuse Rip Hillboro, who's got a fast one like Bob Feller in the heyday of the Cleveland Indians. And Rip wouldn't do that; he may be a pain in the neck, but he wouldn't do it. That's not the point. You know he wouldn't; I know he wouldn't; does the Prophet Elijah know it too?"

A slight roar could be heard through Captain Ashcroft's voice.

"The Prophet Elijah," he said, "would like to boot somebody's stern from here to Goose Creek and back! Not *you,* Mr. Grantham. It's a clever idea; it's mighty neat and clever. The trouble is, it just won't work. If the murderer fired a baseball at Henry's head, how'd he get the ball back afterwards?"

"Yes, there's that," Yancey agreed. "He couldn't have tied a string to it and pulled it back, could he? No! The best pitcher alive can't throw straight if anything interferes with the ball's flight. And he couldn't have hoped a free ball, without strings or anything else, would dent the old boy's skull and then bounce off into grass. No, the distance is too great; that's impossible too."

"Satisfied, Alan?" asked Camilla. She surveyed the others. "Mr. Maynard," she added suddenly, "was alive yesterday. All of you knew him; two of you were fairly close friends. And yet you're talking about him as though he meant no more than the scarecrow that may or may not have been used for a rehearsal. Isn't it rather horrible?"

Captain Ashcroft looked at her. "If this upsets you, ma'am, you can always go indoors."

"It doesn't upset me, not really. It's happened; it's a fact; he's dead! In sheer self-defense we must develop some kind of callousness or go out of our minds. But do we need to make jokes about it?"

"Nobody's joking, ma'am; that's the very last thing we'd think of." Captain Ashcroft shook his fist. "All I say is: however Henry was killed, he wasn't killed in that way. Nothing was thrown at him, either a baseball or any other weapon, because it would have had to land in a soft surface like sand. Even a five-ounce baseball would have made an indentation as plain as a footprint. Do you see any indentation there?"

"No, of course not!"

"So I'll make no more remarks about bug-houses or padded cells, which seems to rile these others as much as jokes rile you or talk about Old Testament characters riles me. But it's time Dr. Fell lived up to his reputation and advised us. Come out of the clouds, King Cole; arise and shine! We're smack up against a blank wall again; which way do we turn?"

Dr. Fell made noises of distress.

"You lean on a broken reed, I fear." His vacant, feeble-minded gaze seemed to be tracing a pattern along the sky. "Until these wits are unsealed, if in fact they are ever unsealed, I must repeat in abject apology that I can't help you with the method. And yet I have a feeling, amounting to virtual certainty." His look grew tense, his voice thunderous. "Something is there—just round the corner, just waiting to be grasped, but hid in obfuscation of my own accursed making! What is it? Archons of Athens, what *can* it be?

"Meanwhile, with your permission, I must concentrate on those chinks and glimmers of light which do most certainly appear. What happened in these grounds on the night of Sunday, May 2nd? Did a resolve to commit murder crystallize at last? Not the manner of doing it; that's hardly likely. But was the vow taken and the course determined then? To a certain interview, out there under the magnolias by the gate, we have now only one available witness."

"Who?" demanded Yancey Beale.

"You," said Dr. Fell.

He said no more. The screen door under the house's portico, whose slam had been the prelude to several interruptions, once more opened and banged shut. Valerie Huret, emerging in her customary hurry, stood for a moment leaning one hand against a tall white pillar. Then she ran down the steps and hastened towards them.

"You've been shouting like a political convention!" she cried. "You've been shouting fit to wake the—oh, what am I saying? Dear God, why am *I* always chosen to be the one who sees it? Whatever you've been shouting about, you'd better stop and come inside. There's another message on the blackboard."

13

They were far from James Island now. It was a quarter to two by the dashboard clock when Alan's car, with himself and Camilla in the front seats, and Dr. Fell and Yancey Beale piled into the back, crossed the soaring two-mile span of the Cooper River Bridge, and dipped down to Highway Number 17 north out of Charleston.

They had left town by way of Meeting Street and turned right for the bridge. Sandwiches at a drive-in provided some sort of lunch. Now, under a sky still dark but with occasional flashes when sun-shafts pierced cloud, they swept down from the bridge through low-country suburbs not too entangled in Saturday-afternoon traffic. Bypassing the village of Mount Pleasant, they continued on 17 until Alan made a right-hand turn at the sign for Highway 703 and an arrow-sign beneath it that read *To Sullivan's Island.*

It was Camilla who broke the silence.

"Sullivan's Island and Fort Moultrie! I've never been there, but why Sullivan's Island and Fort Moultrie *now?* Just because that ridiculous blackboard said—!"

"May I point out," remonstrated Dr. Fell, who had tried in vain to light his cigar against the wind, "that it is not a ridiculous blackboard? It may be an infuriating blackboard, a wrong-headed blackboard; it may display warped humor or a slyness we could do without. But 'ridiculous' I submit it is not. It has struck close to truth so far."

"Yes, but what has it told us?" Alan argued. "Three times there has been a message; three times Captain Ashcroft has rubbed it out and sworn blue murder . . ."

"And the last time," said Camilla, "I thought poor Valerie would have another fit. She flew out at George, and told him to get rid of the blackboard at once. George never lost a hairline of dignity. He said he couldn't even move it without orders from Miss Madge, who's in no state to give orders about anything. Odd, isn't it, that it should be Valerie who discovered some new writing twice in a row?"

"Is it so odd, do you think?" asked Dr. Fell, pointing with the unlighted cigar. "Mrs. Huret is quite an intuitive person, I should say. About that third message—"

"About the third message," Camilla twitched her head round, "I can't help agreeing with Alan. 'If you want to know how the murder was done,' " she quoted, " 'try Fort Moultrie any day between 8 and 5. There is a photograph which may prove enlightening. Yours in homage to the great one, N.S.' What does *that* mean? And Captain Ashcroft . . ."

"Captain Ashcroft wouldn't come with us," Alan supplied. "Note that! He's 'expecting important messages' at his office, is he? He'll have an apoplectic stroke if he doesn't soon learn how the murder was committed. And yet he wouldn't come with us! When Dr. Fell invited him, he refused as angrily as though he'd been asked to help rob a bank."

"Captain Ashcroft, you will have observed, is more temperamental than his appearance indicates. But the most fruitful line of enquiry," said Dr. Fell, "has been suggested by Miss Bruce. What can we expect to *find* at Fort Moultrie?" He looked at Alan. "The present fort, I take it, is not the original one?"

"No; hardly. The original Fort Sullivan, successfully defended by Colonel William Moultrie when a British fleet under Sir Peter Parker attacked it in 1776, was only a double wall of palmetto logs with sand in the space between. A subsequent fort was made fairly formidable during the Civil War, and 'modernized' with concrete gun emplacements in 1898. That's the one you'll see."

" 'There is a photograph which may prove enlightening.' What photograph?"

"I can't think. In a brick-and-concrete tunnel of a museum they've got a display of old relics: cannon-balls, swords, muskets, and other gear from the eighteenth and nineteenth centuries. There are photographs of the exhibits, and a photograph of Fort Moultrie as it looked in 1863. But it hardly seems helpful or hopeful."

"One moment!" Dr. Fell blinked. "We have already crossed two bridges, including the one you said was over Shem Creek. Isn't there another looming just ahead?"

"Yes.—That was the Ben Sawyer Bridge, and the last of them," Alan added thirty seconds later.

"When do we reach Sullivan's Island?"

"This *is* Sullivan's Island."

Dr. Fell gaped like an idiot, the cigar slipping through his fingers.

"Sullivan's Island? But it can't be!"

"Why not?"

"These wide, swept streets and trim villas? This air of suburban prosperity a-doze? Forgive me," bumbled Dr. Fell, groping as though for sanity, "if my notions of the island are derived solely from Edgar Allan Poe, *The Gold Bug,* and that wild, desolate spot where they dug up Captain Kidd's treasure.

" 'The vegetation, as might be supposed, is scant, or at least dwarfish.' (I quote from memory, but I think with accuracy.) 'No trees of any magnitude are to be seen. Near the western extremity, where Fort Moultrie stands, and where are some miserable frame buildings, tenanted, during summer, by fugitives from Charleston dust and fever, may be found, indeed, the bristly palmetto; but the whole island, with the exception of this western point, and a line of hard white beach on the sea-coast, is covered with a dense undergrowth of the sweet myrtle so much prized by the horticulturists of England. The shrub here often attains a height of fifteen or twenty feet, and forms an almost impenetrable coppice, burthening the air with its fragrance.'

"Poe, it is true, wrote that story for the Philadelphia *Dollar Newspaper* in 1843. Common sense suggests that a hundred and twenty-odd years must have brought one or two changes. Yet the dream is lost, the illusion a mockery! I return to wool-gathering, and to Mr. Beale."

For some time Yancey had not spoken a word. Now, stretching his legs, he sat up with the air of one who would have preferred to sleep.

"I was kidnapped," he said. "I'm not complainin', mind; but let the record show I was kidnapped. I'm a lone lorn creature, and there's only one reason you brought me along at all. Whenever the maestro remembers it, he hammers me with another question about a certain Sunday night almost two weeks ago. Yes, I was there! Yes, there was a moon!"

"Dark of the moon, I think?" suggested Dr. Fell.

"What do you mean, dark of the moon? The moon that's waning now wasn't quite full at the time. I remember it distinctly, moonlight and mosquitoes and everything, because—"

"Figuratively speaking," Dr. Fell said impressively, "every act of this drama has been played out at deepest dark of the moon. Dark motives, dark deeds, creep side by side from the same cave. Imagine, please, that you are again approaching Maynard Hall on the night of May 2nd. What then?"

"Hold it, Maestro! I've already told you everything!"

"Everything, sir?"

"Well, almost everything."

Once more Alan swung to the right. As the car went bowling along Middle Street towards Fort Moultrie, Dr. Fell with intense concentration made mesmeric gestures at Yancey Beale.

"The little more, and oh, how much it is! Let me beg you to dig into your memory. Again, I say, you are approaching Maynard Hall on Sunday night. You stop your car in the lane outside the gate. You hear voices. Madge is there. And someone is with her."

"I've told you two or three times, I don't know *who* it was! Somebody about her own age, to judge by the voice."

"Had you ever heard the voice before?"

"I think so; can't be sure. It was a Yankee voice, I thought. But lots of people in this part of the world talk like Yankees. Anyway, wasn't much more'n a whisper. Wait, though! There *was* something else!"

"Yes?"

"I could have sworn I heard Madge beg him not to leave her. And he said, 'I've got no choice; it's a hell of a thing, but I've got no choice.' Then he skedaddled, and I went in. There stood Madge under the moonlight, in a state I can't describe and won't try to. I asked who'd been with her; she said nobody, and I pretended to believe it. There, Maestro! I haven't told you up to now, because . . ."

"Because you forgot?"

A spasm crossed Yancey's face.

"No!" he shouted. "Because I was so God-damn jealous that I —sorry, Camilla—!"

"Please don't apologize, Yancey. There are others of us," Camilla said in her clear voice, "who can be equally jealous at times, and yet have to hide it as you did. You *did* hide it, I gather?"

"I tried to, though it wasn't easy. Ol' Yance isn't much of a ladies' man, I reckon. Madge never looked and talked as distracted as that after she'd spent a few minutes in *my* company. And I didn't know who the man was. I could have slaughtered the bastard then and there; but I didn't know who he was and I still don't. Madge wasn't much help either. She started in about the loneliness of her life; how she was too young to be a hermit, and couldn't bear it. I tried to soothe her there too, but I didn't get very far. Down came the old man, also in a dither and worried about Madge . . ."

"I see," observed Dr. Fell. "Will you endeavor to amplify that part of the story as well?"

"All right; have it your own way. In for a penny, in for the whole bankroll! To an accompaniment of ghost-guns in the background, Madge and her old man flew out at each other with more words that made no sense."

In some detail Yancey recounted the scene under the magnolias.

"Of course," he went on, "I said *I* must have shouted the words Pa Maynard overheard, about what a disaster it'd be if he caught me with Madge. I did it to make Madge feel better. But it didn't make her feel better, and I don't think Pa believed it for a minute. Then there was all the byplay. Why did Madge burst out with, 'Sometimes I think it's not worth—' and what did she mean? What was eatin' the old man? So help me, Dr. Fell, there's not a word or an inflection I've left out. You don't want me to go on about Sunday night, do you?"

"No," agreed Dr. Fell. "The picture of Sunday night, I fear, is as complete as it is revealing. What of last night?"

"Last night?"

Dr. Fell indicated Camilla and Alan.

"It was you, Mr. Beale, who drew their attention to the second message on the blackboard. Almost your first words to me this morning were that you did not understand it. Yet the message was direct, not to say stark. What was it you failed to understand?"

"Look!" said Yancey, as though holding hard to reason. "You and Camilla have quoted the third message, the one that brought us sky-hootin' out here. Let me quote the second one. 'The man you want,' meaning the murderer, 'is Madge's lover.' Remember that, Maestro? You seem to think this joker with the blackboard can call the shots pretty accurately."

"Well?"

"Excuse me if I make it personal," said Yancey, "but what did the joker mean by 'lover'? Did he mean it in the romantic or Victorian sense, of a follower who's just devoted to his lady? Or did he mean it in the modern sense, of a conqueror who stalks in and bowls her over and takes her to bed with all the privileges appertainin' thereto? *If* the joker's right, dollars to doughnuts it's the second. But what about Madge herself? I'd hate to think that sweet-faced little gal was . . . was . . ."

"Less than perfect?"

"Oh, perfect! Who wants perfection, for God's sake?"

"Then what are you trying to say? Would it upset you very much, sir, if the image you have created in your mind turned out to have attributes other than sugar-candy?"

"Don't ask me what I mean, because I don't know myself! Upset me? Yes, reckon it would; I'm only human. But who am I to give Madge orders and tell her what she's to do, or go out and chew worms if she can't see the sterling qualities of ol' Yance?

"Keep your eyes on the left of the road, ladies and gentlemen. In about thirty seconds, past a cross street, you'll see the brick bastion of Fort Moultrie as they built it for the Spanish-American War. What we expect to find there absolutely beats me, but then the whole business beats me. I give you a motto: To hell with everything!"

A minute or two later, parking on the right-hand side of the road because the left-hand side was already cluttered with cars, they crossed Middle Street to Fort Moultrie.

The central wall, red brick faced with concrete, was set well back behind a stretch of grass, with wings projecting at either side. Visitors moved in and out through the arch of the front entrance, which opened into a kind of tunnel through the wall. But Alan did not go towards the front entrance. Camilla, for some reason in a mood almost like the mood of late last night, linked her arm through his. Drifting to the left, past the immense black barrel of a rifled cannon, *circa* 1863, they ascended some outer steps to what in time of siege would have been the rear parapet away from the sea.

The sky had grown still darker, smokily tinged. Distant thunder rippled and rumbled beyond that curtain. Below Camilla and Alan the open interior of the fort, hummocks of grass and hard-packed earth, sloped down and then up again to the sea-wall, where gun emplacements without guns faced south-west towards Fort Sumter. The whole place boiled with an invasion, from serious-minded sightseers aiming cameras to children who screamed as they ran. The stars and stripes on its flagstaff curled out in a damp breeze from the sea.

Alan, leading Camilla downhill towards the door of what had once been a bombproof shelter for storing ammunition, glanced back. Up over the parapet rose the head and shovel-hat of Dr. Gideon Fell. Yancey Beale loomed beside him, stabbing a finger down towards something they had left.

"That, Maestro, was the grave of old Osceola, the Indian chief who gave 'em so much trouble during the Second Seminole War." Then Yancey looked ahead. "Well, burn my britches, we're not so far from home after all! *There's* somebody we know."

A baseball whacked into a glove. Alan also looked ahead.

Dr. Mark Sheldon—in Bermuda shorts, a fielder's glove on his left hand—had just thrown the ball to a twelve-year-old youth in Boy Scout's uniform, also begloved. His gesture checked the boy's return throw. He advanced towards the newcomers, who had gathered together.

"Camilla!" he said. "Yancey! And, as I live, Mr. Grantham and Dr. Fell! This is my nephew Benjie. Benjie—" More formally he repeated the four names.

Benjie, though responding politely, had something on his mind.

"Uncle Mark, have we *got* to go now?"

" 'Fraid so, old son. Your Aunt Annette—"

"She's kind of crabby, ain't she?"

"Mind your manners, Benjie! Dr. Fell," continued a harassed uncle, "I'm free at the moment, as you see; not because it's Saturday, but because even a doctor has got to have *some* time off duty. And yet I can't call this meeting a pleasure. After all—"

"You've heard what happened last night?"

"About poor Henry Maynard? It was in the paper this morning. I wonder you're not besieged by reporters!"

"We almost were. A police-officer named Captain Ashcroft gave them the story and sent them flying. May I ask whether you yourself, sir, have anything to contribute?"

"To the whole tragic affair? No, I'm afraid not. I left before it happened, you remember. But what could I have done if I had stayed?" Troubled, indecisive, Mark Sheldon drove his fist into the palm of the glove. "We always fret ourselves," he continued, "asking where we went wrong, how we could have done better, and the rest of it. And yet this time I did nothing wrong; I can incur no blame."

"No blame," Dr. Fell agreed, "but some amount of curiosity. In one respect at least your behavior might be called mysterious."

"Mysterious?" echoed the other, staring at him. *"Mysterious?"*

"Yesterday, if I am correctly informed, you called on Mr. Maynard to tell him something, but changed your mind and left without speaking. Will you pardon my impertinence, sir, if I ask what you wanted to tell him?"

"Benjie," Dr. Sheldon said sharply, "get on out to the car and wait for me. I'll join you in two minutes. We must go; we ought to have gone already."

"Uncle Mark, is it about Aunt Annette?"

"Never you mind what it's about; just get going, you hear me? No arguments, young fellow, and I'll buy you another bag of popcorn on the way home."

With only a mild squawk Benjie departed, running out through the deep tunnel of the front entrance. Dr. Sheldon, shortish and stocky, rumpled up wiry dark-red hair.

"This is ridiculous!" he exclaimed. "And there's no mystery about it. I was only trying to save Madge—Miss Maynard, I mean—I was only trying to save her embarrassment."

"In what way?"

"At least half a dozen times, since the Maynards got here in

April, they've invited me to dinner. The last time was the Friday night a week ago, May 7th. When Madge phoned about it, she said, 'Dr. Sheldon,' she said, 'I didn't know you were married; I've just learned you were married; why don't you bring your wife?' I didn't say anything except that I was sorry, Annette couldn't make it. Then I got to thinking.

"Annette is . . . well, it's not true to say she's an invalid; she's nothing of the kind. But she suffers from nerves, poor girl. She won't go out with me, but she insists on my going—says it'll be good for the practice, as though I cared two hoots about that! —and then she worries and I worry too. Do you follow me?"

"Not exactly."

"It would have been too brutally blunt to tell Madge, 'If you don't know my wife never goes anywhere—and doesn't receive at home either, so I can't return your invitations—then you're the only one in Charleston County who doesn't know it.' I couldn't have hit her in the face like that, now, could I?"

Obscurely agitated, beginning to pace on the grass-plot where another exhibition cannon-barrel was mounted on concrete blocks, Mark Sheldon removed the fielder's glove and thrust it into his hip pocket.

"All right!" he said. "Maybe I'm making too much of myself and my own affairs, which are pretty small potatoes after all. But I had to tell Madge; I had to let her know somehow. So I thought it would be smoother if I dropped a hint to the old man, and *he* passed it on. Then, when I heard he wasn't in the mood, I backed off. That's all there is to it. If you ask me why I returned to the Hall a second time, last night, I can only answer that I'm damned if I know.

" 'The world is too much with us; late and soon' we something-or-other. I liked both Maynards; I still like Madge, though she isn't as easy to talk to as some people think. The old man, if you'll pardon my saying so, was definitely peculiar. Why, for instance, did he hate charity?"

"Hate charity, sir?"

"The first time I went there to dinner was in April, after they'd just got here. There were the same guests as are there for the house-party now, with Valerie Huret and myself in addition. I was making conversation. Now that he was back in his old home, I asked, did he mean to patronize any local charity? And he changed color. No joking: he changed color! In a strangled voice he blurted out the oddest words heard at anybody's dinner-table. *'Not St. Dorothy? Not St. Dorothy?'* And his hand jerked, and he upset a glass of wine."

"Well?" prompted Dr. Fell.

"I'd never heard of any St. Dorothy, and said so. Instantly he had a grip on himself; he explained that he'd been in the clouds again—which, to be fair about it, he often was—and that I'd misunderstood him. Somebody once asked me whether there was a real St. Vitus, who gave the name to chorea or St. Vitus' dance. And there was; I looked it up. But I've got no idea about St. Dorothy. Maybe it wasn't what he said; it didn't mean a thing to anybody else at the table. And that's all I can tell you, even if it's not a bit of good, and I'm afraid I must go now. My sincerest condolences to Miss Maynard; everybody else, good afternoon and good day."

Off he bustled, almost strutting despite whatever sense of inadequacy he may have felt, and disappeared under the arch. More thunder rolled its echoes down the sky.

"Now what," Dr. Fell asked abruptly, "are we to make of so delicate-minded a gentleman as *that?*"

Yancey Beale pointed a long finger.

" 'The world is too much with us; late and soon, getting and spending, we lay waste our powers.' Mark Sheldon never does finish a quotation, does he? Has it occurred to anybody he's a kind of tragic figure?"

"What's occurred to me," said Camilla, "is that every word in this affair has some meaning beyond its apparent meaning on the surface. It's so tantalizing never *quite* to understand! Mr. Maynard did say St. Dorothy, or something very like it; I was there; I heard him. I never saw him jarred so badly, just for a second or two, as he was then. What he meant, of course . . ."

"And it occurs to *me,*" observed Dr. Fell, clearing his throat loudly as though in reply to a heavier peal of thunder, "that we had better examine the museum and such photographs as it may contain. Where is the museum?"

"Continuing that arch where Dr. Sheldon and his nephew went," Alan pointed, "the tunnel of the museum runs through the earth and through the front wall. Follow me."

A moment later they were inside. And, inexplicably, they had the place to themselves.

Under a vaulted roof, all whitewashed brick and concrete, glass cases reflected back a glow of lights. At the far end another arch was the front entrance to the fort, with a window embrasure on either side. Nearer at hand, old relics glimmered darkly behind glass.

"From the small size of the wine-bottles they drank from," said Dr. Fell, "it is clear that the famous three-bottle men of yore had a thirst less heroic than their reputations warrant. Photographs; hang it, where are the photographs? For the life of me I can't imagine how the picture of some *object* could suggest means of committing an impossible murder. Are there any photographs of people?"

"There's one," Alan replied, "and *I* can't imagine why I forgot it completely. Don't you see Edgar Allan Poe?"

"Where?"

Alan pointed to the left-hand wall. Also behind glass against the wall, amid canteens and badges and other military debris, peered out the photograph which has adorned so many biographies, clear-eyed but a little sinister. Alan went closer to it.

"When he ran away from home and joined the Army under the name of Edgar A. Perry, he became regimental sergeant-major here at Fort Moultrie. There he is, Dr. Fell. Does it suggest anything to you?"

Evidently it did not.

"Sir," boomed Dr. Fell, wheeling round to stare at the photograph, "I have already told you that to me Sullivan's Island and Fort Moultrie have their being because they mean Poe and *The Gold Bug*. But what of that? How do those ominous words sing their refrain? '*A good glass in the bishop's hostel in the devil's seat forty-one degrees and thirteen minutes—northeast and by north. A good glass in the bishop's hostel in . . .*' Oh, God save us!"

Camilla cried out.

An almost frightful change had come over Dr. Fell's face, as you might imagine in a man struck by lightning.

"And I never saw it!" he roared. "Archons of Athens, what a chump I've been! I had a good glass, I had a good glass in my hands, and yet I never saw it until this minute!"

"Looky here, old son!" cried Yancey. "Does this mean you do see something now?"

"I rather think I see everything. We must return to Maynard Hall; we must return at once! I want a look at the one part of the house I have not seen; I want a look at the cellar. It seems probable that—"

He had no time to finish. At the other end of the passage, heavy footsteps pounded from the direction of Middle Street. Into that museum, which was not actually underground though it gave the effect of an underground cavern, plunged none other than Rip Hillboro. Rip, out of breath more from excitement than from any physical activity, dashed up to them and ducked the edge of his fair crew-cut.

"Look, Stonewall Jackson!" he began. "There were three cars of Pa Maynard's in that garage. But I took your car; I thought it'd be simpler and you wouldn't mind. I missed the road twice in chasing you people out here. And once I thought the cops were after me for speeding, though old Deuteronomy promised to fix it if I got a ticket. Didn't I hear somebody say you were starting back now? Then come on; hurry; get the lead out!"

"Yes?" demanded Dr. Fell. "What is it? What's happened?"

Rip waved his arm. An echo of thunder prowled through the tunnel.

"To tell you God's truth, I'm not absolutely sure. The Tetrarch of Jerusalem is playing 'em close to the chest; when he says he won't talk, it means he won't talk and that's that. With all the hell-raising that's gone on, you'd think I'd have some solid evidence to introduce and get admitted to the record. And I haven't. What I've got is mainly scuttlebutt, helped out by an educated guess or two. But the story's practically a certainty. It seems Valerie Huret went crazy and tried to kill Madge."

14

"You're wrong, young fellow," declared Captain Ashcroft, "and it's not only a mistake either! You've got it the wrong way around; it don't mean anything! That poor woman—"

"Valerie Huret, you mean?" Rip asked.

"Sure; who else are we talkin' about? Far from doing anything she shouldn't, she kept her head at the right minute; she stepped in and prevented worse trouble than we've already got."

"Then couldn't you just give us a statement and fill us in a little?"

"I'll give you a statement," said Captain Ashcroft, "when I'm damn good and ready. That's what I told a couple of reporters who were here half an hour ago; that's what I tell you now. Meantime . . ."

In the white sleekness of the lower hall, gloomy under late-afternoon light, he looked from Rip to Alan and Yancey.

"I saw the whole bunch of you drive up in two cars. But I couldn't get downstairs for a minute. Where's Dr. Fell?"

"In the cellar," Yancey answered. "That cellar was on his mind all the way back, though God alone knows why."

"And where's Miss Bruce?"

"She went upstairs," said Alan. "Didn't you pass her on the way down?"

"No, I haven't seen her. If *she* starts monkeying with—but I guess it don't matter." Captain Ashcroft directed a baleful stare at Yancey. "Dr. Fell's after something in the cellar, you say?"

"Yes; it has to do with *The Gold Bug*. He's been on about it since we found Poe's picture at Fort Moultrie."

"Since you found *what?*"

"A photograph of Edgar Allan Poe, who wrote *The Gold Bug, The Murders in the Rue Morgue, The—*"

"I know what he wrote, thanks! And never mind any murders in the Rue Morgue; just give me a hint about the one out on the terrace!"

"Well, Dr. Fell knows that too."

"He does?"

" 'A good glass in the bishop's hostel in the devil's seat forty-one degrees and thirteen minutes—northeast and by north.' That's the answer, or part of the answer. Does it mean anything to you?"

"Not as you quote it, no. But I'll go down and ask Dr. Fell; then maybe it will. I've got some information for him too, information with enough TNT behind it to blow this house into the middle of the harbor. Might be a good thing if the whole shebang *did* blow up. Now mind what I tell you, and don't make any mistakes. You, Mr. Grantham, you go where you please and do what you please; I think I can trust you. The other two—clear out, both of you; make yourselves scarce for a while; above everything, don't go upstairs until I say you can! Mrs. Huret's lying down in a spare room; she's resting; she—"

Yancey interrupted with something like a yell.

"Captain, what *happened* upstairs? All you can do is talk about Valerie, Valerie, Valerie. That's very interesting; I'm glad to hear she's resting; but I can't get passionately interested and that's not the point." His guard dropped; raw emotion cried through. "What about *Madge?* How's Madge?"

"She's all right, young fellow; she's fine and dandy and 'most ready to be questioned, though I think I'll let Dr. Fell do that."

Captain Ashcroft took out his notebook. "Now I'm on my way down to see the old boy; just remember what I've been tellin' you, and don't get too far off base. See you later."

Rather pontifically, holding his notebook as he might have held a weapon, he disappeared through a doorway at the back of the hall.

There was a little silence. The grandfather clock in the hall showed five minutes to five. Rip Hillboro, hitching his heavy shoulders, stalked off towards the screen door at the front; it slammed after him; a moment later he was striding up the drive towards the gate. Yancey Beale drifted in the same direction. But, as though he would have found Rip's company insupportable at that time, Yancey veered to the right and into the library. The voice of Bob Crandall could be heard upraised in some argumentative statement just before Yancey closed the library door.

Alan, left alone, awaiting Camilla, stood for a time looking between the grandfather clock and the portrait of Richard Maynard above the fireplace. Full questions, half answers, thronged through his mind. Then he made his way towards the doorway at the back of the hall, in the direction Captain Ashcroft had gone.

Of this section of the Hall Alan had caught only a glimpse that morning, from the garden. In the smaller, modern wing built out westwards there were two rooms set in a line. The first, long and narrow like a lounge-hall rather than a lounge, had on its left or southern side a line of French doors opening on the flagged terrace. Beyond it lay a room of more than twice the lounge-hall's breadth, providing much space at the back of the dining-room on the other side. From this far room a staircase led down to the kitchen and the other premises of the cellar.

Alan did not trouble about that far room. The lounge-hall, with its doors opening on the terrace, had walls of white-painted brick against which hung vividly colored English sporting-prints. There were overstuffed chairs with white slip-covers, an overstuffed sofa, many standing ashtrays, and several floor-lamps. There was a television set. On a card-table in one corner lay a backgammon box with board and men, as well as three or four packs of cards.

Still no rain had fallen, though thunder went on prowling beyond the sky. Despite its nearness to the garden, despite open doors, this particular lounge was heavily stuffy. Alan wandered to the games-table. He picked up a pack of cards, slipped it out of its cardboard container, and had begun idly to shuffle the cards when a slight noise arrested his hands.

Stealth, and still more stealth! The noise, which at first he did not identify, seemed to come from the far room. Alan did not move from the table, but he did not need to move.

That far room, its left-hand segment visible through the open arch, was very dusky. Down the rear wall slanted the sideways projection of another enclosed staircase, terminating in a closed door he could see sideways and to his left.

Then he remembered. Those were the back stairs, down which early this morning Captain Ashcroft and Sergeant Duckworth had carried a certain Sheraton desk. The noise he had heard just now had been a cautious footstep descending.

Then the staircase door opened.

Valerie Huret was not 'resting.' Seen in left profile as she pushed the door to the right, her head and neck emerged from the staircase well. Lithe in her white dress, gripping a large white handbag in her left hand, she stood poised and hesitant before completing the descent.

Every movement had the furtiveness of which Valerie herself would complain. If she had turned her head fully to the left she would have seen Alan. But she did not turn; she was too rapt and intent. Opposite her, facing the staircase, a glass door in the far room led out to the terrace. Valerie tiptoed across, slipped out, dodged behind a trellis thick with roses, and was lost to view.

Well? What did it mean?

He had no time to speculate. As chimes rang from the grandfather clock in the hall, preparatory to striking five, very audible footsteps rattled down the main stairs. Tentatively he called Camilla's name. Camilla, looking a trifle shaken, hurried into the lounge and extended her hands to him.

"I went up to see Madge. I did see her. Then they threw me out."

"Threw you out? Never mind! How's Madge?"

"Not too bad, I thought. But it was all rather peculiar. She wasn't in bed; she was lying on a chaise-longue in her negligee. Do you know, Alan, that in all the front bedrooms upstairs (Madge's, for instance) the air-conditioner is in the right-hand window of two windows? Whereas in Mr. Maynard's study—and in my own bedroom at the back, as I think I've told you—the air-conditioner is in the left-hand window. Did you know that?"

"I hadn't particularly noticed, though I remember the fact now you mention it. Why *do* you mention it, Camilla? What difference does it make where the air-conditioner is?"

"I know. That's what *I* said!"

Camilla marched to the games-table, picked up the pack of cards Alan had been shuffling, and cut the cards before putting them down.

"I mention it," she went on, "because it's the very first thing Madge said when I walked in. I wondered what she was talking about, and *I* asked what difference it made where the air-conditioner was. Madge said, 'It doesn't. When you're cooped up like this, your mind fastens on some silly little trifle and chases it all over the place. Look here!' she said.

"I've told you Madge was lying on a chaise-longue, or rather sitting up against the head of it. In her hands she had a little puzzle: a kind of flat glass-topped box not three inches long by two inches broad, with shiny little pellets inside. You tilted the box to make them roll into holes.

" 'Look here!' Madge said. 'There are three or four perfectly good books on that bedside table, and I can't open one of them.

Mark Sheldon gave me this; I've sat here trying and trying to make the puzzle work, and once I started weeping because I couldn't.'

"Maybe I'm as inconsequential as she is. I said, 'When did Mark give it to you? He hasn't been here since early yesterday evening, and he didn't give you anything then.' Then she told me he had given it to her days and days ago; that he had any number of puzzles of the same kind, and claimed they were a wonderful test of reflexes.

"I couldn't be inconsequential any longer. I said, 'Madge, what's been going on here?' And I explained we'd gone to Fort Moultrie because Dr. Fell wanted to see something there, though I didn't mention that horrible message on the blackboard. 'Rip came running after us,' I said, 'with some story about Valerie Huret going berserk and trying to kill you. Is it true?'

"While I'd been speaking Madge went as white as a counterpane. Then she practically burst out. 'In one sense, anyway, Valerie *did* try to kill me. I hate her! And I hate her,' Madge said, 'because she hates me; isn't that always the reason? Camilla, don't believe everything they say against me.'

"I couldn't stop myself. 'Nobody's said anything against you,' I told her, 'but then nobody ever knows what you're thinking. You don't really care a scrap for Rip Hillboro or Yancey Beale either, do you? There's another boy-friend, isn't there? And it's Mark Sheldon, isn't it?'

" 'Mark's *married,'* Madge said; 'he's married to a silly woman so jealous she won't let him out of her sight. Anyway, married or not, isn't he awfully young?' 'Young?' I said. 'He's three or four years older than you, whether or not you think you're the one who's emotionally mature. If one woman knows anything about another woman,' I said, 'the man in question *is* Mark Sheldon. It doesn't matter; you needn't tell me. But, before somebody who's rather fond of you herself goes completely out of her mind, please tell me what happened up here between you and Valerie.'

"She was going to tell me; I could feel in my bones and soul she was going to tell me. But just then there was a knock at the door. In came that young policeman—Sergeant Duckworth, isn't it?—and in a polite way ordered me out. 'I can't help it, ma'am; it's the captain's orders.' Madge wasn't unsteady on her feet; she jumped up and said, 'Are they putting me under guard again? Do they really think I'm in danger of being murdered?' The sergeant said, 'There's other things besides murder,' and held the door open for me to go."

Camilla paused, her gaze leaving Alan. Suddenly she walked to one of the glass doors and stood staring out so intently that he wondered if she had seen Valerie, who must still be somewhere in the garden. But evidently Camilla was only thinking. She returned to him, lifting eyes again lost in speculation.

"After I left Madge," she resumed, "I went to my own bedroom. One of the maids, Judith, was there doing some tidying up. Judith is more talkative, or less apprehensive, than either Sylvia or Winnie Mae. She's quite a pretty girl. I hate pumping servants; it seems horribly low and underhand. But I was still carried away. I asked her if *she* knew anything."

"And did she?"

"Only what I'm going to tell you. If you remember, you and Dr. Fell and Yancey and I left for Fort Moultrie at shortly before one o'clock? Captain Ashcroft left for his office at about the same time?"

"Yes. Well?"

"Following our very late breakfast, a light lunch was served about half-past one. Valerie and Rip and Mr. Crandall ate in the dining-room. Judith carried a tray up to Madge, who swore she didn't want anything but promised to try. Then Judith hovered in the hall upstairs, waiting for Madge to finish. She hovered for quite some time.

"When the others had finished in the dining-room, Rip and Mr. Crandall came in here to watch a Saturday baseball game on television. I don't know who was playing, but it doesn't matter. Valerie wouldn't go with them. Valerie prowled from room to room downstairs, talking to herself and not seeming to like it.

"Some time later—she isn't sure when—Judith went into Madge's room to get the tray. The tray had been barely touched. Judith had just picked it up when the door was flung open. In stalked Valerie, in a simmering kind of rage, and ordered Judith out.

"Judith with the tray got no farther than the head of the stairs; I wouldn't have, either. Judith listened; I'd have listened too.

"There was some kind of trouble between Madge and Valerie. But each was doing her best to keep her voice down, and no distinct words could be heard through the closed door. This went on for some time too. There was a silence. Then somebody ran pelting across the bedroom. Another silence, and somebody else ran too. There was a noise like a glass breaking, and a voice cried out."

"Just a moment, Camilla!" Alan interposed. "Who did the running? Who chased whom?"

"Judith couldn't tell. 'It was awful, miss! Like a hanty house, only worse!' Just at that emotional moment Captain Ashcroft, who'd evidently returned from Charleston with Sergeant Duckworth, came charging up the stairs. He ran by Judith and opened the door of Madge's room. Judith sort of dodged after him and looked past his shoulder.

"If you've been in Madge's room you know the bathroom is over on the left-hand side. The bathroom door was open. Valerie was just inside, holding Madge's arms and shaking her. She's the athletic type; she could have thrown Madge out of the window if she'd wanted to.

"That's all Judith saw; Captain Ashcroft slammed the door. Judith stumbled downstairs with the tray, and slipped and nearly fell. Rip Hillboro and Mr. Crandall were in the lower hall. Rip said, 'What's the rumpus; what's up?' Judith said, 'It's Miss Madge and Mrs. Hooray; somebody gettin' killed!'

"Bob Crandall ran upstairs and tried to find out what was what, but the sergeant was on guard now and wouldn't let him in. You'd have thought Rip at least would have been the first to go to Madge's assistance. But he didn't even make a move to; he just paced and fidgeted. It must have been afterwards he decided to borrow Yancey's car and follow us.

"That's all I can tell you, Alan, because it's all Judith saw or heard. What happened in Madge's room is anybody's guess. I don't even know where Valerie is; I haven't seen her anywhere. But I've been thinking . . ."

Alan considered.

There seemed no reason to report that he had seen Valerie, in a passion of stealth, creep down the back stairs to the garden. Also vivid in his mind was an image of Madge as he pictured her on the chaise-longue, with a puzzle-box such as the puzzle Mark Sheldon had been juggling at Davy's Restaurant the night before. All dangerous elements could be seen here, being tilted and juggled together like the contents of the glass-topped box. But these were no quicksilver pellets in a trumpery puzzle; they were emotional bombs that might explode at any moment.

"Yes?" he said. "What have you been thinking?"

Camilla put her hand on his arm and looked up.

"I've seen Madge," she replied. "Mr. Maynard's death was a dreadful shock, and this business today hasn't helped. *But—!*"

"But what?"

"I was afraid," Camilla fought some internal struggle, "I was afraid of finding her crushed or stricken, and it wasn't like that at all. It suddenly occurred to me, while I was talking to her, I've been worrying about her more than she's been worrying about herself. Madge is resilient; we tend to forget how resilient; the worst blow doesn't affect her for very long. I've put my own affairs into the background; I've cursed myself for not thinking more about Madge. And yet, if only this *mystery* could be cleared up . . . can you guess what I'm trying to say?"

"I think so. It's that Philadelphia-Scotch conscience of yours. You've put your own affairs into the background, when there wasn't any real need to do it. Also, since you and I have so much to say to each other . . ."

"*Have* we so much to say to each other?"

"You know we have, when you stop worrying about what you ought to do. Look here, Camilla, I've got a suggestion to make."

"Then go ahead and make it!" interrupted the voice of Captain Ashcroft. "Don't let us stop you or interrupt you! Go ahead and get it off your chest!"

The detective, looking mentally rumpled, loomed up in the archway to the far room. Just behind him towered the bulk of Dr. Fell. Then Captain Ashcroft's eye remembered a grievance.

"Now I've got a question," he continued, "I want answered in one word. No evasions, no funny business, just the truth! When Dr. Fell and I went into what we thought was a secret session up on the top floor late last night, were you two gettin' an earful at the door?"

"The answer in one word," said Alan, "is yes."

Captain Ashcroft's face seemed to swell up.

"Later I thought you must 'a' been, though at the time I couldn't be sure. Now, I ought to get mad; I ought to read the riot-act; I ought to chew you out good and proper. But—oh, hell! Looks as though we're nearer the end o' this business than a few hours ago I'd 'a' thought was possible. Since you've heard so much, maybe it won't hurt if you hear a little more. Not everything —that wouldn't be right or fair, damn you!—but a little. I'm right proud of Dr. Fell here, and a little bit proud of myself too. Dr. Fell . . ."

Dr. Fell, hat under one arm and stick under the other, sailed through the doorway like a great galleon.

"It would be untrue," he explained, "to say I have been communing with the ghost of Henry Maynard. But traces of his personality are all over the place. Would you imagine so fastidious a gentleman as addicted to using his hands for household chores, or that he had any skill at such jobs? And yet he was and had. The invaluable George assured me of this, a statement borne out by the workbench and set of tools you will find in the cellar. There is more! Since he himself had drawn our attention to the baseball equipment in the cellar, it seemed the proper place to look for other sporting gear. Somebody said he was interested in fishing, I think?"

"Somebody said he was a fisherman," returned Alan, "but you weren't there when the remark was made. How do you know he was interested in fishing?"

"Miss Bruce told me."

"*I* told you?"

Dr. Fell looked at Alan.

"As a snapper-up of unconsidered trifles," he said apologetically, "I must confess I have questioned both you and the young lady at various times—notably late last night—when you were scarcely aware of being questioned and don't even remember it. Anything you two have heard or seen has now been registered on the dim old tablets of my own memory. In a dampproof cabinet beside the workbench, Captain Ashcroft and I have discovered the sections that make up a fishing-rod, together with various trout-flies and several spools of Monofilament fishing-line. There were also two revolvers, both unloaded, though with a box of ammunition for each. The captain, with what seemed to me an excess of zeal, rather irritably forbade me to examine the revolvers as much as I should have liked."

"Examine 'em, for God's sake?" roared Captain Ashcroft. "He was lookin' down the barrel and pullin' the trigger, that's all. He's clumsy enough as it is; he messed around with the tools till he busted a saw. We don't want him to blow his fool head off before he gives us the last fact!"

"Speaking of the last fact," Alan said with a certain wildness, "I take it this bears some relation to a solution inspired by *The Gold Bug?*"

"It does, young fellow, and closer to buried treasure than you might think. Anything else?"

"Yes. Since we've admitted to eavesdropping last night, what about the Sheraton desk? You were looking for a secret drawer; you said you had a man who specialized in such things. Did he find one?"

"Jerry Wexford, you mean? Jerry's had the desk since this morning. If there's any secret drawer and any paper in it, as Dr. Fell thinks there is, he's found it by this time. What's your suggestion?"

"My suggestion?"

"When I walked in here and interrupted you, you told the young lady you had a suggestion to make. Of course," said Captain Ashcroft, making a broadly tolerant gesture, "if it's too private and personal to be repeated in public . . . !"

"It's not private at all. I was going to invite her to dinner." Alan turned. "What do you say, Camilla? You wouldn't go to Davy's yesterday evening; you intimated you'd never go under any circumstances. But this is your sincere well-wisher speaking; won't you change your mind and go tonight?"

"I will! I'd love to! If you promise not to sneer at me, that is, and if Captain Ashcroft doesn't think I'm needed here?"

"You're not needed here, ma'am. You go; I'm urgin' you to go, and I'll tell you why. Dr. Fell's the one *I'll* invite to dinner; in fact, I've already invited him. I want him to eat fried chicken as my wife cooks it: not what he'll get in most restaurants. And Mr. Grantham don't seem like a bad sort, if he's met halfway. So you just go along, ma'am, and try to enjoy yourself."

Camilla looked at him. "Are *you* enjoying yourself, Captain? You almost sound as though you were."

"Enjoyin' this mess? Not so's you could notice it I'm not! It's a bad business, worse'n you'll guess till the lid blows off, and it gets no better even when we start to close in."

Here Captain Ashcroft, after nursing his jaw in deep thought, made a still broader gesture.

"A little less'n half an hour ago, Miss Bruce, I told Yancey Beale and Rip Hillboro to make 'emselves scarce for a while. Why don't you and Mr. Grantham do the same thing? It's too early for dinner, but there's other things to do. Go down to the beach, look at the gardens, walk as far as the Poinsett High School! Apart from one more phone-call to set some wheels in motion, Dr. Fell and I have a job to do now. It's not the pleasantest job in the world; we don't want witnesses or even potential witnesses. Yes, and another thing . . . !"

More grievances rose and burst like skyrockets.

"Somebody thinks it's funny, eh," raved Captain Ashcroft, "to keep writin' messages on that blackboard?" He appealed to Dr. Fell. "Even if George gets stubborn and won't move the blackboard, that's no odds. *I* could move it; I could grab it or impound it or chop it up for firewood. But we won't do that, because there's a better way. I brought along somebody else besides Duckworth; I brought Con Kingsley, who's an experienced man and no fool. We'll post Kingsley at some place where he can't be seen: a cupboard in the library or behind the curtains in the weapons-room. Then, if somebody sneaks in to write *another* message on that damn blackboard . . ."

"You will nab the joker red-handed?" asked Dr. Fell. "I beg, sir, that you will do nothing of the kind!"

"Dr. Fell, are you nuts? Don't you want to know who the joker is?"

"I rather think I already know," Dr. Fell said modestly. "But at no time has it been a joke; it is frantic, desperate earnest; we may still learn from it. Can I persuade you, Captain, to keep your hands off our ghostly visitant and let the blackboard stand unguarded?"

"That's your advice? No kidding?"

"That is my advice. No kidding."

"Well," said Captain Ashcroft, lifting his fist and stamping over to one of the glass doors, "we'll play it your way for the time being. Your way's been right so far, though I don't like to watch where it's takin' us. There's one consolation in this business, and only one. We've seen everything; we can't be surprised any more. There's not one other move either the murderer or the joker can make!"

Captain Ashcroft was wrong. He said those words at half-past five. Before many hours had elapsed, as the metronome ticked in a lonely room amid musical instruments, blow and counter-blow were struck in a deadly contest that seemed to have no end.

15

Well, had it been a successful dinner?

Black clouds scudded across the moon as Alan drove Camilla back from Davy's Restaurant to Maynard Hall. And, driving back, he reviewed the dinner and the evening.

Camilla had taken some time to dress semi-formally; it had been past seven o'clock when they left, after Alan phoned ahead to reserve a table. Despite Captain Ashcroft's insistence that he and Dr. Fell had an urgent mission at the Hall, he made no move to get on with this. Police-officer and doctor had foregathered under the portico, sitting on the front steps, smoking cigars, and talking in muffled voices. They still sat there when Alan drove away in the dusk.

Davy's, as might have been expected on Saturday night, was packed. Alan guided Camilla through the outer room past a bar crowded three deep.

In the dining-room, with its Confederate-gray and gold décor, Camilla's receptive mood seemed only increased. The blue eyes remained intent, never once retreating from him; her color was high. Neither had much of an appetite, though they drank a fair amount of wine. And each was a little too conscious of the other's presence; both jumped involuntarily when their hands touched in reaching for butter or salt.

"Bother!" said Camilla. "You brought Dr. Fell here for sight-seeing, didn't you? And yet he hasn't seen anything except Fort Moultrie, and the outside of the theatre next door to here?"

"What's been happening, I suppose, tends to swallow up other interests. Anyway, give us time; we've been here hardly more than a day!"

"What do you want him to see?"

"The old slave market, to begin with. And the original powder magazine, part of Carteret's bastion and fort, which dates from 1700."

"Aren't one or two stately homes open to the public?"

"More than one or two. The thing to remember is which stately homes are open all year, not just in the main season between the end of March and the middle of May. Camilla—!"

"Yes?"

They were bending towards each other, but they sat up very straight. Dinner was finished; a waiter had brought coffee. Into the restaurant at that moment came Dr. Mark Sheldon, escorting a slim, shapely, fashionable brunette somewhat younger than himself. Dr. Sheldon nodded briefly, but gave no other sign as Alan's friend the head-waiter ushered the newcomers to a distant table.

"Well," and Camilla lowered her voice after a quick glance, "she doesn't *look* bad-tempered, I must say. That must be Annette, surely? The wife Madge says is so very jealous?"

"Yes, I suppose so. All right: let's face it!"

"Face what?"

"The whole situation. We've both been trying to ignore it and shut it out, but it won't be shut out for half an hour at a time. Are we back on the theme of jealousy again?"

"The theme of jealousy again? I don't understand."

"Last night," he reminded her, "we listened in on the conference between Dr. Fell and Captain Ashcroft because you had a reason that concerned somebody's jealousy. You couldn't believe your ears at the tone in which somebody spoke certain words. You said it was a very good reason, but you never explained what the reason was."

"Oh, Alan, it was only a wild and ridiculous idea! Don't spoil everything! Just because Mark Sheldon walks in with his wife . . ."

"He's not the only one who's come in. Look towards the door again."

It was Rip Hillboro, whom Alan saw for the first time wearing jacket and tie. Thrusting aside a waiter who stepped into his path, Rip shouldered aggressively towards their table. But he did not seem happy.

"I was having a drink at the bar," he said, nodding towards the outer room. "I won't sit down, thanks. I've already had dinner at the house. But I'm the only one who did."

"The only one who had dinner at the house?"

"Yes. Also, bar Madge and a sergeant still guarding her life, the only one left when the others lit out on their own concerns. Stonewall Jackson was released by the cops and kited off home. Valerie Huret persuaded Bob Crandall to take *her* to dinner in the Swamp Fox Room at the Francis Marion Hotel. Next, you'll ask, what about the cops? Well, old Belshazzar and his friend Gargantua . . ."

"They had some design in mind," Alan said, "but they hadn't carried it out when we left."

"They still haven't. The design," explained Rip, squaring himself and throwing back his shoulders, "was to question Madge about some new development today. But they wouldn't say what the development was; my best efforts couldn't get a word out of 'em. They were actually on their way upstairs when the phone rang. The message was for Shadrach himself; he put down the phone in a funny sort of way and said they'd wait till tomorrow. Then *they* hit the trail in a police car. Which left *me* holding the fort on my own."

"And you didn't like being alone?" asked Camilla.

"No, madam, I did not. I'm pretty tough, I think; I've got no nerves to speak of. But I was spooked, as they say on television. For the first time in my life I was spooked and I admit it. Now look, Grantham!"

"Yes?"

"It's getting on for nine o'clock; did you know? There's a John Ford film at the Riviera Theatre, which is the big one on King Street. The last showing of the feature, according to the evening paper, begins at nine-five. Like to come along and see it, both of you?"

"No, I think not. Unless you, Camilla . . . ?"

"Not for me, thanks!"

"Well, suit yourselves," said Rip. "I think you're making a mistake, but never mind. *I'm* going. Whatever happens, now or in the future, don't say I didn't try."

And off he went with a flourish.

They had sat for more than half an hour longer over coffee, in the dusky dining-room with the shaded lamps. But it was that interlude, first seeing the Sheldons and then seeing Rip, which made Alan ask himself questions as he drove back to Maynard Hall.

The fingers of his left hand drummed on the wheel. Frequently he glanced sideways at Camilla—the short nose, the rather broad pink mouth, a warm and vital presence as withdrawn as her gaze fixed on the road ahead.

Black clouds threatened to engulf the moon, which always wormed out from behind them. It was twenty minutes past ten when Alan drew up at the portico. Faint light showed at the windows of Madge's room above the front door; there was a bleak-looking glow from the chandelier in the main hall. The house, seeming otherwise dark, rose up desolate against a troubled sky.

"None of the others can be back yet," Camilla said. "But it's not late. Won't you—won't you come in for a while?"

"Thanks."

At the back of the hall hovered the imperturbable George, who asked them if they wanted anything. Camilla said they didn't, and he discreetly vanished. Alan followed her down into the library, where she switched on lamps in the big room with the portrait of Mrs. Henry Maynard above the mantelpiece. Camilla, smiling but fidgety, seemed as restless as he was.

"Not very cheerful, is it?" she asked. "Can't you understand what Rip meant by 'spooked'?"

"Yes, but—"

"Alan, is there anything on your mind?"

"There's a great deal on my mind. What went wrong?"

"Wrong?"

"Not one controversial subject all evening! Not one argument of any kind, literary or artistic or political . . ."

"Oh, *those* things!" Camilla dismissed them.

"We were getting towards a kind of spiritual intimacy, we were edging closer and even hurrying together when something wrecked the atmosphere and spoiled the mood. What was it? Can't we refer to the situation in this house, can't we even think about it, without being driven apart as though we'd never even been within touching-distance?"

"Really, Alan! If you insist on playing the great detective again, and hammering me with questions as though I were your principal witness, you can't expect anything else. What do I think is going on here? What do I suspect? Questions like that!—"

"Well, what *is* going on here? What *do* you suspect?"

"Something that's just too ridiculous to be talked about!"

"The things that cause the most trouble in this world, Camilla, are the things that are too ridiculous to be talked about. Loosen up, can't you? As for playing the great detective, I admit I made a fool of myself this morning . . ."

Camilla's mood suddenly changed.

"But you didn't!" she breathed. "You didn't make a fool of yourself at all! Granted the evidence you had . . ."

"Throwing a baseball and beaning the poor devil, eh?" Alan said bitterly. "If it wasn't the height of folly, at least we can call it pretty stupid. But it's just possible, given another chance . . . Now I wonder . . . ?"

"You wonder what? You're not leaving me, are you?"

"Given my own choice, I would never leave you. And I'm not leaving now."

Alan strode to the door of the weapons-room, opened it on darkness, and touched the switch just inside. Light blazed from a crystal chandelier smaller than the one in the main hall. Three times Captain Ashcroft had erased chalked letters from the blackboard across the room. A fourth message stared at Alan in night stillness now.

> THEY SAY "CRACK THE CASE," DON'T THEY? OR IS IT ONLY IN BOOKS AND FILMS? J.P.H.S., R. 26. YOU HAD BETTER CRACK THE CASE WITH WHAT YOU FIND THERE, OR I CAN HELP YOU NO LONGER.
>
> *One who has done his best,* N.S.

A run of chimes, ending in the single stroke for ten-thirty, animated the distant clock in the hall. Alan turned, to find Camilla at his elbow.

"Well," she said, "we ought to be used to it by this time, oughtn't we?"

"Steady!"

"I'm not steady, though I'll try to be. Dr. Fell seemed to expect another message, didn't he? He even seemed to want one?"

"Yes. But this time we're the ones to discover it. This time, whether they like it or not, we can steal a march on 'em."

"Steal a . . . ? Alan, are you crazy?"

"No."

"So far," Camilla gabbled, "the directions have at least been understandable. This one is just gibberish. 'J.P.H.S., R. 26.' We can't make any sense of that, can we?"

"I'm not so sure. What about Joel Poinsett High School, room 26?"

Camilla seized his arm. "It could be! Yes, it *could* be! But—"

"Wasn't Madge talking about the place yesterday? It's closed; they're going to tear it down. Somebody in a nearby cottage keeps an eye on it. What else did Madge say?"

"She didn't say anything else at the time, but she mentioned it to me again later in the day. The man who keeps an eye on the place is the proprietor of a flower-and-seed nursery to the east of the grounds. You can't get into that school by the main door in front, which has been locked and heavily barred since they closed it up. The only way in, apart from burglary, is by a semi-underground door on the west side."

"Whereas the caretaker's on the east side? Better and better!"

"Why?"

"Camilla, the Joel Poinsett High School's not five minutes' walk from here on Fort Johnson Road. The joker—who isn't a joker at all, according to Dr. Fell—says there's something in room 26 that will crack the case. I'm going to go and get it."

"Now?"

"Of course; when else?"

"Alan, I don't have to remind you what's been happening! Mightn't it be dangerous to go there?"

"That can't be helped. These people—murderer, joker, whom you like—have been bedevilling us until we can't take any more. This is it, my dear. You wouldn't like to come along, would you?"

"Oh, may I? I—I don't really mind anything as long as I'm with you."

"Then let's get started. Wait! Do you want to change your clothes?"

"I won't if you'd rather I didn't." Camilla looked down over her pink semi-formal dress. "It's these spike heels, that's all! If I *might* put on flat heels and slacks, I promise not to take longer than five minutes. And you remember the little flashlight Madge was using in the study last night? Captain Ashcroft carried it down to her bedroom, but I picked it up and took it with me. I'll bring that, shall I?—Five minutes!" said Camilla, and darted away.

Despite his tendency to fume, she was better than her word. Camilla must have flung the clothes off herself to don others; he had smoked less than half a cigarette before she reappeared, supple in dark slacks and the same fleecy tan sweater she had worn that day.

Beneath unsteady moon and racing cloud, wild shadows fled across the park as they emerged from the house. Momentarily Alan switched on the flashlight she had given him. But Camilla touched his arm when he started for the front gate.

"We don't need to go that way," she informed him, pointing south. "There's a side gate that'll bring us out very close to the main road. If you *must* do this . . ."

A hundred yards to the south, over dew-drenched grass and past spectral flower-beds in a thin whine of mosquitoes, they found the other gate in the head-high brick wall. Beyond it coarse grass sloped up gently to the screen of live-oaks guarding this side of Fort Johnson Road. Alan hesitated as he opened the gate.

"On the famous Sunday night of May 2nd, when Madge met some unknown man back there, presumably this is the way he went out?"

"Yes, I daresay. Does it matter?"

"Camilla, *everything* matters in this tangle. Up to the road, and turn right."

They swung west along Fort Johnson Road, Camilla walking close to him and Alan occasionally flashing the beam when interlaced boughs above their heads grew too thick to admit any moonlight at all.

"Now, then," he said, "as for the also-unknown N.S. who's been providing us with so many directions . . ."

"A new set of directions every time we turn around! And that can't be!"

"What can't be?"

"N.S.," Camilla whispered, "seems to know the explanation of the whole business. How can N.S. possibly know?"

"It may be just suspicion. Or it may be inside information he—or she—won't come out in the open with. That's one of the things we can't tell."

"And what game is Captain Ashcroft playing? What phone-message did *he* get from his office, so that he looked so very odd and said they wouldn't question Madge until tomorrow?"

"It all comes back to Madge, doesn't it? Possibly the answer's in room 26 at an abandoned school. A little farther along the road, a minute or two more . . ."

On their right the grounds of Maynard Hall fell away behind them. On their left, presently, the line of great live-oaks disappeared in a cleared space of several acres, long if not very deep. First they saw a tall wire fence, beyond which rose banked trees, shrubs, the greenhouse-roofs and cottage-roof which marked the flower-nursery.

Some distance beyond it, orange-yellow brick drained of color and long windows glimmering, loomed the two storeys of the Joel Poinsett High School. In that uncertain light you could just read the name carved across the façade, with the date of 1920.

They passed the building, walking softly though with an attempt at casualness, and keeping to shadow on the north side of the road. West of the school, separated from its grounds by a row of trees, was an establishment Alan could not remember having noticed. A brown-painted board fence enclosed its premises and hid them from sight.

"*I* can tell you what it is," Camilla whispered. "The sign says *R. Gaiddon, Merchandise.* But the gate in that fence was wide open when we drove past yesterday. It's nothing but a junk-yard!"

"Then at least there won't be anybody there at this time of night. Look halfway along this side of the school-building. Some steps lead down to a semi-underground door, which must be the one we want. Come along."

Camilla took his arm. They made no noise as they approached

in a diagonal direction, over bare earth trampled free of grass by several generations. But shadows, in which something or somebody might be lurking, seemed blacker and more dense below the moon-silvered windows. They were still some yards from a three-sided stone coping, like a very shallow well in which three broad, steep steps descended to the door, when Camilla suddenly pulled his head down and whispered even more softly than she had whispered in the attic the night before.

"Alan, who *was* Joel Poinsett?"

"A Charleston diplomat, the first American Minister to Mexico in the eighteen-twenties, and afterwards Secretary of War under Van Buren. Why?"

"Because I don't like this. I don't think we're alone. I've got a feeling there's somebody near us, maybe watching."

"I've got the same feeling. But it's imagination; it's bound to be imagination! There's not a soul within—"

Then a voice split the night wide open.

"Stand out, you!" it bellowed. *"Who are yeh? This here's a shotgun; iffen yeh doan' stand out and lemme see yeh . . ."*

Alan's heart had jumped into his throat. He saw the indistinct figure which seemed to have materialized out of the wall. Then he realized, with equal shock, that the voice was not addressing them at all. It was addressing two bulky men who stood at the foot of the steps outside the door. In his right hand the less bulky of the two men held what looked like an enormous electric torch. Its switch clicked; light dazzled out across the gold shield cupped in the palm of his left hand.

"Police!" Captain Ashcroft yelled back. "Who are *you?"*

The other voice, shorn of ferocity, was disconcerted.

"Name o' Hendricks, Hendricks's nurseries. If you're *po*-lice sho' nuff—"

"Take a look at this badge. And don't tell me I need a warrant for unoccupied premises!"

"Not tellin' yeh nuthin', seh. Got to be careful 'bout the damn kids, is all. Enathing wrong?"

"Maybe, maybe not. I'm here to find out. Are the lights working in this place?"

"Lights, water, 'most ever'thing. Don't go usin' 'em too much, will yeh?"

"I'll take care of it. Now get lost."

"I was on'y askin', seh—"

"Get lost, you hear?"

Shuffling footfalls retreated; the indistinct figure vanished. While a witless-looking Dr. Fell remained where he was, Captain Ashcroft mounted the three stone steps. The beam of light swept across the yard, rising first at Alan, then at Camilla, and was extinguished. Captain Ashcroft surveyed them.

"Well . . . now!" he said, studying Alan. "You got back, did you? Saw what it meant by J.P.H.S., and tried to get here ahead of us, eh?"

"Yes, something like that."

"Well, no harm done. *We* got back and—" His tone changed. "I'm not too pleased to see *you* here, Miss Bruce. This is no pleasure-trip, you know!"

"Captain," cried a distraught Camilla, "do you usually have junk-yards next door to your schools?"

"No, not often. If you mean old Pokey Gaiddon, they bought up his property and they'll clear it away when they tear down the school. No, I'm not pleased to see you. But it's all right if you're with us, I reckon."

"Is it all right?" boomed the voice of Dr. Fell.

Captain Ashcroft turned back, switching on his light. With Camilla and Alan crowding after him, he descended the three steps. The broad, heavy door, without knob or handle on the outside, was held perhaps a quarter-inch open by some thin and twisted metal object wedged between door and frame.

"Had to pry this open with my fingers," the captain explained. "It's not locked, but there's a bar you push down on the inside. So it had to be pried open—"

"—and is kept from closing," supplied Dr. Fell, "by the historic and valuable corkscrew I carry always on my person. Archons of Athens!" he wheezed, making a hideous face against the light. "If we are going in, hadn't we better get on with it? While you were speaking to our friends, I ventured to pull the door a little farther open. I can't be sure I heard a footstep in there; no doubt I am hearing too much. But I was wondering . . ."

"Wondering what?"

"I was wondering," said Dr. Fell, "whether someone else may have got here before any of us."

16

"Somebody else, eh?'" snapped Captain Ashcroft. "We'll soon see about *that!*"

He was over-optimistic, Alan thought. Holding open the big door until the others had preceded him down two more steps into a dark passage, Captain Ashcroft let the door swing not quite shut on its compressed-air cushion. Then, directing the beam of his big flashlight straight ahead, he moved up to join Dr. Fell. Camilla and Alan followed some feet behind them.

A fairly wide transverse corridor, concrete-floored, ran the width of the building. Either the school had only recently been abandoned, Alan decided, or very good care had been taken of it during the interim. Despite the stuffy air of this semi-underground passage, there was no smell of mustiness or damp.

On either side of the corridor, as he entered, he vaguely noted a closed door with an opaque ground-glass panel. He had the small flashlight in his right hand, but did not switch it on to investigate. Instead, with Camilla clinging to his left arm, he followed the larger beam as Dr. Fell and Captain Ashcroft blundered ahead. Their voices ran out and boomed back in echoes.

"Harrumph!" said Dr. Fell, with no easy intonation. "Since for my sins I myself was once a schoolmaster—"

"You feel right at home, eh?" Captain Ashcroft supplied. "O.K.! But what are we looking for?"

"Something," replied Dr. Fell, "to which the joker who is not a joker has specifically drawn our attention. Either it was here already, like the Poe photograph at Fort Moultrie, or else it has been put here for us to find. So far, at least, our anonymous friend has been *accurate*. Archons of Athens!" He paused, pointing ahead. "Surely that is a stairway up to the main floor?"

It was. Where the transverse corridor met a central corridor through the building, a broad staircase with concrete treads and a heavy iron-and-wood banister led upwards into denser shadow.

"And that's not all," Alan whispered into Camilla's ear.

"Not all?" Camilla whispered back.

They had been passing more doors, left and right. Towards one of these, on the right, Alan sent a momentary gleam of light. Its panel bore no number, but the black letters *Manual Training* stood out against opaque glass. Camilla seized his wrist and flashed the torch's ray briefly towards another door, well down from it on the left.

"Domestic Science," her insistent whisper ran on. "Manual training for boys, domestic science for girls; just as in any school built forty-odd years ago. But what did you mean by saying that staircase 'isn't all'?"

"Follow me; walk softly; I'll show you."

As though trying to make both of them invisible to Captain Ashcroft and Dr. Fell, who were now mounting the stairs, he led her half a dozen steps beyond. At the angle of the wall where central corridor met transverse corridor, Alan set his shoulder against tall wooden swing-doors and pushed one of them open.

It was the gallery round the deep well of a gymnasium below. Distorted moonlight, struggling past blinds imperfectly drawn, touched a polished floor some fifteen or twenty feet down. From that floor, through all the confines of the gallery, breathed up a palpable atmosphere of past basketball games and muscular exertion from long ago.

"This isn't the basement, you know," Alan confided. "If you look back at the stairs, there, you'll see more stairs leading down. There's a floor underneath this one: locker-rooms for the gymnasium, furnace-room, all the mechanics of the place when it was in use."

"I—I suppose so," breathed Camilla. "But there's something oppressive and (what's the word I want?) horribly *sneaky* about it, isn't there? I could have sworn I saw . . . I know nothing moved; not really. Still!" Her left arm crept round his neck. "Let's go up and join the others, shall we?"

Upstairs they hurried, letting the door to the gallery swing shut. On the spacious main floor above, with smooth tile underfoot, Captain Ashcroft stood pontifically at the junction of central corridor with transverse corridor, and used the beam of his torch like a pointer.

"We've got to count rooms, that's all," he said. "Must be a good many more'n twenty-six rooms in this place. Only some of 'em haven't got numbers; just names. Like that one there!"

"If you mean the office," Dr. Fell boomed back, following the light as it swept towards the front, "may I suggest we investigate the office without delay?"

"All right! Fair enough, I s'pose. But why the office?"

"My dear sir! Since electricity and water are both working, the telephone may be working too. Should the telephone be working . . ."

"Well?"

"Shall we see?"

A smell of chalk and blackboards still haunted these halls. Ahead, north, the building's big front double-doors faced towards Fort Johnson Road above a sweep of stone steps leading down to the yard. Just inside was a broad vestibule; then, in the wall to your right as you faced forwards, the glass-panelled door of the office. Captain Ashcroft lit the way as Dr. Fell lumbered over, pushed the door open, and touched a switch on the wall inside.

It was a fair-sized room, once a secretary's. One light glowed in the ceiling, another in a lamp on the secretary's flat-topped desk, to show austere buff-colored walls lined with filing cabinets. Two windows a dozen feet above ground looked east towards the flower-nursery. On the wall above the secretary's desk hung a framed photograph of Thomas Edison; on the desk itself stood a telephone, with a Charleston phone-book lying beside it. In the wall to their right, south, a door of polished brown panels bore in gilt letters the legend *J. Finley Sooner, Principal.*

Dr. Fell, more red-faced than ever, pitched his hat on the secretary's desk, laid his stick beside it, and blinked owlishly at the door to the principal's office.

"A name like J. Finley Sooner, I fancy, must have provided endless delight to the juvenile sense of humor. 'There was a young fellow named Sooner, Who set up in life as a crooner.' Come, enough of *that.*"

Wheezing, clearing his throat, he picked up the telephone and held it to his ear. Against night stillness all four of them could make out the hollow humming which indicated an open line. Dr. Fell dropped the phone back on its cradle.

"You hear and observe," he said triumphantly, "that the instrument is in excellent order. If I may enquire, Captain: is any other telephone hereabouts closer to Maynard Hall than this one?"

Captain Ashcroft stared at him.

"No, this is the closest. There's one at the marine research-station, sure; but no outsider could get in to use it. Not many people at this end of the island, remember? The only other phone I know of is at a crossroads store a couple of miles down the road in the other direction." He paused, galvanized. "Were you thinking, maybe, of the humorist who's been havin' so much fun with us?"

"I was."

"Yesterday afternoon he—or she—phoned *me* with all that guff about a tomahawk! You think the call was made from here?"

"I think it extremely probable."

"All right; but what does it prove?"

"Prove?" exclaimed Dr. Fell, rearing up. "My dear sir, as court-evidence it proves nothing! But then we need to prove nothing regarding the humorist. The identity of the humorist—as opposed to the murderer; they are separate and very different entities—has already been betrayed because a certain person knows too much."

"Yes," snapped Captain Ashcroft, "and that's what sticks in my craw. It'll be a fine thing for me, thanks to you, if we can clean up this whole business before the coroner's inquest on Monday. We know the murderer, or at least we're pretty sure we know. But who the hell is the joker and why has he been joking? If you won't tell me because you keep saying it's not important, what do we do now?"

"We find room 26 and the evidence that awaits us. With your permission, sir, we shall use the school's electricity as little as possible. Will you produce the torch again, please, while I extinguish these lights?"

Camilla drew closer to Alan as Dr. Fell, catching up hat and stick, backed towards the switch on the wall beside the door.

"In this affair (forgive me!) I came close to making a very stupid mistake before chance or luck restored my balance. Having stumbled once, and stumbled badly, I have no wish to stumble again. If in fact someone should be following and watching at this moment . . ."

Dr. Fell's voice trailed away; the wall-switch clicked. Except for a little unsteady moonlight filtering through the windows and brushing the carpet, darkness descended like a palpable hood. And in Alan Grantham's brain stirred the whole realm of nightmare. For they *were* being watched.

Outside the right-hand window, its sill a dozen feet from the ground, rose up the dark shape of somebody kneeling on the outer sill to peer in. The figure seemed to move its neck curiously; moonlight threw a misshapen shadow across the floor.

Captain Ashcroft, uttering a ringing oath, switched the beam of the big torch full on that window. Nightmare vanished almost with a yell of anticlimax.

The sinister-seeming figure was only Yancey Beale. Yancey, in sports coat and slacks, still knelt on the outer ledge, keeping precarious balance by holding to the edges of the brick wall at either side. He said or called out something when Captain Ashcroft strode towards him, but no words were audible through the glass.

The window did not work as ordinary sash-windows work. When you pulled a metal handle on the lower edge of the frame, the whole lower window swung inwards and upwards at a sharp angle, leaving space for someone outside to worm through.

A simmering Captain Ashcroft yanked it open. By some miracle of contortion Yancey, looking pale and hollow-eyed, swung his legs round and through the aperture. Then he stood up inside the room, leaning back against the window to close it.

"Well?" demanded Captain Ashcroft, who had been given a bigger start than he would have admitted. "What do you think *you're* up to? You went home, didn't you?"

"I went home hours ago, yes! But I'm back again!"

"So we see. What you *doin'* back here?"

"Ezekiel, for God's sake have a heart! I had to find out how Madge was, didn't I? I couldn't desert Madge, could I?"

"Well?"

"I started to fret about her," said Yancey, making bothered gestures as the other sent the light into his eyes, "so I drove back barely twenty minutes ago. Your Cerberus was still on guard at the bedroom door; wouldn't even let me talk to her. And if it comes to questions, old son," he burst out, "what are the cops up to? Are you holding Madge incommunicado, or something?"

"No, of course not! Why should we do that?"

"That's what *I* want to know, damn it! She's segregated and immunized; she couldn't be more cut off from the world if you'd put her in jail. What's the game, Habakkuk? Strikes me that girl needs a lawyer a good deal more than she needs a doctor."

"Maybe she does, at that. We know what we're about, young fellow; we've got our reasons! Now are you goin' to tell me . . . ?"

"All right, all right!"

In the gloom of the office Yancey waved a hand towards Dr. Fell, towards Camilla and Alan, by way of greeting. Then he flew off again.

"I met George," he continued, "on his way up to bed. George wasn't lockin' up; nobody ever locks up in that place; see the mess we're in. Well, every damn person lit out for town tonight." He looked at Camilla and Alan. "I knew you two had gone, of course. But it seems Valerie drove Bob Crandall in her car to take her to dinner somewhere. Rip Hillboro left next to catch the last show at the Riviera. Rip's not back; Bob's not back; Valerie would have to show up for a minute or two, if only to drive Bob home, but she hasn't. Nobody's back, and it's nearly eleven o'clock!

"According to George," again his eye sought Alan and Camilla, "you two returned at well past ten, but ducked out again without a word to anybody. It takes no mastermind to see why."

Here Yancey drew himself up and eyed Captain Ashcroft.

"You ask what I'm doin' in this place, do you? The same as everybody else, I expect. Do I deduce, Jehoshaphat, that two parties of you—you and Dr. Fell in one party, the two almost-but-not-quite lovebirds in the other—came here separately after you'd both interpreted a fourth blackboard message, and bumped into each other on the doorstep?"

"What makes you think we did?"

"Because the same thing happened to me," retorted Yancey. "Burn my britches to a cinder! After I'd talked to George upstairs, I went down through the library to the weapons-room and found a screed that could only have meant Joel Poinsett High School, room 26.

"I was all alone, mind. But I stood there and talked to myself aloud, which is supposed to be a sign you're going crazy. And I think I must be going crazy, at that. Because, after I'd talked to myself (yelled at myself, rather) about the message and what it meant, I went out into the back garden to cool my head before I came over here. And a voice spoke to me from behind a rose-trellis, when there wasn't anybody there to speak."

"Yes," said Captain Ashcroft, "you're headed for the bughouse sure enough. Or else," he yelled, "you want us to swallow the silliest damn story that ever landed a man in trouble! Either way . . ."

"Can you get it through your head, Captain, that I'm not foolin'?"

"All right; you're not foolin'. What happened?"

"I've tried to tell you. 'Dark of the moon,' didn't Dr. Fell say once today? There was nobody in that garden and couldn't have been. Madge was upstairs under guard; all the others were nowhere near the house. And yet the voice spoke, a whispery and disembodied kind of voice, as I passed a rose-trellis near one of the glass doors to the lounge."

"Like a voice on the phone, was it?"

"Yes! Only from behind the trellis; not on any phone. 'If you must go to that school, look out.' And again, 'If you must go to that school, *look out!*' I ran at the trellis and looked behind it, but there was nobody there."

"If you were all alone, how could anybody have known you meant to come on here?"

"Because I'd been talking to myself; didn't I tell you? I'd been talking to myself in the weapons-room, with the French window wide open before I closed it against the mosquitoes. Anybody within yards could have heard me babblin' about the Poinsett High School and room 26. But who was there to hear?

"Captain, I can't help it if you don't believe me. Maybe I don't expect you to. And yet I've been telling the strict, literal truth! Explain the voice any way you like; it gave me one hell of a turn. But I didn't mean to let it put me off. So I came on here with the idea of burgling a window and investigating for myself. Where is room 26, by the way?"

"We don't know, but we'll soon find out. Do you know anything about this school?"

"Not a thing; never been inside the place before."

"For the moment, my lad," Captain Ashcroft said weightily, "we'll suspend judgment on this story of yours. You'd better come with us while we look for the room; at least it'll keep you out of trouble, and you'll hear no voices from behind anything if *we're* present. Ready, Dr. Fell? Ready, everybody?"

For the next fifteen minutes—Yancey going ahead with Captain Ashcroft and Dr. Fell, the other two remaining behind—they explored every cranny of the main floor. The captain's big flashlight directed operations; Yancey, still on a wire of nerves, kept striking match after match.

They found a smallish but gaudy auditorium, taking up the same area here as must be occupied by the gymnasium below. They opened the door of classroom after classroom. From buff-colored walls looked down the same photographs of whiskered nineteenth-century authors ("Powerful lot of Yankees, ain't there?" observed Captain Ashcroft) that might have been found in any school of its vintage throughout the land. But they had marked down no more than twelve numbered classrooms when, in a tumbling rain of echoes, they tramped up another broad staircase to the floor above.

Another intensive search yielded no result. There was a study-hall of sturdy tables and chairs. There was a chemistry lecture-room with tiered seats, a chemistry lab stripped of equipment, and a 'commercial course' room whose typewriters sported blank keys. The pictures in a dozen more classrooms were topographical but still familiar: the church at Stratford-upon-Avon, the Roman Colosseum, a view of Venice's Grand Canal.

But of room 26 there was still no sign. With a certain desperation they foregathered in the hall round a drinking-fountain vaguely touched by moonlight. Dr. Fell, towering in shadow, lifted his hand for silence.

"We have counted very carefully," he intoned. "This is the top floor, the only other floor, and there is no number higher than room 24. Unless we have been the victims of a senseless hoax . . ."

"It's not a hoax," Camilla said suddenly. "I think *I* know what it is!"

She had spoken only to Alan, but four heads were turned in her direction.

"When we came in by the basement entrance—it isn't really the basement, Alan says, but you know what I mean—there were quite a few doors in the corridor we didn't look at. Come to think of it, there was a glass-panelled door on either side of the entrance itself. It'd be just like this case, wouldn't it, if the room we're looking for was the very first room we passed without even noticing it?"

"Camilla honey," Yancey exulted, "this is sheer inspiration! By the beard of the Lord God Almighty, you've hit it on the nose first time! Room 26 is in the basement; it's bound to be, with whatever's there for us. Let's go, shall we?"

And instantly he spun round, poised to clatter downstairs.

"Whoa, now!" said Captain Ashcroft. "This hall's as slippery as a dance-floor; you want to fall and break your skull? Go easy, can't you?"

"No, O prophet, definitely no! Ol' Yance can't go easy at anything. I wish I could, but I can't. Besides, if somebody's lurkin' in ambush to spring, I want to nail him before he springs. Let's *go!*"

Away went Yancey, through shadow and broken moonlight. Throughout their own more leisurely descent, measured by the tap of Dr. Fell's stick, they heard the bang of footsteps receding as Yancey ran: down to the main floor without trip or stumble, round the post of the staircase, and thence in echoes down more steps to the cellar.

It was a commonplace enough school, Alan told himself; it breathed ominous suggestion only because of the night or their disturbed state of mind. And yet ominous suggestions were piling up to suffocation. Twenty seconds later, when the four of them reached the foot of the stairs to the cellar, they found an interesting tableau.

On their right, westwards, the transverse corridor stretched in darkness to the side door by which they had entered. Yancey Beale did not seem concerned with that transverse passage. Instead, he had taken half a dozen steps along the central passage which bisected it. Striking a kitchen match by whisking the match across the seat of his trousers, he was holding it up and peering towards the wooden double-doors that led to the gallery of the gymnasium.

First Captain Ashcroft, then Dr. Fell, then Alan and Camilla had instinctively followed him a few steps past the angle of the transverse corridor. For an instant Yancey glanced back at them, the tiny flame shining down the side of his face and into opaque dark eyes. Then his attention returned to the double-doors.

"Yes?" he suddenly called. *"Who is it? Who's there?"*

And he charged straight at the doors, shouldering through and letting them swing shut behind him. If the others could not see him, they could hear him clatter round the gallery in pursuit of God knew whom or what.

"Come back!" yelled Captain Ashcroft, directing a beam of light at unresponsive doors. "Come back, you dope! I've told you before . . ."

"It's all right, isn't it?" cried Camilla. "I mean, he's all right? I'd hate to think—"

"Then don't think it," Captain Ashcroft advised her. "Fellow's as crazy as a bedbug! He's chasin' his imagination, that's all; there's nobody here but us. Once Dr. Fell thought there might 'a' been, but there's not. 'Cept for the five of us, there's not another soul within—"

Then they all stood motionless. For they all heard it.

First it was the tinkle of a banjo, then a breezy tenor voice upraised in song. Muffled as though by some intervening obstruction, yet loud against night quiet, the noise burst out grotesquely from somewhere on this floor.

"Oh, I come from Alabama
With my banjo on my knee;
I'm a-gwine t' Louisiana
My Susannah fo' to see.
Oh, Susannah—!"

Backed by full orchestration, many male voices picked up the chorus and carried the song through three more verses. Then, after seeming to brood for a moment, music and voices soared up in honeyed sentiment.

"The sun shines bright in the old Kentucky home;
'Tis summer, the darkeys are gay . . ."

That was when all four listeners moved. They dodged back from the central corridor into the transverse one. Captain Ashcroft's light swept along it, as did the beam from Alan's small torch.

"She was right!" And Captain Ashcroft indicated Camilla. "It's from one of those two doors down at the end, left or right as you come in. But who's givin' a serenade at this time of night?"

"Serenade, did you say?" wheezed Dr. Fell. "It's too mechanical, surely, to be live voices? And there is a certain scratchiness. I rather think . . ."

Alan and Captain Ashcroft had already plunged down the passage. Alan's light, swinging towards what was now the right-hand door as they approached from this direction, picked up against its ground-glass panel the black numeral 25. Then it swung left to the door opposite, and they had found room 26 at last.

The voices, having finished celebrating their old Kentucky home, now made a great din with "The Bonnie Blue Flag." But the room was dark.

"Steady!" said Captain Ashcroft. "No hurry, now!"

Easing the knob round, he pushed the door far enough inwards to grope for and find a switch on the wall to the left. Light sprang up beyond the glass panel. Dropping the extinguished torch into his pocket, Captain Ashcroft set the door wide open and propped it there with a wedge-shaped piece of wood he found on the floor.

They were looking into a good-sized square room, a conventional classroom except that its only blackboard was a portable one on an easel beside the teacher's desk, like the blackboard at Maynard Hall.

Under a ceiling light not too bright, Alan saw four smallish square windows high up in the west wall. A few feet out from this wall the teacher's desk faced east towards rows of conventional students' desks, somewhat scuffed and time-worn, and an electric clock on the east wall. Set cater-cornered in the south-west angle of the room, at one side of the teacher's desk, was a small and antiquated piano on whose top lay a battered saxophone without case or cover. In the north-west angle of the room, at the opposite side of the teacher's desk, stood an old-fashioned cabinet Victrola of the sort popular when Joel Poinsett High School had been opened. This also showed wear and tear. You wound it up with a crank; its lid was open now; exuberant voices soared into "Dixie."

"Music, eh?" said Captain Ashcroft, looking around him. "They taught music, did they?" He pointed to the Victrola. "And turn that damn thing off!"

Alan did so, stopping the record without lifting the needle from its groove. The old-fashioned record on the turntable was inscribed "Way Down South, A Medley," with other notations he did not stop to read.

Alan looked up. The dim yellow light discouraged curiosity. But Camilla, already at his side, was pointing frantically towards the teacher's desk. And he needed no urging to have his attention caught fast.

On the desk, beside a metronome which obviously belonged in this room, lay something which could never have belonged here. It was a packet of letters, some fifteen or twenty good-quality envelopes fastened together top and sideways in broad pink ribbon tied as though with loving hands.

Alan strode over and took up the packet. The crossways ribbon on the top envelope concealed the name of the person to whom these letters had been sent, and all the address except *Goliath, Conn.* in firm, neat handwriting. The postmark provided little help; it was so blurred that he could make out only *Mass.* The date might have been any month of any fairly recent year.

Again Alan looked up. Dr. Gideon Fell, hat and stick under the same arm, now towered above him with the half-witted look of one who has been hit over the head with a club.

"Magister! These letters!" Alan held them out. "Are *they* what we're supposed to find?"

Dr. Fell took the letters, turning them over in his fingers.

"My dear fellow, I have no doubt of it. They are not (if I may say so) indigenous to the Joel Poinsett High School. They have been most considerately provided."

Captain Ashcroft bustled forward, staring at the packet without attempting to take it.

"That handwriting!—" he said.

"Oh, ah. We know the handwriting," agreed Dr. Fell, "having seen it only too recently. Therefore, with your permission . . ."

"Yes?"

"Therefore," Dr. Fell slipped the letters into his pocket, "we shall not examine the contents just yet. And this for two reasons."

Putting down hat and stick on the teacher's desk, he moved behind it and took up a position like a lecturer, eyeglasses glinting and moustache lifted for impressive speech.

"First," he said, "because the letters are unlikely to contain any information we have not already deduced. Second—"

As though idly he bent forward, took up the metronome, set it in motion, and replaced it on the desk. The thin metal rod began to tick back and forth.

"Second," pursued Dr. Fell, first indicating the four windows above and behind his head and then—as though this were not the real direction he meant—pointing towards the open door of room 26, "second, because we should only suffer an interruption. Someone is approaching the building towards the same entrance we used. Unless it is young Mr. Beale returning from the wrong direction, we are about to have another visitor."

Tick went the metronome, *tick-tick* in measured beats against silence. The big side door to the school-yard, which Captain Ashcroft had left not quite shut, was flung violently open. And into room 26 stalked Valerie Huret.

Shoulders back, still all in white with a white handbag clutched under her arm, she seemed buoyed along by some power outside and beyond herself. Against her pale face the eyes had acquired a blaze of what might have been ungovernable rage or even near-madness.

"Well!" she began through stiff lips. "Well! Camilla's not the only one who heard about that side door, you know."

"Well, ma'am!" retorted Captain Ashcroft, wheeling bull-like to face her. "Should I say this is an unexpected pleasure? You're back from town, are you?"

"I'm back from town. So are the others. The film at the Riviera was over at ten-thirty. Rip Hillboro came on to the Swamp Fox Room and joined Bob and me. Then we drove back."

"Are the others with you, ma'am? Here at the school, I mean?"

"No, they're not. Rip insisted he must watch the late show on television. On Saturday nights it goes on at eleven-fifteen, not eleven-thirty. Bob said, 'You've already seen one film tonight; must you have a damn dreary one to go to bed on?' But Rip insisted. They were both half asleep, so they poured a drink and sat down.—Can you guess why *I'm* here?"

"I expect, ma'am, you understood the blackboard message too."

"Oh, I understood the message; a child would have understood it. That's only what told me where to come; it's not why I'm here. I'm here," Valerie almost screamed, "to denounce somebody and tell the truth at last. There's all the wickedness of hell behind this, and yet you don't see it. You're supposed to be intelligent, especially Dr. Fell. But you're not intelligent; you just don't *see!*"

"See what?" demanded Captain Ashcroft. "If you want to accuse somebody, hadn't you better do it? And who would you want to accuse, anyway? You've stuck pretty close to Mr. Crandall, I've noticed. *We* thought it was because you liked him, maybe liked him a lot. But maybe you had some other reason. Do you accuse Mr. Crandall of murder, now?"

"Accuse Bob Crandall? *Are you crazy?"*

Tick went the metronome, *tick-tick-tick.* The breath whistled through Valerie's nostrils. She had run to the front of the desk. Abandoning all pretense of addressing Captain Ashcroft, she was hurling her words straight at Dr. Fell.

"He's a good man. I've said so before; I say it again now. He's too good for that house and the things *he* won't see either. No, I do not mean Bob Crandall! I mean somebody who's evil and damned as nobody's been really evil and damned since the days of sorcery three hundred years ago. I mean—"

The report of a small-calibre revolver, fired by somebody who had been standing outside one window and bending down, exploded with sharp concussion as a clean hole appeared in the glass.

Valerie was not flung backwards, as she might have been by the impact of a heavier bullet. Instead she lurched sideways and to the right. The handbag flew from under her arm. With ungainly movements for so lithe and graceful a woman, she staggered forwards in a diagonal direction, with both arms outstretched ahead.

Her hands struck the Victrola with its four small casters. She pitched on her face and lay twitching. Against the white dress, a fact not understood until later, blood welled up from a wound in the middle of her back. When the Victrola rolled backwards to thud against the wall, some trigger of mechanism released arrested song. With ghastly earnestness and unction, full-throated if scratchy voices soared to a finale.

"Den I wish I was in Dixie! Hooray! Hooray!
  In Dixie land I'll take my stand
To live and die in Dixie:
Away, away, away down south in Dixie—
Away, away, away down south in Dixie!"

17

Following the tumult that ensued, Alan did not see Maynard Hall again until the night of Sunday, May 16th, nearly twenty-four hours later. But there was news of Valerie Huret long before that.

Valerie had been shot about half-past eleven on Saturday night. Returning to their hotel at well after one in the morning, Alan and Dr. Fell were having a final smoke in the lobby when Dr. Fell had been summoned to the telephone. It was Captain Ashcroft, calling from the big hospital on Calhoun Street not far away. Lending an ear just outside the booth, as Dr. Fell picked up the phone and asked a question, Alan could distinctly hear the captain's voice in reply.

"Dead?" the voice exclaimed, with a kind of bursting incredulity. "No, the lady's anything but dead! As a matter of fact, though they've got her under sedation now, she's not even seriously hurt."

"Sir—!"

"It's a freak wound, the doctor says, not common but not unheard-of either. I don't have to tell you the set-up, do I? You yourself found two revolvers in the cellar at the Hall: a Smith & Wesson target .32 and a .38 police-positive. Remember?"

"Oh, ah. I remember."

"From what they see on TV, people *will* think it's easy to shoot somebody dead. The murderer, a would-be murderer this time, stole the .32 and fired down through the window, aimin' at Mrs. Huret's heart. The bullet hit her a little below the breast-bone. Instead of penetrating very far, it travelled around a rib underneath the skin and came out her back without going through the chest at all. Then our murderer threw the gun down and ran; no fingerprints, but no death either. There'll be some pain, maybe, but she'll be fine and dandy in a very short time."

" 'For this relief much thanks.' Is there any other news?"

"Is there any other *news,* blow me down? So much I can't tell you over the phone!"

"Well?"

"I'm right proud to be in charge of this case, though you're the one who told me where to look. For most of tomorrow, Dr. Fell, I *am* goin' to be in charge; I can't put off the dirty work any longer. By 'dirty work' I don't mean the arrest; that's easy; that's a pleasure; anyway, it comes later. I mean—oh, never mind! So, if it's agreeable to you, I won't need you until early tomorrow evening, a little after dinner-time; I'll send a car for you and say when. Then, if our plans go right . . ."

"*If* our plans go right. Oh, ah!"

"Tomorrow," said Captain Ashcroft, "it's likely to be a long night and maybe a rough one too. So I won't need Mr. Grantham until after I see you; we'll fix that up later. Meanwhile, go about your own business and take it easy; you'll get word in good time. Understand?"

" 'Take it easy,' " said Dr. Fell, "is not quite applicable to the present business. But I understand. *'Varium et mutabile semper femina!'* I understand only too well."

Both he and Alan slept late next morning, having breakfast at midday. The afternoon they spent at what sightseeing could be done on a drowsy Sunday. It seemed a time to explore the churches: gray St. Philip's, wrapped in peace under its tall spire; porticoed St. Michael's, whose bells ring special tunes for special holidays, and in whose garden it is a joy to linger. At the Gibbes

Art Gallery, not far from St. Michael's, Dr. Fell stared long at Benjamin West's portrait of Colonel (later General) William Moultrie.

But no distraction would serve. Both had a tendency to fume and bite their knuckles with impatience. It was not merely that Dr. Fell refused to comment on the Maynard affair; contrary to custom, he refused even to hint, despite his obvious and growing worry.

"What did you mean," Alan burst out once, "by that Latin tag about woman being always fickle and changeable? Which particular woman, and under what circumstances?"

"If only," wheezed Dr. Fell, "she had stuck to one man at a time! It would have been much simpler, don't you think?"

They had a very early dinner to make up for the lack of lunch. At just past seven o'clock a police car driven by Sergeant Duckworth arrived at the hotel for Dr. Fell, leaving Alan to await his own summons.

In his own room at the hotel, with the paperback book of puzzles he had bought at a drug-store across the street, he did not even open the book. That the case was headed towards some kind of smash he did not doubt, but he could get no further. Darkness descended on Charleston; a plain of lights blossomed south to the Battery; endlessly Alan reviewed the events of last night, after Valerie Huret had pitched forward with blood staining her white dress.

By instinct they had rushed outside, finding under the third of four windows in the west wall a discarded revolver with one spent shell in the magazine. They were phoning for an ambulance from the office upstairs when Yancey Beale, explaining that he had chased some purely imaginary intruder all over the gymnasium, returned cursing and apologetic. As a last try for evidence they had hurried to Maynard Hall, where Rip Hillboro and Bob Crandall—the late show just concluded—sat spiritless before the television set and had nothing whatever to contribute.

Still Alan pondered.

"Varium et mutabile semper femina." That was Virgil, wasn't it? Since both Dr. Fell and Captain Ashcroft swore no woman was guilty, it would be poetic irony if the murderer should prove to be a woman after all. Could Dr. Fell be holding back something for a tactical ambush to stagger slower wits? What if the murderer were Valerie Huret herself, and the apparent attempt on her life only error or a part of misdirection?

No!

Mentally, even physically, Alan shook himself. He was thinking along the lines of a detective story, of the least likely person, and it would never do. Instead, a pleasanter field for speculation, he began thinking of Camilla. He could not have told how long he had been sitting there, his mind wandering down all sorts of byways with Camilla at the end of each, when the phone rang to rouse him.

"Yes, it's me," said Camilla's voice. "Yes, I'm at the Hall. Alan, what's happening here?"

"You ring me at the hotel to ask what's happening *there?"*

"Well, something did!"

"After Dr. Fell got there, you mean?"

"No, before Dr. Fell got here. In the afternoon, when it wasn't even dark!"

"Camilla, what are you talking about?"

"Lots of hush-hush comings and goings by the police," Camilla said mysteriously. "Fee! Fi! Fo! Fum! And—you remember late Friday night, when Valerie almost screamed the house down?"

"Well?"

"It wasn't Valerie today. I was reading Joyce in the library this afternoon when a woman's voice upstairs cut loose with one absolutely blood-curdling screech that nearly sent me through the roof. Just one scream; then silence and a kind of cover-up."

"Who screamed?"

"I can't find out; nobody seems to know; it was one of the maids, I think. Ever since Friday night poor George, the butler, has been having a dreadful time preventing the maids and the cook from leaving in a body. Outwardly you can't rattle George at all, though inwardly I think he's as disturbed as the others. He can hide it, that's all. *I* didn't scream, and I don't think Madge did. So I vote for Sylvia or Judith or Minnie Mae; who else is there?"

"What about Madge, by the way? How is she?"

"She's not incommunicado any longer. She's up and dressed and about, after a fashion; but very shaky and not speaking much to anybody, for which I don't blame her. Once Captain Ashcroft passed her on the stairs and muttered something. Madge just said, 'Not *again,* you silly boy?' and paid no more attention to him. That's not all, either. Are you listening, Alan?"

"Yes?"

"After the inquest tomorrow afternoon, Captain Ashcroft says, we're all free to leave here and go home. You wouldn't think that would make people *more* jumpy than they already were, but it has. Dr. Fell—" Camilla herself jumped and hesitated. "Just a moment! Here *is* Dr. Fell, wig-wagging at me. He wants to speak to you."

"My dear fellow," Dr. Fell's voice interjected, "do you know what time it is?"

"Getting on for nine, I should think; does it matter?"

"Not particularly, though in fact it is a quarter to nine. If you would care to drive out here now, your presence would be most welcome."

"Yes, Alan," cried Camilla, "do come as soon as you can!"

The phone clicked; the line went dead. Hurrying downstairs to get his car from the auto lobby, Alan found that the night, though fine, had turned unseasonably cool and even chilly. On the way to James Island he met certain thick remnants of Sunday traffic; it was a little later than half-past nine when he drove into the grounds of Maynard Hall.

In the dark lane outside the gate, another car was parked with somebody in it. Paying no attention, Alan went on. Under the portico he encountered a subdued, formally dressed Dr. Mark Sheldon just leaving the house.

" 'Ships that pass in the night,' " said the young doctor, " 'and speak each other in passing.' Whenever you and I meet, sir, I seem always to be dashing away somewhere else."

"Yes, it does look like that. Tonight—"

"Tonight," pursued the other, pointing towards the gate, "my wife is out in the car there. Annette wouldn't go in with me; she said it wasn't right or proper. I felt one *had* to pay one's respects. And yet wherever I turned, in whichever direction I went, there was your friend Dr. Fell standing in front of me.

"Now please understand, Mr. Grantham: I say nothing against Gideon Fell. He's a jovial soul, and has a reputation for being much more acute than he looks. But is he always—frankly, now, is he always quite right in the head?"

"I've usually found him sane enough. Why do you ask?"

"He had a pair of field-glasses," Mark Sheldon replied earnestly, "he told me he'd got from a lumber-room in the attic. He wasn't *using* the glasses, you understand; we were indoors. He held up the glasses without looking through them; he looked at me instead, and said something like, 'With the top part cleared away, there's a wooden crotch that would do for a resting-place.' "

"Well, Dr. Sheldon?"

"Really, now! I wondered if 'resting-place' might be some obscure reference to the funeral on Tuesday, and I asked him. All he said was, 'The windows may be raised or lowered without noise. Please observe, sir, that the windows may be raised or lowered without noise!' Possibly I'm too much of a materialist, but when somebody's mind wanders it makes me uncomfortable. Or *could* it have had a meaning?"

"It had a meaning, though I can't pretend to guess what. Where's the maestro now?"

"In the lounge where they keep the television set and the backgammon-board. He's questioning Rip Hillboro. And now I must go. Let's see!" Mark Sheldon cast up his eyes. "Inquest tomorrow, funeral on Tuesday. Unless you'll be with us for the funeral on Tuesday, Mr. Grantham, there are reasons why I may not see you again. Good night, good night, good night!"

Away bustled the doctor. Alan crossed the porch and opened the screen door, but did not check his stride as he moved towards the lounge at the rear of the hall.

Madge Maynard, a figure of tragedy, stood just inside the door of the dining-room on the right. She wore unrelieved black, in contrast to white skin and golden hair. He would not have intruded on her even if she had seen him, but she did not see him. Madge stood motionless with her head back, fists clenched and eyes tightly closed; she might have been praying.

Alan passed her as he might have passed some image from a dream. In the lounge, all of whose glass doors to the garden were closed against cool night air, Rip Hillboro stood facing Dr. Fell.

"Look, Gargantua," demanded the former, "why do you keep bugging me?"

"Mr. Hillboro," Dr. Fell said gently, "is that your impression of what I am doing? Be more charitable! I have been obliged to corner you in this way, believe me, only because for some time I was unable to find you. Nobody could find you, or seemed to know where you were."

Rip lifted one shoulder.

"Most of the time after dinner," he retorted, "I was packing. They're releasing us tomorrow, as you may have heard, and I've got to get home. I was given a week's leave of absence; I've taken two weeks. The boss-man in my firm—old Jeff Channing, of Channing, Lowell & Bosworth—will have my ears on toast if I'm not back in Hartford within twenty-four hours. So I was in my room, packing . . ."

"May I point out," said Dr. Fell, "that you were not in your room half an hour ago? I visited every bedroom in this house; you were in none of them."

Rip strode to the table on which lay the packs of cards and the backgammon-box. Opening the backgammon-box, he took out its dice and rattled them in his hand without throwing them.

"After I'd finished packing, I went for a walk. Anything wrong with that?"

"No, of course not. It was only that . . ."

"Look, Gargantua! I know what you want: you want to hammer me about last night. But I've told you and the Prophet Daniel everything there is to tell. Between eleven-fifteen and a quarter of one—a ninety-minute show—I was with Bob Crandall watching a gangster picture on the idiot-lantern there."

Rip pointed.

"Maybe I'd had too much film already. At some time after it started I dozed off, and didn't wake up until there was a burst of gunfire near the end. Bob had been dozing too; *he* woke up too. During that time I hadn't stirred; I don't think he had either. Then the rest of you came charging in with your news about Valerie. But that's all! That is absolutely—"

"I am not concerned," Dr. Fell assured him, "with the events of last night. But there are several questions, all of them important ones. Will you cooperate?"

Rip flung the dice across the table, turning up a one and a two.

"Not so good for me, Gargantua, if this had been a crap-game. Never mind; I'll cooperate. Fire away."

"Mr. Hillboro, how long have you known the Maynards?"

Rip stared at him. "*That's* important?"

"It is most vitally important, on my word! I could not ask you before; until last night I lacked evidence to support a thesis. How long have you known the Maynards?"

"Well, let me see. They moved from New York to Goliath in '56, I think it was. I met Madge in '59, during my last year in law school. Yes, '59! That'd make six years, more or less. So what?"

"Was there any occasion, to your knowledge, on which Henry Maynard was absent from home for several months?"

"Yes!"

Clearly Rip's interest had been caught, though he might not be able to say why it had been caught.

"Yes!" he repeated. "Soon after they moved to Goliath, I've heard, the Chancellor of Colt University asked Pa Maynard to teach a course on advanced mathematics; lecture on mathematics, that is. He refused. He enjoyed lecturing, as you've heard Madge say. And Colt's quite a place; it's very heavily endowed. But it lacks the centuries of tradition that appealed to the old man. So he refused. Still curious, Gargantua?"

"Very much so; continue!"

"At some time in '60," pursued Rip, "the same offer was made by Cotton Mather College at Polchester, Massachusetts. Cotton Mather's a small institution and very Congregationalist, but it's crusted with tradition and almost as old as Harvard. Pa Maynard accepted for the academic year '61–'62. At Goliath he installed a housekeeper to look after Madge—she's not much of a home-maker, you know—and went off to Polchester rejoicing. But he stayed only one semester, the fall term of '61. Then he was back again, saying young people were mostly dumb-bells and rejoicing more than when he'd gone away." Here Rip rose to a point of order. "Now look, Gargantua! I don't know what this is all about or in aid of. But you might give me a hint. And what else do you want to know?"

"Nothing else, Mr. Hillboro. That is all."

"All?" Rip blurted, and looked at him in a dazed way. "Did you say all?"

"I did."

"Then would you mind releasing me now? I've got several matters to attend to. I want to see Madge, for one thing; I *must* see Madge, now that she's out from under wraps. Sorry I could give you so little help."

"So little help?" scoffed Dr. Fell, lifting his stick high. "You have given the most dazzling help; you have added the last brick to the edifice. You have given so much help, in fact, that I will reward you with no mere hint but a valuable tip. You leave Charleston tomorrow?"

"Yes, in the afternoon. There's a flight via Washington that will get me home by early evening. Were you saying something about a tip?"

Throughout this exchange Alan had been standing in the doorway of the lounge, apparently unnoticed either by Rip or by Dr. Fell. Over his shoulder, when he moved farther into the room, he thought he detected a movement as of someone listening in the hall behind him. But he paid no attention; Dr. Fell was off again.

"Something about a tip? Oh, ah! Tomorrow morning—" began Dr. Fell, breaking off to make a hideous face of warning and caution, finger on lip. "Sh-h!" he said.

"What's the matter with you, Gargantua? Why all this business of 'sh-h'?"

"Tomorrow morning," Dr. Fell said in a stage whisper, "Captain Ashcroft will have a warrant to search the belongings of every person in this house. He will search another house too, though that hardly concerns us here. The warrant, let me repeat, will be used early tomorrow. If there is anything you don't want found in your possession—I refer to no guilty secret, of course, but to anything at all—be sure you get rid of it before then. Do we understand each other?"

"Look, what is there to understand?" Rip asked with a certain hauteur. "*I've* got nothing to hide, you know. They can search my room or my luggage or my person; good luck, and be damned to 'em. Still, thanks for the tip. You mean well, I suppose, though you're a little heavy-handed in your methods. So long for now; see you later."

And he strode out into the hall. Dr. Fell, wheezing and puffing, addressed Alan like a man winding himself up for an effort.

"Come in," he said heartily, "by all means come in! I am no very successful conspirator, I fear, having neither the face nor the figure for such a role. But I do the best I can. Our young friend Sheldon already doubts my sanity, and I should not wish to carry the thing too far."

Alan looked at him.

"You bothered Mark Sheldon by your antics with a pair of field-glasses. And you've already carried it too far. Magister, what *about* those field-glasses?"

"The glasses," replied Dr. Fell, "were the same ones I was handed on Friday afternoon to inspect Fort Sumter from a distance. I retrieved them from the attic on my arrival this evening. It was dark when I arrived, of course; putting the glasses to their proper use at first seemed something of a problem." Excitement shook him like strong drink. "However, with the aid of Captain Ashcroft's electric torch, we were able to see . . ."

"To see what?"

"To see the place where the foliage had been cut away. It was the first and most obvious move, you'll agree?"

"Hardly obvious, no. I can't agree until you make yourself a little more clear."

"But I *am* making myself clear! Hang it all! For your further enlightenment, I might add that in the attic I also found an instrument neither of us had observed before. It was a pair of scales—"

"Scales?"

"Medium-weight scales," Dr. Fell said earnestly, "of the sort we often see on the counter in an English bank. Bankers use it, no doubt, for weighing silver and coppers. Why Henry Maynard originally procured the scales, or what he wanted with it, I don't presume to conjecture. But it was of inestimable value to somebody else in weighing the weapon of the murder. Surely that much at least is plain, I hope? Or . . . no," and with a wild gesture Dr. Fell clutched at his hair, "perhaps it is *not* plain in all respects?"

"No, definitely it's not. Now look here, Magister!" Alan burst out. "When the time comes to put the cards face up on the table, you'll explain in short words which can't be misunderstood. Has that time almost come?"

"It has."

"Meanwhile, the facts that are so radiantly clear in your own mind will have less radiance in the minds of others. Better say nothing at all than talk what sounds like gibberish. I can't think why *I* was summoned here," Alan exclaimed, "or what help I can be at the finale—"

"Well! A disinterested witness . . ."

"*Am* I a disinterested witness, Dr. Fell? I'm concerned with Camilla Bruce; with nobody else. How deeply I'm concerned with her may not be of any importance, but it's a fact. Where is she now, by the way?"

"For the moment, she seems to have disappeared. Tut!" added Dr. Fell, extending his hand consolingly. "She has not disappeared in the detective-story sense, which would mean that she walks in danger or is otherwise menaced by some villain-in-ambush. Nothing of the kind! To speak with strict accuracy, a while ago she went out into the garden there. Presumably she is waiting for you; she exhibited a certain concern of her own; you had better follow her without delay. In the detective-story sense—"

"Speaking of the detective-story sense . . ."

"Yes?"

"This evening, Dr. Fell, I floundered through a lot of that when I was at the hotel trying to thrash out a workable answer to all the problems. On Friday, I seem to remember, you said no woman was concerned in this business. Was that true? I kept wondering, you see, whether a woman might not be behind the whole thing."

"You wondered quite correctly. A woman *is* behind the whole thing."

"But you said—!"

"I said," interrupted Dr. Fell, rearing up, "that no woman committed this murder, or has any guilty knowledge of it. By that affirmation I most firmly hold, though it must be amplified a little if we are to bring any sense into confusion. One woman, however innocently, inspired the whole murderous dance. Still another woman, though without guilty knowledge, almost upset the apple-cart by guessing too close to the truth."

"Almost upset the apple-cart by guessing too close to the truth? Can the one who guessed too much be Camilla Bruce?"

Standing with his right elbow against one of the glass doors to rear terrace and garden, Alan jumped and whirled round as the door opened behind him. In the aperture stood Camilla herself.

"What's this about me?" she cried. "I couldn't hear what you were saying, and I couldn't lip-read very well. But I caught my name, anyway. Were you saying *I* might be the murderer after all?"

18*

The grandfather clock in the hall had begun to strike ten. Only one light was burning here in the lounge, a floor-lamp at the far end of the room. Alan saw all things as through heightened senses: the dusky glow shining on walls of whitewashed brick, on the red coats of huntsmen in the sporting prints that adorned the walls, on Camilla's face as she seemed to materialize there.

Camilla hesitated in the doorway, her right hand on the catch and her left elbow against her side. She wore blue. Her fair complexion glimmered against darkness outside; lamplight touched the rich brown hair; she hardly seemed to breathe.

"Were you thinking," she blurted at Alan, "that I might be the murderer after all?"

"No, of course not! We weren't even thinking anything of the sort, and in your heart you know it!"

"I know it?"

"You must know it. Some rather odd ideas have cropped up in this affair, but no idea so far has been completely crazy, and suspecting you would be a dozen steps past the point of sheer lunacy."

"Well," Camilla said, "it's nice to know where I stand in the investigation, at least. I asked because—because everybody else is being suspected of something or other; so I wondered. What were you thinking, then?"

"At the moment you showed up," returned Alan, "I was about to go out and find you. We didn't walk in the grounds on Friday night; Valerie prevented us; somebody's always preventing us. Shall we try a stroll now?"

Camilla raised her eyes.

"As a matter of fact," she said, "I came in to suggest the same thing. It's not cold out there; it's just pleasantly cool. And tonight, for some reason, there don't seem to be any mosquitoes. Since there *is* so much to talk about . . ."

"I must remember you seconded the invitation. Come along."

"One moment!" interposed Dr. Fell.

His expression, so far as it could be read at all, seemed neither half-witted nor inspired. It was heavy and lowering, with something of sadness. Camilla caught her breath.

"Yes, Dr. Fell? You have some instructions?"

"Captain Ashcroft (harrumph!) has predicted a long night and perhaps a rough one. I do not necessarily agree with the latter adjective. But I *have* some instructions."

"Yes?"

"It is now ten o'clock. You both wear wrist-watches, I see. Can you manage to amuse yourselves, say for another hour and a half?"

"For much longer than that," Alan assured him, "if they don't keep interrupting us. You see—"

"Longer than that," said Dr. Fell, "will be unnecessary. Stick to the grounds; don't stray too far away. At half-past eleven you will please . . ."

"Return here?"

"No, not here. Under no circumstances," the big voice boomed, "will you return to the house then. At half-past eleven—you may even make it a little later—betake yourselves to the Joel Poinsett High School. Enter by the side door, as we did last night; it will be left easy to open. Go to room 26, sit down, and await results."

"I see," said Alan, who didn't see. "You're setting up a party, are you?"

" 'Party,' " Dr. Fell declared, "is a word most monstrously ill chosen. But it will have to serve our purpose. For the moment I must return to my own concerns, calling your attention only to the faithful servant named George. George is devoted to the Maynards, as you have heard; also, for reasons of his own, he is extraordinarily devoted to Yancey Beale. Now into the garden with you! *A bientôt!*"

And he shooed them out through the glass door, which Alan closed.

Fitful moonlight, draining the flowers of color and accentuating every shadow, turned the garden to a world of unreality. Faint white mist rose no higher than eighteen inches from the ground. They waded in vapor as they found the path and moved west along it. They were as alone, Alan thought, as though nobody else existed; Camilla's shoulder touched his left arm. At the sundial they both halted by mutual instinct, and stood there with the mist drifting past their knees.

"Alan," Camilla said suddenly, "we're getting near the end of the problem, aren't we?"

"I think so."

"Then will you please, *please* tell me what you and Dr. Fell were thinking when I intruded?"

"I don't know what Dr. Fell thinks. As for what I think, it would be a good deal easier to tell you if you returned the compliment."

"Returned the compliment?"

"Yes. You've had several different inspirations in this business, haven't you? They've got to be different inspirations, Camilla; if they're parts of the same inspiration, it makes no sense at all."

"Alan, I don't understand what you're talking about!"

"Listen, my dear. Two nights ago, when we eavesdropped on Dr. Fell and Captain Ashcroft, you had your inspiration about somebody's 'incredible jealousy' of somebody else. I needn't expound that; we've reverted to it several times; you still say it's wild and beyond belief. But one thing at least you can tell me. When the incredible-jealousy motif occurred to you, didn't you regard it as a clue to the murderer? Didn't you?"

"Well—yes."

"All right. Yesterday afternoon, after we returned from Fort Moultrie and you had rather a hectic interview with Madge, you became convinced Madge's mysterious boy-friend could be nobody but Dr. Mark Sheldon. Are you still certain of that?"

"It's the only reasonable assumption. Honestly, Alan—!"

"Let's not stand by the sundial all night," said Alan, though in fact they had been there barely thirty seconds. "This way, with your permission; we'll see if a little walking won't stimulate the wits."

They wandered on down the path, with cypresses and weeping willows looming up black against the sky.

"We've been assuming," Alan continued, "that this unknown boy-friend is also the murderer. We don't *know* that; we've assumed it mainly because a joker who writes messages on blackboards has pretty well convinced us. Well, where does the thesis lead?

"Whoever the boy-friend and murderer may be, it's hard to see why he should have killed Henry Maynard. And if Mark Sheldon's the murderer (which I can't believe, but never mind), that fact alone makes nonsense of the incredible-jealousy motif. In any set-up that concerned Madge and Mark Sheldon, nobody's jealous except Mrs. Mark Sheldon, unless you want to argue Madge herself was the jealous one. If Madge had been jealous enough to kill, wouldn't she have killed Mrs. Sheldon? Would she have gone berserk and knocked off her father just because he objected or might have objected?"

"Oh, Alan, that's ridiculous!"

"Of course it is, as I've been trying to point out. Weren't there two inspirations?"

"Two inspirations?"

Still wading almost knee-deep in mist, still hurling words sideways at each other, they had gone through the arch in the tall evergreen hedge. Beyond, under still more mist, a beaten-earth path led towards the slave-cabins.

"On Friday night," Alan went on, "it occurred to you that a certain person—never mind who—just *might* be Madge's boyfriend and the murderer too. You couldn't believe this; you still can't, though the idea keeps nagging you. Then, yesterday afternoon, circumstances piled up to make you think Dr. Sheldon, whether or not he killed anybody, must be Madge's lover in the real, dangerous physical sense. But it wasn't Mark Sheldon you'd been thinking of the night before. They were two different ideas, weren't they?"

"Did I ever *say,"* Camilla cried out, "they weren't two different ideas?"

"You haven't actually said anything; maybe it's all too tangled. But if only you and I understood each other . . . !"

"And you think we *don't* understand each other?"

"Well, do we? In about a million assorted subjects, where has been the common ground? You name it; we've argued it. Politics, science, art, letters . . ."

They had reached the cleared space between the rows of slave-cabins. In clear silver a dwindling moon emerged from behind cloud. Camilla stopped and turned.

"I know that," she told him. "On the phone this evening I could practically hear you freeze when I said I was reading Joyce, who next to Proust is your pet abomination among writers. Apparently," Camilla cried, "apparently there isn't one single point on which we agree or ever could agree!"

" 'Apparently,' did you say? Only apparently?"

"Yes, Alan. I more than hinted at it last night, but you wouldn't listen. You said we ought to have drawn closer together because there hadn't been any kind of argument, literary or artistic or political. I said, 'Oh, *those* things!' as though they didn't matter.

And they don't matter; they don't matter at all! For the joke is . . ."

"The joke is—?"

"I don't like Joyce a bit; I absolutely loathe Proust; I can't bow down before *any* of the sacred cows. I'm as conservative as you are or more so, politically speaking; only I lack your nerve at opposing popular trends and telling the intellectuals to go to hell. Apart from mathematics and science, and I *won't* give in on those, there's nothing you've ever preached with which deep down inside me I haven't thoroughly agreed!"

"If you mean this somewhat staggering judgment, Camilla . . ."

"Oh, I mean it!"

"Then why, for God's sake, have you been so insistent in the opposite direction? Why so tireless at blowing poisoned darts?"

"Partly because I'm a hypocrite, I suppose. And partly because —because you're so very *serious!* (Who else said that to somebody else?) You can't keep your sense of humor about anything that really matters to you, like books or the use of the English language, just as I can't keep mine over mathematics or science. Who could *resist* puncturing you, or chancing the effect of the odd remark?"

"You thought it was funny, did you?"

"Not funny, no. I get mad and say things, but I always wish I hadn't. That's the difference between us. *I've* never really meant one unpleasant word! Whereas *your* continual sneers . . . and how you enjoy sneering . . . !"

She was very close, quite irresistible. Alan did not say, "Liar"; he did not say anything. Gathering her up in a close grip, he kissed her mouth with thoroughness and at some length. Camilla's response, without even a startled interval, was as unrestrained and uninhibited as anything he could have wished for in a dream. And so, under the moon, they clutched each other; and so passed a chaotic interval. Then a small voice stirred.

"Alan . . ."

"Yes?"

"What—what happened to us?"

"Something that ought to have happened long ago. I love you, you hypocritical Puritan! But I never thought you . . ."

"If you think I'm a Puritan," Camilla whispered, "you try me! Just try me, that's all! But *I* never thought *you* . . ."

"Shut up."

"You're not very romantic, are you?"

So he shut her up in the only appropriate way, elaborating the same treatment.

What they subsequently said or did—the discoveries they made, the vows they took, the pledges old though forever new—are matters of no strict relevance here. But it was very important to these two, and must be dealt with kindly. Their moods ranged from the erotic to the hilarious: from blind intensity of emotion through tenderness to the sudden notion that everything on earth, including themselves, was uproariously funny after all. They had misunderstood each other, they decided, but there should be no misunderstanding in the future. Though they might have bickered incessantly, they were now too wise ever to bicker again.

Presently, after an accumulation of minutes that seemed all too short, they found themselves seated side by side, once more entwined, on an upended horse-trough in the nearest slave-cabin. Both, so to speak, reached the surface at the same time.

"I'm awfully rumpled, sort of," said Camilla. "But I want to be still more rumpled, if you see what I mean, when there's the whole night at our disposal and nobody can possibly interrupt us?"

"I see what you mean. I will devote all efforts to that purpose."

"Alan, what time is it?"

When the hurried striking of a match and a quick inspection of watch-dials showed the time as twenty minutes to midnight, Camilla disentangled herself and sprang to her feet.

"We promised Dr. Fell . . . or do you think it's too late?"

"It's not too late. We're back in the real world, that's all."

"Why does he want us at that school, of *all* places on earth for a midnight meeting?"

"We can both guess, my dear. There are certain facts and realities to be looked at without gloss. They won't be pretty, I'm afraid —steady, now!—but we can't retreat to paradise until we've faced 'em."

With this sobering thought they left the hut. They had no need of retracing their steps to the gate by which they had left these grounds the night before. Camilla thought she remembered, and succeeded in finding, another gate in the boundary wall to the south.

Though it brought them out on the road at a point much closer to the Joel Poinsett High School, the landscape through which they moved now seemed less an unreal place than a dead one. Mist breathed higher from the earth: unvexed by any wind, torn to wisps and tatters only at their passing, but with a clammy touch which made Camilla flinch.

Stark black and skim-milk white, windows faintly glimmering, the west side of the school-building rose up like a repository of secrets. R. Gaiddon's junk-yard lay lightless and apparently deserted.

No dog barked; no guardian barred the way with a shotgun; no footsteps sounded but their own. They had almost reached the side door when Camilla seized Alan's arm and pointed.

"It's dark!" she said in a whisper. "The windows of room 26 are as black as pitch. Dr. Fell spoke as though they'd gotten the place ready for what you called a party, but there doesn't seem to be a light there or anywhere else."

"Since when, my anti-Puritan, need a dark room bother *us?* We're to go in, sit down, and await results. He also said, if I remember, the side door would be easy to pry open."

It was unnecessary to pry open the door, which someone's hand pushed wide from within. Yancey Beale, faint light filtering behind him, leaned his left shoulder against the inside of the door and regarded them with a kind of jumpy nonchalance.

"Howdy there!" said Yancey. "If y'all are thinking what I expect you're thinking, forget it! The room's not dark; it's just blacked out."

"Blacked out?"

"Tar paper," Yancey made illustrative gestures, "on a wooden frame fitted to the inside of each window. It's some game craftily aranged by Grand Goblin Dr. Fell or High Priest Caiaphas Ashcroft, but don't ask me what game or what's up. They phoned me at home; they insisted on my presence, so I drove over."

"Who else is here?"

"So far, nobody 'cept me. Come on in; join the Lost Souls' Club!"

The corridor was dark; room 25 across the way also was dark. But the same bleak ceiling light glowed behind the ground-glass panel in the door of room 26. Pushing open the door, Yancey propped the wedge under it and with something of a flourish ushered them in.

"Been cleaned up some since last night," he explained, indicating the blackout on the windows. "Smell of soap and water, eh? No more blood where poor Valerie stopped a bullet. Victrola back in place, lid closed. And there's that damn saxophone still on top of the piano! In my opinion—" He stopped abruptly.

"What *is* your opinion?" asked Alan. "And what's this about a Lost Souls' Club?"

"I think I belong to it; maybe we all do." Yancey began to pace back and forth in front of the teacher's desk. "When I got here, 'bout fifteen minutes ago, I parked my car on the west side of the junk-yard and walked towards the school. I was just abreast of the junk-yard when I saw a woman wanderin' along the road from the direction of Maynard Hall, as uncertainly as though she couldn't make up her mind where to go.

"Then I realized it was Madge, it was my little Madge! Without seein' me—I was in shadow—she turned around like a blind girl and started back in the direction she'd come from. If she needs aid and comfort, thinks I, ol' Yance is the man to give 'em! I'd just opened my mouth to hail her, when who should walk out of the junk-yard but Grand Goblin Dr. Fell, with a very peculiar look about him?

" 'Don't do it,' says he; 'don't interfere; don't add to her distress.' 'It's Madge!' says I. 'Will she be at the midnight conference too?' 'She will not,' says Dr. Fell; 'need *we* add to her distress either?' He told me to get along to the school, and back he went to the junk-yard without another word. What he was doing there I can't tell you, or what he meant either."

Yancey paused.

Already there had been a faint noise as the side door opened and closed on its air-cushion. Into room 26 lumbered Dr. Fell, hatless, carrying his stick in one hand and a leather brief-case in the other. He closed the door to the corridor. Depositing stick and brief-case on the teacher's desk, he moved behind the desk and faced his companions with a long, rumbling sniff.

"Forgive this cloak-and-dagger secrecy," he began. "We are here, madam and gentlemen, at the request of Captain Ashcroft."

"Old Nimrod himself?" said Yancey. "Where *is* the mighty hunter before the Lord?"

"He has been detained elsewhere on urgent business relating to this case. Since Captain Ashcroft says he has no wish to do the talking, a reluctance not hitherto observable in him, he has deputized me to put before you certain facts which must be understood before we can understand anything else. I myself have little relish for the prospect. It will make bitter hearing, and may explode some fireworks before we have finished. But it is necessary; we have no choice. If you will make yourselves as comfortable as possible under the circumstances . . ."

Camilla, Yancey, and Alan sat down at three students' desks in the front row, having some difficulty adjusting their legs underneath. Dr. Fell remained standing, a prey to disquiet. From his pocket he took a meerschaum pipe already filled. But he did not light the pipe; he pointed its stem at Alan.

"If for a moment I may (harrumph!) pursue the Socratic method, what are the most suggestive features in this affair?"

"Who killed Henry Maynard, and tried to kill Valerie Huret? What's the explanation of the impossible murder?"

"Tut!" Dr. Fell said with a touch of impatience. "I did not ask for the most puzzling features; I asked for the most suggestive. How and with whom did it all begin? Whose emotions touched off a chain reaction which ended in violent explosion? Whose character must we examine first of all?"

"You mean the murderer's?"

"I mean the victim's."

"Are you saying," cried Camilla, "*everything* began with Mr. Maynard?"

"Of course it did. However far we look back, we see Henry Maynard at the end of the vista. Let him walk across the screen of your minds as vividly as he walked in life. But the outward physical characteristics—spare, straight-backed figure always carefully dressed, silver hair, rather frosty blue eyes—are less revealing than the mental or emotional. He was a man of imagination and intelligence. He was a man of strong feelings usually repressed, though they could and did break out. Despite the compelling charm he could use when he needed it, he was moody and unpredictable. For at least a month, probably much longer, something had been haunting and hag-riding him. What was it?

"Outwardly, at least, he would seem to have had few troubles. Already well-to-do in his own right, he had inherited the fortune and estate of his elder brother. He had made a success even of his hobby; academic circles held him in high esteem. Wealth, health, and admiration he had in plenty. Shall a man ask for more than these?

"Yet he remained the reverse of happy; the haunting grew worse. Since his arrival at Maynard Hall, in fact, he had done little but work on paper at endless 'calculations' he never discussed or referred to. Is there any indication of what these calculations may have been? Well! Presumably because his daughter objected to too cloistered a life, he invited certain guests to a house-party which was to begin on Monday, May 3rd, and these guests included the two known suitors for Madge Maynard's hand. Let us note, in passing, that he once asked Madge the height and weight of both Ripton Hillboro and Yancey Beale."

Dr. Fell paused. It was Camilla who answered, in an excitement that almost brought her to her feet.

"Yes!" Camilla said. "I wasn't here when he asked it; it was before any of us arrived. Madge first told me in confidence, and then blurted it out in the library on Friday afternoon; I'm sure it's true. But how does that *help?* Whatever tormented Mr. Maynard, wasn't it something to do with Madge herself?"

"Bull's-eye!" said Dr. Fell, whacking his knuckles on the desk. "His torment—you have used the right word—originated there. So much we have agreed all along; so much has never been denied. You, Mr. Beale, have described in some detail the famous incident under the magnolias on the night of Sunday, May 2nd. You remember?"

"I remember," agreed Yancey.

"Madge had been speaking to some unknown man, who broke away just before you walked in. Down from the attic came Henry Maynard, again in torment, and added confusion to a scene already confused. He was provoked to rather a curious outburst when Madge, in an outburst of her own, ended with, 'Sometimes I think it's not worth . . .' What did she mean by that? How did it relate to the torment of Henry Maynard?"

"My dear Grand Goblin," Yancey raved, "I've already said I don't know, and asked you the same question. God's britches, what *is* all this? We're tryin' to find out what ailed the old man, but there's no evidence at all!"

"Oh, yes, there is," said Dr. Fell.

Putting down the pipe, he unfastened the metal catch of the brief-case on the desk, opened it, and reached inside. But he did not take out any of the papers it evidently contained. Instead, picking up the meerschaum pipe, he again pointed the stem at Alan Grantham.

"Come!" he said. "On our way to Davy's Restaurant on Friday

evening, if you remember, I asked if you had any suggestion to explain Maynard's sometimes astonishing behavior. You hazarded the solution, not uncommon in Victorian novels, that Henry Maynard might not be the real Hanry Maynard, but only an impostor. Though compelled to deny this as erroneous, I replied that it led directly to another thought. And this thought, surely, does much to explain his attitude towards his daughter."

"Another thought, did you say?" cried Camilla. This time she did jump up, like an excited pupil in class. "What thought, Dr. Fell? And how in heaven's name could it affect his attitude towards his daughter?"

Dr. Fell pointed the pipe-stem.

"Because Madge is not his daughter," he said. "Henry Maynard never had a daughter, Miss Bruce; she is no more kin to him than you are. She has every right to the name of Madge Maynard, though it is not the name she was born with.

"For now I must tell you (*fiat justitia, ruat coelum!*) that eleven years ago the pretended father, then living in New York, fell violently in love with a sixteen-year-old girl he met at St. Dorothy's Orphanage in Queens. Madge McCall, herself an imaginative orphan, was of invaluable help at teaching younger children their lessons. But she yearned for wider horizons, as she always has. He adopted her formally; for a year he sent her to the best school in Switzerland, after which seventeen-year-old Madge accepted love on his own terms. She has been his mistress ever since, a relationship so discreetly maintained that nobody ever suspected. His passion, far from diminishing, only increased with the years. The girl herself (genuinely good-hearted, genuinely well-meaning, merely amoral) was quite reasonably happy. She might have remained happy if tragedy had not overtaken them, wrecking his life as it may well wreck hers, when nature had its way and her eye strayed towards someone else."

19

Startled silence held the room and lay like a spell on wits. The dim light in the ceiling shone down on a stilled metronome, on a walking-stick, and on an open brief-case in front of Dr. Fell. Bumblingly Dr. Fell dropped the pipe into his pocket. Once more he reached for the brief-case, but took nothing from it.

"If you would have documentary evidence—" he began again. "However, since Madge herself has owned the truth of all this . . ."

Grotesquely bent forward, Dr. Fell blinked at Alan. He blinked at Camilla, again seated with her hands tightly clasped together. Then, after a look at Yancey Beale, he straightened up and was galvanized.

"Mr. Beale! I regret subjecting you to this bluntness. But it was necessary; you of all people had to know! Better hear it from me, perhaps, than to hear it under circumstances still more brutal."

"It's all right, Grand Goblin," said Yancey. "It's all right."

He spoke in so easy and level a voice that momentarily Alan wondered. Yancey's head was turned away. Suddenly unfolding his long legs, he rose with a jack-knife kind of motion and stalked to the left of the teacher's desk, past the portable blackboard on its easel, towards the battered little piano in the corner. There he seemed to be examining the saxophone on top of the piano. Then, face completely smoothed out except for a vertical wrinkle between the eyebrows, he turned back towards Dr. Fell.

"It's all right, Grand Goblin!" he repeated. "I hear what you say; I understand what you say. Doesn't seem to mean too much, that's all. I'm still in shock, I guess. Anyway," he burst out, "what difference does it make what *I* think?" He looked over at Alan. "You, old son. This business about Madge: did you suspect it?"

"No, not for a minute! But I can see now why Captain Ashcroft called it big trouble."

"What about you, Camilla? *You* guess, honey?"

Camilla stared at her interlaced fingers.

"No, I did not, though I should have. We all noticed something peculiar, and we were *so* wrong! What we kept regarding as his 'over-protectiveness' towards Madge was only . . . oh, never mind!"

"That's what I say too, honey: never mind. I'm tryin' to get this straight. There's no pain at all—not yet, anyway—so I just want to *know*. Can't you loosen up and tell us, Grand Goblin? What made you think of this, for God's sake? What put you on to it?"

Dr. Fell pondered in ruminating and cross-eyed fashion.

"At the beginning," he replied, "it can be called little more than atmospheres, suggestions, innuendoes: what Miss Bruce has described as something peculiar. A hint of this peculiarity cloudily presented itself when I first met the two of them at Goliath during my winter lecture-tour. When he summoned me from New York, and talked to me in his study on Friday afternoon, the accents of peculiarity could be heard like a trumpet-blast. Whether he spoke of her or she spoke of him—either to me or to others in conversations reported to me—it was a father-and-daughter relationship more strange than any I had ever encountered.

"No subject could be mentioned without each instantly springing to the forefront of the other's mind. It was too much; it was obsessive. They did not sound like father and daughter; they sounded like clandestine lovers with constant cause for bickering. Betraying speeches, it is true, did not occur so frequently as to attract general notice. Their intimacy was of a full decade's duration; both could play their parts fairly well."

"Yes," cried Camilla, "but that's what I can't get over!"

"If it shocks you, Miss Bruce . . ."

"It doesn't shock me, exactly, though I can't say I like it. All that difference between their ages! Such things happen, we know; for a long time, I suppose, Madge must have been so grateful to him she really thought she loved him. But—ten years together! How could they have hoped to get away with it?"

"The answer," replied Dr. Fell, "is that they did get away with it. Be discreet, madam and gentlemen; be discreet, I counsel you, and the most censorious neighbor will accept you for what you seem. With your permission, however," and Dr. Fell reared up, "we will return to facts that can be established or proved.

"In the study on Friday Henry Maynard unhesitatingly reeled off facts and figures. Madge, he said, had been born in Paris in 1938 and baptized at the American Church in the Avenue George V. He had grown used to reeling off those 'facts,' I suspect; he never feared a challenge. When a certain girl is generally known as somebody's daughter, and in public at least behaves like one, who will have cause to question it or carry the matter further with investigation?

"Despite the doubts in my mind, I myself might not have investigated but for the single circumstance that betrayed him. As I was leaving to go downstairs he handed me the diary kept by a young lady in 1867, dealing with the death of Commodore Maynard on the beach. Forget that diary, for the moment; it merely sent me haring in the wrong direction about murder-methods. But our good host had told me something else.

"On my way out of the house, to watch some spirited baseball antics in the drive, I looked into the library. Over the fireplace, as I had been told, hangs a portrait of the late Mrs. Henry Maynard, born Catherine Wilkinson of Atlanta. One glance at the portrait inspired thoughts which were still boiling in these dim wits when a group of us returned to the house, discovered that a tomahawk was missing from the weapons-room, and then adjourned to the library for meditation.

"Well, I meditated; by thunder, I did! Standing beneath that portrait and with my back to it, I pursued an elusive memory. Now, Henry Maynard had blue eyes. Probably you noted the blue eyes of the woman in the portrait. You can hardly have failed to observe that Madge Maynard, their presumed daughter, has eyes of a vivid and luminous brown.

"Standing beneath the portrait, then, I tracked down my elusive memory, put a name to it, and said one word. Miss Bruce was playing the piano; no doubt my pronunciation leaves much to be desired; I paid the penalty in misunderstanding. I was believed—"

"Yes?" demanded Alan.

"I was believed to have said, 'Mendelssohn,' though from me any allusion to classical music is as unlikely as a reference to the higher mathematics. It must be pointed out, with the humblest possible apologies, that what I actually said was 'Mendelism.' "

"Mendelism?" exclaimed Yancey, as though fighting for breath. "That seems to mean something to you, Grand Goblin, but I don't get it at all. What's Mendelism?"

"A theory of heredity," answered Dr. Fell, "deriving from experiments in plant and vegetable life made by the Abbé Gregor Mendel of Austria (1822–1884). His followers, applying the same science to human beings, gave us Mendel's law. And Mendel's law, once or twice under attack but never successfully disputed, has established for all time the axiom that blue-eyed parents cannot produce a brown-eyed child. If I somewhat ill-manneredly roared out in triumph, there seemed good reason. This was something that could be proved."

"And was it proved?"

"Yes. On Friday night I took counsel with Captain Ashcroft. A telephone-call to the French police early Saturday morning, followed by their return call with detailed information later in the day, provided confirmation.

"Here," continued Dr. Fell, digging into the brief-case and producing several sheets of typewritten flimsy, which he laid on the desk, "is a copy of the full police report. Maynard's wife really had died in Paris in '39, as he said. But no birth of a child had been recorded at the Hotel de Ville, at the *mairie* of any *arrondissement,* or at the American Church aforementioned. The '*daughter*' was a myth; Q.E.D.

"Passing over the then-still-vexed question of who Madge was and how she had entered his life, let us return to the situation at Maynard Hall towards the beginning of this month, and to a man now half insane from jealousy. She was straying from him; she had found someone else! Should you still doubt the intensity of his feeling for the girl who passed as his daughter," again Dr. Fell dived into the brief-case, "I have here a packet of letters clearly showing his state of mind."

The letters, still bound round with broad pink ribbon, he put down beside the typewritten report.

"Postmarked at Polchester, Massachusetts, dated between September and Christmas of 1961, they were written to Madge in Goliath by an elderly worshipper who had accepted an academic post at which he refused to stay because he had to return to her. I need not embarrass you by reading extracts; they are lyrics of infatuation. He had forgotten that dangerous legal tag, 'The written word remains.' Madge had forgotten it too; she kept the letters. They were found by someone we have been calling the joker, someone who intuitively suspected what was going on between these two bedevilled souls, someone who stole the letters and deliberately left them in this room for the police to find."

"Yes, the joker!" cried Camilla. "Who *is* the joker?"

"May I crave your indulgence for a moment?"

"Well . . ."

"The letters, it is true, were written four years ago. But it can hardly be doubted that his feelings were the same when he planned his house-party for the first week in May. We can go further: his feelings were a hundredfold magnified. Four years ago there had been no rival on the horizon. There was a rival now. He knew this, hovering over Madge as he did, though he never guessed who it was. She, in turn, could only beat her fists against apparent impassivity. If we think back with a retrospective shiver to that scene under the magnolias on the night of Sunday, May 2nd, it is evident that Madge's interrupted outburst would have been, 'Sometimes I wonder if it's worth going on with this masquerade?'

"Well, *he* thought it was. The masquerade should go on forever. And to that end, he decided, somebody was going to die."

Alan sat up straight. "*He* decided somebody was going to die? Are you saying—?"

"Henry Maynard committed no crime. I doubt that he would ever have carried out his design. But he was in a state of mind to think murder, and most ingeniously he planned one. Look here!"

Delving once more into the brief-case, Dr. Fell held up two folded sheets of note-paper. So far as Alan could tell from a distance, they seemed to be covered with figures and with firm, neat handwriting.

"The famous 'calculations,'" said Dr. Fell, instantly returning them to the brief-case. "The notes at which Maynard had been working for some time. The papers about which he was so secretive, about which he lied to me, and which, finally, he concealed in a secret drawer of the Sheraton desk in his study. A detective-constable named Wexford, Captain Ashcroft's authority in the antique-furniture line, found the secret drawer and its contents on Saturday. You have just seen the contents.

"What Maynard had worked out was a complete blueprint, with measurements and specifications, for as effective a murder-device as lies within my experience. Not an 'impossible' murder; that was far from the plan! Something mathematical, as was suggested of him; something eminently practical, which could be worked by anyone with moderate skill of the proper sort. This same device, in the hands of the actual murderer, came boomeranging back to kill Henry Maynard himself. Maynard never saw the danger, never thought to guard against it. As *he* had drawn up his scheme, it was to be used against . . ."

Yancey Beale, with a face of near-collapse, still stood beside the little piano. As Dr. Fell spoke Yancey moved one shaky step forward.

"Yes?" he prompted. "I thought I could take anything you had to say against Madge. Now I'm not so sure. But what's all this about Pa Maynard as a potential murderer? Who was to be *his* victim?"

"As originally planned, I submit, the victim was to have been either Rip Hillboro or yourself. You have not forgotten Mr. Hillboro's speculations on the same subject?"

"No, but . . ."

"Whether he was serious or not, he struck dangerously near truth when he said you had both better take care. Madge, you recall, immediately flared up to ask what her 'father' could possibly have against either of you. You could not answer the question then. Can you answer it now?"

"Yes, but . . ."

"Consider! You and Mr. Hillboro were Madge's two known suitors. You are both young, both presentable; he hated you cordially. Though Madge seemed to favor neither of you, might this not be a blind to conceal passion for one or the other? Such an idea must forcefully have occurred to Maynard. Indeed, when we ourselves look for the real murderer . . ."

"Easy, Grand Goblin! Just you take it easy! Are you sayin' the murderer must be either Rip or me?"

"One moment, sir. We see this through no unprejudiced eyes; we see it through the eyes of Henry Maynard, a man past his prime and tortured by jealousy. If you yourself have ever been jealous . . ."

"If *I* have ever been jealous, for God's sake!"

"And yet, in his heart, did Maynard ever really mean murder? I indulge conjecture, but I doubt it. He loved tinkering with plans and figures; the brutal reality of action was another matter. For what happened? The famous Sunday evening under the magnolias, with guests arriving next day, found Madge in the arms of—whom? You, Mr. Beale, said it was you. He doubted that; he had reason to doubt it. But if not you, then who? He didn't know; he couldn't guess. Alan Grantham and I can testify that the thought maddened him.

"And what else happened?

"On Wednesday, May 5th, he flew to Richmond. A hitherto-depressed man returned on Saturday in a very different mood: gay, buoyant, almost carefree. Clearly, on reflection, he had abandoned the murder-project and put it from him. Perhaps some belated sense of humor awoke to absurdity: could he plot the death of every man at Madge's elbow? Perhaps it was only Maynard common sense. 'Let the future take care of itself,' his thoughts must have run. 'I can't live forever. But I have her now, and I'll make the best of her while there's still time.' No instinct told him, on Saturday morning of the 8th, that he had less than a week to live.

"For just here we see the cross-currents, the cross-purposes, which made a bad situation worse. Let me try to clarify this.

"Two persons had already entered the case and seized events. One, the murderer, found Maynard's blueprint and did mean business. The other, whom we have agreed to call the joker, subsequently wrote messages on the blackboard. Between these two, once the crime had been committed, began a constant tug of war. And yet each misunderstood the other. And we misunderstood too."

"I asked before," Camilla cried, "but I'm afraid I've got to ask again. If you won't say anything about the murderer, who's the joker?"

"Suppose you tell me?" suggested Dr. Fell. "You were not

present in the attic on Friday afternoon when a certain person, slightly offstage on the stairs, was heard to exclaim, 'You don't know what's going on here; I can't bear it.' But other facts have been before us all.

"The same person subsequently left Maynard Hall, drove away in a hurry, and was absent when Captain Ashcroft received an anonymous phone-call (from the Poinsett High School, it now seems certain). The same person returned shortly before six o'clock, at which time she pitched into Henry Maynard and called him a fraud. On Saturday afternoon she pitched into Madge, and for the same reason."

"You mean Valerie Huret, don't you?"

"I do. A most intuitive lady, as I have already remarked. Intense, somewhat frustrated. How conveniently she was present, on two occasions, and 'found' messages that were believed to have frightened her so much!"

"Then Valerie did all that herself? And she was always right?"

"Oh, no," said Dr. Fell.

Fishing the filled pipe from his pocket, he lit it with a kitchen match and blew out a great gust of smoke.

"She was quick to sense the true relationship between supposed father and daughter. But she thought it was incest, which horrified her. That has been Mrs. Huret's motivation throughout. Because she *seemed* right in so much, and led us straight to the murder-method when she herself had only a glimmer of the right idea, we missed the different (and erroneous) interpretation she had tried to convey.

"Take the chalked messages, beginning with the second one where accusations commence. 'The man to be sought is Madge's lover. Find him; don't so easily be put off questioning her. And, if you would learn about the murder, more tomorrow.'

"We interpreted that as being a reference to the unknown lover, the elusive boy-friend of the magnolia trees, who was also the murderer. And we were thunderingly right so to interpret it; it is the truth.

"But does the message actually say that? Did it mean that? Before 'if you would learn about the murder,' note its qualifying 'and.'

"The third and fourth communications complete an accusation and show what Mrs. Huret was really trying to tell us. The third sent us to Fort Moultrie. 'There is a photograph which may prove enlightening.' And, 'Yours in homage to the great one.' Mrs. Huret, a former schoolmistress, had her wits stimulated by Edgar Allan Poe. For she *was* on the right track there."

"But not on the right track about anything else?" asked Alan.

"Not on the right track about anything else. After stealing the packet of letters from Madge so that we should find them here, she wrote her fourth message in valedictory. When *she* spoke of Madge's lover, she did not mean an elusive boy-friend or a murderer either. She meant Henry Maynard and what she thought to be a wickedly incestuous relationship. Maynard *was* Madge's lover, of course. But it seems doubtful that Mrs. Huret ever so much as suspected another lover, the more important lover, who—"

"Well, really!" exclaimed Camilla. "One lover; two lovers; is there somebody else too? I'm not accusing Madge of being a Messalina, which I know she isn't, but how many men did she want?"

"You let her alone!" snapped Yancey. "Madge only did what she had to do, because that old devil forced her. She didn't like it, you know!"

"I wonder. And will you please tell us, Dr. Fell," Camilla said on a note of the frantic, "just what Valerie really meant?"

"We know what she meant," replied Dr. Fell, taking more typewritten sheets from the brief-case and letting them fall on the other papers. "Here is a copy of the statement she made to Captain Ashcroft in hospital, which adds impressively to our list of documentary evidence.

"Her main purpose was to expose the incestuous relationship and blow it sky-high. She would not come out openly and accuse those two. She must play ghost; she must hide; she must whisper in the ear of the law. But it became necessary to remove the mask, and she had chosen her own candidate for the role of murderer.

When she came here last night in a state so overwrought, she was concerned with something else besides incest. If the bullet had not silenced her in mid-flight, she would have denounced Madge Maynard for a deed still more dark."

"*Madge?*"

"Against all plausibility, against all reason, she maintained to Captain Ashcroft—probably she still maintains—that Madge herself must have set a death-trap for the victim. No matter! She hates Madge, you know. And let it be repeated that she is now past all reason.

"But we must never underestimate Mrs. Huret's contribution to this investigation. Though she was mistaken in every respect except that thundering hint about Edgar Allan Poe, she has given invaluable help from the start. Her errors have been our gain. In being wrong, she set us right. That paradox will be appreciated at the proper time."

Dr. Fell paused.

His pipe had gone out. Dropping it into his pocket, he produced a big gunmetal watch, at which he blinked hard.

"Speaking of the time," he continued, "it is far past midnight and getting on towards one in the morning. Archons of Athens! Surely . . . ?"

Back went the watch into Dr. Fell's pocket. For some minutes Alan had been conscious that the blacked-out room, in addition to being stuffy, was distinctly chilly as well. He glanced at the closed door to the corridor. So did Dr. Fell, who seemed to be waiting for something. Then Alan looked across at Camilla and at Yancey; they were waiting too.

Knuckles tapped lightly at the ground-glass panel of the door, which opened. In the aperture stood Sergeant Duckworth, young and hard-jawed, with a manner as conspiratorial as it was urgent. He approached Dr. Fell as gingerly as he might have approached a mine-field, and spoke in a low voice.

"All set, sir. You ready too?"

"Sergeant, we have been ready for some time."

"Couldn't get goin' before, sir! The reason—"

"I understand the reason. But I warned Captain Ashcroft about his idea. This may not work, you know."

"Well, sir, it's workin' already."

"What do you want us to do?"

Sergeant Duckworth looked at Yancey. "You—"

"Me?"

"That's right. Follow me out; do what I do; make as little noise as you can.—I'm takin' him to the place, sir," Sergeant Duckworth explained to Dr. Fell. "He'll be right on hand for the action."

"What action?" demanded Yancey.

"Hard to tell, ain't it? Now, then; this lady and you two others. Count slow up to fifty, then follow us. Go out the side door, and up the three little steps to the edge of the playground. But don't go no further; stay there and watch. Ain' no danger to the lady; ain' no danger to *anybody*. You'll be hardly more'n a hundred feet from the place; you'll see everything when the lights go on. O.K.?"

"When I came in here," Dr. Fell said heavily, "there was moonlight of a sort. Won't we be seen?"

"Not a chance, sir. Sky's clouded over; it's as black as your hat. Wind gettin' up too; there'll be rain before the night's over."

"Dark of the moon, eh? Will it do any harm to talk?"

"Talk if you want to; just don't talk loud. Then, when you get word there's somebody in sight, don't talk and don't move either. O.K., then? Mr. Beale, let's go."

Clearly feeling less sick with something to occupy him, Yancey followed Sergeant Duckworth and was gone. A few moments later Alan, who had been counting in his head as the others were counting, could restrain himself no longer.

"Dr. Fell," he said, "Sergeant Duckworth kept referring to 'the place.' What place?"

In leisurely fashion Dr. Fell took up his stick from the teacher's desk.

"The place in question—twenty-one, twenty-two, twenty-three —is the junk-yard some forty yards west of this building." He looked at Camilla. "That junk-yard, Miss Bruce, figures not unimportantly in our problem. Don't scorn the junk-yard, I beg."

"If you mean I was sniffy about it to Captain Ashcroft, I'm not saying anything at all. But Alan is absolutely bursting with questions; aren't you, Alan?"

"Yes! You yourself, Magister, keep referring to a method of murder you call a death-trap. Are we supposed to understand this method by thinking of Edgar Allan Poe?"

"If we think of him in relation to *The Gold Bug*. What happens in that story?"

"An eccentric character named Legrand solves a cryptogram that leads to buried treasure."

Dr. Fell finished counting to fifty. He lumbered to the glass-panelled door, with Alan and Camilla following. They were all in the corridor, and Dr. Fell had bent forward to open the side door, when he spoke again.

"Don't stop there; go on! Having solved the cryptogram, what does Legrand do?"

" 'A good glass in the bishop's hostel in the devil's seat.' The 'good glass' is a telescope. He—"

Once outside the door, all mist was gone before a damp wind raking from the south. Nor had Sergeant Duckworth exaggerated the darkness, a palpable force. They all stumbled on the little steps leading up to ground-level. When they gathered together at the top, with Alan's arm round Camilla, whispers flew back and forth.

"Well?" prompted Dr. Fell. "About Legrand?"

"When he looks through the telescope at the given elevation, he sees a skull nailed to a tree-branch inside the foliage. Through the left eye of the death's-head, the *scarabaeus* or gold bug is lowered on a long string to find the direction of . . ."

At Alan's ear there was a mighty hissing. "Archons of Athens, sir! Don't you see?"

"See? See what? *We* haven't got any skull to lower a string from."

"No," exulted Dr. Fell. "But we have a tree. Indeed, we have six trees in a row; we know their height. And what, as you yourself pointed out, is directly in line with those trees a little distance away? Isn't it abundantly clear?"

"It may be clear to you, Magister; it won't be very clear to anybody else. You say Henry Maynard devised this scheme and hid his notes in a secret drawer of the desk. You say the real murderer found the notes and used 'em. But if Madge herself couldn't find the secret drawer in the desk, how the hell could the murderer have found it either?"

A noiseless shape loomed up at them out of darkness. After a startled instant Alan sensed more than saw that it was Sergeant Duckworth, making gestures to enjoin silence as he pointed north towards the road in front of the school.

Then the sergeant melted away. Nobody spoke afterwards, though it was a great temptation. Alan, on edge, could not estimate how long they waited. It must have been a very brief interval, whatever it seemed.

Even at rather less a distance away than the forty yards Dr. Fell had estimated, the high brown-painted fence round the junk-yard was totally invisible. In the boards of the fence, Alan remembered, there was a main gate towards the road; as far as his hazy recollection went, there might have been a smaller gate on the side towards the school.

Since he could see nothing, it hardly mattered. Myriad night-noises wove their pattern: wind fretting at tree-tops, obscure scuttlings in grass, the wiry pulse of a cricket, no more.

Had there been another noise? Perhaps a part of the others, or mere illusion? Somebody was approaching, he thought; not along the surface of the road, but in the grass verge to the north of it, as he and Camilla had walked the night before. Unless he was imagining the whole thing . . .

He had not been imagining it. There was a brief, incautious chink of a footstep crossing the road. Despite all darkness, somebody grimly determined was making for R. Gaiddon's premises and drawing closer. Alan, feeling Camilla's hand tighten on his shoulder, himself took a step forward.

There was an explosion of light; if the watchers had been closer, all three would have been completely blinded. They were only partly blinded, and they saw.

The junk-yard had in fact two entrances: the main gate towards the road, under R. Gaiddon's sign, and a smaller door cut in the fence on the side towards the school. Both stood wide open. Through the latter gate, now beginning to take shape . . .

The door of a small office inside the fence had been thrown open, sending a dazzle of light across the littered yard. This, together with the beams of three powerful flashlights, caught somebody in their converging glare and held him as though spitted.

"Hold it!" bellowed a voice. "Hold it right there!"

The scene inside the fence seemed to boil over. Alan saw Captain Ashcroft run forward, with Yancey Beale beside him. He also saw, at a distance, the face of the man caught by those converging lights. This man, with something in his right hand, drew the arm back as if to throw. The arm was caught from behind; a weight fell with a thud; half a dozen men closed in. And Dr. Fell broke silence at last.

"How could he so easily have found a secret drawer in the desk? Well, who began his career as a cabinet-maker, and would have known where to look for one?"

Then Dr. Fell's voice boomed out.

"Yes," he said, "that's the murderer and so-called friend of the family—Bob Crandall."

20

An overcast sky reflected the general mood. On the afternoon of Friday, May 21st, exactly a week after he had entered the affair, Dr. Gideon Fell prepared to take his leave of it. Five persons were assembled in the back garden at Maynard Hall. With the addition of Captain Ashcroft, the same listeners had heard Dr. Fell expound at the Poinsett High School the previous Sunday night.

Dr. Fell himself, throned in one corner of a heavy ironwork garden bench at one side of the path past the sun-dial, smoked his meerschaum pipe with the stick propped against his knee. Facing him, Camilla Bruce and Alan Grantham occupied chairs of featherweight metal and plastic. Yancey Beale occupied another such chair, lost in brooding thought. Captain Ashcroft, who would not sit down or remain still, prowled back and forth in the path. It was Captain Ashcroft whom Dr. Fell addressed.

"If there is anything else you would care to know, sir—?"

Momentarily the other stopped pacing.

"Not much more I need to *know,* thank'ee. It's in my head; in my notebook; anyway, I've got it. What I keep thinking . . . Crandall!" he said viciously. "That fellow Crandall!"

"Oh, ah?"

"It was my fault, I know. Still, who'd have guessed he had cyanide on him, to swallow if everything went wrong? You think of cyanide-capsules in wartime. You don't think of 'em when you search a prisoner you've just booked for murder. All right! He had the cyanide; he swallowed it; he's as dead as poor Henry.

"Maybe it's not so bad, at that. Evidence in a murder trial is always pretty risky, even when you've got plenty of it. Probably we'd have convicted him, and then again maybe we wouldn't. So in that respect, anyway, you can say everything turned out for the best. *But*—

"What about Madge's boy-friend? The boy-friend we were lookin' for, the 'young' boy-friend we all thought of at first? He had a remarkably young voice, I admit; if you just heard him and didn't see him, you'd have taken him for about thirty. And he was a very active fellow. But the 'young' boy-friend, King Cole, was a man almost as old as Henry Maynard himself. Blow me to hell and back, how do you like THAT?"

"Sir," said Dr. Fell, "is it so very surprising? The first man in her life, *aetat* seventeen, was thirty years older than herself. If a decade later she turned to somebody very little younger, but one who knew much better how to captivate her, is it so very surprising after all?"

"Just a minute, my friend! I can understand how Crandall went overboard for *her*. What I don't understand, what I can't understand, is how she came to go overboard for *him*. What was *she* thinkin' about?"

Camilla spoke with intense bitterness.

"Why don't you ask her, Captain Ashcroft? She's in the house now; why don't you go in and ask? Some women do have a weakness for older men; once or twice I wondered about Madge and Mr. Crandall, though I couldn't quite believe it. But we haven't had enough mess and scandal and uproar already, have we? Why not just go in and ask?"

"No, thanks, ma'am; not me. There's been enough trouble already, as you say. And I do have one or two decent instincts, even if I am a cop. But you suspected funny business between those two, did you?"

"I wondered, that's all!"

"It was something to do with jealousy, wasn't it?" asked Alan.

"It was partly that. Oh, need we go on with this?"

"Yes," snapped Captain Ashcroft, "I think we'd better. If that's what you suspected, Miss Bruce, what made you suspect it?"

"The same things, probably, that made Dr. Fell suspect." Camilla gripped the arms of her chair. "Madge and Bob Crandall were very casual in public, like docile niece and slightly raffish uncle. But nobody could help noticing how she hung on every word he spoke; she was absolutely absorbed. Yes, he knew how to captivate her! Then, on Friday afternoon a week ago . . . you weren't there, Captain, but Alan and Yancey were . . ."

"Well?"

"We were in the library when Valerie Huret drove up to the house not long before six o'clock. Madge looked out of the window and said, 'Here she is, Mr. Crandall! Here's your girl-friend back again!'

"Now I can't hope to imitate the tone in which she said, 'Here's your girl-friend back again,' or expect anybody to remember it if I did. But to me it didn't sound like the joking remark it pretended to be; for a second it sounded like real jealousy. So I just wondered.

"Then there was Bob's attitude towards Madge when you saw him off-guard. One afternoon—the Tuesday before the murder, I think—Rip and Yancey were arguing about which of them could climb the north wall of the house, where there isn't any wisteria. But it wasn't either Rip or Yancey who instantly did it. It was Bob Crandall, and he went up that wall like a circus athlete. Which of them, you might wonder, had *really* been trying to impress Madge? It was only a little thing; it didn't occur to me until afterwards. But it added up."

Dr. Fell blew out smoke.

"Nor must anyone forget," he suggested, "the incident of the terrified maid. On Saturday afternoon, following the murder, four of us drove to Fort Moultrie. Madge, confined to her room but no longer prostrated, was given a bad time by Valerie Huret. Captain Ashcroft and I know (the rest of you have not been told) what happened when Mrs. Huret invaded her room. A maid named Judith, lurking outside, overheard high words. Shortly afterwards Judith thought she saw Mrs. Huret attacking Madge in a physical sense, and stumbled downstairs with the news.

"Mr. Beale could not have gone to Madge's assistance; he was absent with us. Mr. Hillboro and Bob Crandall were both in the lounge below. Mr. Hillboro, the professed suitor, did not go to her assistance; he remained prudently aloof until he hared away in quest of us. It was Bob Crandall who ran upstairs and tried to force his way into the bedroom. When we remember the sequence of events . . ."

"Sequence of events, that's it!" exclaimed Captain Ashcroft, snapping his fingers. "I *knew* there was something else. Now get this, all of you." He nodded towards the house. "Duckworth and Kingsley are in there; they've fixed up a little demonstration to show how the murder was done. Let's lead into that. I've got a last report to make before we close the file. Suppose, Dr. Fell, you tell us about Br'er Fox Crandall?"

"From the beginning?"

"Well, almost from the beginning. What he did, how he did it, step by step through the trickiness. Mighty slippery and clever, wasn't he?"

"Undoubtedly. His pose as the outspoken family friend, the plain blunt man, a disguise adopted by so many hypocrites since Iago . . ."

"But didn't you say he was a romantic?" asked Alan.

"I did; he was. Never forget, however, that the obverse side of romanticism is that blind, insensate callousness found in certain Nazi leaders a few decades ago. And, like a Nazi leader, he took poison when he was cornered."

For a moment Dr. Fell smoked meditatively, glancing from Alan to Camilla and to Yancey.

"In these days of constant air-travel, his first moves need excite no surprise. He was due to arrive here for the house-party, and did arrive, on Friday, May 7th. But there is now evidence, as Captain Ashcroft will tell you, that he paid a secret visit before that. In his own overwrought state of mind, he flew south to Charleston on Sunday, May 2nd. He put up at the Scholastic Hotel, a small one in College Street. From Red Shield Drive-Hire he rented a car for his brief journey to James Island. He saw Madge under the magnolias and flew north the following day, but was back again on Friday with his plans nearing completion.

"He wanted that girl; he wanted her badly. From what Madge has blurted out, it is clear she cherished a vain hope: that she and her newspaper admirer could come out into the open with their affair; that Crandall might go to the man she still pretended was her father, explain that they were in love, and be awarded Madge to a sound of wedding-bells. Having guessed the actual relationship between Madge and Henry Maynard—he never *quite* admitted this to her—Crandall knew how vain and illusory her hope was. He could have this girl, with or without wedding-bells, only if he removed the one obstacle. And so . . ."

Yancey Beale suddenly sat up.

"Just a minute, Grand Goblin! I'll buy most of this; can't deny it, I guess. All the same! Are you sayin' it was Bob Crandall with Madge that Sunday night?"

"I am."

"But I damn near walked in on 'em! And what I've just remembered is that she called him a silly boy. A silly boy or a foolish boy, one or the other. Bob Crandall was fifty-four years old. Would she have called *him* a silly boy?"

"Do you remember," asked Dr. Fell, "that she also called Captain Ashcroft a silly boy? It is a trick of speech in frequent use among women, who regard few of our sex as being anything more than infantile. Even I have heard it in my time."

"One other point, though! You've said Pa Maynard worked out a plan for murder without really intending to use it, but that Bob Crandall found his notes and did mean business. What made him look for any notes to begin with? How'd he know there *was* a plan?"

"Though we have no direct evidence, justifiable conclusions lead us straight back to the story. Madge was so full of Maynard's mysterious 'calculations,' so puzzled and troubled by them, that she discussed the subject with anyone who would listen. Crandall saw her on Sunday night; no doubt she told him too. If Henry Maynard never understood Bob Crandall, we may be sure Bob Crandall understood Henry Maynard. From Madge's account, from his knowledge of all the circumstances, he saw the trend of Maynard's mind as I myself saw it later.

"For behold! On Friday, the 7th—just a week before the murder—he put in an official appearance. Maynard was absent in Richmond, leaving him for twenty-four hours a clear field both with Madge and with the Sheraton desk in the attic. All three of them had lived at Goliath, Connecticut, as Crandall still did. If he had heard of a secret repository, he now had the chance to look for it undisturbed.

"There was the secret drawer, as usual behind a real drawer of the desk: eureka! There was a complete blueprint for homicide, to be adapted to his purpose and turned against its originator: hosanna!

"He did not remove the papers from the drawer; why should he? When Maynard discovered the papers were missing, Maynard might suspect what was up, and that must never happen. His good friend Bob Crandall could copy or memorize what was necessary.

"Well, following his arrival on Friday, the fireworks began Friday night. That scarecrow, so necessary to him, he stole from the garden and concealed under an upended watering-trough in one of the slave-cabins. He did not steal the scarecrow until almost three-thirty in the morning; the earliest small hours, I suspect, he spent with Madge in her room.

"Once he *had* taken and hidden the scarecrow, Miss Bruce saw him creeping back into the house. He may or may not have worn a stocking-mask. She herself is not sure whether she saw one; none was found among his effects afterwards, though he may have had a mask and destroyed it. In any case he had time to slip up undetected to his room, and to feign sleepiness—he did not need to feign irascibility—during the search for an imaginary burglar.

"There were no more alarms or excursions until the following Thursday night, the night before the murder, the night Bob Crandall set his death-trap. At one-thirty in the morning he was seen walking east along the beach, carrying the scarecrow over his shoulder; but he was seen only at a distance, by a witness who suspected nothing. The scarecrow you have debated; all other materials for the death-trap are here close at hand. Most have been under your eyes the whole time; the rest I have carefully described to you."

Alan intervened then.

"What did he want with the scarecrow? Was it . . . ?"

"It was just what you yourself suggested: dressed in Henry Maynard's clothes, a doll or dummy to represent Maynard himself. Let us see, now!"

As usual, Dr. Fell's pipe had gone out. Dropping it into his pocket, surging to his feet on the crutch-headed stick, he addressed Captain Ashcroft.

"Sergeant Duckworth and Detective Kingsley, you said—?"

"They're ready now; they just signalled through an upstairs window. Shall I tell Kingsley to bring the other dummy down, and have Duckworth do the trick from inside?"

"Would you do that? Thank'ee. Will the rest of you (harrumph!) be good enough to come with me?"

While Captain Ashcroft went into the house, the others followed Dr. Fell round its south side to the front, and then in a northerly direction until they were standing on the grass beyond which stretched the front terrace.

Today its surface of crushed oyster-shell looked smooth and swept. The green-painted iron table and chair stood in their usual place, at the middle of the terrace but well towards its front. To the right of the terrace rose the row of six poplar trees, twenty feet high.

Dr. Fell pointed.

"It has been remarked," he said, "that the row of trees—with particular reference to the end tree on the side towards the house—is directly in line with that flagstaff, the same height, which you see over on the left, almost against the wall of the house. Note once more that the flagstaff rises a couple of feet above the far window of a certain room on the bedroom floor.

"Whose bedroom? We could have told that long ago."

Dr. Fell looked at Alan.

"When Henry Maynard first received us in his study on the top floor, he took us through a billiard-room and into a lumber-room, so that he could point out Fort Sumter through the window. It was the far window of the far room, the left-hand one as you stand inside looking out. He handed me a pair of field-glasses, *these* glasses," pursued Dr. Fell, taking the glasses from his immense side pocket, "and told me to look on a line over the flagstaff below.

"Whose bedroom, the end one on the north side at the front, was just below? Bob Crandall's, as we learned that night. The flagstaff, therefore, rises just outside the far window of that bedroom.

"Would it have been easy for the room's occupant to get at the flagstaff? It would. Each bedroom has two windows with an air-conditioner in one. But each bedroom at the front has its air-conditioner in the right-hand window facing outward. Bob Crandall had only to raise the left-hand window (those windows move without noise), and the flagstaff was well within reach."

Camilla, though she did not like any of this, stood her ground none the less.

"Yes," she said; "but within reach for *what?*"

Dr. Fell handed the field-glasses to Alan.

"You try first," he suggested. "Begin with the top of the flagstaff, the little pulley over which a rope runs when they raise a flag. Look slowly across from there to the top of the nearest tree.

Do you see anything, anything at all, stretching between the pulley of the flagstaff and the top of the tree?"

Alan lifted the glasses and focussed them.

"Nothing there!" he reported presently. "I can't see anything at all."

"No, you see nothing. You would see nothing even if it were only a few feet away. Something does in fact stretch there: a length of the strongest Monofilament fishing-line. Will someone else have a look now? You, Mr. Beale?"

"No, thanks, Grand Goblin!" Yancey backed away. "I'll take your word for it and Alan's too. *I* don't want the damn glasses!"

"And I don't want them either!" said Camilla. "Alan, please give them back to Dr. Fell. That's enough, surely? And yet I do begin to get a glimmer of understanding."

"If you looked closely at the top of the tree itself," Dr. Fell took the glasses, "you would discern other details. The few branches and little foliage at the top of any poplar have been cleared away except for a short wooden projection to form a crotch. In that crotch lies balanced a short length of iron weight such as may be found amid the litter of any junk-yard. At the beginning of this affair Captain Ashcroft remarked that the injury might have been inflicted with that kind of weapon. And so it was.

"The murderer, then, set his trap on Thursday night. In the cellar he had several spools of fishing-line, from heavy to light. With a short length of this he wove a tiny net to enclose the iron weight and hold it. Having measured out the full length of slack he needed for a line from the flagstaff to the tree, he first tied one end to the net round the weight. He dropped the weight from the window, ran the other end of the line over the pulley, and tied it to the flagstaff.

"Having done one other thing, as will soon be evident, he was now ready to leave the house and prepare the tree. The man who could climb as he did had no trouble with that poplar. The weight on its line went up with him, to be balanced in a crotch he either found there already or hewed out with the tools at his disposal.

"When all preparations were finished, did he fetch the scarecrow from the slave-cabin for a rehearsal? Evidently, though we can't be sure. But, speaking of a rehearsal . . ."

Dr. Fell gestured towards the house. The far window of what had been Bob Crandall's room was now open, and Sergeant Duckworth leaned out. Behind him loomed the bulk of Captain Ashcroft. Now Dr. Fell indicated the portico of Maynard Hall. Out of the front door came a grizzled middle-aged man, Detective Kingsley, carrying . . .

"Yes!" said Dr. Fell. "Another suit of Maynard's clothes, another dummy carefully prepared. In order to demonstrate—" He had started in a rush; then, seeing Camilla's face, he checked himself, reddened, and harrumphed. "This time, Miss Bruce, I fear the old duffer has gone too far. Hang it all, need you watch this? Hadn't you better go into the house?"

Still Camilla stood her ground.

"I won't go into the house," she told him. "But do we really need to have any demonstration, especially one with the dummy?"

"To show how it worked—"

"I can see how it worked. One twitch at that line from the window . . ."

"I see it too!" said Yancey. "With one twitch of the line, at an angle that could be calculated, the iron weight whistled down and conked the head of anybody in that chair. Hitting the head arrested its motion; it swung over gently against the flagstaff, to hang a few feet aboveground. And Crandall could haul it up again, eh?"

"He could haul it up still better," Dr. Fell pointed out, "if towards the other end of his line, a few feet out from the tree, he had attached another, still lighter line to the first one, controlling it yet not interfering with the arc of the missile. I told you he had done one other thing; that was it."

Dr. Fell had grown radiant with relief.

"Miss Bruce is right; a demonstration would be superfluous. Ashcroft and I rehearsed it several times. It works without a hitch, but even the mimicry is not pretty; once we smote the head clean off the dummy. If Madge Maynard should look out of the window . . ."

Here he swung towards the house and bellowed.

"There's no need to show 'em; they understand! Kingsley, take the dummy back in again. Sergeant Duckworth, lower that window and go away. Captain Ashcroft, aroint ye; vanish; get lost.

"But here," he went on to his companions, "we must mention Mrs. Huret, who almost saw the murder committed without ever once suspecting Crandall. How serious she was in making eyes at the Sage of Goliath we may never know; she has refused to answer questions since they released her from hospital.

"And yet we know what happened. Before dusk on the evening it was done, Crandall went up to his room. Mrs. Huret followed. She looked through the keyhole, as he must have been fully aware she might. She could not have got in; despite his words to us, he would have taken the precaution of locking the door.

"He was pacing from one side of the room to the other, pretending to study a book on chess. She could not see him, as she herself testified, when he went to the left-hand side of the room: the side with the window opening on the flagstaff, the side from which his thunderbolt could be launched. He had become maniacally determined, with the supreme daring murderers show at such times. And so he let the thunderbolt fall.

"No 'impossible' murder (need I repeat?) was ever intended by anybody. Observe! If on a dry day like this I myself walk out on the oyster-shell surface—so—even my weight leaves no discernible footprints. In these parts ghost-guns of thunder are often heard without any rain. And the weather for Friday (remember?) had promised to be fine. When our frantic murderer set his deathtrap the previous night, he could not have anticipated the brief, violent thundershower which soaked the ground. But by that time he had gone too far to retreat.

"If you will follow me again to the back garden," continued

Dr. Fell, moving away with the other three trailing
"I will do my best to conclude the story.

"It may be remarked, parenthetically and with apology, that I never dreamed how the crime was committed until we found that photograph at Fort Moultrie; I had been looking too hard in the wrong direction. If Crandall did not concern himself with an old bogey-tale or with the murder of Commodore Maynard on the beach, I had concerned myself with it too much.

"Certain previous ideas, together with a young lady's diary for 1867, produced utter confusion. Newspaper accounts said that Commodore Maynard had fallen at a point below the reach of the incoming tide. Yet the same accounts described a little heap of seaweed on the beach at a point above the body. Clearly the seaweed had been carried there by the tide, as it always is; clearly, too, the water had risen higher than anyone observed or believed. It seemed to me that the ne'er-do-well Maynard cousin, approaching in a small boat through shallow water, must have struck down the commodore on his blind side.

"That may be the true explanation. But what of it? Antics on sand a hundred years ago bore no relation to the problem here and now; far from helping, they only sealed up vision. I had been looking out over water when I should have raised my eyes to a tree."

In the back garden again, Dr. Fell lowered himself thankfully to the iron bench. Camilla, Alan, and Yancey returned to their chairs, sharpening to attention when the doctor raised an admonitory forefinger.

"Let us round this out," he suggested, "as briefly as may be. The thunderbolt fell, and Henry Maynard was dead. Madge collapsed. In a haze of drugs later that night, wondering what her pretended father *might* have hidden in a secret drawer of the desk, she blundered up to the attic and collapsed again."

"Dr. Fell," Camilla said intently, "are you sure Madge, like Valerie, never once suspected Bob Crandall?"

attic, when you and Alan were present, she ... the innocence of the unknown lover; nor did ... the drug-fog in which she almost thought she saw ...anding outside the study door.

"Meanwhile, Valerie Huret had received another inspiration. From her statement to Captain Ashcroft we know that much earlier that day, before any tragedy occurred, she had determined to play ghost. She had phoned Ashcroft about a missing tomahawk, she wrote the first message on the blackboard—"

"Grand Goblin," interjected Yancey, "what *about* that tomahawk? Who did steal the tomahawk?"

"Crandall himself stole it, to mislead and confuse. Oh, ah! It was found among his belongings; he kept it by him, as he kept the more incriminating iron weight. They *will* preserve these things; Captain Ashcroft was right to think so. But I was dealing with the inspiration of Mrs. Huret.

"It had occurred to her, she says in her statement, that Maynard had been killed by a weight on a long string swung down from a tree. Though she does not say where she got this inspiration, I fear she got it from me."

"But she got it mistakenly, didn't she?" Alan asked. "When she overheard you say something about a string, you were speaking figuratively and didn't mean a literal string at all?"

"Yes, she was mistaken. She never connected the tree with the flagstaff and the house—or with Crandall. String; tree; *Gold Bug;* Poe; Fort Moultrie! That's all. And yet, hazy though the thoughts might be, they were a step towards truth. Once more, by being wrong, she led us right.

"Late Friday night she wrote the second blackboard message, which she herself contrived to discover. Not even a hint, yet, regarding Poe or Fort Moultrie; merely a promise of more to come. Friday's tumult ought to have ended when Captain Ashcroft secretly removed the antique desk for expert examination. But tumult had not quite ended. In the early hours of the morning

Crandall, beginning to tidy up after his exertions, se
scarecrow and destroyed it."

Dr. Fell paused for a moment, wheezing meditatively.

"Saturday," he went on, "was also a day of destiny. Captain Ashcroft put through an early call to the French police—had any daughter been born to the Maynards in 1938?—and received promise of a return call later in the day. We foregathered here at the Hall. After Alan expounded his theory of the thrown baseball, Mrs. Huret intervened with news of the message that sent us to Fort Moultrie.

"At Fort Moultrie we discovered more than that revealing photograph. If Madge Maynard were no daughter but a paramour (we still lacked proof of this, though it seemed probable), then who was she and where had she come from? She had been with her supposed father, it was agreed, when they moved from New York to Goliath some nine years ago.

"Dr. Mark Sheldon, describing Henry Maynard's behavior at a dinner last April, reported a curious incident. Asked merely whether he intended to support any organized charities, Maynard blurted out, 'Not St. Dorothy? Not St. Dorothy?' in an agitation nobody understood. Taken in conjunction with the reference to charity, could it have been 'St. Dorothy's'? Could it have meant a school or an orphanage?

"Meanwhile, at the Hall, events had rushed towards near-disaster. Valerie Huret, who some days before had stolen a packet of letters proving that relations between 'father' and 'daughter' were anything but filial, cornered Madge and pitched into her. If she stopped just short of the flat accusation of incest, she said quite enough.

"Madge, bent on self-destruction, rushed into the bathroom. She knocked over a glass and smashed it before grabbing at a razor-blade to slash her wrists. Mrs. Huret followed and stopped her. *That* was what happened: the scene interrupted by Captain Ashcroft, witnessed but misinterpreted by the maid.

, fetched us back from Sullivan's Island, Ashcroft, he also had news for me. The French replied; Madge was not Maynard's daughter. Though ... no case of incest, we still had high explosive in plenty.

"Ashcroft wanted to tackle Madge at once and get the whole truth out of her; or, rather, he wanted me to do it for him. I counselled delay.

"Somewhat soft-pedalling my conviction that I now knew how the murder had been committed, I stressed the name of St. Dorothy. A complete case, surely, was better than half a case? New York was of easy access; let his office first phone the New York police. Was there in fact any institution called St. Dorothy's, and what could be discovered about it? He agreed to wait.

"Ructions were still in progress. A police guard had been put back on Madge: not to prevent murder, but to prevent suicide. Mrs. Huret, never stopping to wonder how Madge Maynard could have operated any mechanism of weight and string, had convinced herself utterly of Madge's guilt.

"She could bring this guilt into the open, Mrs. Huret thought, if she left Henry Maynard's letters at the Poinsett High School and wrote a last message on the blackboard. To this end, when she was supposed to be lying down and resting, she slipped out of the house with the letters in her handbag."

"I saw her go down the back stairs," Alan told him, "and her handbag was conspicuous. But it gave no indication of where she was going! Since things seemed to be blowing up in all directions . . ."

"Things *were* blowing up in all directions," agreed Dr. Fell. "You and Miss Bruce departed for Davy's Restaurant a little past seven o'clock. Captain Ashcroft, darkly brooding as he and I lingered, had almost decided not to await word from New York when there was a call from his own office. New York had reported a St. Dorothy's Orphanage in Queens. If we wanted details about a child adopted from there: well, Sunday or no Sunday,

they would have the information tomorrow.
to wait after all. ct determined

Mrs. Huret, her own chore accomplished, had persu... Crandall to take her to dinner in town. Though she would neve...
anything openly until her statement in hospital, the lady is not
precisely a Sphinx. Always hinting, always oblique, she told Bob
Crandall just enough to make an edgy, desperate man think she
suspected *him*. And her life was in danger from that moment."

Once more Dr. Fell addressed Alan.

"You and Miss Bruce, returning from dinner, found and interpreted the last blackboard message, as Ashcroft and I had done just before then. We met for conference at the high school. Mr. Beale, who had also interpreted it, burgled a window and joined us."

Yancey jumped to his feet.

"I understand everything else, Grand Goblin! I still don't understand *that*."

"Understand what?"

"The disembodied voice, or it sounded like a disembodied voice, that whispered to me here in the garden. 'If you must go to that school, look out!' Though how it could have been known where I meant to go . . ."

"Known where you meant to go?" echoed Dr. Fell. "Archons of Athens! Just before then, you said, you had been standing in front of the blackboard and talking to yourself aloud for the benefit of anyone who cared to listen. You were not really losing your mind, but—"

"But there was nobody there to listen! There was nobody to be the voice!"

"On the contrary, sir. There was someone to whom you had been talking only a minute or so before, someone already badly worried about the situation, someone with a habit of being absolutely inconspicuous . . ."

Yancey stared. "You don't mean George, do you?"

ge, the faithful servitor whose devotion

continued Dr. Fell, "that some such warning was

yed to Valerie Huret. Mrs. Huret, returning from the staurant with Rip Hillboro and Bob Crandall, had to make sure the packet of letters had been found. She left her two companions (as she believed) immobilized at the television set, and fared forth to make sure.

"We ourselves were still blundering in search of room 26. She had slipped in by the side door. To draw our attention to that room she set the Victrola in motion, slipped out, and waited for the right moment dramatically to reappear with her denunciation.

"When she did reappear, however, hysteria made her incoherent. She shouted that she had come to accuse somebody. Captain Ashcroft, who knew who was really guilty, asked if she meant Crandall. In all sincerity she denied it. She was still frantically denying it when he shot her through the window.

"Crandall, at the last pitch of desperation, would *not* be beaten. Rip Hillboro, surfeited with films, fell asleep during the late show. Crandall, in no mood for sleep, followed Mrs. Huret with a revolver from the cellar and was back before the end of the show.

"You may remember one earlier circumstance. Mr. Beale, climbing to a window of the anteroom outside the principal's office, called out something to us before the window was opened; but we could not hear.

"A similar circumstance led the murderer into error. Crandall was sure Mrs. Huret suspected him and might denounce him. Through the semi-underground window of room 26 he saw her lips move. Though he could not hear her, he saw her lips move with his name. And so he fired to silence one of the two persons who most strongly believed in his innocence.

"The rest of a grotesque tragedy is soon told. I myself was not summoned to Maynard Hall until Sunday evening. Captain Ashcroft was already in action. From New York he had received word that Mádge Maynard, though legally adopted at sixteen and entitled to that name, had begun life as Madge McCall of St. Dorothy's Orphanage. Her true position could be demonstrated by the letters from her 'father.'

"Feeling he no longer needed support from me (in fact he had never needed it), the captain had come here and faced Madge with his evidence. The single cry she uttered rang through the house. You, Miss Bruce, do not appear to have believed it was Madge who cried out. But all these events had their center and focus in her; it could have been nobody else.

"The previous evening, for diplomatic reasons, I had been obliged to play down my lucky discovery of the murder-method. I now played up every indication; the wooden crotch in the tree, the absence of foliage, the windows that moved without noise. Ashcroft, though agreeing and abetting, had a further plan.

"He believed that Crandall, as murderers will do, had kept the iron weight picked up from a neighboring junk-yard. He believed Crandall could be maneuvered into returning that weight to the place it had come from, and where henceforward it would lie unnoticed amid other scrap.

"I was dubious, I confess. But I followed instructions. When from the corner of my eye I saw Crandall listening outside the door of the lounge, I said that next morning Ashcroft would search every room in the house.

"Well, the professional detective had been howlingly right. The search would have been made had it been necessary, but it was not necessary. At dead of night Crandall ventured out; he sought the junk-yard to dispose of that last incriminating evidence; he walked into a police trap. And that is all."

Drawing a deep breath, Dr. Fell propelled himself to his feet and stood towering.

"I have said that is all," he added. "Yet an emotional question remains. What happens to Madge, round whom every storm has blown?

"Last Monday, after Crandall had committed suicide, we heard from Maynard's lawyer the terms of his will. How far can a man like that go to keep what he has once owned? He planned inflexibly: except for a pittance which may or may not support her, Madge has been disinherited. His fortune goes to charity; the Hall will become a museum. That, no doubt, was what caused Mr. Hillboro to leave us in a hurry. If she were Maynard's real daughter, she could contest such a will with ease. Under the circumstances, of course, she can contest nothing. She has become an outcast, scorned of good people. And yet she has suffered too.—Mr. Beale, where are you going?"

Yancey swung round. "Up to see Madge, as I promised I would Who's talkin' about outcasts, Grand Goblin?"

"Have I made myself clear, sir? In the eyes of the world . . ."

"Damn the world!" said Yancey. "And its eyes and its views and everything else. Madge won't contest any will; she'll not need to, even if she won't have me. She *won't* have me, I expect; I'm no prize in the lottery, and I'm not pressin' her against her will. Still, if she does happen to need me, I'm here."

And he sauntered up the path into the house by one of the doors to the lounge. For some seconds Dr. Fell blinked at the ground; then, muttering about a conference with Captain Ashcroft, he followed. Alan and Camilla were left alone in a luxuriant garden under the sombre sky.

"I'm glad Yancey did that!" breathed Camilla. "I've never belonged among the good people, of course; but I'm *so* glad he did. Madge will get over this; you see if she doesn't; and she has a very fair chance of being happy too."

"What about you, Camilla? Are *you* reasonably happy?"

"I'm so wonderfully happy, Alan, I'm almost annoyed with myself for feeling it! Now that we understand each other and don't quarrel any longer . . ."

"We don't quarrel, do we? And tomorrow you go back with me to Pearis. Then, when we're married . . ."

"You don't have to do that, you know. You don't *have* to make an honest woman of me!"

"That's where you're wrong. You have certain skills, my magnificent anti-Puritan, to which few female mathematicians can aspire. So I don't mean to let you get away from me. If only I understood about the sergeant's wife . . . !"

"Sergeant's wife?"

"Yes. 'Somebody asked the Sergeant's wife' something, and in some way it's supposed to apply to us. But for the life of me—!"

"You didn't spot it? And you a teacher of English too? Oh, Alan! It's the last verse of Kipling's 'The Ladies.' I know it well; *I* can quote it!"

"You can quote Kipling? You condescend to quote Kipling? With your tastes, I should have thought . . ."

"Please, darling, let's not start that all over again! If Dr. Fell meant it as a dig at me for being so uppish about everything . . . I was uppish, I know, though I never meant to be . . . well, I accept the correction and glad to.

"What did the Colonel's lady think?
  Nobody ever knew;
Somebody asked the Sergeant's wife,
  And she told 'em true.
When you get down to a man in the case
  They're as like as a row of pins,
For the Colonel's lady and Judy O'Grady
  Are sisters under the skins."